THE WITCH HAVEN

SASHA PEYTON SMITH

SIMON & SCHUSTER BFYR

NEW YORK   LONDON   TORONTO   SYDNEY   NEW DELHI

SIMON & SCHUSTER BFYR

An imprint of Simon & Schuster Children's Publishing Division
1230 Avenue of the Americas, New York, New York 10020

SIMON & SCHUSTER BOOKS FOR YOUNG READERS
and related marks are trademarks of Simon & Schuster, Inc.
For information about special discounts for bulk purchases, please contact Simon & Schuster Special Sales at 1-866-506-1949 or business@simonandschuster.com.
The Simon & Schuster Speakers Bureau can bring authors to your live event.
For more information or to book an event, contact the Simon & Schuster Speakers Bureau at 1-866-248-3049 or visit our website at www.simonspeakers.com.
Interior design by Tom Daly
The text for this book was set in Adobe Garamond Pro.
Manufactured in the United States of America
First Edition
2 4 6 8 10 9 7 5 3 1
Library of Congress Cataloging-in-Publication Data
Names: Peyton Smith, Sasha, author.
Title: The witch haven / Sasha Peyton Smith.
Description: First edition. | New York : Simon & Schuster Books for Young Readers, [2021] | Audience: Ages 12 up. | Audience: Grades 10-12. | Summary: Whisked away to Haxahaven Academy for Witches in 1911, seventeen-year-old Frances Hallowell soon finds herself torn between aligning herself with Haxahaven's foes, the Sons of St. Druon, to solve her brother's murder or saving Manhattan and her fellow witches.
Identifiers: LCCN 2020057256 | ISBN 9781534454385 (hardcover) | ISBN 9781534454408 (ebook)
Subjects: CYAC: Witchcraft—Fiction. | Wizards—Fiction. | Murder—Fiction. | Brothers and sisters—Fiction. | New York (N.Y.)—History—1898-1951—Fiction.
Classification: LCC PZ7.1.P51515 Wit 2021 | DDC [Fic]—dc23
LC record available at https://lccn.loc.gov/2020057256

For Leah, little star

Someone I loved once gave me
a box full of darkness.
It took me years to understand
that this too, was a gift.

—Mary Oliver

NEW YORK, MAY 1911

The East River smelled distinctly of death.

The boy had not begged before he was thrown into its depths.

It was better that way. Begging was so undignified.

The boy hadn't said much at all. Just the girl's name, only once, right before he sank.

It was a simple enough task, killing someone. One good clock to the head was all it took. The river did the rest. Humans are so fragile.

The moon was a perfect crescent, hanging over the city. Calm and quiet, cold and indifferent, like nothing in the universe had changed at all.

No one in New York City noticed a person in a dark coat, walking alone away from the docks.

No one in New York City noticed a person dropping a pair of bloodstained gloves in an alleyway.

No one in New York City noticed much at all.

That's simple too, the getting away with it.

Forty-two blocks away, in a tenement slicked with grime, a girl slept soundly for the last time. Across the narrow room, her brother's bed was empty.

And somewhere on a street corner in Lower Manhattan, under the rumbling of the subway, the frantic buzzing of new electric lights, and the rush of a blood-hungry river, the magic began to stir.

CHAPTER ONE

NEW YORK, SEPTEMBER 1911

My mother once told me a girl's success in this world was dependent on how well she could pretend. Right now, I am pretending I don't want to scream.

Mr. Hues is a difficult presence to ignore as he stalks through the shop with all the grace of a drunken lion.

He arrived this morning for one of his favorite surprise inspections, but as usual, it's less an inspection of the shop than of the seamstresses who work here.

Through stolen glances, the other girls and I take stock of one another's work. Mary ran out of bobbin thread two minutes ago. Catherine's tracing pencil snapped just before that.

I lose the silent game of chicken. With a resigned sigh, I rise from my desk, knowing the iron needs to be lit if I have any hope of finishing this hem.

It's impossible to pretend I don't notice the weight of Mr. Hues's gaze as his eyes track me down the aisle.

"Morning." His grin makes my skin crawl.

The smile I force feels like defeat. There's nothing he loves more than basking in our gratitude. Never mind that it's the thirteen of us here who do all the work and ship the profits off neatly to him at the end of every week.

Mr. Hues often tells us not to do things by halves, to dedicate ourselves fully to all that we do. When it comes to contributing to my misery, he follows his own advice.

An unexpected early fall frost fell last night, and the shop is cold. It's difficult to make the delicate stitches Mr. Hues demands with numb hands, but the last time our supervisor, Mrs. Carrey, asked him to increase our coal budget, he laughed in her face. And Mrs. Carrey does not have a face that's easy to laugh in.

I return to my sewing machine, weaving like a spider around desks of girls, all churning out dresses as quickly as we're able in the cramped space. I do my best not to bump Jess's elbow as she works next to me. The last time I did, I ended up with a straight pin stuck between my thumb and pointer finger. She said it was an accident but smiled when I started bleeding.

Mr. Hues lumbers around the dress shop, picking at dummies, running his fingers over fabrics. He stops at my workstation and picks up the stack of pattern pieces I've carefully laid out for a velvet coat for a rich widow, my best client. He rifles through them carelessly, as if he has any idea what he is looking at, then places them back on the corner of the desk haphazardly. A piece of the collar flutters to the floor. He pays it no mind.

It'll take me ages to sort out what he's just done.

His next target is Mary. He perches himself on the edge of her desk and asks her to give him a smile. His blond hair, or what is left of it, has been oiled back and combed over his head. He's drenched himself in cologne today; it coats the back of my throat, acrid and awful.

"Well done," he finally speaks, apparently having found our partially constructed garments to his liking. "How are my girls?"

The tone of his question implies he expects to find us overjoyed to be in the employment of such a fine man.

"Fine, thank you, Mr. Hues," we reply, our voices all an octave too high.

He turns to Mrs. Carrey to ask about the state of business.

With a wave of her wrinkled hand, she dismisses us from sitting at attention. Though our tightly packed desks don't offer us much distance from Mr. Hues, the reprieve from having to look at the grease trap of a man with reverence is a relief.

At least when I'm driven to eating nothing but a crusty heel of bread for dinner, I don't have to pretend to be happy about it. At least when I miss William so badly I fear my chest will crack open with the pain of it, I'm not forced to wear a smile on my face.

I busy myself constructing the midnight-blue velvet coat, and with the soft feel of the cloth under my hands, I remind myself, as I do ten thousand times a day, how lucky I am to have this position, Mr. Hues's visits and all.

I could be like my mother, exiled to that horrible hospital on Long Island, her mind irreparably fractured by William's death.

Or like my school friend Rosie, working in that factory by the river, inhaling sludge, on her feet for twelve hours a day, putting the same button on the same shirt ad infinitum. And that mind-numbing exhaustion is nothing compared to some of the stories she tells me, like the one of the girl who wore her braid too long. It got snatched up by one of the machines, and she died right there on the factory floor.

Rosie told me when they unraveled her braid from the gears, they found her entire scalp still attached.

I had nightmares about it for weeks.

Or I could be like my brother, his waterlogged bones turning to rot in a grave I still can't bring myself to visit. He arguably got the worst deal of us all, though I'm not sure he'd agree. It is a shame he's not here to ask.

I keep waiting for the pain of his death to subside, but it hasn't yet stopped feeling like a punch to the gut fifty times a day.

He'd probably tell me to stop being so dramatic.

Truly, I'm lucky to be employed as a dressmaker in a small shop, even luckier that Mrs. Carrey let me move in with the other girls upstairs after my mother was sent off to the asylum. Positions like this are getting rarer by the minute.

Every day they build new smokestacks, and every day another shop like this one closes.

I take my time on the wealthy widow's coat, hoping the steady clicking of the sewing machine will drown out all the other noises in my head.

I'm sewing on the buttons that will trail all along the front of the coat when the soft chime of the door swinging open startles me. It's only a delivery boy dropping a package of new needles on Mrs. Carrey's desk, but I'm surprised to see the sky awash with the pale purple of twilight. The velvet coat's owner is expecting a delivery tomorrow morning, and I still have ten buttons, both cuffs, and the trimming left.

The shop needs at least three more seamstresses, but Mr. Hues is convinced our inability to keep up with orders is an issue of work ethic, not staffing.

The Thompson sisters ordered those ugly matching sailor dresses yesterday, putting me behind, and Mr. Hues's visit today only made things worse.

Dark shadows of late evening stretch across the room, and one by one the girls filter upstairs to the apartment where most of us live, until only Mrs. Carrey and I remain. She kindly lights three kerosene lamps and tells me not to be up too late.

Being in the shop alone at night is a particular kind of misery. Under the cover of darkness, the mice skitter across the floor, and the temperature drops so low I'm soon shivering beneath my shawl.

The other girls are giggling in the apartment upstairs. We don't laugh often, so I imagine they're sharing a joke at Mr. Hues's expense.

My needle flies across the fabric. I'm working as quickly as I can, snipping the thread of the eighth button, when a key jangling in the front lock startles me.

The bell attached to the front door chimes. Here in the dark, it sounds so different.

Stomach heavy with dread, I force myself to look up from the coat, and my worst fears are confirmed.

Mr. Hues.

He charges into the shop like a bull, tripping over his own shoes as he crosses the threshold.

His face is flushed, despite the cool evening air, and his brown tweed coat is buttoned wrong.

With sweaty hands, he shuffles through the till, grabbing loose bills and shoving them into his pockets.

I freeze. Perhaps I'll get lucky and he won't notice I'm here.

I once read that dogs can smell fear. I think men must be able to as well, because his gaze snaps up, meets mine.

I can lie to myself, but deep down I know the truth is I've never been lucky.

At the sight of me he sucks his teeth and smiles a slippery awful thing. "It's you."

"Just leaving, sir," I shove stray pattern pieces into the drawer of my sewing desk to avoid meeting his watery gaze.

A grimace cuts across his face. "No"—he chews on the word—"I don't think you are." The turn of his mouth and slime in his gaze make it clear what he means to do.

Terror shoots through me, fuzzy and nauseating. I pause, and then I calculate.

To get to the front door, I'd have to walk past him, within arm's reach, and the dark street outside is likely abandoned at this hour. The back door, the one that leads to the apartment upstairs, is closer but will be locked this late. The key is in the pocket of my apron, but I can already picture my shaking hands fumbling with it until it falls to the floor.

The kerosene lamps flicker, casting the shop in a sickly orange glow.

My lungs are in a vise.

Make a decision.

I pick one foot off the floor, then hurl myself in the direction of the door that leads to the back staircase. I'm aware of nothing save for Mr. Hues and my own heart beating in my chest, counting down like the second hand on a poorly oiled clock.

I'm almost there, fingers outstretched, reaching for the handle, when a hand grabs a fistful of my collar and yanks me back. I sputter as the fabric chokes me.

"Where are you going?" Mr. Hues slurs, words as grease coated as the rest of him. "The night is young."

A cold embrace seizes my pounding heart, and the tips of my fingers go numb right along with it. I stumble back and turn to face him, but I don't get far with my blouse still fisted in his hand.

"Please, sir," I whisper. My voice trembles. I hate myself for it.

His only reply is to shove me roughly against the wall. My head makes a terrible cracking noise as it collides with the bricks.

He pins me, one hand gripping at my shoulder, the other splayed across my hip.

I can't summon my voice to scream.

This close, the sour smell of whiskey on his breath is overpowering. His face is red and blotchy, eyes hooded and swollen. A bead of sweat from his face drops wet and hot onto my neck.

I throw my arms up to unsteady him, but he's too large.

The metal boning of my corset bites into my ribs. My lungs scream for air.

"Don't you like me, Mary?" he says with a slippery grin, dragging his hand away from my shoulder to pin my neck against the wall with his forearm. He presses down hard.

I'm not Mary, I'm Frances, I want to scream at him, but it doesn't matter to him who I am, who any of us are. If he saw me as a person, he wouldn't be doing this.

Pressure from his massive arm makes breathing impossible. I gape, like a fish pulled from water. At first I feel nothing, then there is the awful burning as I begin to suffocate.

I attempt a gasp and he smiles.

If I don't die tonight, I know the wild-laughter joy in his eyes at my pain will haunt me for as long as I live.

Bright spots flash in my field of vision. The edges of the room blur in and out of focus.

He inches closer.

I close my eyes.

Is this what my brother felt?

Nothingness licks at the edge of everything. Then, beneath the icy dread, there is something once more. A thrumming starts in my stomach. Blooming down my fingertips.

A thought slips through the haze of panic, like morning sun dispelling fog on a harbor: *Death is warmer than I thought it would be.*

The feeling consumes me, illuminates all the shadowy parts of my being, until there is nothing left but it and me.

I choke in a shallow breath, all I'm able with his arm crushed against my windpipe.

I am not afraid.

I refuse to be afraid.

A low whistling, the sound of an object flying through the air, snaps me out of my trance.

With my eyes still shut tight, I hear a squelching thump and flinch as warm liquid splashes my face.

Free from the weight of his forearm, I heave in a desperate gasp. The relief is immediate.

My eyes shoot open just in time to see Mr. Hues tumble to the floor with a mighty thud, my sewing shears buried almost to the hilt in the meaty left side of his neck.

Wine-red blood spills from the wound, blooms across his white shirt, and drips down into the seams of the worn wood floors.

He makes a gurgling noise, spasms, then goes completely still.

Where there was once a person, there is now only a body. A body with my sewing shears buried five inches deep in its neck.

But the door is firmly closed, the windows latched. There is no mystery savior, only me and the body and the shears.

A cold certainty fills me. I did this. Somehow I did this.

My mind goes dark. My knees go weak.

The last thing I think before falling to the floor is *Please, God, don't let me land in his blood.*

Again luck abandons me.

I come to, moments later, hands and arms sticky and red. Mr. Hues lies beside me, his beady eyes still open, his face arranged in an almost comical expression of shock.

The blood has seeped into the sleeve of my blouse, marring the white with a gash of rusty red.

Silver moonlight streams in through the windows, illuminating Mr. Hues's waxy hand, lying inches from mine.

I lie on the floor for a moment, prying my eyes from Mr. Hues's lifeless form to the ceiling. The apartment above is still; the encounter with Mr. Hues has apparently not woken the others. But why would it have? The screaming existed only within my own head. My vocal cords, paralyzed by fear or crushed by Mr. Hues, managed only the rasping beginnings of a cry.

I swallow down a sob. If the other girls wake, they'll find me here next to Mr. Hues, and I know what this looks like.

The only breaths I manage are frantic and shallow. I rise to my feet, which is difficult with every muscle in my body shaking, and find the soles of my boots are sticky with his blood.

Before I can stop it, my stomach rolls and I vomit all over the floor.

It mingles with the smell of sewing machine oil and something dying.

I heave again, but there's nothing left to come up.

I should probably make some attempt to get rid of the body, find an alley to drag him down, but even if I were strong enough to move him on my own, the idea of touching him is so revolting, I don't even want to try.

I cross the shop and sink down into the hard, wooden chair behind my sewing machine.

The blue velvet coat is still there, pristine and untouched. How anything in the world could be unmarred by the events of the last five minutes, I have no idea. It feels as if everything should be as different, should be as ruined as I feel.

I scrub a hand down my damp cheek. My palm comes away red. Blood, then, not tears.

Staring down at the coat, I make a plan. *One step at a time, Frances,* my brother's voice echoes in my head.

Step one: I will finish the coat. If it is incomplete in the morning, I will be fired, and everyone will know that something forced me to stop working. The body in the middle of the floor will make it fairly clear what that *something* was.

Step two: I will hide my bloodstained clothes and dispose of them in the morning. I can easily throw them away while out on delivery.

Step three: I will never tell anyone. I will never think of this ever again.

I reach to the right side of my Singer where my shears usually lie, but my fingers brush only empty space.

Oh.

Of course.

I steal Jess's instead. Her desk sits so close to mine, I can open her drawer without rising from my chair.

Their cool metallic weight makes me feel a little sick.

Again I hear William. *You can do this. You have to do this.*

I wipe my bloody hands on my dark skirt and get to work. I'm shaking badly enough that holding a needle is difficult, but I make do. It doesn't take long to finish the buttons and the hem.

Mr. Hues's form on the other side of the room is difficult to ignore. No matter how hard I try not to, every time I look up, my eyes snap to where his body lies, dark and solid, and very, very still.

My mouth tastes like bile, and it hurts a little each time I inhale. The pain is the only reason I believe any of this is real.

At the back table, I wrap the coat in tissue paper and then unbutton my own blouse. Blood is splattered across the neck and down the left sleeve. I have no chance of removing the stain on laundry day without the other girls seeing, so I fold it carefully and slip it into the box with the coat. I wrap the evidence neatly with a thick satin bow, and place it on the front desk, ready for delivery.

My corset is also marred with a coin-sized splotch of blood right above my heart, but another would cost at least a week's wages, so it'll have to stay. It's easier to hide, at least.

I have no time to mourn my ruined clothing or a time when I didn't know what a body sounded like when it hit the floor.

I swing the door to the dark street wide open and toss the cash box out onto the empty sidewalk, knowing it will be gone by morning. I don't know how to stage a crime scene, but I hope this looks something like a robbery gone wrong.

I'm wearing nothing but my corset, and the night air sends a shiver that reaches straight through my rib cage to my still-pounding heart.

Mr. Hues's body is splayed out near the base of the staircase. I close my eyes, grit my teeth, and summon a final act of determination to step over it.

If I were a braver person with a stronger stomach and steady hands, I would remove the shears from his neck. But I am not.

I reach into the pocket of my apron, pull out the key, and unlock the door. It doesn't open all the way, what with Mr. Hues's torso in the way, but I pry it open wide enough to shimmy through the gap. One step up the staircase, I turn for a last glance at his glassy, open eyes. The same eyes that roved over me so often in life are now unseeing.

Good riddance.

My breathing is jagged, still too shallow and fast as I walk up the narrow staircase to our dark apartment. Blessedly, the other girls are asleep in their iron bedsteads, breathing deeply, soft and quiet.

With a wet cloth from the washbasin in the corner of the room,

I wipe the dried blood off my face. I'm not sure if I get all of it—the cloth keeps coming away from my face red—but I can't stand to look at it anymore. In an apartment full of girls, no one will give a bloodstained rag a second glance. I throw it in my laundry pile and hope I've done enough.

I wish I were back in our old apartment on Hester Street, that William was in his bed, and I could wake him and ask what to do. His absence usually feels like a hole in my heart: ever present, but something I can function around. Tonight it feels like a gaping wound: stinging and ugly and desperately urgent.

Most days I try to dam my grief, fearing the dark unknown of its depths, but tonight I let it drown me, hoping if I do, I won't think about Mr. Hues's hands on my waist, or his dead eyes, or the way my scissors flew across the room as if by magic.

I sink and sink and sink into nothing but blackness.

I do not dream. And for that I am grateful.

CHAPTER TWO

Chattering voices wake me, and for a single blissful moment I don't remember the previous night's events. But I swallow and it burns in my throat, and the images of Mr. Hues pinning me against the wall come flooding back like a faucet of toxic sludge I can't turn off.

I catch only parts of the girls' conversation.

"Scissors . . ."

"Dead . . ."

"Thank goodness . . ."

There's nothing I want less than to leave my warm bed, but until I'm hauled off to jail for murder, I need to remain employed if I don't wish to starve to death.

My brother's voice rings in my head. *Chin up, sis. It's going to be all right.* It's what he'd say to me when we were children and I was crying because the girls down the street wouldn't let me play dolls with them, or when our mother was too lost inside her own head to feed us.

William had an annoying habit of always being right. Right up until he wasn't.

I swing my legs out of bed and place my feet on a floor that's so cold, it sends a shiver straight through my core.

The room we all share above the shop is small. Three narrow windows stretch across the wall, letting in beams of dust-flecked morning light. The wood floors are scuffed with years of use. Twelve twin beds, wrought iron and narrow, line the walls, six on each side. Mrs. Carrey's apartment is on the third floor, up the staircase on the far wall.

It's Jess who greets me first. "Oh, Frances, thank God you're up. Mrs. Carrey is downstairs with the police. *Mr. Hues is dead.*"

I feign a gasp and tug my nightdress up higher over my bruised throat. "What happened?" It hurts to speak.

"We don't know yet," Mary answers from across the room, where she sits twisting up her dark hair. "All we know is that the police came up this morning and fetched Mrs. Carrey. I can't believe you slept through it."

None of us waste time pretending to be sad for Mr. Hues. Although never openly discussed, all of us suspected what he was.

As if summoned by the act of her name being spoken aloud, Mrs. Carrey bursts into the room, a police officer at her heels.

"Is this the way young ladies look after eight a.m.?" she scolds us.

"No, Mrs. Carrey," we say in unison, throwing on dressing gowns and coats for some semblance of modesty in front of the officer.

17

In both hands, he holds our scissors. They clink together with each step.

Mary's hang off his pinkie, with their copper-colored blades. The long shank and large bolt mark Jess's. The ones with the coil of cobalt-blue thread around the thumbhole, mine, are missing.

He stops in the middle of the room, bends down, and fans them out across the wood.

"Ladies, if you would be so kind as to identify your shears for me."

One by one, each girl approaches the pile of scissors.

Allison grabs the ones with the strip of faded red fabric knotted around the thumbhole.

Catherine takes the pair adorned with shiny black ribbon.

On and on until there are no scissors left.

I approach the empty spot on the floor where the shears used to be, hoping I look appropriately confused. I don't reach out for fear the officer will see my hands shaking. Instead, I clasp them behind my back and grip so hard, it hurts.

"Mine are missing." I wonder which of the officers had the gruesome task of pulling my shears out of Mr. Hues's neck.

"What is your name, miss?" he says curtly.

"Frances Hallowell, sir."

He nods once, says, "Thank you, ladies," then exits the apartment.

The girls are silent, every last one of their gazes trained on me.

One doesn't have to be a detective to put the pieces together. I worked late last night. Mr. Hues is dead. My shears are the only ones missing.

I feel unbearably, hopelessly, backed into a corner. I could run away. But I have no money and nowhere to go. I could confess, but there is no way they would believe the truth of what really happened. I was there, and I hardly believe it myself. All I see before me is a path lined with reporters, lawyers, investigators, and prison. The case will be a tabloid sensation, as murders involving young women always are. I can see the headlines now: SEAMSTRESS OR KILLING MACHINE? or perhaps FRANCES HALLO-HELL: INSIDE THE MIND OF EVIL.

Mrs. Carrey turns up her nose and trots across the room, her boots clicking against the wood floors. "Miss Hallowell, a word." Her back is to me as she says it, which makes it worse, somehow.

Mrs. Carrey's apartment is an extension of her physical appearance, all propriety and cleanliness. I've only been up here once or twice before, despite living just one floor below her for the better part of a year.

She gestures to a pair of leather chairs placed facing a potbelly stove in the back of the room. I pad across her threadbare rug and take a seat, positioning myself just on the edge of the chair, as if I could get up and run at any moment.

"Miss Hallowell," Mrs. Carrey begins. "I wanted to speak to you before the police have the opportunity to question you."

The thought of police questioning fills me with a panic I swallow down. She takes my silence as an invitation to continue.

"Did everything look ordinary when you left the shop last night?" she asks.

I imagine the scene: Mrs. Carrey stepping downstairs this morning, finding Mr. Hues on his back, the wound in his neck dark with coagulated blood, his eyes staring at the ceiling, my vomit on the floor next to him. It must have been horrible.

"Yes, ma'am." Her lined face is difficult to look at, so I train my eyes on the floor. I've never been a particularly good liar. William could charm and fib his way out of anything; it's not a gift I also inherited.

"What time did you finish your work?"

"Around ten o'clock, I believe, ma'am." This time, the lie comes more easily.

"Make certain you know your story, Frances," Mrs. Carrey says, and I freeze. But her voice isn't accusatory; it's kind.

"I will support whatever you say," she continues softly. "Whatever that man did to you, I can assure you, he deserved the fate that befell him."

Mrs. Carrey purses her lips slightly. "I will help you, Frances, but first you must help yourself. You left the shop at ten. You know nothing else. Pretend to be weak and foolish. It's what the detectives will expect of a girl your age. With luck, they'll not push you further."

I stare at her wide-eyed, before nodding once.

From behind her chair, she pulls the delivery box I left downstairs last night. "For Mrs. Arnold, yes?"

"Yes, ma'am, the velvet coat."

"Good," she replies. "Do your delivery. Take the back staircase, try your best not to let them see. Make yourself scarce today—it's for the best."

The package is heavy in my hands, I picture my bloodstained blouse folded neatly inside.

"Everything is going to be fine," her voice trembles slightly, and this time, I can tell it is she who is lying. "You are dismissed, Miss Hallowell."

I rise, still in shock, and exit her quarters. The rest of the girls are in the throes of getting ready, and as I walk through them, they stop—ribbons half-tied, brushes half-pulled through locks of hair—and stare at me.

For the first time, perhaps ever, the apartment is completely silent.

I slip on my long dark wool skirt, button my high-necked white blouse—the only one I have left—braid my hair, and pin on my felt hat, while they all pretend not to look at me.

A horrible realization hits me. With Mr. Hues dead, the shop will likely be forced to close for good.

Their eyes follow me as I walk out the door.

I allow myself one single moment, alone in the rarely used back stairwell, to bite down on my lip and scrunch my eyes closed. But I can't fall apart just yet.

The cool morning air hangs heavy with the specific New York smell of river water, garbage, and too many people all living in one place. Black smog flows from the smokestacks of the factories on the other side of town. Horses, automobiles, trolleys, and people rush past me in a cacophony of activity.

A group of onlookers has gathered on the other side of the street, their faces screwed up in expressions of horror and delight. A woman in a pink dressing gown sweeps the same spot on the sidewalk over and over again, her wrinkled neck craned toward the shop. A grisly murder is easy entertainment for bored fishmongers' wives.

A headache still pulses excruciatingly through my head, an

ever-present reminder of what a horrible mess I've managed to make of my life in twelve short hours.

But being out of the shop gives me the first sense of control I've had all morning, and there is relief in that. There's anonymity in the city. When so many people live on top of one another, avoiding looking in someone's eyes is a politeness; it's as much privacy as we're able to give each other.

The grid of the Lower East Side is imprinted deep in my brain. Mrs. Arnold lives ten blocks away. There's an alley three blocks from here I should be able to duck down, open the package, and dump my bloodied clothing in before rewrapping the velvet coat for delivery.

I push my way through the crowded streets, eager to rid myself of the physical reminders of last night. I duck under a porter carrying a trunk, weave through a pack of laughing schoolgirls, and dodge a shiny black Cadillac barreling down the road.

I'm almost to the alley of a redbrick townhouse, ready to make a sharp turn, when a body slams into mine, snapping me out of my daze.

I stop short when I see the face of the offender.

"Oliver?" I gasp. The sight of him sends a zip of nerves through me.

"Frances Hallowell!" He sounds genuinely delighted. He's taller than the last time I saw him. It looks like he's grown at least an inch in only four months.

He has a boyish sort of face, despite being nineteen already. If I squint, I can picture him as the thirteen-year-old he once was, bounding up our stoop with a baseball in his hand, a mischievous smile cracking his dimpled cheeks. His green eyes are kind but offset

22

by his sharp cheekbones and jaw, certainly features he got from his mother. His father, Judge Callahan, is a lump of a man. My brother was the judge's errand boy years ago, before he got caught up in the wrong sorts of things with the wrong sorts of people.

Oliver's wavy brown hair is badly in need of a barber, but his navy-blue suit is impeccable. Better than anything I could make, and I'm not a half-bad tailor. The chain of a pocket watch strung from his breast pocket glints golden in the morning sun.

Seeing him feels something like walking into my old apartment on Hester Street: what was once warm and familiar now only makes me feel a deep, bruising ache of loss.

He seems to be examining my appearance as well—the dark circles under my eyes, the moth-bitten hat placed upon my poorly braided hair, my dingy shopgirl outfit—as commuters flow around us as if we are rocks in a stream.

His eyebrows knit together. "You look . . . well." He says "well" like he wants to say "bad." I don't tell him he looks well too, because I'm not a great liar and I don't know how to say *It physically hurts to look at you.*

"We should . . ." He trails off, darting his eyes forward.

I stutter a little. "Oh! Y-yes."

I take off down the street, and he follows me, though I'm fairly certain this wasn't the way he was headed before he ran into me.

"It's good to see you, Frances," he says after a too-long moment of silence.

"Thank you."

I like to think there is a version of Oliver who would have noticed that I'm profoundly unwell. The Oliver who taught me to play poker one rainy afternoon when William was busy working, or the Oliver who left a brand-new scarf on my bed the winter I turned fourteen.

But I don't recognize this fancy, Ivy League Oliver who wears the gentle smile on his face like a disguise. It doesn't touch his eyes the way it used to, when the corners would scrunch up, and he'd slap his knee, laughing at whatever joke William had just told.

It's all just as well. He doesn't know me, either, this new Frances who has blood under her fingernails.

I no longer remember how it felt to be the Frances who wrote Oliver's name in the margins of her schoolbooks. She would have had dozens of moony smiles to give him. I have none.

The last time I saw Oliver was at William's funeral, where he stood somberly next to my brother's grave, his black mourning suit worth more than what I make in six months.

Oliver's father paid for William's tombstone, for which I will always be grateful, despite not being able to bring myself to visit it. I sent Oliver a letter a few months back, begging for his help in finding William's killer, but he never responded. Wealthy, educated Oliver was supposed to have been William's best friend, but he did nothing to save my brother, and now he can do nothing to save me.

"I'm making a delivery. I'm late," I add sharply.

"Let me accompany you."

"I can handle it perfectly well by myself, Oliver."

He holds up a hand and replies, "I insist," like a gentleman. It's unsettling that the boy who used to sneak my mother's whiskey on the coldest nights of the year has grown up to look so natural in a suit.

On long legs, he walks next to me. I struggle to keep up beside him, fear and anger and grief simmering all the while. I can't bring myself to look at him, because in his face I only see William, so I look at his shoes instead.

I wish he'd leave me alone.

"I've been meaning to come see you," he says after a moment.

"You don't need to do that."

"Do what?"

"Lie to me."

"I'm not lying, Frances. It's been difficult. I've—"

I cut him off. His buttoned-up facade is too perfect. I want to poke at it. "It's been four months, Oliver. You don't have to pretend you still care."

He's visibly wounded, his sculpted face crumpling. "How could you think I don't care? I loved William like he was my own brother. I—" He chokes on the words.

I am not interested in his excuses, today of all days. "I loved him too. How much we loved him didn't matter in the end, though, did it?"

He shakes his head. "You can't truly believe that."

We pass a storefront that used to be soda fountain, and a memory briefly stops me in my tracks. I'm frozen in time, eleven years old, my socks mismatched, Oliver beside me, us both ordering vanilla ice cream, while William makes fun of us for being boring.

Oliver must see me looking at the building, because he smiles sadly and says, "They watered down their Coca-Colas, but I miss that place."

"I'm surprised you remember it at all."

"Why wouldn't I remember?" His face is inches from mine. His breath lingers on my cheek. My heart races as habit forces me to lean into him. If this were the past, before William's death, before . . .

I step back, push the lump down my throat. "Don't you have new friends now? Surely you don't dwell on your childhood friend and his kid sister."

Now I'm being cruel. I can see it in his face. Oliver never could hide anything he was feeling.

"You have no idea what I dwell on." A weaker boy would have looked at the ground as he said it, but Oliver's gaze bores right into mine. He chews on the inside of his cheek and then straightens his spine. "I'm sorry to have upset you, Frances." He reaches into his breast pocket and pulls out a small calling card printed with his name and contact information.

"I did get your letter. I'm studying at Columbia now. Please, tell me if you need anything. I've . . . I've missed you." He has the audacity to smile that strange, hollow smile again.

He reaches out for the briefest moment like he means to touch me, but I recoil. I don't take the card. I ignore the screaming part of me that wants to collapse in his arms and tell him everything. But I am four months older than the girl he once knew, and I now know how dangerous it is to love things.

"I'd best be going, Oliver."

I pick up the pace of my steps, disappearing into the crowd, leaving him standing in silence on the busy street corner. His eyes burn into the back of my skull, but I won't turn around.

I can't.

I can't think about how, after all these years, Oliver Callahan still makes me nauseous. Nor can I think about the strange way he said he missed me or the serious line of his mouth. I can't give in to the hurt of the things he makes me remember and the things he makes me want. I have a job to do.

After looping around the block, I duck down a narrow alley between a department store and a green grocer. No one will notice a bloodied blouse thrown among the pallets, factory scraps, and rotting food.

With quick fingers, and only rats for company, I untie the ribbon and slide my blouse out, tossing it in a pile of grease-covered rags. I stare at it for a moment, wishing I felt some level of relief in being rid of it. But instead I feel annoyance. The bastard ruined my favorite blouse.

I don't look back. I just slip out into the chaos of the streets, another faceless girl.

Seven blocks later, Mrs. Arnold's butler answers the door to her brownstone.

I'm invited into a parlor so clean, I feel guilty sinking my boots into the carpet. The room is cloaked in forest green, filled with spindly furniture, golden mirrors, and rugs so lush it looks as if no one has ever set foot on them. A girl close to my age silently scrubs an already gleaming fireplace. I offer her a sad smile she doesn't return. Maybe she can sense that there's something fundamentally wrong with me now. Perhaps, after what I've done, I have a look about me that warns others to stay away.

I chew on the inside of my cheek, trying to think of anything but the way my scissors flew across the room last night. What if I am imagining things? I wouldn't be the first Hallowell to lose their grip on reality. I hate that I can't make myself feel normal, that it feels like something is crawling inside me. I can't shake the feeling that I've awakened something I can't make go away.

A few long minutes crawl by before Mrs. Arnold's well-coifed lady's maid appears and opens the box containing the coat. "The eighth button is a little loose, but I can fix it myself. Don't let it happen again."

"No, ma'am. Thank you." I swallow the more gruesome retorts that spring to mind.

Stepping out of the mansion, it's strange to be free of the coat that gave me so much trouble.

I wander the streets aimlessly for a while, passing factory girls dressed in shades of dingy gray, cotton caps covering their limp hair. They look hollow-eyed, and most have been working all night. Among them pass a few rich men in top hats and their fancy wives twirling satin parasols. Small boys on corners shout the latest news, and women on balconies shake out the day's first batch of laundry. The predictable chaos gives me some semblance of comfort.

I bound across traffic to the other side of the road, leaping on deft feet over the trolley tracks that snake through the city, avoiding the horses that trot by.

If I had money, if I loved my brother less, I could use this opportunity to walk to Grand Central, board a train bound for the West, and never return. I saw a photograph once of San Francisco, and I always imagined I'd like it there. It looked like a place one could breathe. There's never any place to breathe in this city.

But what little money I make each week goes almost entirely to my room and board. In the cigar box currently resting under my bed

I have exactly two dollars and sixty-two cents. It might get me west of the Mississippi, but not much farther. I'm not sure I'd even know how to live anywhere that isn't here.

I could stay in New York. I could run uptown, maybe Harlem? But I'd live in fear. If the police ever found me, and I'm sure they would, my fleeing and hiding would only be evidence of my guilt.

Which means I have nothing. Nowhere to hide, nowhere to run.

Girls born into tenements on the Lower East Side don't have the privilege of being dreamers. I've never had romantic notions about what my life would be. I didn't imagine it behind the bars of a jail cell, but there are worse things than prison.

Living in constant fear of the other shoe dropping would be worse.

Or maybe I'll finally, *finally* get lucky; maybe I'll convince the police of my innocence.

My only choice is to return to the shop and face what happened. But the surety doesn't keep me from being terrified.

I steel myself and turn down Delancey Street.

CHAPTER THREE

The sidewalk outside the shop is still swarming with police, the brass buttons on their blue uniforms polished bright.

My steps slow as I approach, and I attempt to arrange my face into an expression of innocence. I fear it only makes me look more suspicious.

"Good afternoon, officer," I nod to a mustached man. He's shorter than me, which is to say very short. His shoes are impeccably clean. I picture his wife shining them for him before he left for work this morning. The imagined scene almost makes me feel guilty for the lies I'm about to tell him.

I'm surprised I don't recognize him. I know most of the officers at the local police station well by now. I've spent every Sunday sitting in their waiting room, picking at my cuticles until they bleed, waiting to speak to an officer about William's case.

Our conversations are always the same, a well rehearsed theater. *No, there aren't any leads,* they tell me. Next comes my line: Is there anything I can do to help? They always smile and tell me no. It fills me with a rage so strong it fuels me for the rest of the week, until I appear again the next Sunday and the anger is renewed.

I enter the shop at the officer's heels. Mrs. Carrey and the girls must be upstairs. The police are still busy documenting evidence and speaking to one another in hushed tones. They brush for fingerprints I know will be mine, and track blood splatters on the wall, but I'd be surprised if they came to the conclusion of *flying scissors.*

"Miss Hallowell, yes? Your supervisor informed me you were out on a delivery. You *should not* have left," he scolds, " but I'm glad to see that you've returned." His beady eyes look me up and down. "I was hoping we could have a word."

"Yes, sir."

He pulls out the chair at Mary's desk for me, but remains standing, his shiny shoes toe-to-toe with mine.

"Miss Hallowell," the officer begins, clearing his throat, "I just have a few simple questions for you, very simple, all right?"

He nods his head at me like I'm a child. I nod back dumbly.

"Where were you last night?"

I pray that my face doesn't turn red, as it always does when I am embarrassed or anxious. "I was here working in the shop until ten p.m., sir. Then I retired to the apartment upstairs." I'm pleased to hear how steady my voice sounds.

He jots something in the narrow notepad balanced in his left hand.

"Good, very good," he says encouragingly. "And why were you up so late?"

"I was behind on a project." I'm grateful for one answer that isn't a lie.

He scribbles some more.

"Did anything unusual happen when you left the shop?"

"No, sir."

"I see, I see." He nods, then looks up from the notepad. His eyes are no longer kind.

"And can you tell me, Miss Hallowell, why your shears were found in the victim's neck?"

"No." My voice cracks.

He presses further. "Well then, can you confirm, Miss Hallowell, that you were alone in this shop after hours, the same shop the deceased's body was later found in, and can you confirm that the deceased had a"—he stops and clears his throat again—"sordid history with the ladies?"

His tone has changed dramatically; he's speaking quickly. My palms and chest have begun to sweat.

"I don't know what you're implying, sir." I sound panicked. I *am* panicked.

He glances at my feet, boots only partially hidden by my long black skirt.

"May I see your boots?" he asks.

I pause for a moment, pretending to be distracted by the ambulance that's pulled up on the curb alongside the police vehicles and carriages. I wonder if the body is still here somewhere, and they've arrived to take it away.

I say a silent prayer to William for a moment of brilliance, a revelation that will help me out of this mess, but I know I'm finished. I'll spend the rest of my days in prison. My life will have amounted to nothing. I want to burst into tears, fall to my knees, and beg him to spare me, but I swallow the urge. William would never have begged.

Chin up, sis. It's all going to be all right.

I bend down slowly, reaching for the laces with shaking fingers, when the chime on the door breaks the heavy, dread-filled silence.

Still bent over, I freeze and look up.

Standing in the doorway, illuminated by the yellow morning light, are two nurses. One is young—my age perhaps, or a little older. The other is likely in her forties. They're wearing long gray-blue dresses with straight prim white collars. Their white hats sit perfectly atop their swept-up hair, and their red-cross armbands are wrapped snugly around their upper arms. They're both wearing elbow-length capes with straps that cross in an X at their chests. Most nurses' capes are lined with red; theirs, however, are as black as night and unlike any I've seen before.

"Excuse us," the younger one interrupts, pushing through the crowd of officers, not distressed in the slightest by the scene before her. Her voice is low and reedy, her hair so blond, it's almost white. She moves in contrast to her older, dark-haired companion, a pale woman with a freckled face who stands next to her silently, mouth pressed in a thin line.

"We're looking for a Miss Frances Hallowell," the blonde demands, hands placed on her hips.

"I'm Frances Hallowell." I'm still half-hunched, my fingers frozen on my bootlaces.

"Your test results have returned," she trills, "and we are so terribly sorry to inform you of your tuberculosis diagnosis."

There must be another woman named Frances Hallowell in this neighborhood, because the person they are seeking obviously isn't me. I don't have a cough. I haven't been tested for anything. The last time I saw a doctor I was nine.

From the corner of my eye, I can already see the police officer inching away from me, not wanting to catch what I allegedly have.

The older nurse meets my eye and raises her eyebrows slightly, as if to say, *Trust me.*

I cough one pathetic little cough to communicate my understanding.

"You have been ordered to report to Haxahaven Sanitarium," the little one continues. "This is for the safety of yourself and others. We have an ambulance waiting outside to take you now."

"Miss Hallowell is a suspect in an ongoing investigation," the officer finally pipes up from behind me. Somehow, with all that is currently unfolding before me, hearing out loud that I'm a confirmed suspect is what fills me the most with fear.

I don't know who these women are or what I will encounter at this sanitarium, but if it means avoiding going to trial for murder, I will follow them wherever they wish me to go.

"No," the blond nurse corrects the officer impatiently, "she is a patient. And the longer she remains in the city, the more people we are putting at risk."

The older nurse finally speaks. "You'll come with us at once, Frances." Her voice is low and kind.

The officer stares at them both, mouth agape.

Mrs. Carrey floats into the room, her brows knit together.

"Frances dear, this does explain that awful cough you've been having." She glances quickly at the officer.

I nod, thankful for her one final act of protection. "Yes, ma'am. Please give the other girls my regards."

Sadness cracks through the veneer of her professionalism, a frown tugging at her lips. "You'll be missed."

Without another word, the blond nurse takes me gently by the elbow and leads me outside to the waiting ambulance. It is a rickety thing, as if someone tacked a large box on the back of a Model T and painted a red cross on the side. It looks profoundly unsteady on its chest-high spoked wheels.

The older woman slides into the driver's seat and starts the engine with ease. I've never seen a woman drive a machine before.

The younger one leads me to the box attached to the back of the car. It is a simple setup: two stretchers are tacked to the wall, and a few cases of what I assume are medical supplies litter the floor.

She sits down on the stretcher on the right wall and gracefully slips into a supine position, lying flat on her back.

She notices me eyeing her.

"Oh, this?" she says. "It's much more comfortable this way. We've got a long drive ahead of us."

She gestures with a slender hand to the wall opposite her. "Take a seat."

I step into the back of the ambulance; the roof is so low, I have to keep hunched to avoid hitting my head. For a moment I consider telling the strange nurse she's got the wrong girl, but I can't bear to be sent back into the shop. I'm less brave than I hoped I'd be.

"Aren't you going to lie down?" the blonde asks me.

"I'd rather sit, if that's all right." Lying down would make me feel more vulnerable than I already do.

"Suit yourself." She closes her eyes and crosses her thin arms over her chest. Her black cape falls around her. She looks like Dracula in his tomb.

The Model T lurches forward, right as another police officer steps out onto the street.

"You're still needed for questioning!" he calls. "You're a suspect in an ongoing investigation!"

The wheels kick up dust in his red face, and his protests are swallowed by the noise of the engine.

I may have just gotten away with murder.

The back of the ambulance is open, and soon the shop, the police, and the fifteen blocks containing everything I've ever known shrink away into the horizon.

It's my first time riding in an automobile.

"Where are we going?" I ask the young woman lying across from me. I've never been as relaxed anywhere as she manages to be in the back of an ambulance bolting through the city.

"Haxahaven. We said that part, right?" she replies breezily, her eyes still closed.

"And Haxahaven is a sanitarium for tuberculosis patients?"

"It will all make sense when you get there," she replies with a yawn. "Now, shh. I'm trying to take a nap."

I knock my head against the wall as I lean back in frustration "Will you tell me your name at least?" I beseech her.

"I'm Maxine. That's Helen up front." She sounds bored at best.

"I'm Frances," I reply out of habit.

"Oh, honey, we know," she replies. "Now shh."

Do you? I want to ask. But I know when questions are unwelcome, so I chew at my nails instead.

We race through the maze of towering concrete and masses of people. Maxine remains motionless on the other side of the car, apparently deep in sleep, though I don't know how with the deafening roar of the engine and the pitching of the wheels over the uneven road. Helen deftly maneuvers between pedestrians and horses as we snake through the chaos of Lower Manhattan. Just when I'm sure we're about to be mowed down by a trolley, she turns, and we're bouncing down another cobblestoned street.

Finally, we reach the Williamsburg Bridge, and I can't help but shut my eyes and clench my jaw as we race over the polluted river. Though I know William's body is resting in a pile of dirt in a graveyard not far from here, the dark water still makes me feel sick.

Brooklyn is quieter than Manhattan. The laundry hanging out of brownstone windows waves like flags. A silent farewell parade to my old life. I'm overtaken with an ache of sadness so deep, it penetrates my bones. One question plays in my head: *What have I done? What have I done? What have I done?*

Still we drive. Queens is even quieter, cloaked in trees withering with the cool of early fall. Large houses with privacy shrubs dot wide streets.

We go on for what must be nearly an hour. Nerves keep me propped up rigidly, except for my foot, which I can't stop from bouncing. If Mrs. Carrey were here, she'd smack me with a ruler to stop. But she's not.

The drive leaves too much time alone with my thoughts. Perhaps

I have lost my grip on reality, like my mother did after William died. My mother had never been the portrait of maternal love and care, but something irreparable inside her soul snapped the day they found William's body washed up on the shore. She sat perfectly still for three days in an armchair by our single window. I brushed out her matted hair, but I couldn't make her eat. Rumors regarding my mother's state burned through our apartment building like kerosene set alight by an errant match: quick and hot. Mr. Feranno upstairs wanted our apartment so his grandchildren could live below him. He wrote the authorities about my mother, said she wasn't fit to care for herself. Then I missed a rent payment, and we were well and truly done for. From our landlord there was no forgiveness, no understanding. To him, there were only those who could pay and those who couldn't. We could not.

They dragged my mother off to the asylum in the middle of the afternoon. She didn't scream at all when they took her. But I did.

Finally, the ambulance begins to slow. We creep down residential streets speckled with mansions and browning gardens. To our left there's a park, looming as large as Central Park but twice as dark and three times as overgrown, more forest than anything. It seems dimmer somehow, as if the skies this far from Manhattan are a different shade of blue.

We make one final turn down a driveway all but hidden by a canopy of live oak trees. At the bottom of the drive there is an iron gate at least eight feet high. The rest of the property, which looks to be nearly the size of a city block, is surrounded by a stone wall just as tall. The wall is old, not crumbling, but old, as if it sprung up from the earth itself.

Stuck in the ground at the base of the wall is a sign. It's hanging lopsided on its frame, supported by a single, sad chain. The white paint is chipping, revealing layer upon layer of flaking grime. In faded black are the words:

HAXAHAVEN SANITARIUM

TURN BACK FOR THE SAFETY OF YOURSELF AND OTHERS.

An ivy plant is choking the sign, doing its very best to pull it back down to the purple-thistle-covered earth.

Helen steps out of the ambulance but the machine still rumbling. She pulls a brass key the size of her palm from the pocket of her apron and undoes the padlock on the gate.

It's a little rude, really. If the great state of New York is going to commit me to an asylum, they could have sent me to the same one as my mother.

It's too late to protest now, so I sit in silence as Helen reenters the driver's seat and takes us up a narrow drive. The gate shuts behind us with a clank. When I glance back, the lock is latched once more. Then, from behind the cover of branches, an imposing building comes into view.

Like the sign, this place has seen better days. The Grecian style estate has a white facade marked by hulking columns, grayish with the decay of time and bowed, struggling to carry the weight of the roof, which looks in danger of sliding right off. There's a lawn of weeds bordering a circular drive covered in pale pea gravel. Ivy climbs over the porch and up the columns, reaching for the dingy windows. The few white chairs placed beside the front doors look as if they might turn to dust and float away on the wind—if they don't fall through the rotting wood of the porch first.

What's strangest is the eerie stillness, the emptiness of the porch and front lawn. I've never heard of a sanitarium where patients don't recover out of doors.

I've read the exposés in the papers about sanitariums. One former patient said they were experimented on. Another said they were locked inside their rooms for twenty-two hours a day. Maybe I should have let the police take me; maybe jail would have been better than this. At least prison has to give you a sentence; a sanitarium can keep you forever. *Jesus, Frances, what have you done?*

The ambulance halts directly in front of the crumbling steps of the porch.

I glance back at the gate; it doesn't look as if it would be terribly hard to climb. I could make a break for it.

Maxine finally awakens. "Here already?" she mumbles.

As gracefully as she slid herself in, she slides out of the stretcher and makes a little hop to the ground. The gravel crunches beneath her boots.

I stare at her, eyes wide in terror. *Why did you bring me here?* I want to shout at her.

Instead, I follow her.

Squaring my shoulders, I steel myself for the horrors of a state-run sanitarium. I picture dingy gray walls, people forgotten in their rolling chairs, left alone to hack up a lung, bloodstained rags scattered across the ground like fall leaves.

Helen leaves to park the ambulance, and I follow Maxine up the ancient stairs and through the creaking white double doors.

I blink my eyes twice, trying to adjust to the sudden flood of light. Instead of blood and sickness, there are shining marble floors that soar into goliath white columns and twin staircases, sweeping elegantly up either side of the entry hall. Sparkling crystal chandeliers dot the vaulted ceiling, reflecting the light streaming in from the floor-to-ceiling diamond-pane windows, throwing rainbows all across the room. My heart stutters a beat; it's the only sensation that keeps me from believing that I am dead and in heaven, which is apparently in Queens.

The outside of this place may look abandoned, but inside is a flurry of activity. Dozens of girls scurry about, dressed all in black from their pinafores to their knee socks to their elbow-length capes, identical to Maxine's, fluttering behind them as they rush off to various destinations.

Maxine's mouth hitches in a half smile.

"Welcome," she says, with a flourish of her gloved hand, "to Haxahaven Academy."

CHAPTER FOUR

My mind takes a moment to catch up to what Maxine just said to me. The words "Haxahaven Academy" bounce around between my ears before I fully grasp their meaning.

"Academy?" I turn to her.

"Haxahaven Academy, yes. That's what I said." She's smiling like she finds my frantic confusion comical.

"You said this was a sanitarium."

"A most clever disguise. You'll find we're very clever here," she says with a wink. If we were friends, I'd tell her to quit it with the dramatics, but we are not friends.

Girls bustling around the great hall slow a few at a time, stopping to take in the newcomer standing in their foyer. They glance at me briefly, a few mutter something to their nearby friends, and then they continue on their way.

I imagine how I must look to them, standing in their fairy-tale entryway. I wish I'd had time for a bath, or that I wasn't still wearing a corset stained with the blood of a man I'd killed.

Helen steps in through the front door, back from parking the ambulance. She stands square and squat next to lithe Maxine. The long trip has made her hair even frizzier, and it springs from the fluffy bun atop her head as if trying to escape.

"Be nice to the poor girl, Maxine," she scolds.

"I am being nice!" Maxine responds, offended by the very idea of her introduction lacking niceness.

"Be nice, or I'll be the one conducting the orientation," she says, with a small jab to Maxine's rib cage with her elbow.

Maxine huffs out an annoyed sigh. "What's the fun in being a witch if I can't be a mysterious witch?"

Helen rolls her eyes and walks toward a door to the left of the entry hall.

Over her shoulder she calls, "Be nice, or I'll tell Mrs. Vykotsky you're not to be trusted with the next one!"

"Helen's always so certain she knows what's best," Maxine whispers to me conspiratorially.

My mind whirs in an attempt to consolidate the hurricane of information dumped on me.

"You said this was an academy?" I look at her for confirmation, and she nods once, obviously annoyed that I've been so slow on the uptake. "Aren't you a nurse? Where are the patients? Where do we convalesce?"

She shrugs. "We lied."

"You lied?" The room tilts a little; my knees are weak.

"Because no one lets us take girls away for something as inconsequential as an education."

It's the closest thing I've gotten to what feels like an honest answer from her. "I left school at fourteen to work. I had no intention of returning." The Clinton Street Public School on the Lower East Side could only be described as "brutal." I think I must have loved learning at some point in my life, but rulers on knuckles rapped all the questions out of me a long time ago.

"And yet here we are," Maxine replies.

"I don't understand."

She sighs heavily. "You'll meet with the headmistress shortly. The whole murder-charge thing mucked up the orientation process—we had to get you out quickly."

"Sorry about that, I didn't have much of a choice," I snap.

She's disarmingly sincere as she replies, "We know."

"How?"

"I can't quite say. The headmistress is particular about the welcome speech she gives to the new girls. What I am allowed to tell you is that you're safe, you're sane, and you're not in any trouble." Then she turns on her heel and trots up the marble stairs.

I follow her, because my other option is to stay standing like an idiot in the entryway alone.

Maxine's long legs carry her so quickly, I have to hurry to stay behind her, muttering frustrated little excuse-mes to the other girls as I push past them. The odd thing, I realize after a moment, is that they're not all girls. The people in the foyer and on the staircase are women of all ages, all in the same black cape and pinafore. One woman has cropped snow-white hair; another girl of only ten or eleven passes me in a rush. A few even wear trousers. Light streams in from the windows, casting the marble hall in a glow so white, it's almost blinding.

Maxine takes me across the second-floor landing and up another side staircase to the third floor. Here the carpet is lush and black, in contrast to the stark white of the floors below.

Only small slivers of the gold damask walls are visible. The rest is almost entirely covered with portraits, tintypes, and photographs of women.

I pass one photograph that can't be more than a few years old of a group of girls smiling and laughing with their arms thrown around one another in front of a lake. It hangs next to a portrait of a very stern-looking woman wearing an Elizabethan collar.

It's unclear where the girls on the stairs and in the entryway were headed, but it wasn't here; the halls upstairs seem to be abandoned except for Maxine and me.

A flash of movement from the corner of my eye makes me jump. With a gasp, I bring my hand to my chest, as a tabby cat emerges from the dark corner, a still-flapping moth in her mouth and a self-satisfied look in her eye.

"They're everywhere," Maxine says in response to my startle.

"Cats?"

"Yes, the cats."

"Intentionally?"

"Not particularly. They keep the moths at bay and most don't scratch too badly. The black one in the kitchens bites, though."

The tabby retreats with her prize back into the shadows, and I follow Maxine down the hall.

We pass door after wooden door, until finally she stops at one painted with an elegant 11.

"This will be your room," Maxine says.

Despite Maxine's assurances of safety, I'm still confused and upset. I've been taken from my home, my job, and told I am to live at this strange school full of strange women. The thought of my mother sitting alone and without visitors in the asylum makes me sick. It's not Maxine's fault. It's not anyone's fault but Mr. Hues's, but knowing that doesn't stop the waves of anger.

Maxine pushes the door open. Upon first glance, I am reminded of the apartment above the dress shop. Four beds, two on each side, pushed against the walls, but unlike the cheap iron bedsteads of the shop apartment, these are hand-carved wooden canopy beds.

Like the hallway, the carpet in this room is a lush black that contrasts beautifully with the gold vanity positioned at the far side of the room. The wallpaper is the same as the hallway. It must be the nicest room I've ever been in.

"Here is your bed." Maxine waves toward the bed closest to us on the left side of the room. "I trust you'll find all you need here. The fall uniform is laid out for you already, and you'll find four more hanging in the wardrobe. Shoes are under the bed. The rest of the girls will show you where everything else is kept."

"All right."

"I suspect you're exhausted. After my first outburst, I slept for three days, thought my head was going to explode with the pain of it. Some girls are out for a week. I'll let you rest."

She makes her way for the door.

"Outburst—" I blurt.

46

She turns to face me, her eyebrows raised in a question.

I'm suddenly very angry with Maxine and all of her sly smiles. "It wasn't my fault. I don't know how the scissors ended up in his neck, but I didn't put them there."

Maxine sighs. "Mrs. Vykotsky will explain everything."

"I'm not going to jail, then?" Speaking the words feels dangerous, as if somehow, by acknowledging that I am a person who belongs in prison, I make it real.

Maxine laughs and turns to exit the room. "Not yet!" she calls on her way out the door.

And then I am alone.

I walk to the bed, *my* bed, and thumb over the uniform someone's laid out for me. A black cotton blouse that puffs out a little before coming in at the elbows, with a black pinafore laid on top. There's a pair of black woolen knee socks, a coil of black velvet ribbon for my hair, and my very own cape, the same as everyone else's. I trail my fingers over the clothing; the quality of the fabric and the construction is extraordinary.

What I'm most thrilled about, however, are the undergarments. Three perfect corsets accompanied by silk chemises nicer than anything I've ever owned. The thought of ripping my bloodstained corset off fills me with such relief, I choke out an elated laugh into the empty room.

In the mirror on the far side of the room I catch a glimpse of my throat, a mottled bruise green. It doesn't matter; this skin doesn't feel much like my own anyhow.

Maxine was right about the exhaustion; I feel about as heavy and lucid as a log.

But I don't slip immediately beneath the duvet. I walk to the single-pane diamond glass window and place my hand at the spot where the cold leaches through the casing. The third floor offers an unobstructed view of the tangle of trees that is Forest Park. Directly below me, encased within Haxahaven's wall, is a sad courtyard.

I unclip the lock and push the window open simply for the reassurance that I can. Three floors up is too far to jump. Not that I would. Not yet at, least.

Finally, I lie down on top of the blankets because I don't know what else to do. The canopy is made of dark red velvet that matches the covers laid across the bed. I run my hands over the real goose-down pillows and sigh.

Once, when I was six, I was sent home from school because I couldn't stop crying. When my mother inquired as to what happened, I did my best to explain. I told her I had raised my hand, which I rarely did, and asked my teacher when were we going to learn what was on other side of the map of the world that hung on the wall of our classroom. She flipped it over and showed me it was blank. "That is the whole world. There is no more." All the things I would ever see or know were printed right there on a paper with no second side, no new world to explore. There was no more. My little heart couldn't take it.

But now, in a bed carved with fairies and snaking vines, I feel as if my teacher may have been wrong. Here I am, on the opposite side of the map, in a world that is entirely new.

I dream of a mansion draped in golds and maroons. A group of men in finely tailored suits sits around a glossy mahogany table. I'm standing in the corner, watching their meeting like a specter, when a boy in a gray overcoat and disheveled curly hair sidles up next to me. He reaches over to hold my hand, except—no. He's handing me something. He presses my sewing shears into my hand; they're as warm as an embrace and wet with thick blood. It seeps hot between my fingers. A single drop falls onto the white carpet. The boy winks. The men at the table go silent. Their gazes snap to me.

I wake, disoriented, but the feathered pillow is solid beneath my head. The damask wallpaper, the velvet canopy, that's all still here too. This room, at least, isn't something I dreamed up.

The boy. He's real too. Or was real at one point. We've met before.

He was in my apartment last December, just after Christmas. I remember it vividly, William barreling into the apartment well after dark, waking me from a dead sleep on a night so cold there was frost on my quilt.

I lit the lamp on my bedside table and carried it out into the kitchen, where I found William half-slumped and hanging off the shoulders of a disarmingly handsome boy. He never brought friends around, unless the friend was Oliver, and even that was rare.

My brother and this boy were swaying in the entryway singing a drinking song about a lost love. They went silent when they saw me.

"What's wrong?" I greeted them.

"Mm'fine," William slurred.

"A bit too much to drink, I'm afraid," the boy replied.

"Well I hope you had fun," I sniped. My annoyance teetered dangerously on the edge of rage. William never came home drunk. I didn't even know he drank. I'd spent all evening cleaning the apartment, scraping together a stove full of food, brushing mom's hair, organizing the wash, all while William was out making a fool of himself with friends I didn't know.

"Thanks, I'll take him from here," I said to the boy. He looked at me a little glassy-eyed, and I wondered if he'd had too much to drink too.

"I'm Finn," he blurted. I remember being surprised by his Irish accent.

"Ahhh, Finny boy!" William muttered into his friend's collar.

I wasn't expecting an introduction. "Um, I'm Frances. William's sister."

"He talks a lot about you," Finn replied.

"My precious baby sister," William mumbled as I transferred one of his arms from Finn's shoulder to mine.

William stumbled, almost taking me to the floor with him.

"Whoa, whoa, whoa," Finn breathed, picking up my brother's other side.

Together we half walked, half dragged William to his bed and laid him down on top of the covers.

Finn made quick work of my brother's shoelaces, which was impressive, because he wasn't looking at William—he was looking at me. The kind of penetrating serious gaze that made me want to hide behind my unbound hair.

"How do you know my brother?"

"We work together."

William had left his position as Judge Callahan's errand boy a year or so before, and I was seeing less and less of him as the months went on. All I knew was that he was working at a gentleman's association as an assistant. The club was filled with important men. Do well enough there and they might mentor him in business, he told me whenever I complained.

"You work at the club too?"

"Aye."

"What do you do there?"

"Doesn't much matter." He opened his mouth as if there was something more he wanted to say. I gave him silence, but he didn't take the opportunity.

William's face was properly buried in his pillow now. "I feel awful. Why'd you make me drink so much," he mumbled.

"Oh it hardly seems fair to blame me," Finn trilled.

"All that whiskey you gave me. I won't be able to work tomorrow."

"I'll cover your shift, don't you worry, but you know the real loss is yours. Tomorrow is Sunday, so Boss will be wearing his—"

"Purple suit." William completed Finn's sentence with as much of a laugh as he was able, given his state.

"I'll paint you a stirring verbal portrait upon your return, my friend." Finn patted William's back and stood up from where he was perched at the end of the bed.

"No! Don't go!" William shouted. "We have to write more songs, or we'll never get the musical off the ground."

"The musical?" I prompted.

"Seemed like a good idea to write a musical together three whiskeys ago."

"My name will be in lights, Frances!" William exclaimed.

I sighed heavily. "Time to sleep, William."

"You never let me have any fun."

"Seems that you have plenty of fun for the both of us," I snapped.

"Not fair, I work so hard . . ." My brother trailed off, closing his eyes.

"You work hard?" I mocked him. "I'd show you that my hands are *bleeding* from all the work at the shop today, but I'm wearing these gloves because this apartment is so cold, I'll lose all feeling in my hands if I don't. But it's fine, I understand. We've both had a long night, you with your friends. Me reading our mother Charles goddamn Dickens until she relaxed enough to fall asleep without you here." Sadness welled thick in my throat. I wanted to punish my brother, but instead I'd only made myself look like a fool in front of his friend. The tears were stupid, as tears almost always are.

"Mmm sorry, Frances." William rolled onto his back and raised his arms from the bed like he meant to hug me, but they collapsed heavily back to the mattress.

"Sorry doesn't do me much good now. Just sleep. We'll talk in the morning." Our mother used to say there was something about the middle of the night that always made things seem worse than they were.

"Good night, my friend," Finn said with a pat on William's head.

I walked Finn to the door, because it seemed like the polite thing to do.

"Nice to meet you, Frances . . . finally," he said in the doorway.

"Finally?"

"Your brother thinks the world of you."

I didn't return his smile. "Don't let him drink that much whiskey again."

Finn reached for the dead bolt at the same time I did, and our hands brushed, just barely.

"They're nice gloves, for what it's worth," he said, head ducked low, not quite meeting my eye.

"Well, you never know when guests might come by, and to be caught without my gloves would be quite the society scandal," I joked, but it didn't hide the edge in my voice.

"Well, I'll be happy to report to the society pages your good manners remain intact," he said, which was kind, because he felt how cold the apartment was, heard my humiliating outburst at William. He could have chosen to embarrass me, but he didn't. I don't remember if I said good night, but he did, halfway out the door with a final glance back at me like he was searching for something in my face.

I scrub a hand across my eyes and try to clear William from my brain. Some memories sting more than others.

I don't know how long I napped for. It's still light outside, but the hallway is silent, and the courtyard is empty. Wherever the classrooms are, they're far from this wing.

I amble through the room for a few minutes, poking through the drawers and closets of my roommates. I don't find anything interesting. I'm not sure what I was expecting. Maybe a diary with entries like *Help! Their capes are beautiful, but they won't let me outside.* Instead I discover uniforms identical to the one laid out on my bed, a few books, scattered papers and inkwells, a bottle of lilac perfume, and pair of pearl earrings thrown carelessly on a chair.

All this rifling through drawers is beginning to make me feel like a criminal. I need to take a walk. To taste the pines this mansion seems to be living inside. All my life, I've lived in the city—among sirens, the buzzing of factories, and smoke billowing into the air. The silence of Haxahaven is so unsettling, I can't stand it. Maybe this would all feel less surreal if I could touch something alive.

I rush down the steps, the eyes from the oil paintings and photographs following me as I go to the door.

My fingers are outstretched, reaching for the brass handle, when Maxine's voice cuts through the hall like a knife. I hadn't even seen her in the foyer.

"What are you doing?" She's sitting on a silk settee against the wall, a book in her hand and a horrified look on her face.

"Taking a walk in the park?"

"No. No, you're not," she snaps. I don't know what it is I've done, but Maxine's tone makes it clear it is no small mistake.

"I just—" My eyes well up with tears like they always do when I'm embarrassed. God, I wish the past twenty-four hours contained less crying. I won't let more tears fall.

"You are never, *ever* to leave this building by yourself. Do you understand?"

"Yes," I say, though I don't understand at all.

"Good. Come with me, then." She gives me a strained smile. "Your timing is impeccable. It's time to meet the great Vykotsky."

CHAPTER FIVE

Set against the starkness of the great foyer is a large black door that yawns like the mouth of something with teeth. It's early evening now, and the marble floors glow pink with the sunset outside. Maxine picks up the handle of the golden eagle–shaped door knocker and lets it fall from her long fingers. The hollow thud of the door reverberates through my bones.

"Come in," an icy voice calls from inside.

"Good luck!" Maxine replies cheerfully—a little too cheerfully, from what I've come to expect from Maxine.

I take a breath, turn the brass handle, and step inside.

The room is low lit, swathed in black velvets and dark wood. The back wall is made up entirely of shelves containing tiny dust-covered jars and vials. The vaulted ceiling is adorned with dried bouquets of baby's breath and sprigs of herbs hanging upside down on long strings of twine, hovering just above my head. A white woman, perhaps sixty, sits at an ebony desk covered in delicate whirring brass instruments, stacks of yellowing papers, and a small pile of dried-up inkwells.

Like her office, she is dressed entirely in black velvet, from her floor-length dress to her cape, identical to those the other women wear, save for the fabric and the monstrous moonstone brooch secured at her throat. Her snow-white hair is piled atop her head in a pompadour. She sits as straight as a board in her chair, her eyes narrowed, looking down her pointy nose at me. All the while, she drums her fingers along the desk, so pale they are nearly translucent, purple veins popping out at each knuckle. She looks like the kind of woman Mrs. Carrey might get along splendidly with.

"You must be Miss Hallowell." She speaks after a moment of examination. Her voice has the dignity and pointed pronunciation of the upper class. The kind of voice that, through force of sheer habit, nearly has me reaching to my pocket for an order form, asking what kind of dress she's looking for.

I take a single, careful step inside; my boots sink into the plush carpet. "Yes, ma'am."

"Please, won't you take a seat?" she offers, gesturing to the straight-backed velvet armchair across from her.

The overstuffed cushion is so tall, my feet barely graze the carpet. I can't help but swing them back and forth like a child.

The woman spends a moment looking me up and down with a gaze that makes me feel like my insides are being spooled out for her inspection.

When she is satisfied, she speaks. "It is important to me that you know, first and foremost, that Haxahaven is a place of healing."

"So is this a sanitarium or a school?"

She purses her thin lips. "Both, in a way, I suppose."

There are ten thousand questions I want to ask this woman. *Why was I brought here? How did you find me?* But the questions stick in my throat like a hunk of stale bread, so I stay silent under her intense stare.

She must sense my discomfort. "You are safe here, and very welcome." But something about the way her mouth curls around her teeth makes a chill spider-walk down my spine.

"Thank you, ma'am."

"I suppose you have many questions for me, but please allow me to first give you the speech I give all our new girls. I realize that what I'm about to tell you may sound rather suspect, but I need you to trust me. Can you trust me, Frances?"

I nod, even though I trust this woman about as far as I can throw her.

She smiles, like she's pleased. "Some may call what we can do magic, but it is simply a function of your divine self. Of your soul. The same soul that inhabits every other human on this planet. We just have the ability to use . . . more of it. To manifest it in ways uncommon in the general population."

I'm not sure what I expected, but it wasn't this. Maybe she's a liar, or this is an elaborate joke. "Magic?"

"Yes, Frances, magic. Like the way those scissors soared across the room and into that man's neck."

Nerves ricochet through me. "How do you know about that?"

"Inference." Mrs. Vykotsky smiles in the particularly annoying way the old smile at the young, with pitying condescension. She is at once a frustrating and terrifying woman.

"I'm too old to believe in magic. It would be easier for you to tell me the truth."

Again, she smiles. "You think you're smart."

"I don't think I'm anything, ma'am."

"Allow me to prove you wrong."

She raises her hand from her desk, and her pen levitates right along with it.

My stomach lurches. I close my eyes, as if I can blink away witnessing the impossible. It hurts to look at, like my mind refuses to take in what I'm seeing. "How'd you do that?"

"Magic."

The simplicity and impossibility of the pen floating in the air sends a fissure through my brain, cracking everything I thought I knew of the world in half. "Do it again."

And she does. One by one she levitates each object on her overcrowded desk. She sends a hard candy wrapped in purple foil drifting across the room, where it settles in my lap.

"Eat it," she offers.

I feel like I did the first time I rode the subway, the lurching nausea and sense of amazement. There's an undercurrent of fear, too, the sensation of hurtling through darkness. "No thank you. I have a lot of questions."

With each of the objects now firmly back on her desk, she keeps her hands folded carefully in front of her. "I'd imagine so."

But I feel the *thing* inside me, the *thing* that sent the scissors flying at Mr. Hues, and it whispers that she's telling the truth. It's there in my gut, something golden and inexplicable, something *awake*. I try to let it all settle in. This truth. What she's trying to tell me by not telling me. *Magic*. I have magic. Which means . . . My eyes dart to hers. She can see me putting everything together, piece by piece. Mrs. Vykotsky leans forward, waiting for me to say it. "I'm . . . a *witch*?" The word is so ridiculous, I almost don't get it out.

"If that's the word you wish to use. The truth is you possess an extraordinary ability. It is who you are."

My vision tunnels. I grip the armrests of the uncomfortable chair; I need something solid for purchase.

"I can do what you do?" I say. "Move things with my mind?" *I can do impossible things?*

"Magic is derived from the human soul; it is as varied as humanity itself, but yes, with proper training, you'll have the ability to move things with your mind."

"How?" *How is it that the world is entirely different from what I've been told?*

"Few people are gifted with the ability to perform what is commonly called magic. This ability is typically awoken by a traumatic event. You can think of your ability as your very soul being expanded. The explanation as to *why* is between you and your god."

The knots in my chest uncoil just enough to breathe again. "How long does it take to learn?"

"Depends on the person. Girls are usually with us for a number of years. Think of this time as your magical secondary education. It is our sincerest hope that you find your time with us valuable and instructive."

Years. I file the information away to panic about later, but I can't get lost in nerves just yet, I have too many questions. "Can you bring the dead back to life?" I try to feel the weight of what I'm being told, but the only thing I can think of is: *William.*

Mrs. Vykotsky swallows. "If only."

Disappointment burns through me. I settle back into the chair. What good is having magic if it can't bring him back?

"Our job is to keep you safe. If thousands of years of history have taught us one thing, it is that the world is not kind to women who possess power. I will give you exactly one warning, Frances—you will do what we say, and we will keep you safe. You do not want to be a witch in the world alone, nor do you want your power to eat you up from the inside out. Do you understand?"

This time I'm honest with her. "No, ma'am. I'm afraid I don't."

She leans forward with the grace of a snake. "Are you familiar with the Great New York City Fire of 1845?"

I shake my head.

"The story I am about to tell you does not begin with the fire, but rather, it ends with it. In the 1840s a group of idealistic witches left our beloved Haxahaven for the thrill of the city. They took their magic and their youth, and they set up a coven in a copper-roofed building on Broad Street. There they lived together, and there they practiced their magic recklessly, on street corners and at parties for anyone who could pay the right price. It was small magic. The manipulation of objects, identifying the first initial of someone's secret love." Mrs. Vykotsky pauses for a moment to gauge my reaction. If I'd been born seventy years earlier, I would have wanted to have been friends with these women, but I don't get the impression that's the reaction the headmistress wants from me, so I nod solemnly.

She purses her lips and continues, voice grave. "But word got around about the witches and their warehouse, and those who would prefer to keep magic to themselves burned the warehouse to the ground. All thirteen of the witches died, as well as thirteen more civilians and four firemen." My blood runs cold, imagining the horror of it all. "The fire commissioner never could explain why the warehouse was encircled with salt and gunpowder, but those of us up here knew what it meant. Witches are not stupid, Miss Hallowell. We are not reckless. And we heed the warnings we are given."

"But who burned down the warehouse? Why not fight instead of hide?"

"We hide because that is how we protect young witches like you and your classmates. We do not fight because there are many with gunpowder and matches and very few of us."

Her answer makes me angry. How completely predictable, how infuriatingly boring that women with magic can be so easily intimidated by ordinary men with guns and matches. "How few of us?"

"There are one hundred pupils here, and we gather every magical girl from the tristate area. I trust you can do the math yourself."

"Yes, but—"

"I'm not here to debate you. I'm not here to be your friend. I am here to keep you safe. It is an obligation I take seriously. Your days will be filled with coursework. You'll take three classes as a student of Haxahaven Academy. Magical History, Practical Applications, and Emotional Control. I trust you'll find them . . . illuminating. We do ask that you don't practice your abilities by yourself without the guidance and safety provided by a skilled instructor."

I nod. The gesture feels too small an acknowledgement for the storm raging in my head. I want to shout or smash something.

"This is a school, a safe haven, and yes, in many ways a magical sanitarium. Our disguise as a tuberculosis hospital is intentional. We will train you, and you will return to your life. In time, controlling your magic will be as easy as breathing."

I think of my life spent sewing until my fingers bled. Returning doesn't sound like a happy ending.

But I also think of Mr. Hues and the noise he made as he drowned in his own blood. I don't mourn the man, but I would very much like to avoid killing someone again. Learning how to control this *thing* doesn't sound so terrible.

"You lived alone, correct?" she asks me.

"Not alone exactly, above the shop I worked in with the other girls. I moved in four months ago."

"So no family?"

I have no interest in talking about the unpleasant, so I say, "No, ma'am."

"That's good then. For most girls, the school sends a stipend home to make up for lost income. We tell the families it's a grant from the state. But it doesn't appear it will be necessary in this situation."

"No one will miss me."

"That's no matter. We're your family now."

Her words ring in my ears. It is exactly what Mrs. Carrey said to me my first day at the shop, on a day much different than this one. But Mrs. Vykotsky is staring at me across her ebony desk with a smile I did nothing to earn plastered on her face, and it doesn't feel like the protection of my previous mentor.

A white petal from one of the drying bunches flutters down

from the ceiling and lands on my shoulder. I brush it away and take a deep breath.

"Thank you, ma'am."

"I expect you to treat this as you would any other school. You'll have class six days a week. Sundays are your own to do as you please. Stay within the garden walls. Don't leave after dark. Breakfast served at seven, lunch at noon, and dinner at six. Follow the rules, ask the other girls for help, and I have no doubt you'll do well here."

She studies me for a moment, her dark eyes raking over my face. "I suspect we will speak again soon, Miss Hallowell."

I rise, but she is already dipping her fountain pen in ink and scribbling away at the documents spread across her desk. She doesn't say goodbye as I walk through the door.

I'm in such shock, my body doesn't feel like it belongs to me. Buzzy and weightless, my feet carry me to my still-empty room, where I flop down on the bed and stare at the ceiling.

I'm a witch. Witch, witch, witch.

If William were here, he'd make a joke about putting a hex on our loud upstairs neighbors. He'd find this exciting and hilarious. William lived his life like something great was always right around the corner. The existence of magic would probably come as no surprise to him at all.

But William is dead, and I am alone and terrified and more than a little confused. My heart beats loudly inside my chest. *Witch-witch-witch,* it echoes. And I don't know if I want it to beat louder, or for the noise to go completely silent.

There's a small plate of mashed potatoes and boiled chicken on my bedside, probably left by Maxine. It was a kind gesture, but I have no appetite. Eating is the last thing on my mind. *What do I do now?*

Later that night, well past three a.m., I wake with a start, the question still on my mind, plaguing me. The room is dark and quiet.

The only noise is the heavy breathing of strangers who sleep in the other three beds. My new roommates must have come in at some point during the night.

It's so cold, there's a spiderweb of frost on the window, illuminated by the silver light of the moon.

And sitting on the pillow next to me is a small square of parchment folded gently in half.

I reach for the note like I would a coiled snake. The rough paper feels dangerous under the pads of my fingers. I unfold it.

Written in bold scrawl: *11.30.1891–5.15.1911. Justice Undelivered.*

My body goes numb. The note falls noiselessly to the carpeted floor.

November 30, 1891, was my brother's birthday. May 15, 1911, was the last day he was seen alive.

The words "justice undelivered" work their way under my skin.

"Hello? Who's there?" I hiss into the darkness. I don't receive an answer. The heavy sound of inhaling and exhaling makes it feel as though the room is breathing around me.

I force myself up and out of bed, though the last thing I want to do is leave the warmth of my duvet.

Shivering like a rabbit in a trap, I check the window first; it's locked from the inside. The courtyard below is empty, and beyond that, the park is an impenetrable black mass, terrifyingly dark and still.

A quick rustle of fabric snaps my attention behind me.

Nothing. No one. My legs quiver as I approach the washroom.

Empty.

I hear the noise again. It's quiet but distinct. And it's then that I realize with horror that the sound is coming from the direction of my own bed.

My heart is in my throat. *Should I wake up my roommates? What would I even say to them?*

I swear under my breath, steel myself to check under my bed.

I bite back a scream, before calming my frayed nerves.

Goddamn it, I hiss under my breath.

A small black cat innocently paws at my bed skirt. It has the nerve to meow at me, like it didn't just frighten me out of my own skin.

I grab the tiny menace and haul it into bed with me. It nestles by my feet like we're best friends and not mortal enemies.

It isn't until I'm back under the covers that I consider what I would have done if I'd found an intruder: Fight them? Scream? Hope for another well-timed pair of flying scissors?

My heart rate slows, but I still can't escape the itchy feeling of being watched.

Perhaps this note is the proof I've been desperately searching for that my brother's death wasn't a random act of violence. Or perhaps it is proof that Haxahaven's pupils haze their new schoolmates in awful, unfunny ways.

I don't know how these girls would know anything about my

brother, but I also know that I no longer understand anything about what magic makes possible.

Shaking, I shove the note under my mattress and spend the rest of the night in a fitful sleep, dreaming of my hands covered in ink and someone else's blood.

CHAPTER SIX

My eyes open to a gaggle of girls hopping out of bed, throwing on corsets and capes, brushing out their hair, and shouting across the room at one another.

It's so similar to the shop, it takes me a moment to remember where I am.

They fall silent at the sight of me stirring out of bed. I steel myself and hop up, attempting to smooth my hair and dress. I was so shaken last night, I didn't even think to change into a nightgown.

My new roommates and I take one another in simultaneously. They look similar enough to the girls I knew from the shop, though their cheeks are a little less hollow.

"I'm Frances." I say my own name like a question. A round girl with rosy skin and beautiful masses of auburn hair piled up on her head speaks first.

"Aurelia Barton," she replies. She has a gap between her front teeth, which she reveals when she smiles at me reassuringly.

The girl at her side could have been carved from ice. She's standing at the vanity mirror tying her corn-silk-blond hair up out of her face with a black ribbon. "Ruby Laird . . . pleasure." Her tone sounds as if it is anything but.

It is only then that I see my third roommate, emerging from behind the silk dressing screen in the corner of the room.

She's tall; I don't have to stand next to her to know she's got several inches on me. She has tan skin and shiny black hair plaited in one long braid that reaches most of the way down her back. She stands with her head slightly down, as if she's pointedly avoiding my gaze.

"Lena Jamison." Her voice is cool, if a little disinterested.

Aurelia sits down on the edge of her bed to lace her shoes, and Ruby finishes her bow with a nod at herself in the mirror. My window of opportunity is closing quickly. I swallow my nerves and ask, "This may sound strange, but did any of you leave a note on my bed last night?"

The looks on their faces are so genuinely confused, I believe they're telling the truth when they all mutter confused *nos*.

"What did the note say?" Aurelia asks.

I don't know how to begin to respond so I chicken out instead. "Must have been a strange dream." I lie poorly.

Ruby and Aurelia share a confused look, button their capes over their pinafores, shout "Farewell!" and walk out the door arm in arm, leaving Lena and me alone in static silence.

I stand near my bed, not sure what to do next. I want to ask Lena if she was once as scared as I am now, or what magic feels like to her. I wonder if her family misses her, if she's from the city or someplace I've never been.

"You'll need to put on the cape for breakfast," she offers from across the room.

"Thank you." It comes out as a sigh of relief.

As a seamstress, I appreciate the construction of clothes, but what I wear has always been a matter of strict practicality. Buttoning the cape over my chest feels like something different entirely. I straighten my spine but avoid glancing in the mirror. I don't want to know if Mr. Hues's fingers are still imprinted on my throat.

"Will you walk with me? I don't know where to go," I ask Lena.

Her smile is reluctant. "Why not? Follow me."

The black cape flutters behind me as I go with Lena to the stairs, and it makes me feel like a very important, glamorous lady—or maybe a small bat; I can't decide.

The pristine stairs sink peculiarly under my feet, like they're rotting from the inside out. Lena and I walk through more shining halls, to a pair of immense double doors that leads into a shimmering dining room, bedecked in sparkling crystal-and-gold sconces. In the center are three mahogany tables, shined within an inch of their life, capable of seating a hundred at least.

Lena chooses a seat, and I plop down gracelessly next to her.

More and more girls pour into the room. Lena and I don't speak.

I can't relax. I scan each of their faces, wondering which person in this room left the note on my pillow. It has to have been one of them.

I'm chewing violently on the inside of my cheek when someone sits down in the seat next to mine.

"Good morning! How're your roommates?" Maxine asks, and the sight of her sharp face and hazel eyes fills me with surprising relief. She crosses her legs in front of her, leaning off the side of the chair, looking casual, rogue-like even. She wears the uniform differently than most girls, with the collar unbuttoned around her throat, her cape hanging just slightly off center, like a costume, like she's in on a joke.

"You got stuck with Laird and Barton, right?" she continues.

"And Lena Jamison," I add, gesturing to her with a nod of my head.

Lena peeks around me. "Hi, Maxine."

"Sorry to you both, getting stuck with those shrews," Maxine says.

"Aurelia doesn't seem so bad. . . ." I trail off.

"She's not when she's not around Ruby, but she has the spine of a jellyfish. She'll do whatever she's told," Lena explains.

"Count your blessings, girls. There are worse than Ruby and Aurelia," Maxine replies.

"Oh?" I fidget in my chair. For such a large dining table, it is noticeably absent of any food.

"Mm-hm." Maxine nods and takes a swig of water. "Like those two over there." She gestures to a pair of near-identical round-faced blondes at the other end of the room. "The Underwood sisters, Hattie and Beatrix. Mean as a whole a pit of vipers. But most of the girls are fine. Just mind your manners and smile pretty."

I open my mouth to respond but come up short as a feast on sparkling silver platters comes through the dining hall, carried by women in black capes just like my own.

Entire glazed hams, bowls of fruits and vegetables spilling over,

French toast, bacon, eggs, and apples boiled with cinnamon.

Maxine reaches out and serves herself a spoonful of diced peaches as if this is all old hat.

"Where did this come from?" I ask.

"The kitchens," she says through a mouthful of toast.

There is more food on this table than I've seen in my life. I can't tell her I don't remember the last time I had enough to eat.

My father left soon after I was born, so my whole life was my mother, William, and me trying to survive. My mother did her best, which wasn't very good. She'd take in neighbors' laundry and clean the other apartments in our building, but she was never stable enough to hold down a steady job.

There was one Christmas when all we had to eat was a handful of chestnuts and a crust of old bread. My mother made William and me drape napkins on our heads and told us we were just like Joseph and Mary in the innkeeper's barn. I was six and William had just turned nine, and we no longer believed in fairy stories. The next day, William went out on his own and got his post as Judge Callahan's errand boy.

But Maxine doesn't need to know about all of that. So I answer, "Of course," and take a bite that turns to sawdust in my mouth. I feel too full of questions to swallow anything.

Maxine notices me pushing the food around my plate. "Aren't you hungry?"

"Objectively, probably." My attempt at a smile is poor.

"Seems like a waste of pancakes."

"It's almost as if having one's reality torn to shreds ruins an appetite," Lena deadpans.

"I don't mean to spoil breakfast. It's just I don't feel like my brain has caught up to what's happening."

"A school for magic girls isn't what you expected when you woke up yesterday?" Maxine laughs.

"When I woke up yesterday, I thought I'd be in prison by nightfall."

"No bars on the windows here," Lena says, her voice tinged with sarcasm.

"Just a twelve-foot wall that keeps us safe, sweet Lena," Maxine replies.

Though I don't have an appetite, what I do have is more questions, and I wonder if there will ever be a time when I don't. "How is it that a school for magic exists, and no one has found out about it?" It seems a more reasonable question than *How is it possible that everything I've ever thought to be true about the laws of the universe is wrong?*

"The school used to be disguised as a convent—if there was one group of women the world left alone, it was nuns. But then the local churches began asking questions, so it was converted to a school back in the 1850s. It wasn't long before the locals came knocking. I'm not sure why when women say 'students,' men hear 'potential wives.' Can girls not be scholars in peace? Anyway, the sanitarium guise started about thirty years ago. The neighbors leave us be." She punctuates her statement with a dramatic fake cough. "But don't think because you're just finding out about magic, it means no one else in the world knows."

Oh. "So who else knows?"

Maxine and Lena make nervous eye contact. "Not appropriate breakfast conversation for young ladies," Maxine says.

"You can hardly blame me for having questions."

Maxine glances around. A tendril of silver-blond hair falls from her bun and into her eyes. "Fine." She springs up, smoothing her pinafore.

"Where are you going?" I ask.

"Keep your voice down. Follow me."

Lena and I follow her without another question. Despite Maxine's breakneck pace, I drink in as much of Haxahaven as I can. It looks like a cathedral and a manor house and a hospital all at once.

We crisscross Haxahaven winding halls until we finally come to an ancient-looking stone door. It's carved with runelike markings in a language I don't recognize.

Maxine waves her hand, and the door slides open with a low scraping sound.

I hear Lena give a small snort. "You can manipulate objects too?" she asks. "I thought you were a Finder?"

Finder?

Maxine laughs. "I've always wished there was a more elegant term for what we do. Surely 'Finder' isn't the best we can come up with." She shakes her head. "But I digress. I can manipulate better than some but not as well as others. My magic is one of . . . connection. I can feel the connections between people and power most easily, but manipulating the way objects are connected to other objects isn't so difficult."

Her answer begs more questions than it answers, but I swallow them down and follow her through the door. I'm almost giddy witnessing Maxine's use of magic as if it's an ordinary task. Each spark I see solidifies the new reality I inhabit, confirms that all of this, that *magic*, is real. The terror of everything that happened yesterday only slowly starts to subside, as my curiosity begins to take over.

Breath catches in my throat at the cavernous room filled with floor-to-ceiling bookshelves made of charred-black wood. The soaring ceilings are buttressed with Gothic arches, and along the crown molding are life-sized stone statues of stern-looking women.

I can't tell if the strange buzzing in my ears is coming from inside my head or from the walls.

Like ducklings, Lena and I skitter behind Maxine to a worn table near the side of the room.

Candles drip white wax onto the surface, their yellow flames reflected in the single glass of water placed among them. Despite the monstrous room, a claustrophobic pressure mounts in my lungs.

"Why the quick exit?" Lena asks. I don't get the impression she and Maxine are particularly close. She looks as lost as I am.

"Fewer eavesdroppers here, and there are a few very important things I need you to understand. One, at Haxahaven the walls have ears. There are no secrets here. Two, not everyone here is your friend." A muscle in her sharp jaw twitches.

The library smells of parchment and kerosene.

"So, as you were saying . . . ," Lena prompts Maxine. "The witches of Haxahaven are not the world's only possessors of magic?"

"Oh God, no. That'd be rather narcissistic, would it not?"

"So who else?" I ask.

"Haxahaven is rather good at finding every magical girl in the area. Rich, poor, any race, from any neighborhood, girls whose parents thought they were boys upon birth, girls who are only sometimes girls, girls who are still deciding, people who are neither boys nor girls. We train them all. The men are left to their own devices. They do what men do."

"Destroy things? Hoard money? Fight each other?" Lena quips.

"Precisely."

"What do we do when we leave?" I ask. "We are allowed to leave, right?"

Maxine and Lena exchange a look that makes me nervous, but Maxine answers me after a tense moment. "They do what most women do: marry, have children, work. I've heard rumors of a few magical communities in the city. I believe there's at least one underground magical market. I once overheard Helen speak of a coven on Martha's Vineyard, but she refused to tell me more." Maxine's brutal confidence flickers out for a second. "I wish I knew more."

"That's all she's told you?" I prompt.

"I only know that we're supposed to treat everyone we meet with extreme caution. If someone arrives at the gates, we do not let them in."

So the wall around this school exists as much to keep us in as it does to keep others out. That means whoever left the note on my bed last night has to have been someone in this school.

I don't know how to ask Maxine and Lena *Who here knows about my dead brother, and why did they leave a terrifying note on my bed?*

But Maxine is still looking at me expectantly, so I move on to my second most pressing question.

"How does a world with magic work?"

"The way it always has. The magic isn't new. Your awareness of it is," Maxine says.

"So tell me more. Tell me the rules. Tell me how it works." *If it's real, teach me to be so powerful no one ever touches me without my permission again.* My curiosity builds and builds. I can't stop it. I don't want to. If I know it—magic, how it works, being a witch, *all of it*—maybe I won't be so afraid anymore.

She smiles at me, finally pleased with something I've said. "You have to be present for the magic to work. It is exceedingly difficult to magick more than one object at a time. You'll learn spells in class, and those will help you focus the energy. The first day or two after a magical awakening are strange; we aren't usually able to do spell-less magic after this, except by accident. But Mrs. Vykotsky doesn't react well to magical accidents." She turns on a voice to mimic Mrs. Vykotsky's. "The worst thing a girl can do is lose control of herself."

"Have you?" I ask.

"Have I what?" Maxine replies.

"Lost control?"

"Mrs. Vykotsky only has two Finders at Haxahaven. She needs my skills to find new pupils more than I need her. But please do know . . . Mrs. Vykotsky does not make empty threats." She sighs, and the corner of her mouth twitches up. "I like you, just a little, and I'd like for us to be friends. So please be careful, but don't be boring."

Maxine's affection feels a bit like when the vicious mouser cat we had in the shop decided her favorite place to nap was under my desk. Something sweet and rare and a little dangerous. One wrong move and my ankles might be torn to shreds. I'm not naive enough to trust anyone here, but I desperately want to trust Maxine and Lena.

"If we are to be friends, there are a few more questions I'd like answered. This is a school, correct? Who teaches the classes? How does any of this work?"

"A combination of teamwork and magic," Maxine trills.

"I'm serious!"

"So am I!" She laughs, and despite my frustration, I find myself laughing too at the ridiculousness of it all.

"Magic is typically awoken by an event in someone's life. For most of us, that event occurs in adolescence, but we don't find some witches until adulthood. Other girls are just children. Everyone stays for different lengths of time, depending on ability. That's why the sanitarium guise works so well. It takes different people different amounts of time to gain enough control to be ready to reenter society."

"Just like a real sanitarium." I echo my conversation with Mrs. Vykotsky.

Lena chews on her cheek, then answers, "Only if you think magic is a disease."

"Is it?"

"If you let it be." I don't know Lena well enough to know for certain, her face is purposefully impassive, but if I had to guess, she seems sad.

"How long have you been here?" It is perhaps the wrong question to ask, but I can't stop myself.

"Nearly two years," she says. "Happy anniversary to me." Her words bite with sarcasm. I remember what the headmistress said yesterday about most girls staying at the school for years. My heart aches for Lena, who looks like she'd rather be anywhere but here.

"And you, Maxine?" I ask. Our table sits close enough to one of the long rectangular windows that I press my hands to the glass just to feel something cool and steady. Fat clouds float by in an autumn sky of brilliant blue.

"Six years. They found me when I was thirteen." I wonder what happened to wake their magic, but it feels impolite to ask.

"How did you find me? How did they find you?" I ask, the memory of Maxine and Helen appearing in the shop to rescue me from the police, as if by magic, playing in my head.

"Witches like Helen and me can sense . . . disruptions in the energy source. Usually it means a flare-up of power for the first time. It comes to me like a vision; it's strange every time it happens. I don't often know their names. I only knew yours because the officers were talking about you outside your shop."

At her mention of police, Lena casts a sidelong glance at me.

"Do you bring all the people you feel to Haxahaven?" I ask.

"Usually." She bites at her thumbnail.

"Not always?"

"You'd have to ask Vykotsky." She arches an eyebrow, and I nearly laugh at the thought of ever returning to that office voluntarily.

Under the table, I pick at a cuticle. "What does this all mean for me, then?"

"It means you're home—we're stuck with each other."

From somewhere far off, a bell chimes. Maxine and Lena spring from their chairs.

"Time for your first class, little Frances," Maxine declares. "Lena will show you the way."

I follow her and Lena out of the library and into the hall. With one kiss blown over her shoulder, Maxine trots away. Girls rush off in all directions, their heads down, mouths shut, capes flapping behind them.

Through serpentine corridors, Lena and I weave between our

classmates. The halls echo with the sounds of heels on flagstone floors and hushed conversation.

After a long, awkward stretch of silence I ask Lena, "Where did you live before this?"

"A place called the Thomas School."

"That sounds nice."

"It wasn't." Her answer is fast and certain.

"Oh—I'm sorry. Why did you go then?"

"It wasn't a choice. All of the children from my tribe were forced to go. The nuns came every fall to collect us."

"I'm sorry."

Lena shrugs, but there's tension in the line of her shoulders.

Soon we reach an open door and join the stream of girls pouring inside.

We enter a room filled with rows of marble-topped benches, simple stools set behind them. Two skylights, set high in the arched ceiling, illuminate the room with twin beams of morning light. Lena and I take seats behind one bench near the back.

At the front of the room, standing in front of a well-worn slate, is an old woman with wire-rimmed glasses.

"A new pupil!" she exclaims the moment I sit down.

I pop back up from my stool and wave, which feels stupid. The chalk in the air makes my eyes sting.

"Your name, dear?" She prompts.

"Frances Hallowell."

She clutches her heart with the pride of a mother. "Ah, my darling Frances, how delighted I am that you have joined us. This is Practical Applications, and I'm Mrs. Roberts."

She turns her attention to the rest of the class. "Girls, your books, if you please." It's strange to be back in a classroom. I never took much joy in school, was never hungry for it the way I am now.

From the built-in shelves below the benches, the girls pull identical leather-bound copies of a book that look similar to the hymnals at the church we used to go to when I was little. Then William stole enough Bibles that my mother was too embarrassed to go back. Ten-year-old William thought it was the height of comedy. Those Bibles lived under his bed until he died, though none of us ever read them.

"Turn to page two hundred twenty-four, would you, darlings?"

While my classmates rifle through the onionskin pages of their books, Mrs. Roberts circulates through the room, distributing squares of scrap fabric, assorted buttons, needles, and thread.

At the corner of the bench Lena and I share we receive two pieces of dark blue muslin and two delicate mother-of-pearl buttons.

Mrs. Roberts returns to the front of the classroom, perches at a lectern, and flips open her own book.

I glance down at my open book, and my vision goes a little fuzzy. I don't know what the text is, but it isn't English. There are drawings of human hands surrounded by looping arrows, as if they were instructions for a dance.

Magic. I resist the smile that pulls up at the corners of my mouth.

"Ladies, we'll be continuing the sewing lessons we began last week. Frances, dear, in my class you'll learn to apply magic to your everyday life. As witches, it is our responsibility not to burden the world with our power, but it is in our best interest to burn off a little, day by day, in order to be our best selves. Miss Jamison, would you be so kind as to begin."

With a nearly inaudible sigh, Lena reaches over and snatches a square of dark blue cotton, a needle, a length of thread, and a button.

She takes a breath and begins to read in a low, steady voice, *"Nal, syn, ga."* Her hand loops in a figure eight.

The needle, as if held by an invisible hand, levitates from the bench. With her other hand, Lena pinches the thread so about an inch is sticking up from her thumb and pointer finger. The needle swoops down and threads itself, before falling to the bench with a tiny cling.

I've been told that magic exists, I've witnessed it already, but still, seeing the needle levitate off the table and thread itself knocks the wind out of me.

"Very well done, Miss Jamison. Let's work on those pronunciations though, darling. They're still a bit clumsy."

Lena nods, then tilts her head back and massages the bridge of her nose.

"Are you all right?" I whisper.

"House magic always gives me a headache. I'll be fine."

Mrs. Roberts appearing at my shoulder makes me jump. She moves with the silence of a cat stalking prey.

"Your turn, Miss Hallowell," she says.

I suddenly feel much like I did when I was in the fourth grade and had forgotten to do my report on President Franklin Pierce. "How?"

"Just take a breath and say the words on the page." She makes bending the laws of the universe sound so simple.

I close my eyes, like I saw Lena do, then I loop my hand in the same figure eight in front of my chest and say, *"Nal, syn, ga."* The words are awkward. My tongue doesn't know how to form the syllables. The sounds stick in my throat like peanut butter.

This magic feels different than the sewing shears, it's more like learning to hold a pencil. A part of me that is both me and more than me stirs awake, and for the first time since my brother's death, I feel like a participant in my own life.

I open one eye. The needle is levitating off the desk. A wave of excitement washes over me, and with my shriek of victory, the needle falls with a *ting*.

Mrs. Roberts places a warm hand on my shoulder.

"Well done, Frances. We'll try again tomorrow." She floats on to the next pupil, and I thumb the mother of pearl button, marveling at the things I didn't know I had inside me.

The rest of the class passes quickly. I soak in all the magic I'm able, watching classmate after classmate levitate and thread the needle. Mrs. Roberts is kind, adjusting hand positions and pronunciations. It's tedious, and nothing like the wild magic that made my sewing shears fly across the room, but there is something comforting in the control it gives me over the pounding in my chest.

A sharp bell dismisses us, and Lena kindly offers to walk me to my next class.

"All the new arrivals go to Mrs. Li's class."

"So you won't be there too?"

"No, I take Emotional Control with Mrs. Porozky and a group of girls who arrived around the same time I did. After that I'll head to Clairvoyancy."

"Clairvoyancy?" I open my mouth to ask her the hundreds of questions on the tip of my tongue.

"Don't ask me to tell your future," she quips.

"But—"

"If you don't ask me to tell your future, I'll show you where your next class is."

"I thought you were doing that already?" I say with a laugh.

"I'm not above leaving you in the hallway. It would take you days to find your way out."

I sigh. "Deal."

We trot through the halls of Haxahaven, and although most of my classmates cast their eyes downward, I can't help but gaze up at the swooping buttresses and sparkly chandeliers. It's almost enough to make me forget about the note, still tucked under my mattress.

Lena leaves me at the door with a polite wave.

Sitting at the front of the room is a woman in her early sixties, perhaps, with snowy white hair and a serene smile on her face.

I wonder if perfect posture comes naturally with being a witch, or if it is something that is taught at Haxahaven.

"Ah, Frances." She waves me over. "I'm Mrs. Li. It is my pleasure to welcome you to class."

"Thank you, ma'am."

"You've been placed with me and a small group of girls with similar powers who all arrived here recently, like yourself."

I nod, and with another wave of her hand, she gestures for me to take a seat in the circle of chairs, where a few of my classmates have filed in.

"Welcome, friends," she greets us.

We all take a seat, arranging our capes and black skirts around us.

"We have a new pupil with us here today. Would you please introduce yourself?"

Every girl in the room turns their gaze to me, and all the blood in my body rushes to my face. "Frances Hallowell," I answer.

"And why are you here?" Mrs. Li prompts me.

"I'm afraid I don't understand the question."

"What happened to awaken your magic, dear?"

I briefly consider lying. There is nothing I'd like to avoid more than telling a room full of strangers the story of the worst moment of my life.

I settle on half the truth. "My boss attacked me."

She nods, her lips pursed. "Ah, I see. And how did that make you feel?"

"Make me feel?"

"Yes, Frances, how did your boss attacking you make you feel?"

I wish everyone would stop staring at me. Their unblinking gazes turn the bubbly joy I felt moments ago flat and sour.

She can't be serious. "It made me feel bad." I finally answer.

She turns just slightly to a mousy girl who sits to my right. I sigh in relief at the reprieve of her gaze.

"And what do we do when we feel bad, Sara?"

"We take deep breaths," Sara says. "We center ourselves. We remember we are in control of our bodies and ourselves."

"Yes, very good," Mrs. Li replies. "Magic is, above all, mastery over yourself."

What follows is hours of girls spinning tales of their most horrible moments and describing the way their hearts raced, their anger, their sadness. Mrs. Li sits with her perfect posture and tells my classmates that they must breathe deeply and picture their soul becoming small and retreating back into their chests.

I'm sick with fascination. Or maybe I'm just comforted in knowing I am not the only one who has experienced the horror that comes with feeling dangerous and out of control.

Two hollow-eyed girls on the other side of the circle detail their experiences in the Triangle Shirtwaist Factory fire that happened a few months ago in midtown. It was all over the papers. One hundred forty-six people died. Sara and Cora should have been among them, but the horror of the accident awoke the magic in them, and they used their abilities to open a locked steel door and flee to safety.

Sara and Cora take turns telling parts of the story of that awful day. I get the impression they've told it many times in this room. They seem well practiced in noting the details; Cora describes the smell of burning flesh, while Sara explains the screams. Mrs. Li tells them they must learn to control the power that resides within them.

It strikes me as odd that no one in the room acknowledges that it was that power that saved their lives.

Mrs. Li nods and looks appropriately sympathetic at all the right moments and tells us again and again that we're in control of ourselves.

It's too much to stare at their vulnerable faces, so I memorize the features of this classroom, as strange and different as the last one. It reminds me of the basement of a church: windowless, with walls that look like they're covered in dripping black wax. The candelabra overhead casts the paintings on the waxen walls in golden shadows. I watch them flicker and change until Mrs. Li announces class is finished.

Lena is waiting for me outside the door after we are dismissed.

My steps fall into sync with hers and soon we're in the dining room, a lunch spread out before us. Lena sits down next to me and serves herself a bowl of soup. I follow suit, finally hungry. After a moment I ask, "What was all of that?"

"Mrs. Li's class?" She glances over at me. "She believes in . . . purging oneself of emotions. You're lucky that's all it was. I heard the woman who taught the class before Mrs. Li was enthusiastic about practical demonstration."

"What do you mean?"

"She spent the class period throwing books and screaming at the students. When they had enough control over their powers to not react, she deemed them ready to start learning spells."

"That sounds preferable, honestly." I laugh.

Lena flashes a knowing smile. "Well, then I'm afraid you'll be disappointed by the academic offerings here."

"All of the classes are like that?"

"More or less. Without proper control, the power can ruin your life." Her voice is monotone, as if she's repeating something she's been told but doesn't believe.

After lunch, Lena takes me to a third classroom, paneled with rich mahogany; again she leaves me at the door.

I sit down next to a tiny girl with dark brown skin and black curly hair tied into a bun at the base of her neck.

"Mabel," she greets me, holding out a small hand.

"Frances."

Her smile is sunshine itself, a relief after being in Mrs. Li's cave of a classroom for so long.

The teacher for this class is a pale redhead I saw walking across the entryway when I arrived yesterday. She introduces herself, and I immediately forget her name. Her voice is sweet, but dull.

Lena told me this was a history class. I never cared much for history at school, but I am teetering on the edge of my chair with excitement for this lesson. If magic exists in the world, surely it has influenced every significant historical event. Were there magic Revolutionary War heroes? A Helen of Troy capable of destroying ships with her very soul? My mind is racing with the possibilities, but my excitement turns to confusion and disappointment when the instructor begins her lecture on witch-owned apothecaries in the seventeenth century. Maybe I just entered on a dull day. That would be my luck.

Some girls take dutiful notes, and the sound of fountain pens dipped in ink scratching across parchment fills the classroom like a chorus of insects. Others, like me, stare at the chalk-covered board, our eyes glazed over.

I've been sitting for forty-five minutes listening to the significance of witchcraft to women's economic development in pre-industrial America when I can't take it anymore.

I shoot my hand up in the air. I never used to ask questions in school, but I've never had questions I cared this much about before.

The other girls snap their heads toward me. The teacher raises her eyebrows. "Yes?"

I ask the same question I asked Maxine. "Who else has magic? It can't just be us."

"Magic is exceedingly rare," she says with the patience of a primary school teacher.

"But that doesn't mean—"

"I apologize, Miss Hallowell, but this is our lesson for the day. I encourage you to make use of the library. How lovely it is to have such an engaged pupil."

The rest of my questions die on my tongue. I'd forgotten how rotten it is to be made to feel stupid by a teacher. She's right; it was rude to interrupt the lesson—it's just I don't remember the last time I was this excited to learn.

After class, in the break before dinner, I go to the library, anxious to see what else I can find about magic in the books that reside there.

I was numb inside before yesterday, but now a light of hope fills my chest, and I can't contain it. I don't want to. It's nice, feeling this awake.

Evening is falling fast, and the whole place is lit with candelabras like a cathedral. I wander up and down the aisles for what feels like forever but find only gothic novels and encyclopedias. There doesn't seem to be a mention of magic anywhere in this library that feels steeped in it.

There are a few other girls in the library, but none of them are reading; they're just sitting, legs propped up on tables, chatting or playing cards. I follow them to dinner a while later, more confused than disappointed by my findings.

It'll be fine. I'll be a better student. Today, I have magic running through my veins, and that is enough.

At dinner Lena laughs a little at one of my jokes. Maxine shares a piece of cherry pie with me. I smile, and for the first time in four months, it doesn't feel like I'm pretending.

CHAPTER SEVEN

The next morning I bound out of bed and rush downstairs for breakfast. Over cinnamon buns and steaming tea, I jiggle my foot under the table, anxious to learn today's new lessons. Lena meets me at the dining room door, and like yesterday we walk together to Practical Applications.

Also like yesterday, Mrs. Roberts circles the room, doling out needles, buttons, and thread.

Dutifully my classmates pull out their textbooks and flip to the same page we opened to yesterday. And Mrs. Roberts walks around, examining our progress with the needle-threading spell. Still Lena's pronunciations are deemed sloppy. Still I'm told I lack necessary focus.

"Would it be possible to take the books out of the classroom, so I could study after hours?" I ask Mrs. Roberts.

She clicks her tongue "No, dear. Why strain yourself?"

"Because I wish to improve."

"How . . . ambitious." She shakes her head and continues on her way, ending our brief conversation.

In Mrs. Li's class Sara and Cora tell us more about the fire.

It was awful.

They lived.

They feel awful they lived.

The silver lining, they say, is that the horror they experienced has led to greater oversight and protection for factory employees. They heard there's a whole department now devoted to monitoring the safety of garment workers. It seems strange to me that their friends were burned alive and they're satisfied with a bureaucratic solution, but perhaps Sara's and Cora's hearts are less bitter than mine.

The room is claustrophobic, and I don't want to talk about my feelings.

The next class period is a marked improvement, in that at least it is a change of scenery. In one straight line, all eighteen of us follow Mrs. Vance, our history lecturer, through the gate and out onto the streets of Queens. Forest Hills is hardly bustling in the same way Manhattan is, but it is a relief to be outside, to crane my neck up and breathe in the sky.

On the grassy north lawn of Forest Park, our class settles in a circle, fanning our black skirts out around us. Above, the fall sun blazes, and even though the air is cool, I'm soon sweating under my cape. The grass is covered in browning leaves, and I pick at their drying edges while Mrs. Vance lectures. I've always hated autumn, hated watching the earth die.

Mrs. Vance picks up where she left off yesterday. Witches in early America used their powers to help run cottage businesses, but they were always careful not to be too successful, lest anyone get suspicious.

I pick and pick and pick until my skirt is covered with leaves and sweat is snaking down my neck. Mrs. Vance doesn't offer time for questions, and today I know better than to ask any.

I go to dinner that night without much to say to anyone. I make a few jokes, hoping to shake my foul mood, but Lena doesn't laugh, and Maxine sits with her other friends.

The next morning, I rise with considerably less buoyancy than yesterday.

Mrs. Roberts doesn't hand out needles today but wooden stirring spoons.

We spend an hour making them stir nothing in the air, swishing and twirling over our work benches.

The next day we banish dust from a coffee table.

The day after that we levitate a rug for dusting.

"Do we ever learn to do more than keeping house?" I lean over and whisper to Lena on a Thursday afternoon.

"That wouldn't be very *practical*," she replies with dense sarcasm. We share a knowing glance, but I don't push the topic further.

On Friday we make a rose bloom, and for a second it's so beautiful, it takes my breath away, but then Mrs. Roberts launches into a story about a friend who uses this trick to ensure her flower arrangements are always perfect for her dinner parties, and I am bored once more.

History isn't any better.

Mrs. Li's class is worse.

On and on for two weeks, I go to class. I make small talk with Lena and Maxine, who seem to tolerate me well enough, and every day my excitement withers like a rose forced to bloom too soon.

How foolish I was for thinking I was the recipient of something good. Or how selfish and ungrateful I am for being bored with magic in less than a month. Either way, I'm not acting like what Mrs. Carrey would call a "a girl of quality." I have a warm bed to sleep in, more food than I could eat in a lifetime, and *magic is real.*

How is it possible that I am still unsatisfied?

At night, when I can't sleep, I allow myself to stare up at the canopy of my bed and let the rage wash over me. What on earth is wrong with me that this is not enough? I've felt anger before, but I'm beginning to fear I well and truly hate myself.

It is there in the dark that I pull the note marking my brother's birthday and the day of his death out from under my mattress and run my thumb over the sharp crease of the parchment. I imagine the dark figure sneaking into my room, standing over my sleeping form. In my fantasies, I wake up and see their face. I dream they tell me everything, that they help this all make sense. But I'm left alone in the dark in a cold room with only a small square of paper, a cat sleeping at my feet, and more questions than ever before.

And it's on a perfectly unremarkable, gray Monday morning, when I realize I can't bring myself to walk from Practical Applications to Emotional Control. My feet simply won't cooperate. I'd rather live through the Triangle Shirtwaist Fire than hear Sara and Cora talk about it any longer.

I tug my cape around me and think seriously about walking out the front door and never coming back, but somehow I know it won't be that easy.

I had so much hope, but the light has dimmed, and I feel as empty inside as I did in the days after learning William had died, like my insides have been scooped out. It's there on the staircase that it hits me: I'm angry at myself for getting my hopes up. *How stupid, Frances,* I curse at myself. Haxahaven seemed so sparkly, I let myself forget that I am not the sort of person who gets nice things. My eyes well with fat tears as I climb the stairs. I don't let them fall until I shut the door to my room behind me.

Haxahaven distracted me from my true purpose, from the only thing I'm sure I'm meant to do. I won't make that mistake again.

I reach under my pillow and feel for the note's rough parchment beneath my fingertips. No more getting distracted by shiny things and blooming roses.

Guilt gnaws at me; all I can think is that without me there to remind them, the police will stop looking for William's killer. Not that I could contact them, what with being a murder suspect myself. My feather bed coughs up a cloud of dust as I throw myself on it. The day slips away, lost to my self-pity, but I bring myself to climb down the stairs for dinner. I don't know if anyone noticed I wasn't in afternoon classes. Probably not. No one here seems to notice me much at all.

The excessive food was a luxury my first days here, but now the waste disgusts me.

I sit at the table and pick at a plate of red potatoes.

A yellowjacket lands on a plate of sticky, sliced fruit. It skitters around before taking flight once more.

I'm not hungry.

I'm the first one upstairs after dinner, having left my roommates downstairs, where they were still eating and socializing with the other girls. Many of the girls stay up late in the dining room or atrium or sun porch playing card games and gossiping, but I have yet to be invited to join them, and I'm not sure I want to be.

I'm lying to myself. Of course I want to be invited.

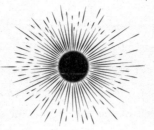

CHAPTER EIGHT

The days tick by, bitter and slow like tree sap. I attend class; I sit quietly, my cape wrapped around me, fidgeting—too consumed with the mystery of the note to pay much attention at all. It feels like a snarl of yarn; if only I could tug at just the right spot, the whole thing would unravel.

After William died, I checked out every book on policing I could from the library, hoping they might give me some tips on how to solve a crime. I needed a list, a list of things to do to, and then maybe the mess inside my brain, the giant, yawning maw of hurt would be fixed. It turns out finding a murderer who leaves no evidence but chains is difficult, an intruder who leaves nothing but a note proves equally difficult to find. And the hurt is still there too, the mess I can't untangle.

The detective books would tell me to analyze the handwriting, so I do, because I don't know what else to do and I can no longer do *nothing*.

I start with Lena, because she's the closest thing I have to a friend here and seems the easiest place to start. She smiles kindly when I ask to borrow her notes after Mrs. Roberts's class and readily passes them across the bench. Like Lena, they're neat and thorough, but the squiggles and swirls in the corner indicate she's giving less than her full attention to the class. A doodle of Mrs. Roberts with devil horns and a little pitchfork feels like the closest thing to a peek inside Lena's head as I've ever gotten. The handwriting doesn't match the note about my brother, but I'm not surprised.

Maxine is next. It's difficult to make an excuse to see her notes, since we have no classes together, but I finally finagle an old essay under the guise of needing inspiration for a paper for Mrs. Vance's class. She hands it to me after dinner, wrinkled and stained, like it's been dipped in coffee and shoved under her bed. Her penmanship is sloppy, the essay marked with crossed-out sections and notes in the margins. "Good luck with that," she laughs as she hands it over. It's nearly impossible to read, but it's immediately clear she didn't leave the note either.

I peek at Aurelia's and Ruby's papers, strewn across the vanity in our room. No match there.

I systematically work through my classes for the rest of the week. I ask to borrow so many notes, I fear my classmates may think I'm illiterate. Mabel passes hers over with a smile and an offer to help me study; Sara and Cora offer theirs after a suspicious glance between them. Maria's are bound in a beautiful leather notebook; Rachel's are a pile of loose-leaf paper. None of them match, but the handwriting on the note has an unmistakable air of familiarity, so I don't stop trying.

I also can't stop trying because I'm not yet sure what else to do. It feels good to be doing *something*, but I can't shake the feeling that I'm not doing enough.

In Mrs. Li's class I share the bare minimum to avoid being called uncooperative, but I'm careful not to say anything too revealing.

Sometimes I pay attention in history and Practical Applications. The small part of me excited by my power soaks up every word like a sponge, while the part of me that thirsts for more stews in anger at the useless scraps of magic I'm being given.

I learn Haxahaven's patterns. How to avoid the sunroom after meals, because that's where Ruby and her cronies hang out. I stay away from the third-floor lounge as well, because of the scratching coming from inside the walls no one can explain.

Mrs. Vykotsky never calls me back to her office. I spend most of my free time in the library, dwelling on the strange note. I keep coming up empty, and I can't decide if frustration is a feeling worse than hopelessness.

I sleep poorly at night. I instead stay awake, running my fingers over the crease of the note again and again just to reassure myself I didn't dream it up.

When I do manage to fall asleep, I'm plagued with vivid, confusing dreams. I'm typically in the shop, but sometimes I'm in our old apartment, or in Tompkins Square Park, or even at Haxahaven. In the dreams I always know that something is deeply wrong, but I can't ever identify what. Finn, the boy with the curly hair and intense gaze is almost always there, too. He watches me through narrowed eyes, and I wake up covered in cold sweat, feeling like I haven't slept at all.

The second note arrives on an uncharacteristically cold Tuesday.

I leave dinner early, planning on reading a novel in the peace and quiet of my empty room, but I must doze off while the sun is setting. I wake with a start, still in my uniform, lying on top of the duvet, book resting on my chest, feeling as if no time has passed at all. The room is purple with twilight, and there on my pillow, just like the last one, is a folded square of parchment.

With a zip of nerves, I'm suddenly wide awake. I unfold it quickly, my hands shaking so badly, I almost rip the heavy paper.

In the same scrawling hand as before it reads, *Do not trust the sisterhood. Meet me at the door to the Forest Park Clubhouse. Midnight.*

I stare at the note for a moment, committing it to memory, then I shove it under my mattress, where it joins the other.

If I were a smarter person, a more reasonable person, someone with consideration for their own well-being, I might dwell on the note, consider my options. But I know immediately what I am going to do. When it comes to my brother, I've never had much of a choice.

This is how I love him now, in the dark with my rage and shaking hands.

From my window I can see the pitch of a roof poking out from the tangle of trees in the park. As it's the only building in view, I assume that's the clubhouse. The wall around Haxahaven, with its rough stone, looks easy enough to climb. *I can do this. I have to do this.*

I glance at the clock. It's only just past five in the evening; my roommates must still be downstairs talking or playing cards. What would have happened had they come in and seen the note before I did? What would have happened if they'd come in and seen *who* was leaving it? It has to be a student at this school, I reason. The alternative is too unsettling to dwell on. But if it is another student leaving the notes, why do they want me to meet them outside the protective walls of the school? I pray I soon have answers.

After dinner, I slip on a white cotton chemise and slide into the soft sheets of my bed. I'm too awake from having napped and too anxious about the meeting to sleep, but I need to avoid arousing my roommates' suspicion if I have any hope of sneaking out successfully.

I lie in bed for hours, staring at the ceiling and counting down my heartbeats as darkness creeps over Haxahaven.

Eventually, my roommates filter in. I hear Ruby brush her hair one hundred times and Aurelia wish Lena good night. After what feels like eons, the room fills with the heavy sounds of their breathing and the ticking of the grandfather clock on the far wall.

It's only by the watery light of the moon that I can read the golden clock face. At 11:43 I slide out of bed, button my black cape over my white nightgown, pull on gray wooly socks, and lace up my boots.

It isn't until I have my shoes on that a terrifying realization hits me. The person who is leaving these notes may very well be my brother's killer. Maybe they've returned to finish the job. But I go anyway. It's like I'm watching myself from outside my body, screaming at myself to stop, but I can't make myself listen. Being dead would be better than not knowing forever, I think.

On quiet feet, I pad across the carpet. For one heart-stopping moment the door squeaks and I hear someone stir, but then the room falls into silence once more.

Sitting still in the hall outside my room is the small black cat who hid under my bed my first day here. She looks at me like I'm an idiot.

"What do you want?" I whisper.

She swishes her tail and walks away.

I creep down the stairs, ignoring at every step the logical part of my brain that begs me to turn around and return to bed.

Haxahaven feels like a living thing at night, full of warm breath and secrets, and deeply, deeply asleep.

I pause at the double doors for a fraction of a second. My brother's voice rings in my ears. *Not your smartest idea, sis.* The doors groan as they swing wide. The night welcomes me with open arms, like it does to all who make terrible decisions after dark.

The late September air bites with the promise of winter. The cold pricks at my skin. Dew from the lawn soaks into the leather of my boots and leaves me shivering despite the weight of my socks.

It doesn't take me long to reach the wall that borders the school like a sharp-toothed mouth.

Staring up at it, I am well aware that I am about to do the stupidest thing I've ever done. The wall looks taller at night, and it's been a long time since I scaled a fence. Not since I was eleven and playing hide-and-seek with Oliver and William. I felt less nauseous then.

Thankfully, it's not difficult to find a foothold. I wedge the toe of my boot in between two stones and haul myself up. The tips of my fingers find purchase on the ragged edge of a weatherworn piece of rock. I reach one arm up, but it falls short of the top of the wall by nearly twelve inches. It's harder to haul myself up the second time. My foot slips, and for one sickening second I think I'm about to fall, but my fingertips hold on despite the screaming pain. Finally, I find another foothold and wrench myself to the top of the wall. I sit there for one moment, wondering if perhaps there are spells or alarms to keep me inside.

But then I think of my brother, the bravery with which he would have run into any forest to save me, and I jump.

The fall takes longer than I thought it would. It isn't until I'm in the air that I give any serious thought to how terribly landing is going to hurt. I collapse to the ground with a thud. Pain shoots up my ankles and through my knees. Cautiously I rotate both ankles— they've felt better, but nothing is broken, blessedly, so I push myself up and continue on.

Queens is only a few miles from Manhattan, but there is nothing familiar about this place. The stillness feels less like peace and more like a threat. I don't know what waits for me in the dark.

Twigs snap under the soles of my feet as I work my way farther into the darkness of the park. The blackness is so heavy, it feels like a physical object, so complete, it seems to be chewing at the edges of reality, eating everything around it. My eyes can't adjust. The path turns deeper into the trees. I stumble and end up on my knees. I reach down to wipe off the dirt, and my hands come away wet. I wipe the blood away on my nightgown. The jackrabbit beat of my heart makes me feel like a prey animal about to walk into a trap.

A canopy of stubborn leaves blocks out the light of the moon, and it doesn't take me long to be very cold, and very sure I've made a mistake in coming here tonight. My body is shaking all over. I clench my jaw to keep my teeth from chattering.

I curse under my breath and turn back, but the path snakes again, and I'm suddenly not sure where I am. I've strayed too far from the walled safety of the school. Surrounded by trees, I feel very small. It's been a long time since I wished for the warmth of my mother's embrace, but I crave it now.

I take three steps down the path and whip my head from side to side. *Nothing.* Nothing but the solid darkness of silent woods on all sides of me. The flickering candles in the windows of Haxahaven are nowhere to be found.

My heart quickens as panic rises in my chest. *You deserve this,* a cruel part of my brain whispers. *This is what you get for being a fool.*

With the power I've felt in me before, I try to summon *something, anything,* but nothing happens.

I squeeze my eyes shut and count backward from fifteen. It's a habit I picked up from Mrs. Carrey. Whenever we made a mistake on a garment, or struggled with an order, she would tell us to close our eyes and count backward. We had fifteen seconds to pull ourselves together. It was usually all we needed.

Fifteen, fourteen—the deafening silence is splintered.

Thirteen, twelve—a voice cuts through the darkness—*eleven*—no, voices, plural.

Ten—someone hisses, "Shhh"—*nine*—a sharp laugh—*eight, seven*—a low voice whispers—*six, five, four*—dry leaves rustle.

Three, two—a female voice says something that might be my name—*one.*

My eyes snap open.

I am not alone in this park.

"Hello?" I whisper to the solid darkness. There is shuffling in the underbrush.

A bobbing lantern comes into view first. It flickers orange and white against the obsidian dark.

With sheer force of will, I gather my confidence and take a few careful steps in the direction of the light. "Who's there?" I rasp.

The whispering voices are louder, but I still can't make out what they're saying.

Closer and closer I creep to the lantern, which has stilled. Whoever is carrying it has reached their destination, or they're lying in wait.

"If this is a joke, it isn't funny," I hiss into the night. The voices have gone quiet.

Too close, a shadow moves. It's human shaped, but hunched and moving in a jerky, repetitive pattern.

I don't expect the clod of dirt that flies up and hits me in the mouth.

"What the hell!" I exclaim.

"Who's there?" a female voice asks from outside the range of the lantern's light.

"Who are you?" I hiss back.

"Frances?" a different voice asks.

At the sound of my name, recognition hits me like a punch to the gut.

"Lena? Is that Maxine? Are you two the ones leaving me notes?"

"What notes? And what are you doing out here?"

"What are *you* doing out here?" I demand in return.

Maxine rises from the ground, brushing dirt off her night clothes, an oversized linen shirt paired with loose trousers, holding a large object in her hand. "Looking for this." That's what the movement was—*she was digging.*

"And I was looking for you," Lena says, rising from the ground herself. "I heard you get out of bed. I followed you down the stairs to see where you were going, and I ran into Maxine on the landing.

"And *I* felt a strange flare-up of magic so strong, it woke me up!" Maxine says, "so I got out of bed to investigate. I found Lena looking for you and invited her to come with me."

"Invited?" Lena snorts.

"I wanted the company!"

"You wanted to use me as monster bait."

"Not true!"

"Wait, wait—" I interrupt the bickering. "So neither of you have been leaving me notes on my bed?"

At their confused expressions, I unfold the note clenched in my sweaty palm. They pass it back and forth, examining it under the light of the lantern.

"I didn't leave this for you," Maxine says. "I'm not even sure what this means."

"I think it has something to do with my brother," I say.

"I didn't know you had a brother," Maxine replies.

"I don't anymore." It's easier to be glib than sad. "I think this might have something to do with his murder." The twin pity in their eyes makes me feel small.

Maxine inhales sharply. "And you thought creeping out into the dark woods to meet a murderer was wise?"

"It's probably just another girl playing a mean joke," Lena says.

Maxine nods in agreement. "A nasty prank. I'll help you get them back. We'll put paste in everyone's oatmeal."

Lena looks horrified. "Everyone?"

Maxine shrugs, undeterred. "I'm committed to any and all revenge plots."

I sigh, and they return their focus to me. "I barely speak to the other girls. What use would they have to do something like this?" I don't tell them about studying their handwriting. Not to mention how it would be near impossible for any of my classmates to know the exact date of my brother's death.

Their silence makes me uncomfortable, so I ask another pressing question. "Maxine, what did you say about a magical flare-up?"

"All magic is connected. I don't understand it, but I can feel it. It's how I found you. It's how I find everyone. But tonight I felt something *different.*"

"Different how?" I ask.

"Different as in *different.* Almost like someone using power for the first time . . . but more urgent somehow. It *wanted* me to find it."

"It?" I ask.

"*This.*" Maxine holds up an oversized leather-bound book flaking with age and grime.

"A book?" I ask.

"A *magic* book," Maxine corrects me.

"A magic book *buried* in the park, revealing itself to us the same night Frances was supposed to meet a murderer in the woods," Lena adds. She looks skeptical, and it doesn't escape me she's taken two steps back from where Maxine holds the book.

"I thought you said it was probably one of the other girls." I feign offense.

"No. *Maxine* said that. I think you were willing to traipse out in the dark to meet a total and complete murderer."

Maxine huffs. "Can we stop the bickering and address *the magic book*." She holds it over her head with one hand and gives it a shake for emphasis. Clods of dirt rain down on her shoulder. She's in her nightgown too, cocooned in a dark coat.

"I don't trust it." Lena shakes her head.

"I don't care if we trust it; I care if it's useful," Maxine says.

A raven taking off from the trees above startles all three of us. Maxine curses under her breath.

"The park at night has no effect on you, but a bird does you in?" Lena scoffs at Maxine.

"I hate birds. It's the damned flapping," Maxine says, voice thick with disgust.

"Of all things to scare the indomitable Maxine," I whisper.

"Can we continue this discussion back at school? Have the two of you fulfilled your death wishes for the night?" Lena places her hands on her hips, waiting for us to realize she's right.

Maxine tucks the book under her arm and takes me by the hand. "My death wish can wait another day. Frances?"

I scan the dark park once more for the note leaver, but it's futile. The person isn't here, and I am no closer to getting the answers I desperately seek than the day William died. It must have all been a joke. Hope playing with my imagination and grief. I let out a deep sigh. "Yes, let's go."

Maxine has no trouble skipping down the path back to the wall that encircles the school. She finds it so easily, just like everything seems to come easily to her. I am grateful to have her warm hand in my right and Lena's in my left. The dark is less frightening with them by my side.

I'm getting ready to hike up my nightgown to climb the wall when Maxine laughs and pulls a skeleton key from the pocket of her overcoat.

"Perks of the job," she deadpans as she unlocks the front gate.

We creep across the lawn, pry open the front doors, and step through the echoing entryway. It still strikes me as odd that the door isn't locked. Anything this easy usually comes with a price.

On the second-floor landing, Maxine jerks her head in a *follow me* motion. Lena and I obey, trailing her down the hall to her room. Maxine attends classes like the rest of us, but her special status as a Finder makes her some cross between student and faculty, which must be why she has no roommates, just a powder-blue canopy bed strewn with clothing and blankets. Her vanity is littered with sparkling baubles and velvet ribbons. She catches me eyeing them.

"Mother won't stop sending them in the mail no matter how I beg her to stop. Take whatever you wish."

I don't take anything, but I do think about sticking a brooch in an envelope to send to my own mother.

The heavy book lands with a thud and a cloud of down feathers as Maxine dumps it onto her bed.

"Do you feel that . . . that buzzing?" Maxine asks.

Lena and I glance at each other and shake our heads no. A shiver spider-walks up my spine.

"Buzzing?" Lena's face is etched with concern, her dark eyebrows knit together.

"It feels alive," Maxine whispers.

Nausea rolls through me. "That doesn't feel right."

Lena's voice is scarcely above a whisper. "It can't be."

"Could the person who has been leaving me notes have wanted me to find this?" I ask. I don't know why the question terrifies me so deeply.

"It looks like it's been buried for ages. It wouldn't make much sense."

"You know I don't believe in coincidences like that," Lena states. Her eyes haven't left the book. She's staring at it like it might pounce at us.

"Might as well see what's inside." Maxine's usually confident voice is thin.

She reaches out and traces her fingers gingerly over the words stamped in faded gold on the black leather cover; *The Elemental* it reads. She flips it open. Her nimble fingers fly through page after handwritten page of diagrams, words, and symbols.

This book doesn't look anything like the onionskin textbooks we use in Mrs. Roberts's class. It looks ancient and awful. Like it wasn't written by a person but simply willed into being by the ground itself.

Maxine's hands move quickly, but she's careful not to tear the delicate papers as our eyes devour the pages. She lingers on shapes and markings that make my head throb. Scrambled words and loud, angry handwriting pierce my chest before Maxine flips by a drawing that makes my heart stop.

"Wait, wait!" I grab the book from Maxine's lap and flip back to the page she just passed.

The ancient spine cracks as I spread the book on the powder-blue duvet.

The ink has faded, as if the words on this page are being whispered through time. Most of them are in a language I can't make out. In the center of the page is a drawing of a coffin, a mirror, a headstone, a tooth, and a comb laid out in a circle around a Celtic cross.

It's the title at the top of the page that sent my heart skittering in my chest. In devastatingly careful penmanship, bolder than the rest of the faded letters are the words "The Resurrection." The ink looks newer than what's in the rest of the book.

Four objects are drawn and carefully labeled. A scrying mirror, a vial of graveyard dust, a hairbrush marked *item belonging to the deceased*, and a dagger labeled *Freagarthach*.

"What is this?" I whisper.

"I think it's a spell," Maxine replies.

"A spell to bring someone back to life?" I wonder aloud.

"That's impossible," Lena whispers. She lays a gentle hand on my shoulder.

In the left margin, in darker ink, someone has scrawled hasty notes. The writing is so frantic, I can only make out some of it.

Only effective if done soon after departure from this plane

Best under waning moon

Graveyard dust no more than five days old

RISKY.

Best in the company of others

There are other notes too, but they're in a language I don't recognize. I flip quickly through the other pages of the book. Most of the printed spells offer at least some instruction in English, but the margins of nearly every page are filled with notes in this unfamiliar language.

My reality shifts, expands the same way it did my first day at Haxahaven. Like my brain has to make new room to understand a world where any of this could be possible.

Maxine snorts. "Doesn't seem like the spell being risky was going to stop whoever wrote this."

"I wonder if it worked," I say more to myself than to them. The tiny spark of hope that lives in my rib cage burns brightly, ignited by the idea of a spell that could bring William back to me.

"Of course it didn't work—the dead don't come back to life." Lena shakes her head. I can barely hear her over the roaring in my ears.

"But I don't think this is a spell to bring them back to life." Maxine's tone is questioning; she doesn't understand this any more than we do. "Look here." She points to an illustration in the lower left corner. A magician sitting in a robe in front of a mirror. In the mirror, another person is drawn. "I think it just allows you to speak to someone on the other side."

"Other side of what?" Lena's eyes are wide in some combination of horror and amusement at the ridiculousness of the idea.

"Perhaps the dead will tell you if you get the spell right." Maxine raises her brows.

There is a storm of emotions raging inside me. A hurricane of joy and fear and horror. A wildfire of hope. My breathing picks up, though I haven't moved a muscle. *My brother might not be so gone after all.* He might exist somewhere that isn't here, somewhere I could use magic to reach him. "We should try it." The words tumble out of my mouth before I can stop them.

"You can't speak to the dead." Lena whips her head between us. "I can't believe the two of you are considering this."

"I'm not considering anything," Maxine says.

"Tell that to poor Frances," Lena quips. She sinks down on the bed next to me. "Let this go now. Before you do whatever it is it looks like you're planning on doing."

"I—" I begin. But I don't have anything to follow it up with. Of course I want to try the spell.

Suddenly there's a knock on Maxine's door.

"Damn it," Maxine says under her breath. The three of us share panicked glances.

Lena darts into Maxine's wardrobe, and I hurl myself under her bed. In the same moment Maxine snaps the book shut and shoves it under her pillow. Lena juts an arm out from the wardrobe, robe in hand. Maxine snatches it and wraps herself, covering the overcoat she's still wearing.

Bang. Bang. Whoever is outside is impatient. Maxine blows out a lantern, leaving just one lit. She carries it to the door and opens it a crack.

"It's late for you to still be up, Maxine." I can't see her, but I recognize Helen's scolding voice immediately.

"I was reading." If I weren't so scared, I might laugh. She is technically telling the truth.

"I thought I heard voices," Helen continues. Her voice is low, authoritative. "I was on my rounds."

111

Maxine sighs. "Well they weren't from here. Would you like to come in and check?"

From under the bed, I will my breathing to slow, terrified that Helen will hear me.

"No, no. That won't be necessary," Helen answers after a pause. "You should sleep, though. It's late."

"Yes, ma'am," Maxine answers, then shuts the door with a click. Simultaneously the three of us let out a sigh.

At the sound of Helen's footsteps down the hall, I feel safe enough to wriggle out from under the bed. Lena takes a careful step out of the wardrobe.

I've had enough blind terror for one night.

"You two should go back to your room. It should be safe now. She'll circle the east end of the second floor before looping back around to the stairs. Go quickly. We'll continue this another day soon, I promise."

I feel a pull toward the book hidden under Maxine's pillow. This strange, magical, terrifying book, buried in the woods like someone wanted us to find it. Maybe fate exists. Maybe the universe wants this for us. We attend an academy for witches; we have evidence enough to believe the impossible.

"Let me take the book." I want to spend more time examining every word inked in its pages.

Maxine swats away my extended hand. "Your room isn't private. What if someone finds it?"

I'm annoyed with the truth of Maxine's statement.

"I'll arrange something. Soon. I promise," she says.

Lena looks at me through narrowed eyes. I'm no mind reader,

but I'd guess she's thinking *Why should Maxine have the power to decide what we do and do not try?* She makes her way to the door.

We say our good-nights, and I follow Lena up the additional flight of stairs to our room.

I pause outside our door. The hall is blessedly silent, free of Helen. "You followed me tonight?"

She shrugs her shoulders. "I thought you might be in trouble."

"Thank you."

"It was nothing."

"It's not nothing to me."

I toss and turn through the night, unable to rid my brain of the image of my brother trapped inside a mirror.

One line from the spell book haunts me: *Only effective if done soon after departure from this plane.* My brother has been dead for 126 days. What constitutes *soon* in magic spells? How long until *soon* becomes *not soon enough*?

If I wish to perform the Resurrection, I have no time to waste.

It must be close to sunrise when I roll over in a huff.

At the sight of a new note on the pillow next to me, I am wide awake.

It's been placed gently right next to my head, folded in half in a straight crease.

With shaking hands, I unfold it.

The purple light of near-dawn presses through the curtains.

I missed you tonight. He deserves justice.

CHAPTER NINE

It takes every ounce of self-control I have not to scream.

Once again I shove this note under my mattress and try not to think of whoever left it standing like a dark shadow over my vulnerable sleeping roommates and me.

Soon, the spun-sugar pink of morning fills our room, and my roommates rise for the day. The world feels different, as if my own heart is beating in a minor key.

I'm wiping the sleep from my eyes when Lena asks if I want her to wait for me so we can walk down to breakfast together.

"No thank you, I'll only be a moment."

When the room is empty, I leave a note of my own, scrawled on the back of last night's.

This is not a game I am interested in playing. Tell me something real. I have nowhere to send my message but can only hope that the writer will return to leave me another one and will see what I've written. If I thought I was foolish for my actions last night, I realize what I am doing now might be worse.

My sleepless night has cost me. I'm so exhausted, it's making me nauseous. Reluctantly I pull on my uniform. It takes me three tries to properly button my cape in an X across my chest. I secure my hair with a black velvet ribbon into a loose braid slung over my shoulder. With the hollow purple circles under my eyes, I look rather like a witch this morning.

If I hurry, I can still snag a biscuit from the dining room before Practical Applications.

I'm almost to the stairs, brushing an errant lock of mouse-brown hair out of my eyes, when a picture hung on the wall, hidden among all the others, catches my eye.

It's small and sepia-toned but well preserved thanks to the darkness of the hallway.

I stop short.

Swallow.

Blink.

Try to process what I'm seeing. Because among the group of smiling girls, immortalized in the photograph, is *me*.

Except it can't possibly be, because this photograph is easily thirty years old.

Eight girls, wearing long black dresses cinched in tightly at the waist, hair in styled coifs, wearing capes identical to my own, and in the middle of them is *me*. Dark hair; straight, serious eyebrows; a just-too-big nose; full lips hitched up in a half smile. Except that's an expression I've never had on my face; it's not even one I'm sure

I'm capable of making. It is the kind of look that speaks of a terrible, wonderful secret. The kind of look that only girls truly sure of themselves are capable of making.

Below the photograph is a tiny brass plate reading HAXAHAVEN ACADEMY, 1882.

I stumble back a step, my heart beating like a snare drum. *My mother.* The woman with my face is my *mother.* She would have been eighteen in 1882, just a year older than I am now. My mother had mentioned once, rather sadly, that I was the spitting image of her younger self, but I'd never seen a photograph.

I run down the stairs as quickly as my feet can carry me, my cape flying behind me like bat wings, my braid unraveling with every step.

I burst into Mrs. Vykotsky's office with a frantic breath. She's thumbing through a leather-bound book, posture as straight as a board in her wingback chair. Without lifting her eyes, she says, "So you found your mother, then, did you?"

I place my hands on my knees and suck in a breath. I'm winded from running down so many flights of stairs. It's clear Mrs. Vykotsky has been waiting for this moment, and it fills me with something akin to betrayal.

"She was a student here?" I choke out.

"Indeed she was," Mrs. Vykotsky replies, finally deigning to look up at me. "Perhaps it's best if you take a seat." She gestures to the low chair, the same one I sat in weeks ago when I first arrived.

As I sink into the worn velvet, I tug my cape around me like a safety blanket. Mrs. Vykotsky is about to tell me things about my mother I might rather not know. It makes my throat tight and my eyes sting to think my mother is likely an entirely different person than I thought she was. I'm not sure I want the burden of knowing her secrets.

Mrs. Vykotsky snaps her book closed and begins a story it seems she's been waiting a long time to tell. "Your mother came to us in 1878 after the death of her little sister."

I didn't know my mother had a little sister. My heart breaks. Two generations of Hallowell girls with dead siblings. The ghosts in my mother's eyes suddenly make more sense. As does the way she folded in on herself after William was gone. So much loss for one life.

"It was cholera, if I recall correctly, though my memory is less than perfect these days. Your mother's family became concerned after they found every single glass in their house shattered. It was an expensive outburst. We found her soon after."

"My mother was a witch," I say slowly, the pieces clicking together.

"Is still, I would assume," Mrs. Vykotsky says. "Witches do not lose their powers with age. They can, however, lose control of them without proper management"—she waves her hand dismissively—"but I would not know your mother's state, as we at Haxahaven have not seen her in many years."

"What do you mean, you haven't seen her in many years?" I sort of want to cry. Perhaps it's because the rug that is the foundation of all I believe to be true is being pulled out from under me again. Or perhaps it's the deep sense of shame that permeates every thought I have of my mother. The shame I carry for being so angry at her for being unwell, for being unable to take care of me in the way I craved.

"Oh, it was quite a scandal," Mrs. Vykotsky replies conspiratorially. It makes my stomach turn; I don't wish to be her partner in gossiping about my mother's life. "Your mother was a star pupil. One of the most gifted witches we'd seen in years. She was on track to become a faculty member, just as she'd wished. Until she met a young man, ran off into the night, and was never seen again." She says all of this rather matter-of-factly, though I suspect my mother's defection affected her. By the set of her mouth, I can tell she wants me to ask about my mother running away, but this is the one part of the story I already know.

I was young when my father left us for good. He'd been flitting in and out of my mother's life for years. He left soon after William was born, then returned a year later, and my mother fell pregnant with me. I was still an infant when he allegedly went to find work on a lobster boat and never came back. Neither William nor I had any memories of him, but my mother spoke of him as if she was still in love with him, despite all he'd done. She said he was tall and handsome and that they'd met at a ball—when she was at a boarding school far away, a place her mother would never let her leave to marry. It was because of him that we were destitute, and yet she'd still speak, starry-eyed, of that time he took her to the beach in Queens, or of the letters he used to write her while she was in school, full of sonnets and declarations of love, and it was through these letters they arranged to elope. It turns out running off was the only thing my father ever knew how to do. And the next time he ran off, he did it without her.

I think of my mother's inability to hold down a job, the way she never slept, her tenuous grasp on reality. Everything I know about my mother shifts like puzzle pieces around this new information. *My mother is a witch.*

Mrs. Vykotsky shifts in her chair. "Your mother ran away from us before her training was completed. It happens occasionally, though we do our very best to avoid it. Usually the outcome is . . . unpleasant."

I shift in my chair. "Unpleasant?"

"Oh well, we don't need to get into all the poor witches who died; the lucky ones just lose their minds a bit." She waves her hand around wildly, as if she's describing something funny. "Your mother has turned in on herself, hasn't she?"

Tears sting my eyes. I find I can't speak, so I nod.

"It happens. The magic needs something to latch on to. Without a healthy excision of her powers, it's devouring her instead. A pity," she says dismissively. "You'd be wise to remember that witches who choose to go it alone don't last long in this harsh world. If evil doesn't get them, their own brains will."

"Why don't you help them, the ones who get lost?" Anger fuels my tears, my grip on the chair tightens.

"It is a lesson we all must learn at some point in our lives: you cannot help someone who doesn't want it. You can only try to minimize the damage they do."

"Did my mother *not* want your help?" I push the words through gritted teeth. "Did you even ask her?" All this time, I thought she'd had to leave me because she was sick and unable to care for herself, but if it was magic that broke something within her, could this school have not helped?

No, the voice inside my head answers. *This school* should *have helped*. And it didn't. Mrs. Vykotsky didn't.

"I know your mother. She is stubborn."

"You knew her at eighteen. You know nothing about the person she became," I bite back.

Mrs. Vykotsky doesn't react to my tone. "People don't change." She purses her lips.

"So you did nothing." My chest heaves; my breathing grows shallow. I feel Mr. Hues's hands on my neck; the fury inside of me rises and rises. "You never tried? Was she not worth helping?" The anger feels too big to hold in my body. Every muscle burns with it. Suddenly the delicate vials on her shelves shatter with a bang, leaching scents like bleach and mint into the dark room.

My stomach lurches as I try to dam my pain inside me instead of letting it flow out into the room. My hands curl into fists so tight, my fingernails bite into the flesh of my palms. I clench my jaw and squeeze my eyes shut. I focus on my breathing like we've been taught in Mrs. Li's class. *Inhale, exhale, try not to think about slapping the smug look off your headmistress's face, exhale.*

When I open my eyes, I see Mrs. Vykotsky sitting, an impassive look on her face, hands still folded in her lap, just watching me.

My anger starts to subside as fear takes its place. It scares me, this magic that ruined my mother's life, that has already left me with a body count. As I slow my heartbeat, the power shrivels back into my chest. I try to find the calm. *Easy, sis.* William's words swirl around me, and I straighten my back. I unclench the sore muscles in my jaw. "Can we help her now?" My voice is small. I sound very much like a child.

Mrs. Vykotsky studies me, notices that I've put whatever power I have back into its box. "I'm afraid not," she finally says. "Asylums are difficult to infiltrate, and if we spent our time trying to rescue every wayward witch, we'd never have any time to educate the ones here."

The corners of her thin lips draw up into a smile. "I understand this is difficult."

Because I don't know what else to say, I say, "Yes, it is."

She rises like a specter, smoothing the black velvet of her dress, and glides to the shelf on the back wall. The broken glass crunches under her heels.

She gives me another small smile. The expression looks unnatural on her face. "Why don't we clean it up together?"

Using magic to clean the broken glass would probably be quickest, but my power has shrunk back into a place inside me that feels awfully small, and dark and full of fear.

On my knees, I banish all thoughts of magic mothers and runaway fathers and get to work.

Mrs. Vykotsky crouches down next to me.

"You're not going to make me use magic?" I ask.

"It seems in this situation, magic might make things more difficult. We'll clean this up the old-fashioned way."

She doesn't say any more. But patiently she works next to me. We fill our hands with dried herbs and brush the broken glass into a pile.

The silence is heavy, thick with acrid herbs, but I can't think of anything else to say. I know I'll only be met with more frustrating dismissals.

When we're finally done, she smiles at me once more. "I know it's been a challenging adjustment. But I do hope you know you can come see me about anything."

There's a flicker of something human in her eyes.

"Thank you, ma'am." I don't mean it.

* * *

I've missed Practical Applications, so I make my way directly to Mrs. Li's waxy cave of a classroom. I can't bear to spend the morning talking about my deepest fears, or whatever new torture she has orchestrated today, but class is preferrable to being alone with my thoughts.

Cora does most of the talking while I pick splinters of glass from the palm of my hand.

During dinner, I rip a piece of paper from my notebook and scrawl a message. *I know the truth. I'm at the school. Please let me help you. I'll come visit as soon as I am able. All my love, Frances.*

I address it to my mother and slip it under Mrs. Vykotsky's door with a prayer she sends it on my behalf.

I return to my room soon after dinner, turning down Maxine's offer of a game of twenty-one.

"Are you all right?" she asks me.

"Just a long day." I feign a smile.

I collapse on my bed, nerves spent, exhausted to the bone from the incident in Mrs. Vykotsky's office. I tumble into sleep like a rock thrown into a pond.

I gasp awake in the watery light of dawn. Waiting on my pillow, scrawled on a new slip of paper, is a response to yesterday morning's message.

I am your ally. When you are ready, I will be waiting for you.

CHAPTER TEN

I tell myself I won't sneak out again.

I will be a good pupil. I will bide my time and bite my tongue and swallow my anger. Because I plan to learn magic and then leave and do something with it.

I won't make the same mistakes as my mother. I refuse to live her life.

I find myself thinking of her often, picturing what she looked like as she roamed these same halls. I stop at the photograph frequently, searching for clues in her defiant face. Did she have friends? What were they like? How did my father find her behind the tall walls of the school? Was he worth it?

If thoughts of my mother consume me during the day, I think of my brother most at night. I dwell on the spell book. I wonder if speaking to him would bring me peace, or if seeing him trapped somewhere I can't reach would break me forever. Lena and Maxine notice me falling quiet at meal times but don't pry. They're trying to be kind, I think. But it only makes me feel more alone.

Mrs. Li's class becomes more unbearable. Every day I sit, staring at the black walls of her classroom as she tries to pry the pain from my broken heart.

I've never been comfortable living with grief like an open wound. The sepsis of it seeps through my veins, a pain deeply my own. I've never known how to let go of something this big, so I've clung to it instead. At least the pain reminds me William was real. I have no interest in releasing it to Mrs. Li. I refuse to tell her my secrets, and I'm fairly certain she hates me for it.

Every night after dinner I go to my room and I practice my magic, because I can't bear not to. Threading needles under the watchful gaze of Mrs. Roberts doesn't scratch the itch.

I study the small magical textbook we're given during Practical Applications and memorize as many spells as I can. The magic starts small. I make my bed with a wave of my hand instead of touching the blankets, or I flip a page with my mind.

I tell myself I won't sneak out again, but I am a rotten liar, even to myself. If I am going to trek beyond the walls of the school, I want to be prepared.

Progress is slow. It takes three days to magick a leather-bound book across the room. It takes another two to be able to unlatch and open the window, then close and re-latch it with my mind. How quickly magic goes from awe-inspiring to tedious.

I'm staring at a handful of hairpins, trying to levitate more than one, when Lena comes in early after dinner one night.

"What are you doing?" she asks me.

"Practicing."

She pauses in the doorway for a moment, her eyes narrowed, then crosses the room and plops down on my bed next to me. "Get on with it, then."

An orange cat I've never seen before slinks in the open door behind her and hops between us, nestling in the middle like we're all old friends.

The cat lays her tiny head on my duvet and watches me fail. I don't have any success manipulating more than one pin at a time. Lena peers at me in silence as I try so hard, I give myself a headache.

Lena snorts. We've been eating meals next to each other but haven't spoken much since the night in the woods. It's as if we're both so scared of what the book means for our future that we're putting off dealing with it entirely. I've been so glum, I can't imagine it's been easy to talk to me.

Between the book, the notes on my bed, and my mother, I am in desperate need of a friend, but I am terrified of being a burden.

I throw her a glance. "Any tips?"

"I'm sorry, manipulation isn't my strong suit."

"I see you in class—you do just fine."

"I'm capable of it, but it doesn't come as easily to me as it does to you."

"Will you tell me what it's like to see the future, then?"

She scrunches up her nose. "It's like . . . remembering something that hasn't happened yet."

"Can you tell my future?" The question escapes my lips before I grasp what I'm asking.

She rolls her eyes. "I'm not a carnival act."

"No, I'm sorry, I just meant—"

"I know what you meant. Besides, I can't control it like that. I see things I'd rather not more often than I see anything of use."

"Like what?"

She sinks back into my pillows and takes a few breaths. "Something bad is coming," she says rather calmly, looking up at the ceiling.

A zip of adrenaline goes through me. "Soon?"

"Soon enough. A few years, I think."

I hesitate to ask the next question, but I do it anyway. "How bad is 'bad'?"

She shakes her head. "I've been seeing the same visions for a while. The land turning to razor wire and ash, the air into toxic fog—sometimes I see my old classmates choking on it. It's a war, I think. But it's not like one I've ever read about."

The room feels colder; my muscles are tense suddenly. I tug my cape around my shoulders, though it doesn't help much with the chill. "How do you know the visions are real?"

She sighs deeply. "The other clairvoyants are seeing the same ones."

"That's not good," I respond.

"No, not good at all," she says matter-of-factly.

"Is there a way to stop it?"

"I don't know, but the others say that visions of danger and doom have plagued clairvoyants since the beginning of time. Part of being who we are. But I intend to find my way home before the world goes to hell."

"Home?"

"The Genesee Valley. A few hours from here. It's where my tribe is, my people, my parents."

An awful part of me is jealous that she has someone to miss, someone to miss her. A home to dream about returning to.

I hate my envy. "I'm afraid to let myself love things anymore. I fear it's making me a subpar friend."

Lena is silent for a moment; I'm learning she's someone who considers her words carefully. "Perhaps we're well matched. I'll leave this place as soon as I'm able. I've not been good at cultivating relationships in the meantime. My heart is somewhere else."

"Will you tell me three things you love?" I ask. William and I used to play this game; it's a relief to find someone else to talk to this way again.

She thinks for a moment. "Maple candies, romance novels, and my mother's cooking. You?"

"Long baths, ice cream, and the rare occasion I win at cards."

She smiles. "Play you after dinner tomorrow? You've got to get out of this room."

I smile too. And it feels real, finally. "Absolutely."

She pops up from my bed and walks over to her own. "One last tip," she offers. "Don't let them catch you practicing. They don't mind you using the magic, but they don't like it when you get good at it."

"Why train us at all, then?"

"Women are supposed to be competent at everything, but experts at nothing. Haven't you heard?" Her voice is thick with sarcasm, but the tiniest smile breaks through the gloom.

"Good night, Frances."

"Good night, Lena."

I beg Maxine to let us examine *The Elemental*, the spell book she found buried in the park, but she tells me it's too risky. I'm beginning not to care about the risks.

I grow more and more restless. It feels at times that my soul is trying to wiggle out of my body using any cracks it can find, like a mouse in a tenement looking for warmth.

One Thursday morning I awake to another note. The folded square of parchment is resting on the pillow next to my head, bathed in the dawn light. I bolt upright and pick it up by a corner. It unfolds for me, revealing the same bold scrawl as before.

Tonight. I'll be waiting for you in the woods that border the east field. You will not know me, but I will know you. We are on the same side.

I'm so desperate for *something* to happen, this time, I feel more relief than fear at its arrival.

At breakfast I sit next to Maxine, who sections a grapefruit with great concentration.

Between bites of my sticky bun, I sigh heavily. Maxine pauses her work on the grapefruit to look up at me.

"You're rather out of sorts this morning."

I look at the frosting on my hands and not at her. "I didn't sleep very well."

"Did the ghosts keep you up?"

My eyes snap to hers. "Are there ghosts here as well?"

She snorts. "Not that I know of, but who's to say, really?"

"That wasn't funny."

"Not to you."

"Is it possible to leave after dark again?" I ask her.

Maxine purses her lips. "No."

But she's chewing on her cheek and has a wicked glint in her eyes, so I have a feeling her answer is a half-truth.

"I could go alone. I managed it last time." Under the table I pick at my nails.

She rolls her eyes. "You only *partly* managed. What is it that you're looking for, Frances Hallowell?"

"Please, Maxine. *Please* let us study it." I don't dare mention the spell book here with all the other girls listening. I also don't mention the new notes that have arrived. I haven't spoken of them to Lena and Maxine since the first one, and they haven't asked. I know what their response would be. They would try to convince me it's a prank, or worse, they would try to stop me from trying to meet the note leaver entirely.

"Perhaps," she says, and takes a slow sip of water.

"Please." It comes out more desperate than I mean it to. "It has to be tonight."

"Tonight?" She sounds surprised. "I don't know if I can make arrangements that quickly."

"Then give me the key." Maxine rolls her eyes at me—it was a long shot. "Please, Maxine, I just—" I struggle to find an excuse that will make sense to her. "I just need to be out of this school for a while. I'll do it alone if I have to."

She pushes back from the table and stares at me; she knows I'm telling her the truth. I will find a way. Reluctantly she sighs, her eyes roam the room before she leans to whisper in my ear.

"At eight p.m. meet me at the base of the staircase. Tell your roommates. All of them."

"You're going to wear holes in the carpet if you keep pacing like that," Ruby snaps. It's 10:55 p.m. and I've been circling the room for the better part of an hour.

It wasn't difficult to persuade Aurelia and Ruby to join me tonight—a meeting cloaked under the secrecy of darkness is enough to lure anyone as bored as we are. But Lena is nowhere to be found, and it makes me nervous. I want to wait for her, but the fear of Maxine leaving without me stops me.

It's October, and I throw an overcoat borrowed from Aurelia over my uniform, leaving my dark hair loose around my shoulders.

Maxine is standing with all of the high-headed grace of a queen at the base of the stairs. Not in uniform, she's wearing a man's white shirt tucked into riding trousers, a loose waistcoat and brown leather shoes. Her blond hair bobs around in a loose bun on top of her head. Maxine is beautiful in the way boys are allowed to be, in a way that feels like defiance instead of a performance.

Surrounding her are eight more girls, among them Mabel, Sara, and Cora. Some are still in their uniforms, or states of partial uniform like me, while some are in clothes from home.

Right when I think she's not coming, Lena strides over from the sunroom, shooting me a look that lets me know I'm toast if this all goes sideways.

"I believe some of you are acquainted," Maxine announces as I join the group. She gestures around the circle. "Frances, Lena, Sara, Cora, Mabel, Maria, Aurelia, Ruby, Rebecca, Emily, May, and Alicia."

I don't know Alicia, Emily, or Maria, though I've seen Maria hanging around Maxine before.

While the rest of the girls make small talk, I sidle up to Maxine. "Are you going to explain to me why I had to invite Aurelia and Ruby along?"

"We need thirteen," she replies with a shrug.

"Why thirteen?"

"From what little English is in this book, I gather it takes thirteen to make a coven."

Coven. The word alone is a thrill. But thirteen will make keeping this a secret difficult.

"Where are we going?" Lena asks.

"To the Blockula," Maxine says with a wicked smile.

"Is that allowed?" Aurelia asks as we creep closer to the door. A rumble of agreement ripples through the group.

"For tonight, yes. Fear not little chickens, and follow your mother hen," Maxine trills. "I believe it's time we had a little fun." Slung over her shoulder is a leather satchel, and I pray it contains the book I can't stop thinking about.

She leads us through the entryway and out the front doors into the cool evening, skipping and prancing, waving her arms a bit in the air. There are no staff members to stop us. No Helen on patrol. The entryway and porch are empty save for the thirteen of us. A familiar thought nags the back of my mind. *It shouldn't be this easy.* But it feels good to brush away the voice in your head when it says things you don't want to hear.

Maxine skips down the lane leading up to the school, and we follow her like she's the Pied Piper and we are the children of Hamelin.

She pulls the skeleton key out, unlocks the gate, and the thirteen of us spill into the park, a plague of girls.

"The Blockula, the Blockula!" she sings, and I notice now some of the girls who have been here a long time like Maxine have joined her. "We're going to the Blockula!"

We follow a narrow dirt path through tall oak trees. In the daylight we might've passed a few families, babies in prams, old women walking arm in arm, but in the dark there is no one to give us disapproving glances.

The path opens out onto a large lawn, completely devoid of people. With its browning grass and dying purple asters returning to the wet fall earth, it looks like a cursed kingdom from a fairy tale.

The sky is dark and clear, bathing the meadow in silvery light from the wash of stars overhead.

Maria throws her hands up in the air, delighted, and yells, "The Blockula!"

Lena speaks up first. "This is absurd. What is the Blockula?"

"Oh, my dear Lena, I am so glad you asked," Maxine replies, hands on her hips, the commitment to theatrics unwavering. "The Blockula is where the devil holds court with his mistresses, and tonight we are his mistresses!" She does a twirl and releases her hair from its pins, sending it in a cascade down her shoulders.

Lena and I both share a laugh at the show Maxine's putting on, but Aurelia's whisper is genuinely frightened. "The devil?"

"Come, come, my dears!" Maxine skips farther out into the field, swinging her leather satchel as she goes.

The group is skittish, all darting eyes and worried faces trailing behind Maxine and Maria. I'm not sure what I pictured sneaking out to look like, but it certainly wasn't this.

Directly in the center of the meadow, Maxine drops her satchel and demands that we all gather round.

"Dear sisters, old and new, tonight we honor our powers, our sisters, and our foremothers, the witches who came before us." She reaches down into her bag and pulls out bottle after bottle of communion wine, whiskey, and something clear in a glass kitchen jar. "Let us toast!"

She pulls the cork on a dark green bottle of wine and takes a hearty swig.

"To magic!" she says, raising the bottle to the sky before passing it to Ruby next to her.

Ruby, too, takes an enthusiastic swig.

"Isn't your mother the president of her Woman's Christian Temperance Movement chapter?" Aurelia asks, scandalized.

"My mother is a cow." Ruby tosses her corn-silk hair over her shoulder before taking another swig and passing the bottle to Aurelia beside her.

Aurelia takes a smaller swallow, poorly disguises a grimace, then passes the wine on to the next girl.

Some of the girls make toasts.

"To our mothers!" or "May we never grow old!" or simply *"Salut!"*

Soon the bottle makes its way around the circle to me. Its dark red contents, severely diminished, slosh around the bottom.

Lena looks over at me. I raise the bottle to my lips and take as big a swig as I'm able.

It tastes a bit like grape juice gone bad. The burn is worse than the taste.

I can't stop my eyes from flitting to the edge of the field. The note left on my pillow said only *tonight*. I'm still not sure how to break away from the other girls. Being here with them is giving me the first taste of joy I've had in a very long while, but I haven't lost sight of my true mission.

Maxine has more in her bag than just alcohol, and after she's satisfied that everyone's veins are buzzing, she dumps her bag on the ground, sending objects spilling. Strewn in a heap on the damp grass are black taper candles, pewter candlesticks, gold coins, and crystals. There's even a single pomegranate, sitting red and waxy next to a paring knife.

And there, amongst all of it, looking ancient and heavy, is the spell book. "Who is ready to do some real magic?" she asks us with a wolfish grin.

A zip of excitement runs through me, or maybe that's just the communion wine.

"Where did this come from?" Sara asks, eyeing the objects with suspicion. She's not the only one.

"My job does come with certain perks, my dear Sara. When I was out fetching a new pupil a few months ago, I found this bounty on her mother's bookshelf, and I believed we needed the contents more than she did. Sometimes robbery is a decision made for the greater good."

I'm relieved that she lied about the spell book's origins. I don't know if she's lying about where she got the rest of it.

With the confidence and clear instructions of a drill sergeant, she directs the thirteen of us where to sit, cross-legged, on the dying grass.

In the center of the circle of girls, she lights the candles and places them in a perfect pentagram.

At each of the five points of the pentagram, she places an object: a clear crystal, a kitchen knife, matches, a chipped seashell, and a bottle of what's left of the wine.

Match smoke is carried away on a fall breeze. Next to me, Aurelia tugs her coat tighter.

"I've read through a good deal of the book this week, and I believe I have found a spell for us to practice with." Maxine stands at the head of the circle. Eyes aloft, licked with flames from the candles, with a proud set to her jaw, she looks, for a moment, like Joan of Arc being burned at the stake.

She opens to a page with diagrams of hands, a tangle of words, and a small sun.

Maxine sits, sets the book in the grass, places her hands in a prayer position near her heart, and recites the words from the page. *"Déanann máthair dúinn ár . . ."* She makes the bulky words sound elegant, and soon a dim globe of light, no bigger than a few inches across, springs to life in front of her chest. It winks out nearly as quickly as it appeared.

My classmates scramble over one another, crawling across the circle to get closer to the book.

Mabel snatches the book off Maxine's lap. She says the spell once, and nothing happens. Black candles drip wax onto the damp ground. They flicker dimly, waiting like the rest of us. The second time she tries there is only more silence. The rest of us wait with bated breath. When a light finally flickers between her hands, after the third try, the entire circle gasps.

Maxine shrieks. It's a shockingly un-Maxine-like sound. The other girls join in the celebration.

The spell is exciting, sure, but I don't understand the near-frenzied joy of my classmates' responses.

"Why is everyone reacting so . . . enthusiastically?" I lean over and ask Lena.

She pauses for a moment, then whispers in my ear, "I think this is the first time we've created something from nothing."

Ruby snatches the book next. It takes her even longer than Mabel to get the spell right, but she manages eventually. Her globe of light glows a little red, and still it comes and goes in a blink.

On and on the girls practice, passing the book between them. Some get it right away, like Maxine, some take longer. It's a comfort to know they are as hungry for this as I am. No one can make the light last.

The book finally lands in my lap. The words feel pointy and too big in my mouth. *"Déanann máthair dúinn ár."* I stumble. First, there is nothing. Then, from the back of my throat, the palms of my hands, my diaphragm, *everywhere*, the power sparks awake and with it a small, blinding sun held between my hands. Hovering above the ground, shining as clear as day. The warmth is fleeting.

Something inside me goes very still. I stare at the light until my eyes water, then I shake out my hands and release the pressure in my chest. The moment lasts only the length of a few heartbeats.

"Congratulations," Maxine says.

"On what?" I ask.

"Your light came the quickest and burned the brightest. Our little witch queen."

Her compliment makes my heart swell with pride. This is something I want desperately to be good at.

I'm not yet sure who I am. But I could be *this*. Powerful. Reckless. It's intoxicating.

No one says it, but by the looks on their faces, I can see they understand. The magic we've been taught at school is small. It is magic that allows us to manipulate existing objects in small ways. To above all things be good girls, good wives and daughters. Some girls, like Lena and Maxine, are connected to the magic in a way that gives them the ability to see and feel things others can't. But this spell book, for the first time, has given us all the ability to *create*.

I don't want to be good. I want to create something, *be* something.

After everyone has had a turn with the book, Maxine declares we've had enough fun and stashes it back in her satchel. Ruby tries to snatch it from her, but Maxine is quicker. The circle of the twelve of us erupts in protest, but Maxine points to the stars, cresting the horizon over the dark of the tree line, and declares, "We only have so much time left. Let's not waste it all on school." She pulls another bottle of wine out of her satchel before anyone can disagree with her.

Cora takes a long swig and passes it to Maria. There are sparks in everyone's eyes.

Girls scatter across the field, dancing and laughing and violently alive.

The bottle makes its way to me. Sticky sweet, acrid and burning, it reminds me of the paint thinner the workers used last summer when Mrs. Carrey insisted we spruce up the shop.

A group of girls to my left begins a game of "Ring around the Rosie," and they grab my hand, pulling me into the fray.

I forget to fall down at the end of the song, and Maxine shouts from across the field, "The instructions are in the lyrics, stupid!"

"I refuse to be so easily manipulated by a song!" I shout back, as Cora side-tackles me to the ground.

The alcohol loosens our limbs and our tongues, and my head begins to spin so badly, I stay on my back right there on the grass, the damp leaching through my coat.

It would be easy to let myself slip away, nice even, to let the alcohol blur my thoughts to nothing and return to my warm bed.

The ground is cold. Black wax from the candles pools on dead leaves.

Yes, it would be easy to slip away, but William would be so disappointed in me.

Maxine, having crossed the field to sprawl out next to Lena and me, rolls over on her side and props herself up on an elbow, a storm-cloud-dark smile spreading across her face.

"It seemed like time you finally had some proper fun. Our lives don't only have to be classes and avoiding Vykotsky's withering stare."

"You had me fooled," I reply, staring at Maxine like the curious thing she is. A blurry-around-the-edges kind of person, made up of equal parts affection and sharpness, the unwilling mother and mentor to all who come to Haxahaven under her wings. For the first time, I think about how lonely that must be.

It's in this moment that I consider telling her I plan on meeting the note leaver tonight. There's a chance she'd understand, a chance she'd help.

But if she stops me, I might never find out who it is, and I'm not willing to take that risk.

Aurelia joins us next, lying down next to Maxine, sporting a crown of small white flowers. She drops a matching one on Lena's head.

Then, one by one, girls lie down with us, draping their loose limbs over friends, resting heads on shoulders and stomachs, lying out like a constellation.

They laugh and talk about classes, things they miss about their pre-Haxahaven lives, and all the boys and girls they love back home.

An image of Oliver standing in the morning sun floats into my mind, and I brush it away just as quickly as it came.

Aurelia tells us about a cousin who knew a girl who knew a girl whose family made a fortune in steel. The girl was shipped over to England to marry a duke and live in a castle.

"Wouldn't that be dreamy?" Aurelia sighs. "To be a duchess?"

"It sounds like a bore, to be honest," Maxine replies sharply.

Aurelia offers a sad, small "Not to *me*" under her breath.

"I have no patience for tea parties," Maxine continues. "I'd like to move to Cairo and train Arabian horses and climb the pyramids."

"I'd like to be a nurse, I think," a girl to my left says—Alicia, I think her name is. "Maybe help people who *actually* have tuberculosis."

"Hey!" Maxine interjects. "I've said it before and I'll say it again, any one of us very well *could* have tuberculosis."

Next to her, Maria dissolves into a fit of giggles.

"Well, I'd just like to marry a boy who really, really loves me," Aurelia sighs, eyes fixed on the stars. "Duke or not."

"What about you, Frances?" Maxine asks. "What do you want to do when you're free of this place?"

"I haven't given it much thought, to be honest. I always assumed I'd die a seamstress."

"Bleak," Ruby quips.

"What do people usually do when they leave?" I ask, recalling that I've asked this once before—when I first arrived at Haxahaven. But now I yearn for a more specific answer. One not clouded in ambiguity and cautionary tales.

"It depends on the girl and what she can do," Maxine replies. "Some of the girls from wealthier families, like Duchess Ruby here, go home and marry a suitable fellow, only using their magic for basic household tasks, hiding their true identities for the rest of their days."

"You say that like money is some evil thing," Ruby replies, twirling a small ruby ring around her pinky finger.

"Not evil. Just perhaps not the *only* thing," Maxine says, rolling her eyes. "Some of the girls from worse circumstances use their gifts to start businesses. I know of at least three running wildly successful flower shops in the city. The clairvoyants can typically make a living as psychics, performing parlor tricks at parties. Manipulators are good at menial jobs—you can wash clothes and clean apartments in record time. See, Frances, you could very well still die a seamstress."

"A dream come true," I deadpan.

"And then there's us sorry Finders. The only good I can do is here at Haxahaven, collecting girls from the greater tristate area and bringing them into our ranks. You may be destined to die a seamstress, but I am destined to die here," she finishes sadly, her joking bravado cracking to reveal the deep dissatisfaction within.

I reach over to touch her hand. "You're going to die on the top of a pyramid if I have to push you off myself."

I am overcome with sadness, not only for Maxine, trapped by her powers, but for all of us. Similarly trapped by our circumstances and our magic and the terrible misfortune that befell us when we had the bad sense to be born female.

Ruby could be a Gibson girl or a picture star like Mary Pickford; her cruel smile and masses of blond hair seem made for the stage. Instead she is a tool to be used by her wealthy family to maintain status. I heard her speaking to Aurelia yesterday about her mother's latest letter. Her mother is speaking of getting a private physician to look after Ruby's condition. She's afraid the boy Ruby is supposed to marry, a boy drowning in railroad money, is going to lose interest if Ruby's "tuberculosis" doesn't soon resolve itself.

Then there's Aurelia, so poisoned by expectations that she be sweet and good all the time that she's had no space to develop any resolve of her own.

Maxine could do anything she wanted, if anyone gave her half a chance and she cared less for Haxahaven.

And Lena deserves every good thing in the world. She should be home, where she wants to be, instead of trapped within the walls of a school she never asked to attend. Though we are learning magic, we have been taught all our lives to remain small, and even here we seem to be in cages of our own making.

Does it break their hearts too?

"So, Frances—seamstress it is?" Maxine asks, tone joking.

"I want to use magic to help people. To protect the ones I love. I'd like for this to matter."

"Here, here!" she cheers, raising the bottle of communion wine to the sky. A few others join her toast, draining what little remains in the bottles.

"Well, we've had our fun," Maxine declares. "Time to return to our humble home." We blow out the candles and carelessly shove the objects from the pentagram back into Maxine's bag.

An awful part of me considers snatching the spell book, shoving it under my coat. But I resist the temptation.

And just as she led us in, she leads us out of the meadow, though we're significantly stumblier than before.

The moon is full and bright, looking down on us from the middle of the sky.

Desperation makes me daring.

I haven't forgotten why I'm here.

It's reckless, stupidly so, but at least this is danger of my own creation.

With buzzing in my head and iron in my veins, I take a breath and step off the path. Break away from the chorus of girls ahead of me, careful to slip away undetected.

I'm two steps into the trees when I hear the whistling.

CHAPTER ELEVEN

The tune floats through the darkness of the forest so softly, I have to pause for a moment to make sure I'm not imagining it.

It's coming from the left and up ahead, a haunting, jaunty tune that sounds like something my downstairs neighbor Mr. O'Sullivan would have played on his fiddle. The floors in my old building were so thin, I could hear everything. I hated how late he'd practice, especially since his playing got worse when he was a few glasses of whiskey deep, but I almost miss it now.

The sound of the whistling pulls me like a tether deeper into the woods. I don't know if it's the alcohol or the magic pulsing through my veins, but I feel ready for this, for whatever I'm about to find.

At the sound of my boots crunching through the underbrush, the whistling stops.

"Who's there?" I whisper-shout.

The only answer I get is the footfalls of heavier boots, very much not my own.

The pounding of my heart feels more like anticipation of the inevitable than fear.

"Hello?" I ask the darkness once more. Still I receive no answer.

"Déanann máthair dúinn ár," I mutter clumsily. I'm not sure it's even the right spell. Nothing happens.

The forest is very, very dark. The canopy of leaves blocks out the moonlight here, and it feels an entirely different world from the meadow I shared with my friends.

Someone whistles a single low note. I can't tell how close they are.

I curse and focus on the fluttering in my chest. *"Déanann máthair dúinn ár,"* I command the magic once more.

Responding to my words, an orb of blinding white light sparks to life between my thumb and forefinger before winking out. I'm surprised the command worked. I hadn't really expected it to.

The whistling and crunching of boots stops.

I look up, blinking away the spots in my eyes.

A deep voice cracks the darkness. "Hiya, Frances."

The gasp that exits my body is as involuntary as the shriek that follows it. I stumble back a few feet, banging my ankle badly on a rock. Pain shoots up through my leg. I curse, and force myself back upright.

In the trees is a boy close to my age, and devastatingly familiar, built like a wall—broad shoulders and muscle tone. Light brown hair falls in curls around his head, and under his eyes are deep, bruiselike purple shadows, visible here even in this low light.

It's him, it's him, it's him, my brain sings.

With heavy footfalls, he steps back a few feet and puts his hands up in front of his chest in a show of surrender. "I'm sorry about that. I didn't mean to scare ya,'" he says in a thick, singsongy Irish accent.

"I'm not scared."

He lifts the lantern he's holding to illuminate his face. He has the jawline of a statue and the kind of aquiline nose that's begging to be broken. He's just frightened me so terribly, I think seriously about doing it myself.

It's him.

He grins. "Good. I'm sorry this was the only way for us to speak."

I've never trusted snake-oil salesmen or boys who grin without reason.

He steps forward two paces. I step back two paces. He extends his hand. I step forward to shake it because I don't want to be impolite. It is surprisingly warm and solid.

"I'm Finn D'Arcy." He quirks a reassuring half smile as he says it.

"We've met before." It isn't a question.

He nods. "Aye, I wondered if you'd remember."

"You were in my apartment." I'm confused. "And now you're here. Why?"

"William and I worked together," he says like it explains anything.

"I remember—you brought him home drunk one night."

"William didn't always know his limits."

"Yes, I know." I take a deep breath. "Are you the one leaving the notes?"

"Yes." He shrugs a hand through his curls and looks at the dark forest floor. "I'm sorry it had to be like this, but there was no way they were ever going to let the likes of me walk into that fancy school o' yours." His lilting accent teases me. Or maybe that's just him.

"Then how are you getting the notes to me?"

"Cat burglary. Lock picking. General brilliance."

Confusion makes way to annoyance. "And you couldn't have just met me in my room? Why make me trek all the way out here?"

"Couldn't risk having your classmates run into me instead. I apologize."

"But why? Why leave the notes at all?"

His posture is casual as he shoves his hands in the pockets of his rough-spun work pants. "One month ago, you waltzed into my head in a bloodstained white blouse, with a pair of scissors in your hand. I remembered you from that night last winter. I knew who you were, and thought you might need help."

Before I can stop myself, I take another step forward. "You're having the dreams too?"

"I'm a walker."

The wind picks up, sending leaves flying through the thicket and tangling my skirt in my legs.

"You say that like I know what it means."

"A *siúlóir*. I can enter dreams."

"Enter dreams?"

With all the magic I've learned about in the past month, I should be less surprised to hear that someone has been walking through my head.

"William was my friend. I wish I could have done more to save him." His face is open, honest. Despite my better judgment, I believe him.

"I plan to get justice for him. I've been waiting and waiting for someone to help me." My voice cracks on the last two words.

Finn cocks his head. "William would have done anything to protect you. He's gone, so I figured someone else should probably try."

"I don't deserve a life of my own until I find who took his." It's a horrible thing to say out loud. It comes out more dramatic than I intend.

Finn must not agree, because he lets out a sad laugh. "You think your brother would have wanted you to become a crusader?"

The sound of his chuckle makes me defiant. "He wouldn't want his killer to walk free."

"If you're so determined, at least let me offer you my protection."

I lift my chin, hoping the words come out as sternly as I feel them. "I intend to be so powerful, I won't need protecting."

Finn smiles at me like he's proud of me. It reminds me so fiercely of my brother, it nearly makes me stumble backward.

"Maybe I can help with that, too. One step at a time and all that," he says.

I'm dizzy with new information, or maybe it's just the wine. "Did my brother have magic too?" It's a big question to ask. It hurts to imagine my brother living a whole life I knew so little about. I'm angry at him for knowing about magic and not telling me. I used to joke that William couldn't keep a secret to save his life. Apparently, I was wrong. The feeling makes me both sick and furious.

"No, not a lick. He was an errand boy."

It's a shame. My brilliant light of a brother deserved this so much more than me. This power should have been his.

He continues, "I saw your little group. The spells are barely working. I can teach you more than how to create a single spark of light. I can teach you how to use the book, if you'd like."

The book. The thought is thrilling, but I still don't know what to make of Finn's declarations.

"You were watching us?" *Watching us in the meadow, watching me at school, watching me in my dreams.*

There's a beseeching look in his eyes, like he's searching for something in me. "If you're determined to learn, let me help you do it safely."

"Was the book your doing too?" If he was breaking in to leave me notes, it wouldn't be horribly out of character to bury a book in Forest Park.

His brows knit together in confusion. "My doing?"

"Did you bury it?"

"I can't tell if you're pulling my leg or not."

I'm frustrated; I know I must sound ridiculous. "The first night I was supposed to meet you, I came but we found only the spell book instead."

Finn would have to be an incredible actor to fake the look of genuine bafflement on his face. "Aye, that is strange. But it wasn't me. All the more reason for you to accept my help. A book that appears from nowhere is likely a book that is dangerous."

Maxine's voice cuts through the woods and the ringing in my ears. "Frances?" she calls. *"Fraaances!"*

I wish my head would stop spinning. I reach up and slap my face a little, hoping to regain feeling in my cheeks. Finn laughs, his face cast in moonlight and shadows.

"You all right there, love?"

"Don't call me 'love.'"

"Sure thing, love." He has the nerve to wink.

William taught me how to throw a punch. I wonder how upset he'd be if I used his lessons on his friend.

"Frances?" Maxine calls again. She's close and getting closer. A part of me is glad she's come for me, another part wishes she'd go away so I could stay and listen to what it is Finn has to say.

"C'mere," he says through gritted teeth.

I step forward, hesitantly. We're close enough now that I can feel the heat of his breath.

"Frances, is that you?" Maxine calls. She's just outside the copse of trees where we're hidden. We'll be discovered in seconds.

Finn grabs my hand, pulls me to him, wraps his arms around my waist, and draws me so close I can feel the heat of his breath and his heart thumping out a steady rhythm beneath his shirt. His lips hover above mine.

"There was another spell in the book," I whisper.

"What kind of spell?" His breath is hot.

"A resurrection spell."

"My, Frances, you are a dangerous girl."

Maxine is coming; her footsteps are mere feet away.

But Finn is so close, I can see the flecks of green in his eyes, illuminated in lantern light. "Can you help me do it?"

"Yes," he breathes.

"It has to be soon. The spell said 'soon.'"

Maxine bursts through the trees. "Frances, there you are. We were worri—" She stops short at the sight of me in Finn's arms. I gather my bearings enough to shove Finn away from me.

Her mouth forms a little O, her eyebrows raised.

"I didn't realize," she mutters. I've never seen Maxine at a loss for words.

"It's not—" I begin to say, but she holds up a hand.

"Just hurry up please. It isn't safe to be out here alone. I'll wait for you, and we can walk back together."

She's angry with me, and I don't blame her.

Finn and I are still standing too close. My shove didn't make much of a difference. The warmth of his chest radiates through me.

"Meet me here three nights from now."

It's heavy, this moment, whatever it is.

"How?" It comes out as an exhale.

"You're smart, Frances. I'm sure you'll figure something out," he replies with another maddening grin. "You'd best be going now. Your friend is waiting, and she's none too pleased with you. I didn't mean to create trouble."

I glance through the trees to where Maxine is waiting for me, my stomach heavy with guilt and dread and communion wine.

I turn to Finn to respond, but he's already walking back silently in the direction from which he came, whistling the same haunting tune.

"Come on, Frances!" Maxine shouts.

"Coming!" I push through the branches to meet her.

Her mouth is turned down in a frown, moonlight glowing silver on her skin.

"That was exceptionally stupid, even for you," she says.

"It's not like that." As if I could possibly explain what it is like.

"Please, Frances, elaborate, because I am positively dying to know!" She throws her hands up in the air; wind-whipped tendrils of her hair dance around her face. "How did he even find you?"

She looks furious, the way I imagined Hera, Zeus's perpetually betrayed wife to look in the stories William and I used to read when we were young.

"I had a brother once, Maxine. I'm just trying to figure out what happened to him."

"By kissing boys?" she mocks.

"I told you: it wasn't what it looked like."

Leaves crunch beneath her boots, even her steps are angry. "I am begging you to enlighten me."

I weigh my options. Perhaps telling Maxine about Finn is short-sighted. There's still a chance she'd try to stop me from meeting him again. I don't think she'd rat me out to Mrs. Vykotsky, but if she truly believed I was in danger, I don't doubt she'd lock me in my room, or barricade the doors. Plus, there's a tiny part of me that wants to keep Finn a secret. Someone just for me.

Maxine's brows are furrowed, her sharp face both enraged and concerned. It's her concern that makes me relent. That, and I've missed having someone to share my secrets with. I sigh. "I'll tell you everything, but not here." There's something about this park that makes me feel itchy all over.

"Come along, Frances," she says, tugging me forward through the inky night back to Haxahaven.

Maria has left the front gate unlocked for us. The massive double doors creak as we open them, but the foyer is mercifully dark and still as we step inside. We're the only ones foolish enough to still be awake after curfew.

We creep through the front hall, careful to quiet our footfalls.

Maxine gestures with one hand in a *follow me* motion.

Clouds must have overtaken the dim light of the moon, because it's as dark as sin in Maxine's bedroom.

I reach my hand out through the impenetrable darkness only to bump Maxine.

"Watch it," she hisses at me.

"Shhh," I whisper back.

"We need to find a candle."

"And aren't you supposed to be a Finder?"

She reaches through the darkness and raps me on the head.

"Go to hell," she snaps.

The sudden sound of a match striking makes us both go still.

We snap our heads around to see a shadowy figure sitting at Maxine's vanity, their feet propped up as casual as you please.

After an agonizing second, the figure lifts the match to a candle; it catches light and illuminates her face.

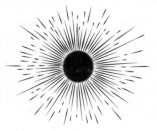

CHAPTER TWELVE

W ell aren't you two just waking snakes," Lena says.
I sigh in relief.

"Jesus Christ!" Maxine exclaims. "What on earth are you doing here?"

"You didn't think I was going to let you leave me out, did you?" she replies, face awash in candlelight, still leaning back in Maxine's vanity chair like the queen of the castle. Her mouth is curved in a half smile, eyes glowing with the glee of seeing Maxine jump out of her skin. I would be hunched over laughing if I weren't clutching my own chest in surprise.

The vanity where Lena sits is covered haphazardly in jewels as sharp as Maxine's eyes.

"Leave you out of what, exactly?" Maxine asks while pulling pins out of her hair. She throws one at Lena, who dodges it with a laugh.

Maxine then reaches down to the hem of the man's shirt she's wearing and tugs it over her head. She isn't wearing a corset underneath.

It's with confidence that I will never possess that she strides over to her wardrobe and throws on a silk dressing gown, while Lena and I stare at her in identical stunned silence.

"Oh of all the things we've done tonight, this is what scandalizes you the most? Grow up," she snipes. "Now, Frances, please tell us what it is you were doing with that boy in the park." Lena snaps to look at me. "Well, well, well, Frances." She sounds impressed, maybe. Or she's mocking me too.

I sigh and sink down onto Maxine's feather bed. Maxine sprawls out beside me. Lena rises from the vanity and joins us.

"His name is Finn. He was a friend of my brother's."

Maxine jabs me in the ribs with an elbow. "Don't think I don't notice you didn't answer my question."

Lena closes her eyes and massages the space between them. "I think he's going to teach us."

I turn to her. "How did you know that?"

Lena's eyes blink open. "The same way I knew you'd be here." She taps the side of her temple with her pointer finger. "Clairvoyant, remember?"

Maxine settles her head into the crook of Lena's neck. "So this mysterious woodland boy is going to teach us *what* exactly?"

Lena thinks for a moment. I'd give anything for a peek inside her brain. "I see the three of us with him in the woods. We have the spell book. It's nighttime. We're . . ." She shakes her head, baffled or bemused by whatever she's seeing. "We're smiling. We look happy."

If what Lena is seeing is true, then the resurrection spell might be legitimate. I could speak to my brother once more. I'd do things much worse than sneak off to meet a boy for that.

Maxine kicks my foot. "I didn't get the impression we were invited too. Seemed like a Frances-only affair. Who are we to get in the way of romance."

I kick her back. "Don't be cruel. That wasn't what it was like at all. I only met him once before tonight, a long time ago." I don't tell her about the way his hazel eyes and the set of his jaw sent a thrill through me. It's stupid to think of a boy that way at all when we have bigger issues at hand. "If you want to come, I'm inviting you." I also don't tell them they're so much more important to me than any boy. That is what I really wanted, a warm bed filled with friends, with three identical hearts on fire, burning for something more than what we've been given.

Lena gives a decisive nod. "I'm coming."

Maxine sighs and rolls over, nestling her head against my chest and laying her legs across Lena's. The three of us are tangled like a pretzel, like a single unit of being. "You're both rather stupid—you know that, right?"

Lena scowls down at Maxine. "You're telling me you don't think we have a right to learn more about our power? We've snuck out twice now—how difficult could it be to do it again? Helen's clearly a terrible patrolman."

"Lena makes an excellent point," I agree.

Maxine purses her lips and lifts herself up—sitting straight and sure. "If you tell anyone what I'm about to tell you, I'll skin you both alive, understood?"

Lena and I nod solemnly.

"Vykotsky thinks a little rebellion is good for a girl, so I have special permission to sneak out a few times a year. Tonight was a school-sanctioned outing."

I feel more betrayed than I should by Maxine's admission. I thought tonight was a gesture of friendship, and to find out it was little more than a field trip stings. But still, I know she burns for more too.

"What about the night we found the spell book?" I prod.

"That was a risk. I knew the faculty had a meeting that night, and were likely tipsy on brandy. It was luck more than anything. Getting out won't be so easy next time."

Lena seems less surprised. "But you have a key to the gate in the wall. There has to be a way out?" she prods.

"It's getting out of the walls of this mansion that's the problem, not the wall surrounding it," Maxine snaps, but there is a flicker in her eyes. Faint, but I can see it.

"There is a way, though." I press her. "Isn't there? Lena sees us training with him. So there is a way. Not easy isn't the same thing as impossible."

I'm learning that Maxine keeps her face in a carefully constructed mask of cool amusement, but it cracks when she's thinking hard about something. You can see it in the way her eyes scrunch up in the corners. She's making that face now. "We could try, if it's worth it."

To learn magic that does more than mend a dress, I'd face more fearsome creatures than Helen and Mrs. Vykotsky.

Lena and I respond simultaneously. "It's worth it."

* * *

I'm back in Mr. Hues's shop, cranking the wheel of my sewing machine, fabric passing softly through my hands.

I know it's a dream because the shop is empty. No Mrs. Carrey or Jess or Violet. No chatter drifting down from the apartment upstairs. I'm completely alone. The edges ripple, the light bends all wrong here.

The chime of the doorbell startles me. I should be less surprised to see Finn standing in the doorway, his curls haloed in soft morning light.

"Hiya, Frances," he greets me.

"Are you real?" I stop the turning of my right hand, and the ticking of my sewing machine quiets.

"As real as anything ever is." His hair has turned golden in the dream light. He looks like an apparition, a son of Zeus.

"That's not an answer."

"Having touched you makes this easier, us talkin'."

I fall back on old habits, directing my attention to the garment I'm working on rather than meeting his gaze. It almost makes me want to laugh, the idea of pouring work into this dream dress, until the garment comes into focus. It's a coat made of dark blue velvet. The laugh dies in my throat.

"So. Three days from now. You coming to meet me?" He raises his brows seductively like he's asking to call on me.

I'm reminded of the errand boys, the sons, and husbands of clients who would come into the shop to fetch orders and the way they would leer at me. Once a boy whistled at me as I handed him the dress I'd worked all week on wrapped in tissue paper.

"I'd bet you look fetching out of the wool dress," he said, and my face went so red, the other girls in the shop teased me about it for weeks. I went home and took a bath so long, my fingers pruned as I scrubbed myself raw, like I could wash his gaze off my skin and down the drain. I couldn't. I still felt it crawling all over me as I slept.

It doesn't feel like that with Finn. Sure, I'd like to sock him, but he smiles at me like I'm in on the joke.

"If you can talk to me in my dreams, why can't we practice magic here?" I ask.

"Magic on the astral plane is different. The only limit of what is possible is what you can think to create. Real magic doesn't work like that. Go ahead. Picture a flower blooming in your hand."

I unfurl my palm, and in it sits a tulip, white in the middle and blood red at the edges of its fraying petals.

"See?" Finn smiles.

I've taken enough of Mrs. Roberts's needle-levitation lessons to know magic doesn't feel like this when I'm awake.

"So you'll do it? You'll come train with me?" he asks.

The dream space is closing in on me; the voices of my roommates waking up filter in through the edges. I'll be awake soon.

"I'll try."

The shop blurs in and out of focus. Before he can reply, Finn is gone, and instead I find Aurelia standing over me, shaking my shoulders gently. I blink my eyes open.

"It's time for breakfast, Frances," she whispers softly. In the corner, Ruby rolls her eyes.

"Hallowell can't handle her liquor," she says with a laugh. "Get the hell out of bed and nurse your headache without complaint like the rest of us."

My stomach rolls, and my head pounds fiercely.

"Leave me be," I mumble into my pillow.

Aurelia prods me. "Frances, we have to get dressed and head down to breakfast."

Ruby buttons her cape around her delicate shoulders while Lena plaits her hair in front of the mirror.

Ruby is likely right and I simply can't handle my liquor, but the idea of standing up makes me want to vomit, and surely that's a legitimate reason to miss breakfast.

"Frances, come on," Lena shouts. She, too, looks a little green but is putting on a brave face.

"I can't. Tell them I'm sick." It itches where each sweaty tendril of hair is plastered to my forehead.

"You heard her," Ruby says. "She said to leave her. We have to make it to breakfast before those god-awful Underwood sisters eat all the sticky buns."

The three of them walk through the door. Lena pauses for a moment and turns to me.

"Do you want me to stay with you?" she offers.

By her tone, I can tell there is nothing Lena would dislike more than playing nurse to me all day, but that only makes her offer kinder.

"No, thank you. Please go."

She shrugs a little, then replies, "Drink some water," before running out the door to catch up with the others.

I'm too jittery to fall back to sleep, so I stare at the ceiling and think of my brother. When we were very young, before my mother was too crushed by the weight of living to care for us, we'd sometimes go to the beach. William and I would sit, our chubby little legs sprawled out in front of us, and we'd dig holes in the sand right at the edge of the water. It was a futile task. The sand would collapse in on itself, and William and I would laugh and laugh as the holes filled with seawater.

There's a sinking pit in my chest now that feels like the holes at the beach my brother and I used to dig. Every time I think I've worked through some of the pain, new pain arrives. There's no bottom, just endless salt water and a hurt that doesn't end. Since his death, I've thought maybe if I found his killer, the pit in my chest would stop collapsing in on itself. Finn's arrival feels like my first real chance.

I miss breakfast but make it to Mrs. Roberts's class on time. She hands me a small scrub brush at the door. It's magical dish-washing day.

In between sudsing a plate and rinsing it, Lena passes me her textbook with a deliberate jerk of her chin.

I flip the book open to find a folded square of parchment inside. I slip it into the pocket of my pinafore. It stays there, heavy, all through the rest of lunch, class, and dinner. There is no place at Haxahaven where someone isn't watching you. Finally, after dinner, alone in our bedroom, I unfold it. Maxine's handwriting is sharp and small. *Thursday night at 10 p.m. Meet in my room. —MCD*

The fat tabby currently resting on Lena's bed eyes me. "Shh, don't tell," I whisper to it.

I lower the note to the flame of the gas lamp on my bedside. My anticipation is as dark and wild as the smoke that rises from the burning parchment.

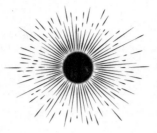

CHAPTER THIRTEEN

I'm so nervous for the next two days, I barely get through my classes. In Mrs. Roberts's class I can scarcely focus enough to lift a sewing needle. Mrs. Li is so upset with my lack of participation, I make up a story about remembering my father's face just to get her to stop glaring at me.

It isn't until Thursday after the sun has set that I begin to wonder if I'm making the right decision. No choice seems easy, so I choose to listen to the humming in my chest that begs for answers and for the possibility of seeing my brother once more.

Lena and I sit on the edge of her bed embroidering, waiting for the clock to countdown to ten. Her nimble fingers sew green seed beads into elegant spirals on a piece of leather. I pull black roses into a piece of pale pink cotton. Lena's hands are quicker than mine. We could use the spells from Mrs. Roberts's class, but the pain in my fingers is a comforting familiarity.

At a quarter till ten we rise, lace our boots, and put coats on over our nightdresses.

Maxine is waiting for us in her room, just as she said she'd be. She's wrapped in a hooded cloak, which she tucks the spell book under. With her silvery hair in a braid over her shoulder, she is the very picture of a witch, which I'm sure was her intention.

Haxahaven is even more unsettling at night than it is during the day. Without the chatter of girls to fill the empty space, it looms dark and hollow, like the unbeating chambers of a heart.

We creep through drafty hall after drafty hall to a nondescript wooden doorway. Maxine raps on it three times in rapid succession. There is an agonizing pause before the door cracks open, throwing a gash of light across the dark floors of the hallway.

Standing in the doorway is a middle-aged woman with dark skin I've never seen before. She's wearing a white muslin dress, and has kinky curls pulled up into a bun, set with a mother-of-pearl comb. Her eyes are kind, but her mouth is set in a hard line. "Quickly, girls, please."

We step through the door and into the warm belly of a kitchen.

"Thank you again for your help, Florence." Maxine trots across the kitchen, trailing a finger across the polished butcher-block counters.

"I still don't think this is a very good idea, girls." Florence takes us in, raising her brows.

Maxine shrugs. "Then thank you for helping us anyway." She turns to Lena and me. "Florence runs the kitchens. The back door is monitored less than the others."

"How do we know we can trust her?" Lena asks.

Florence smiles at Lena. "I like her."

Maxine laughs. "We can trust her because I trust her."

It's good enough for me.

The three of us follow Florence across the warm brick floor of the kitchen to an oak door set with a small, round window, black with night.

"Helen is on patrol tonight. I encouraged her to have a brandy with me after dinner, so hopefully her senses are dulled. You girls be careful, you promise me?" Florence says.

Maxine grasps Florence's hands with a warmth I've never seen from her. "I promise, Miss Flo."

With that she opens the door, and we step into the chilly night.

The air is damp and heavy, but it is a relief to fill my lungs after sitting inside for so many days.

Maxine unlocks the gate, and we step into the park.

"Thank you," I say. "For sneaking us out tonight. I know it's a risk for you, too."

Maxine shrugs. "We're lucky to have Florence."

Lena nods in agreement. "Feels good to break the rules of a place I hate. Cathartic, is the word, I think."

In silence the three of us walk to the edge of the park. At the tree line on the east field, we stop. I reach out and grasp their hands on either side of me. "So we don't get lost," I whisper.

Maxine snickers. "You know you can just ask to hold my hand." I nudge her with my shoulder, but I don't let go.

The park is as omnipresent as ever. For a place that fills me with such discomfort, I seem to be spending an awful lot of time here.

It doesn't take long for us to find Finn's lantern flickering in a copse of aspen trees.

"Ah, Frances, I knew you'd come." The last word of his sentence is clipped. He stops short at the sight of Maxine and Lena linked to me.

The three of us stare Finn down, daring him to say something.

After a tense second he opens his mouth. "We hadn't discussed bringing friends." His eyes narrow as if he's doing an equation in his head. Finally, he shrugs. "But the more the merrier, I suppose. Ladies, I'm Finn D'Arcy, a friend of Frances's late brother."

"Maxine DuPre, not a lady."

"Lena Jamison."

He nods his head. "Why'd you follow our Frances out into the woods?"

The answer to Finn's question seems obvious, that we all share the same bruising ache for more magic.

"We're not in the habit of letting our friends sneak out alone to meet strange boys," Maxine replies with a twist of a smile.

Wind whips through Finn's curls. "Ah, I understand William would be pleased to see his sister surrounded by such good friends."

The sound of William's name being spoken aloud into the world fills me with warmth. It makes him feel a little less gone. He'd find all of this one hilarious adventure. He would have packed snacks.

"It's chilly out, so I'm sure you lasses would rather we do this quickly," Finn trills.

"Actually, we have a few questions for you," Maxine interjects. I didn't expect this, though I probably should have.

Finn nods. "Of course."

"Not that we don't take our dear Frances at her word . . . but we'd really like to make sure you are who you say you are."

"Maxine, he knew my brother."

"Well pardon me if I don't trust boys who appear from nowhere. He shouldn't even know where Haxahaven is."

"Fair enough." Finn shrugs. "I know the location of Haxahaven because I belong to the Sons of Saint Druon, an organization of men who have magic much like you witches."

His honesty stuns me. I know about the Sons—my brother used to work for them—but I thought they were just a plain old gentleman's social club, not unlike dozens scattered across the city. Men who meet to push money around and wield political influence, it makes sense they'd play with other kinds of power too.

Lena looks nervous. Maxine doesn't look surprised. I don't know what look is on my face—it's gone numb with the cold. But I'd guess it's something close to shock.

"I've heard of the Sons," Maxine replies sternly. "I was told to stay far away."

Finn laughs, but there's an uncomfortable edge to the sound. "And I've been told to stay away from you."

"Then why are you here?" Maxine crosses her arms over her chest.

Finn shrugs casually. "I don't mind risks for things that matter."

It's Lena who speaks next. "So what will your boss and our headmistress do if we're caught conspiring together?"

Again Finn smiles wide, showing us every one of his straight teeth, but if I'm not mistaken, fear flickers across his eyes. "Let's hope we never find out."

"If we're such enemies, how did you know where Haxahaven was?" I ask him.

He continues casually, "The Sons and the witches of Haxahaven have a gentleman's agreement to leave each other be, but that doesn't mean they don't keep tabs on each other."

"We're not gentlemen," Lena replies.

"If we're being honest with each other, neither am I." If I weren't so freezing, I might have blushed.

"And we're just supposed to believe you?" Lena replies, her face serious.

"I'm too lowly an errand boy to be privy to much of anything that goes on at the club. If this were truly a Sons of Saint Druon scheme, there's no way they'd ever send me."

"But you're a magician too?" Maxine asks. She sucks on her teeth, as if finding the very concept of a boy with magic inherently suspect.

Finn gives a nod. "I can enter dreams and cast. William couldn't, but it didn't stop us from becoming fast friends." Finn continues, "When I learned William's sister was taken to Haxahaven, I wanted to help. William was always fascinated with magic, despite not being able to do any of it himself. I thought he'd probably want his sister to learn in earnest. I'm not much of a teacher, but it seemed worth tryin'."

Maxine looks from Finn to me. "Frances?" she asks.

"I believe him," I say simply. Lena gives me a sideways glance that communicates that she disagrees with me. I widen my eyes at her as if to say, *Trust me*.

Finn raises his hands in a show of truce. "What else do I have to gain by being here other than freezing to death and losing sleep?"

"Our sparkling company?" Lena deadpans.

His answer must be good enough for her, because Maxine pulls the ancient, leather-bound book out from underneath her cloak.

She flips through the thin pages with nimble fingers, then lays it open on a tree trunk. The lantern casts long shadows and orange light through the clearing.

On the page is a spell in a language I don't recognize.

"This isn't the resurrection spell," I whisper to her, irritated.

"Let's not dive feetfirst into hell," she replies.

She cracks her knuckles and begins to read. The words sound unnatural, sticking like honey in her throat. Nothing appears in her cupped hands. She frowns and tries again. Still there is silence.

Lena places her chin on Maxine's shoulder for a better look at the book and tries herself. Again there is nothing.

"Why isn't it working?" Maxine says. She's frustrated, her hands balled into fists at her side.

Finn approaches carefully. "May I?"

Maxine nods reluctantly.

Finn studies the page for a moment. "There are notes here in the margins," he explains.

"I'm not stupid. I can see that," Maxine snaps back at him. "But I don't know what half of them are saying."

I peer over Finn's shoulder to see what Maxine is talking about. It's difficult to read the spell book in the light of a single lantern. Shadows of tree branches dance over its ancient pages, giving it the illusion of being alive. Scrawled in the margins are notes, made so hastily, the author has left the page covered in ink spots. Some of them I can read, quick English words like "breath." Another is in Latin, "fiat lux." But most of them are in a language I don't recognize, a mess of consonants and vowels.

Finn meets my eye. I hadn't realized we were standing nearly close enough to touch. "This is Gaelic." He turns to grin at us. "How lucky you are to have an Irishman around."

He turns his attention back to the book. "This is different from the magic they teach at school. This is magic of creation, the kind of magic that comes straight from the core of you. Words can help direct energy, but it isn't as . . . specific as what you've been taught at Haxahaven."

"What do you mean 'specific'?" Lena asks.

"Think of basic spells as a hammer and a nail. No creativity, but it will get the job done. The magic in this book is more like paints and a canvas." I can't help but wonder how Finn knows all this. Where his knowledge comes from. As if reading my mind, Finn turns his attention to me. "Magic is an art, not a science. Think of this book as giving you suggestions, not instructions."

Maxine's eyes narrow. "How does that work practically?"

He shrugs a hand through his curls. "Let me see if I can translate this." In his pause the only sound is our breathing, so deep and heavy, the trees might be breathing with us.

"The first thing to understand about magic is that language has power. But intention matters more."

We nod, though I'm not sure yet if I understand his meaning.

Finn runs his pointer finger along the page. "These notes here speak of an inner light that exists within a person. The spell you were practicing the other day is a command, which is well and good, but magic is not a dog to be called. It's part of you. The words you use should be too."

He closes his eyes; his eyelashes are so long, they graze his cheekbones. Under his breath, so soft it's almost inaudible, he whispers, *"Solas m'anam, Aisling,"* and a spark crackles to life between his thumb and forefinger. He picks up a dried leaf from the forest floor and sets it alight. The smile that cracks his face is almost as bright as the magic.

Ashes drift to the ground as we stare on in awe.

"What's 'Aisling' mean?" Lena asks.

"It's my mother's name. This spell requires something of you, something personal. It requires emotion. It helps to think of something you love."

It's strange to think of Finn having a mother, of having existed anywhere before he popped into my life.

"But why wouldn't they teach us this kind of magic at school?" Lena asks.

Finn grins. "Because this kind of magic is wild. It's unpredictable . . ."

"And the world doesn't like wild, unpredictable girls." Maxine finishes his sentence.

He nods at me. "Go ahead, Frances, you try."

I think about saying my brother's name, but the place where he lives in my heart doesn't feel like a place of light, just an ugly quagmire of hurt. The place my mother lives is even worse, stinging pain mingled with sickening guilt. Instead, I picture Percy, the old tomcat who lived in our apartment when I was young. He was black and grumpy, and came and went as he pleased, but William and I loved him.

I rub my hands together like I'm warming them up over a fire. *"Solas m'anam, Percy,"* I whisper, picturing his long tail whipping back and forth in our old windowsill.

The forest around me rattles like it's impatient. On my third try a tiny spark springs to life between my fingers. The heat of it surprises me. I jump back and clap my hands over my mouth in glee. I feel it in every part of my body, like the light is part of me, too. For the first time I feel ownership, control of *this thing*, the magic.

Finn smiles proudly. "Well done, Frances."

Next is Maxine. *"Solas m'anam, Nina."*

She gets it on the second try, and light sparks to life between her hands.

As soon as it winks out, it's Lena's turn. *"Solas m'anam, Jonathan."* Her sparks appear immediately, a light in the darkness.

The three of us share a smile.

We all try the spell again with different incantations and things we love. At one point Maxine uses "coconut cake," and we all dissolve into a fit of giggles—Finn included.

My hands are numb, and spots flash in my eyes from staring at the light, but from the flush-cheeked faces of my friends I can tell that they feel as vibrantly alive as I do.

Success with the spark-creation spell fills us with confidence, and soon we're flipping through the rest of the book. Splayed out on a bed of dead leaves, I thumb through pages that speak of astrology, numerology, energy work, charms, and hexes. There is an entire section dedicated to herbs and their properties, another that details which color candles to burn for which ritual.

Lena doesn't need Finn to translate the marginal notes scrawled next to the renderings of the herbs. She recognizes the delicate drawings of wild ginger and thistle root by sight alone. Maxine explains the constellations sketched in the pages and points to the tree canopy to show us where they'd be this time of year if we could see them.

The book is a relief, confirmation that being a witch is so much more than the ability to thread a needle with your mind.

We're all sitting so close together, gathered over the book, I can feel the heat of Finn's expansive chest. It's all that keeps me from shivering.

I extend my hand to trace over a sketch of an evil eye, and Finn's hand brushes mine. He pulls it back like he's been burned.

I scoot away from him and remind myself he's a means to an end. It would be a massive waste of my time to consider the shape of his fingers.

I direct my attention back to the book and continue to flip through its pages. I catch a glimpse of the words "True Love" at the top of one page and, without thinking, flip back. Next to me, Finn chuckles. "Already interested in love spells, Miss Hallowell?"

I hope it's too dark for him to see how I blush. "Is that what this is?"

He takes the book gently from my hands and examines it for a moment. "No, not quite. This is a spell that is supposed to tell you the first letter of the first name of your true love."

Maxine huffs. "True love? What an absurd concept."

"You don't wish to try it and see if it works, Miss DuPre?" Finn asks, teasing.

Maxine sticks her tongue out at him and snatches the book.

"We need something to burn," Finn instructs. "It's a relatively straightforward spell—let's give it a go."

There's a note in the same scrawling ink jotted in the margins.

Maxine tips the book toward Finn. "What does this say?"

He leans closer to get a better look.

"It wants you to imagine the feeling of being in love."

How could one possibly know what that feels like? But I'm not up for a philosophical discussion on the nature of love, so I stay silent.

Maxine leans down, plucks a few of the driest leaves off the ground, and brushes the dirt from them. Next, she takes the lantern and carefully removes the brass top, so the flame is flickering free.

She studies the book for a moment; then she presses the leaves in between her palms and tilts her face up at the sky. For a heartbeat, she is silent. Then she mutters the word *taisdomliad.*

She opens her eyes, flames reflecting in her pupils, and tips the handful of leaves into the flame.

Nothing happens at first. The leaves catch light but flicker out just as quickly. Maxine shakes her head in frustration, ashes caught in her blond hair.

Next to her, Finn stands with his arms crossed. "Don't give up that easy—go again."

Maxine sighs, and swipes a few more leaves from the ground. She hunches over to take another look at the spell book, worrying her lip in concentration. Once again she closes her eyes, takes a deep breath, and mutters *taisdomliad.* The leaves catch light immediately, bright and hot. They flash white with a pop and a spark. Left in their wake is a plume of smoke curling up into the night sky in the shape of what might be the letter *M.* It's brief and it's terribly dark, so it could be a trick of my eyes, but I swear I see it.

Maxine laughs; her eyebrow arches in a satisfied expression. "Looks like I'm my own true love. *M* for Maxine."

Lena rolls her eyes as she bends to gather leaves from the under-brush for herself.

For her, the spell works right away. Again the flame sparks; swirl-ing through the dark is a coil of smoke in the shape of an *M*.

At this Maxine truly laughs in the genuine way she rarely does, deep from her chest with no hint of sarcasm. "Do you think that's all the spell knows how to produce? Infinite *M*s?"

Lena shoots her a glare. "Or *M* is an extraordinarily com-mon letter."

"It's your turn." Maxine extends the book toward me. I feel Finn's amused glare tickle my neck.

"I'd rather not." I'm annoyed we've wasted so much time learn-ing a spell so pointless. This is a parlor trick to be performed at carnival games or tea parties. What is the point of such a spell in as powerful a book as this—a book that could also hold the key to seeing my brother again? But Maxine's words of practicing our magic before taking on the resurrection spell make me push myself up from where I'm sitting on the fallen log. If practice gets me closer to becoming capable of performing the only spell that matters in this book, I guess it couldn't hurt. "All right," I say. "Let's test this a third time."

Maxine takes my spot on the log. "I hope I'm everyone's true love."

I pick the leaves from the ground and settle in front of the spell book. The instructions are brief—look to the sky and recite the spell.

It's the *imagine the feeling of being in love* instruction that stumps me.

I close my eyes.

I look to the sky.

At first there is a calm sense of ease as I listen to the wind hit the trees. It reminds me of a neighbor's windchimes, hung on a fire escape, in an apartment a lifetime ago.

What would love feel like, I wonder? I hope it feels like coming home.

Oliver Callahan's face pops into my head.

At the surprise of seeing him, my eyes shoot open. I blink him away, the sharp jaw and soft eyes and the way he always looked at me like I mattered.

I say the spell, *taisdomliad*. It doesn't sound as elegant as Maxine's nor as determined as Lena's, but I'm eager to have it done with.

The lantern is so hot, it takes concentration not to pull my hand back for fear of being burned as I lower the leaves. The flame pops, hisses and produces a white spark, but the plume of black smoke is so much bigger than Maxine's or Lena's. It doesn't form anything resembling a letter; it just spills into the sky, furious and abundant. It stings in the back of my throat. I swallow a cough.

Everyone is so painfully silent. Awkwardness fills the darkness as Finn studies me. He extends his hand like he means to place it on my shoulder, but he pulls away at the last second, balling his hand up into a fist at his side.

Lena snickers. "Well, at least it's not Maxine, then."

I'm surprised by how annoyed I am that the spell didn't work. "Maybe I don't have a true love," I speculate aloud. It's a better thought than the possibility of not being powerful enough to produce a letter from a stupid party trick. If I can't do this, how will I be able to perform the resurrection spell? *No.* I push such a thought out of my head.

"Besides . . ." Maxine clears her throat. "No one has a true love—it's a ridiculous concept." It isn't as comforting as she intends. Finn's eyes latch on to mine. There's something bruising in the set of his stare.

"Finn next," Maxine prods, but he shakes his head, his gaze still caught on me.

"I'm afraid not. I've really got to be going."

"Are you afraid?" Maxine cocks her head at him.

Finn snickers and pushes his hand through his messy locks. "Maybe I already know who my true love is. Maybe I've got a train to catch. Who's to say?"

Maxine, smiling, with starlight tangled in her hair, glances up at the moon. "We've already been out too long. It's probably time we return as well."

The annoyance I had at wasting time trying the love spell returns. "But what about the Resurrection?" We can't lose sight of the reason we're out here. There's an edge of desperation in my voice; I can't hide how badly I want this.

"Magic is a muscle, Frances. You have to be strong enough," Finn protests. "We'll practice for a wee bit. Then we'll try whatever it is you wish to try."

"We just have to hope I'm strong enough now, because the only spell I'm interested in trying is the one that will allow me to speak to my brother," I snap.

Finn, Lena, and Maxine share an uncomfortable glance between them.

"Frances." It's Lena who whispers my name under her breath like I'm a spooked horse who needs calming down.

"If you won't help me, I can do it myself."

"Fine," Finn concedes. "Next week we will discuss the Resurrection. You'll return?"

"Fine," I say back. It's the best I can hope for. I should feel guilty for souring our happy evening. Maybe I will in the morning. But right now I just feel angry.

"I can hardly let Frances traipse into the woods alone. If you wish to teach magic, I wish to learn it," Maxine adds.

Lena doesn't say anything at all.

"Well then, I'll see you again in a week. Same time, same place," Finn declares.

I don't know if we'll be able to sneak out again, but Maxine doesn't protest, so neither do I.

Finn takes two steps toward me and in a hoarse whisper says, "I want to speak to William again. God, I want it more than anything. But I want to make sure you're prepared, that *we're* prepared for the kind of magic that takes. When we do it, we've got to do it right."

Before I have a chance to respond, Maxine grabs Lena and me by the hands and drags us toward the path leading back to school. "Good night, mysterious woodsman," she calls to Finn.

"Good night, terrifying sorceresses."

CHAPTER FOURTEEN

Two nights after our first lesson with Finn, I fall asleep too late after getting caught up in a never-ending game of gin rummy with Lena.

Finn is waiting for me in the hazy dream space.

I find him in a gold-spun forest, magic palpable in the glow that envelops us.

"I was wondering when you'd arrive." He greets me with a grin.

"An after-dinner card game got a little contentious." I take a breath; the air is thick and sweet like molasses.

"Did you win?"

"Lena had me in the last hand."

"Ah, you'll get her next time."

I'm in a white high-necked tea gown. Finn is wearing the same clothes I last saw him in, rough spun trousers and a crisp white shirt.

"Why are you here?" I ask after a beat.

"Is it foolish if I say I wanted to see you."

I fight the smile pulling at my mouth. "Why would you want to see me?"

We're suddenly closer together, though I didn't take any steps.

Finn looks down. "I meant I just wanted to see how the magic was coming. If you'd gotten a chance to practice."

"Only a little," I reply. "Unfortunately, Haxahaven-approved lessons come first, though I'm sure you'll be delighted to hear my magical bread-kneading skills are developing quite nicely."

He laughs, and it sounds like the pealing of church bells, holy and familiar. "Ah yes, delighted."

Another pause stretches between us.

"Will you tell me more about my brother?" I'm desperate to see him through someone else's eyes. I can't stand the thought of William only existing in my own head.

Finn chews his lip, thinking, then smiles. "There was a member of the Sons of Saint Druon, Horace Kipling. He ran a necktie factory. No magic, but family money, which can be just as valuable where power is concerned. Anyway, Horace didn't much care for the Irish. Went out of his way to make my life miserable, especially when I first arrived. One night he spit in my dinner in front of everyone. A real bastard. William saw all this and didn't take kindly to it. Your brother didn't much care for bullies."

The yawning pit in my heart feels momentarily filled with light as golden as the forest we're standing in. "No, he didn't."

"So what did our William do?" Finn continues. "He could have dressed Horace down in front of everyone, but that wouldn't have done much good, and he knew it. So he went over to Horace's necktie factory and talked to every single one of his employees. The next Monday Horace had a line out his office door with folks turning in their notices. William found every one of those workers a better-paying job, or a job closer to home, or in a factory with better hours. He snatched all of Horace's employees out from under him and made sure word got around that Horace Kipling was a man worth avoiding. Horace's rich father was so disappointed in him, he sent him to Pittsburgh to look after the family's steel ventures." Finn slaps his knee in laughter. "Pittsburgh! Can you imagine a fate worse than Pittsburgh? Old Horace couldn't. Threw the biggest fit I've ever seen a grown man throw."

I can't hold back my smile. "My brother really did all that?"

Finn's grin matches mine. "It was brilliant. He was brilliant. He didn't even let me thank him properly. Just laughed and said something about old Horace having it coming."

Despite my smile, tears spring to my eyes. "There was no one else like him."

Aye," Finn replies. "We'll make William proud, you know."

My chest is tight. Riotous, glowing butterflies flutter from a bush dripping with flowers. "I'm trying. It's all I can do without him."

Lena doesn't mention Finn for the rest of the week. Not while we play cards or walk to class or eat meals. Maxine is even harder to pin down, always flitting between groups of friends or out with Helen. It's almost easy to pretend our meeting in the park had been a dream. That is, if it weren't for the actual dreams I am having.

In Practical Applications on Wednesday, Lena barely looks at me over the vase of flowers we're failing to arrange. Neither of us has any eye for symmetry, and only half of Lena's rose is blooming on command. Mrs. Roberts clucks at the poor job we're doing and chalks it up to our less refined backgrounds. "An eye for beauty is not something everyone is blessed with, dears. It's rare for girls from your circumstances to recognize it. Please do your best, but know I don't expect much."

Her tone is warm, like she thinks she's doing us a favor, but Lena and I dissolve into laughter the minute she walks away from our table, and the spell of awkwardness is broken between us. "How will I find a husband now?" Lena quips.

"You'll have to settle for a second son, to be certain."

While I still have her attention, I scrawl a note on a blank page in my open notebook. *Will you come tomorrow?* I pause for one moment and add *Please.*

She stares at the note briefly, purses her lips, and nods reluctantly. A flood of relief washes through me.

Thank you, I mouth.

She laughs again, the most I've seen Lena laugh, perhaps ever. "Have you considered I'm not doing it for you?"

Our second meeting with Finn takes place on a chilly late-October night. He arrives with a bag slung over his shoulder, pulls out three small packages wrapped in brown paper and twine, and hands one to each of us.

I unwrap mine with numb fingers to find a pair of knotty-knit blue mittens inside.

"I wasn't sure of the colors you'd like, so you're free to trade," he says.

I glance around the circle and see Lena and Maxine holding their purple and red pairs.

"I call red," Maxine exclaims.

"I'm quite satisfied with blue," I say.

"It's hard to practice magic with shaking hands, and I had some free hours this week," Finn replies.

"You made these?" I ask.

"Aye. Grew up on a sheep farm. Not much to do in the evenings to keep your hands busy and plenty of wool to spin. Play your cards right, and next time I'll bring you a sweater."

I slip the mittens on, and Finn smiles. "They suit you. Fewer holes than the ones you were wearing the night we first met."

I suppress a grin. "I'm surprised you remember." I don't recall the last time someone gave me a present.

But there's something hidden behind Finn's gifts and smiles. Even in the low light of the lanterns, it's clear his shoulders are slumped and his eyes are rimmed with red.

"What's wrong?" I ask him under my breath. Lena and Maxine are already off thumbing through the book, discussing what spell to try tonight.

"Just a hard day—no matter, it's a blessing to see your faces."

"What happened?" The night is cold, and the forest is dark. Finn avoids my question by busying himself lighting a lantern to hang off a tree branch. It throws shadows like outstretched fingers across the clearing. I pull my coat a little tighter.

Finn turns back around. "I'm glad you like the mittens."

I wiggle my fingers. "They're quite impressive—you're not a terrible knitter."

"I know I'm not." Despite the haunted look on his face, he smiles a little.

Maxine glances at us from where she stands with Lena. "Hello, sad boy," she calls. "Are you going to tell us what's wrong or not?"

Finn drops his head and plays with the loose string of his jacket, and when he speaks, his voice doesn't have the same ringing of light. "The brother of a close friend went missing a few days ago. Poor kid left for work and never came home. Factory foreman said he never showed up. I didn't know the lad well, but every time we met, he was kind. His brother is torn up."

The stress he's carrying is evident in every part of him. It breaks my heart. "I'm so sorry to hear that, Finn." I tamp down my own memories of the first few days after my brother went missing. I remember a lot of crying on the kitchen floor. I think at one point I may have screamed at a policeman to try harder. Finn lost William too, I remind myself. The memories must still sting for him; they have to.

"Thank you, I'll be fine. Still praying it will all be some misunderstanding and he'll show up in a few days. Maybe he eloped or joined the circus."

"Let's all pray for the circus," Maxine says.

I extend my hand to place on his shoulder but snatch it away at the last minute. It doesn't feel right to touch him.

Finn gives a solemn nod. He takes a deep breath, like he's trying to shove his emotions back inside. "Indeed. All right, no more of my troubles, let us begin." Finn opens *The Elemental* to a page near the back.

There are no hand diagrams on this page, just a block of text written in such cramped handwriting, I can hardly make out the individual letters.

Finn looks like something out of a gothic novel tonight. His curls blow in the fall wind, and the purple circles under his eyes are as dark as ever. The collar of his black wool coat stands starched around his neck.

"There's something I'd like to try tonight," he says, peering at the page, then at me.

"I want to try the Resurrection," I retort. "We don't know how much time we have left."

"Practicing this kind of magic will make big spells like the Resurrection easier, I promise."

"How?" I prod.

"Don't you trust me? Frances, I'd like you to see if you can move my hand."

"Your hand?" I'm confused. "Why—"

"We've been told that controlling another person is dangerous, forbidden, even." Maxine interrupts me, her eyes determined and steely.

"Your school sure loves its rules, doesn't it?" Finn shakes his head. "But that's not what we are doing. Plus, I've never found a human soul that abides by any law. So let's try anyway, shall we?"

"Is there a spell?" Lena asks.

"No, just concentration. Focus on your soul reaching out beyond the bounds of your corporeal form."

I'm not entirely sure what that means. I stare at his elegant hand until my eyes hurt, memorizing the white crescents of his fingernails. Nothing happens. "I'm not sure what I'm supposed to be doing."

He leaves the book on the log where it's balanced and closes the distance between us, until his nose hovers a breath from mine.

Lena and Maxine watch us from across the clearing with narrowed eyes.

In a whisper only for me he says, "Move my hand."

"I can't," I whisper back. It's an aggressively pointless exercise. It does nothing to help William.

Agonizing and slow, he lifts his hand to brush an errant lock of hair off my forehead. The lightest touch is like embers being raked down my spine.

He leaves his thumb at my temple. "Move my hand," he whispers once more.

I shake my head. I can't form thoughts around the hammering of my heart, coupled with the embarrassment of Lena and Maxine staring.

He draws his hand away from my temple and to my mouth. I tremble, summoning the courage it takes to look from the ground back to him. He flicks his thumb against my lower lip.

His hazel eyes narrow, and something shifts.

No. Not like this.

Then, like he's been shocked, he snaps his hand away and stumbles back a few feet. The leaves crunch under his weight.

He grins wolfishly. "Well done."

"I did that?" I felt the lash of power, but still I'm shocked by it.

"You did."

Lena turns to Finn. "You seem surprised."

"I am," he replies. "I've only seen it done once before. I've never managed it myself. And here it took our dear Frances less than fifteen minutes."

So much for silly true-love spells, I think.

Lena and Maxine speak in a flurry at the same time. "How?" "Let me try!"

Finn doesn't use the same tactics on Maxine and Lena. Maybe he knows they wouldn't let him crowd their space like I did; maybe he knows I'm the weak one. For over an hour they meditate and concentrate and even clutch an onyx stone that Finn produces from his pocket.

"Your pinky, it moved!" Maxine shouts at Lena.

"It did not!"

"Don't lie to me!" Maxine smiles as she says it.

"Maybe I'm shivering because I'm about to freeze to death," Lena retorts.

"If only a Good Samaritan had knit you mittens." Finn jumps into their bickering.

It's strange to see him slot into our little sisterhood.

"I'm cold. We have class in the morning. I give up," Maxine declares, popping up from where she sits on the ground, brushing leaves off her coat.

Maxine and Lena walk to the edge of the trees. I hover close to Finn as he bends to pack up his satchel. "Are you taking the train back into the city?"

"Aye. It's not a terribly far walk to the station."

"Thank you for coming." I don't know why I say it. It isn't as if I asked him to appoint himself my protector.

"Always."

I lower my voice. "Is there a reason manipulation comes more easily to me than the others?" This new aspect of magic feels like knocking on a door when I'm not quite sure I want to know what's on the other side.

Finn shrugs. "Some people are just more powerful than others. The universe is a strange place, Miss Hallowell."

"C'mon, Frances!" Maxine calls.

I say my goodbyes to Finn and trip after them, nursing a terrible headache and the fear that comes with possessing new information about myself.

One week later Finn meets us in our usual clearing in the park looking even worse than he did the week before. His hair is disheveled, eyes swollen, coat wrinkled. He hasn't met me in my dreams all week. I've been worried, and it looks like my worry was justified.

Maxine spots him the second after I do. "Jesus Christ, what happened to you?"

"Lovely to see you as well, Maxine." His attempt at a smile is unconvincing.

"Is everything all right?" I wish I could wrap him in an embrace. He looks like he badly needs one.

Finn greets us with a sad wave. "You know, I'm beginning to think Lena might be my favorite. She doesn't pry."

Lena raises her brows. "You flatter yourself. Perhaps it's because I don't care."

Finn laughs in earnest. "Fair enough."

I walk over to him as he hangs the lantern on a tree branch. Under my breath I ask, "Did they ever find your friend's brother?"

"Aye."

186

By the tone of his voice I already know the answer to the question I'm about to ask. "Alive?"

He looks at the ground and shakes his head. "Without his hands, washed up on a beach in Brooklyn."

"Without his hands?" I'm glad it's dark enough that Finn can't make out the full expression of horror and disgust that crosses my face. My stomach turns.

Finn nods. "It gets worse." He fishes a folded-up scrap of newspaper out of his pocket and hands it to me. In the low light of the forest, it takes me a moment to make out the headline. SECOND HANDLESS BOY FOUND ON BEACH, KILLER ON THE LOOSE?

"A second boy?"

"Without their hands?" Maxine exclaims, suddenly over my shoulder.

Lena grabs the article from me and begins to read aloud. "'The body of Mario Gianetti, found on the shores of Brooklyn yesterday, marks the second found on Sheepshead Bay this week. Even more disturbing to the local community, Mr. Gianetti, seventeen, was found missing his hands, just like John O'Farrell, nineteen, found on the same beach only two days earlier. Mr. Gianetti and Mr. O'Farrell were reported missing by their respective families last week. Both boys were residents of the Lower East Side. Police have denied that the bodies are evidence of a killer on the loose, but that doesn't seem to be much of a comfort to those who live near such gruesome findings.'"

"It was Johnny O'Farrell who was my friend's brother," Finn says. He looks genuinely heartbroken.

"And the other?" I ask. "Do you know anything about yesterday's victim?"

Finn shakes his head no. "Never heard the name before."

The wheels in my head are turning, and I'm struck by an awful feeling I can't shake. It's slippery and nauseating. But beneath the abject horror is a thrill at the first real clue I've had in months. Should I be ashamed of the kicking in my chest, something close to excitement? "Your friend, he's a member of the Sons?"

"Yes, but his brother Johnny wasn't."

"And the other boy? Any chance he could be a member?" The question comes out so urgently, I sound frantic. I *feel* frantic, thoughts flying too quickly to keep up with them all.

"Doubtful but not impossible. I've never heard the name, but we're a large organization. I don't see why it matters, though. Two people isn't exactly a pattern."

I look between Finn, Lena, and Maxine, who stare back at me with identical wide-eyed confusion. "Two might not be a pattern, but three is. Sheepshead Bay is the same beach where they found my brother."

CHAPTER FIFTEEN

W ith steely determination and an upset stomach, I march over to Maxine's bag and pull out *The Elemental*.

The book flips open to the page detailing the Resurrection like it's been waiting for me.

"You can help me or not, but if William's killer is out there, murdering other people, I'm not going to sit around and do nothing. We can ask William who killed him. We could stop this from happening to more people." My heart is pounding; my words come out aggressive and quick.

Maxine and Lena share an uncomfortable glance. They're doing that more often as of late.

"I'll do it myself then," I respond to their infuriating indifference.

I pull off the scratchy mittens Finn gave me, and ghost the tips of my fingers over the pages. They're as cold as the frost-slicked underbrush. Finn's lantern casts them in a flickering orange light.

I stare back at the familiar illustration of a human figure sitting in front of a mirror surrounded by other objects. The objects needed for the spell are sketched in black ink and labeled in slanted handwriting. A scrying mirror, a vial of graveyard dust, a hairbrush labeled *item belonging to the deceased*, and a dagger called *Fragarach*.

Like most of the pages in this book, the marginal notes are in a mix of languages. Most are in what I think is Gaelic, but there's one in English that stands out the darkest: *Only effective if done soon after departure from this plane.* It's the note I think about when I can't sleep.

The others gather around to read the spell over my shoulder.

"What's *Fragarach*?" I ask.

"It's a type of dagger, an old one," Finn answers reluctantly. He scrubs a hand across his neck; there's something tortured in the simple gesture. "I can help you get it, if you're determined to do this."

"We need it soon," I say.

"Before any more bodies wash up on the bay," Finn agrees. I'm relieved he's seeing my point.

Maxine looks grave as she speaks up. "I've been a little bored, and this seems like a terrible idea. Why not speak to the dead and solve a few murders?"

Lena looks between the three of us like she's doing a calculation, her eyes fluttering, brow creased. Finally, she closes her eyes in a huff. "I wish I could see how this turns out. I cannot."

There is no moon tonight. The thicket of trees is the darkest I've ever seen it. Shadows stretch long, like hands reaching out, grasping at the dark. A shiver goes through me and it's more than the cold.

"We'll need to minimize the risk." Finn's eyes are big and soft. He looks more lost than I've ever seen him, which is strange, because I feel balanced on the precipice of finally finding something. "The head of the Sons has always been a bit of a collector. He keeps the magical artifacts in his office. How morally opposed are you to cat burglary?"

"Sweet of you to assume witches have any morals at all," Maxine answers. "How very modern of you."

"Can you make it to the Commodore Club on the Lower East Side this Saturday? There's an event, everyone will be busy, and security will be lax. It could be our one chance to sneak into the office," Finn explains.

The excited rhythm in my heart beats an answer: *Of course, anything.*

Lena frowns. "Why do you need us to break into your own organization?"

"I can't magick objects as well as you. There'll be locks and wards, and I don't have the power to get through them myself. At least not quietly."

"Yes." My answer is immediate.

"It has to be two days from now?" Maxine asks, incredulous.

"Unfortunately."

From somewhere nearby, an animal scurries in the underbrush. It sets my teeth on edge.

"What about the mirror?" I prod. We have to think of the big picture. If we're going to do this, we need to do it properly.

"I'll do some research" is Finn's curt reply.

"Does your brother have a grave?" Lena asks quietly.

"Yes, in Manhattan. The dust will be easy."

Maxine brushes a strand from her forehead. "And the 'item belonging to the deceased,' do you have anything of your brother's?"

This question stings. "I don't, but I know where to get one."

And suddenly we have a plan. A plan that begins with us breaking into the Sons of Saint Druon.

I grip *The Elemental* all the way back to Haxahaven. It stays cold no matter how long I clutch it to my chest.

Maxine unlocks the gate, and we slip into Florence's dark kitchen. She hasn't stayed up for us tonight, but she has left a warm pot of tea on the stove.

"This is getting dangerous," Lena says. Her voice is hollow. It bounces off the bricked floors.

"Yes," Maxine agrees. "But at least it's not boring."

I'm surprised to find Finn in my dreams later that night. We're in a fairy-tale forest next to a bubbling stream. Birds whistle in a chorus overhead, and a butterfly lands gently on a dinner-plate-sized flower at my feet. But the light bends wrong here; the colors are too vivid, just one shade off of anything naturally occurring.

"I just saw you." I'm glad to see him, but he doesn't need the satisfaction of knowing that.

There's an odd look on his face, the same tortured set to his brows as earlier. "I wanted to make sure you were all right."

"More than all right," I answer honestly.

"I'm worried." He doesn't need to tell me. It's written all over his face.

"It doesn't matter. I'm going anyway."

"What if we get caught, Frances? I'm one of them. I'll be fine. But you're a witch, and I don't know what they'll do to you."

I turn to him, confused. The veneer of his confidence has cracked, revealing the teenage boy underneath.

"This was your plan."

He sighs. "And I already regret it."

"I'm doing this with or without you. It will be easier together."

"If we get caught, I might not be able to protect you."

"You don't even know me." He looks wounded, but I don't regret saying it. I like Finn, I probably like Finn too much, but his fussing over my safety seems to go far beyond what he'd owe his dead friend's kid sister. Oliver and I grew up together, and he's spared only half a passing thought to my well-being since William's death. It doesn't make sense that Finn should take this all upon himself.

He lets the silence stretch between us as my statement goes answerless. "You don't owe me a single thing, " I tell him.

He pulls a hand through his curls, setting them in a riot around his face. His hair is longer now than when I first met him. "No. I don't. But I do. It's difficult to explain."

"I'm smart. Try me."

He kicks at the dirt with the toe of his shoe. "Can I admit something? I'm terrified to try."

I've never heard a man admit fear before. It makes me smile a little. "Be brave for me?"

His sigh holds the weight of a hundred sleepless nights. "I'll try." He lowers himself onto a log blanketed in vivid green moss and looks out toward somewhere, then back at me.

"I grew up in a farmhouse in County Galway with four brothers and three sisters," he begins, a soft smile dimpling his cheeks. "My da died when I was young, and my mam soon married Alfie, who was a wicked son of a bitch. He beat the shit out of her, and when he tired of that, he'd beat the shit out of me, or my brothers, or my sisters, or sometimes all of us if he was in a particularly foul mood. Every day was the same. Wake with the sun. Mind the sheep. Sell wool at the Saturday market. Care for my siblings. Tend to my mother's wounds. Tend to my own. But I had one bright spot in that hell. My dreams."

I sit down next to him, close enough that we're pressed leg to leg, feet swinging in the bluebells.

"Tell me about the dreams," I say in a voice scarcely above a whisper.

"They started when I was twelve. The night after Alfie knocked me unconscious for the first time. I thought I was hallucinating at first, they were so *real*."

His voice is thick with emotion, and it makes my bones ache. I raise my hand, almost placing it on his knee, before I think better of it and tuck it back to my lap.

"I entered Mam's dreams first. She was dreaming of my da. I'd forgotten what his face looked like. But then . . . the dreams shifted. I started seeing the men I'd met at the market. Or the village girls who spun the wool into yarn."

I turn to face him, but he's staring off at the false horizon, imagining the dreams long past of people far away. His jaw is sharp now, but I can imagine what he must have looked like at twelve, with chubby cheeks and a dimpled smile. So much fear lingering in his eyes—of his stepfather, of the dreams he'd explore. I'm filled with a sense of deep, primal protectiveness.

"The dreams were unpredictable. I didn't know how to control them yet. I'd end up in others' dreams all the time. Some people I'd see just once, then never again. But there was one constant. *There was a girl.*"

It's reverent, the way he says it. Quiet, like a prayer, his eyes are closed now, head tilted just slightly to the sky. There's a scar along his chin I've never been close enough to see before, and another snaking silver along the edge of his left eyebrow.

I don't know how my body works in dreams, but our chests are rising and falling together in unison. I'm covered in goose bumps.

"And she was beautiful and sad. She was unlike the others, because I knew I'd never met her. Hers was a face I would have remembered. I didn't know where she was, only that it wasn't Ireland. Her world was grayer than mine, louder too.

"When I was twelve, I could only see her from afar, more a silhouette than anything. She was so blurry around the edges. When I was thirteen, she came into focus a little clearer. She started wearing her hair in one braid instead of two." There's a tightness in my chest now; I can see it all so clearly. I remember the feeling of my mother's hands in my hair as she braided it, how I'd begged her to let me wear it in one plait down my back like the older girls at school.

"When I was fourteen, I heard her speak for the first time. She didn't see me in her dreams, which wasn't unusual, most people never noticed I was there, but she was different, because I wanted so desperately for her to see me. I would have given anything to speak to her." At this my eyes sting with tears. I remember being fourteen and achingly lonely too.

"When I was fifteen, Alfie broke my leg, and I was laid up in bed for a week with an awful fever. I thought I was going to die." My heart breaks at the image, Finn near death at the hands of someone who should have protected him.

"Mam had the village priest give me my last rites. I was so far gone, I didn't realize until it was too late that I'd wandered into the dream of Boss Olan, head of the Sons of Saint Druon, who was on business in Galway. He was the first person to recognize me for what I was." It's all coming into focus now, a picture of every tipped domino that led Finn to me.

"The fever broke the day he came to fetch me at the farm. Five days later I was in New York."

It feels like Finn is handing me his beating heart, raw and bloody, with both hands.

He takes a breath, steadying himself. "We arrived in the city. I started working for the Sons. Someone like me is a valuable commodity. I'm like a spy, except I can't get caught. And things were fine, until one day I was walking down Broome Street, and I saw her, the girl. I saw *you*, Frances."

I close my eyes briefly, savoring the warm weight of the confession.

"You saw *me*?" I whisper.

"You were crossing the street. You were *real*. I couldn't believe it." I can almost picture myself through his eyes, fifteen and knobby kneed, eyes bright with the belief that the world was full of good things.

"So, I followed you a few blocks to your apartment. I couldn't help myself. You stopped outside and waited for someone. When William approached with his arms full of groceries, I felt like the breath had been knocked out of me. I knew him from work at the

Sons. He had become my friend. It all came together so clearly, you had the same nose, the same hair. *You* were the kid sister he spoke so much about. But there's no way to tell your buddy *I've been dreaming about your sister for the better part of a decade and would love an introduction.*" Finn shakes his head, the shadow of a smile appearing on his lips. "I cared too much about our friendship and my reputation to say anything. So I did everything I could to forget about you. I thought if I ignored them, the dreams would go away, and I could move on with my life.

"But they didn't. And then William died. I couldn't save him, but I thought maybe I could save you. Maybe this is what I was meant for. It's nice to imagine things have a purpose. So I started coming up to Haxahaven on nights I was supposed to be working because I couldn't stay away from you. You've been haunting me my whole life."

You've been haunting me my whole life. That sounds about right. For the last four months, I've been more ghost than girl.

I'm aware that I should be unsettled by his story. There's something invasive and intimate about the idea that he's been witnessing my dreams for years, even more so that he followed me once he made it to New York. But instead of squirmy discomfort, there is the fizzy warmth that comes with being special to someone.

He finally turns to look at me, and it's like staring into the sun. His eyes are wide and questioning: *You matter to me; do I matter to you, too?*

His hand edges closer to mine, our pinky fingers brush, and it feels like being burned alive.

I should say something kind. I should tell him that I've never felt this special to anyone, that I'm glad he saw me all those years ago, that

I wish I could travel back in time and spare him the pain of his childhood. But the way he's looking at me makes me feel stripped bare, and I'm nervous. "I appreciate all that, truly I do, but it doesn't mean you can protect me," I say in a voice that sounds awfully far away.

"I know. But I don't know if it will stop me from trying."

"What if we promise to protect each other? A partnership. Sherlock and Watson."

"Yes, but if we're being honest with ourselves, we're both Watson, so it's a less than perfect metaphor." Finn smiles, but he can't hide his anxiety.

"You can't protect me. You can only teach me what to do with what I've been given."

"That's a deal I'll take." Suddenly he glances to a place I can't see. "I have to go. I'll see you Saturday," he says, then shimmers like a specter out of sight

"Please, Finn—" I call after him. I still have so many questions.

I snap awake, sweaty and wanting in the dark of my room.

I'm jittery all over, certain of two things.

He's been seeing me forever.

And I'm going to break into the Commodore Club.

I feel guilty all of breakfast the next morning. I feel as if I should tell Lena and Maxine of Finn's confession last night. I don't like keeping things from them, but for now it's something I want to keep tucked away in my rib cage, just for me.

Once my picked-at scrambled eggs go cold, Maxine hauls Lena and me to our usual quiet corner of the library to discuss our plans for Saturday.

Maxine looks exhausted, like she, too, didn't sleep much last night. She sinks her chin into her hands and sighs. "I've been trying to work it all out," she says. "I have an idea, but it's not ideal."

"Go on, then," Lena prompts.

Maxine chews on her lower lip. "Helen and I are supposed to attend a meeting of the National American Woman Suffrage Association on Saturday; there's a girl there, a new pupil we're fetching," she explains. "What if I made her take you with us?"

"Would she do that?" I ask.

"We'd have to lie a little."

Lena laughs at this. "You draw the line at lying?"

Maxine grimaces. "I'm just not a very good liar is all."

Her confession fills me with a profound sense of fondness. "Even after we lie to varying degrees of convincingness, would she still take us into the city like that?"

"It would be easier to bring you than make me mad," she replies flippantly.

Lena tilts her head, looks out the window. "It seems like a risky bet."

"Hardly," says Maxine. "When I was sixteen, Mrs. Vykotsky refused to let my little sister come for a visit. In turn, I refused to use my power to help her and Helen collect new pupils for weeks while I sulked. Helen couldn't narrow down anyone's location closer than six blocks. She eventually brought some girl up here who didn't possess a lick of magic, the wrong Sarah Simmons, or something. It was a nightmare. It was also a little hilarious. Eventually, Nina came to visit, and I've gotten what I wanted since."

"What happened to the girl?"

"Sarah? I think we paid her off and sent her back to her family."

"You're a monster." I laugh. "So, we go to the meeting, and then what? I run off?"

"Obviously," Maxine says. "Lena and I will stay and distract Helen; you and Finn will get the dagger. And besides, it's stretching the truth at best," she adds with a wave of her hand. "You do think women should have the vote, do you not?"

"Well of course—" I say.

She cuts me off. "Then it's settled."

And so, in our corner of the library, our plan comes together. Maxine and Helen are going into the city, and Maxine will insist they take us along. The suffragettes hold meetings in a church basement on the Lower East Side on Saturday evenings, and it won't take me long to sneak off and meet Finn at the Commodore Club instead. Maxine will insist Helen and the others wait for me, and I will meet them outside the church at nine o'clock, sharp.

I will profusely apologize, make up a story about how much I missed a friend and snuck off to see her, and will accept my punishment with a stiff upper lip. Maxine is sure Helen won't assign me to anything more serious than a week of kitchen duty. If everything goes right, by this time on Saturday, I will be a step closer to seeing my brother again.

CHAPTER SIXTEEN

Saturday comes too soon and not soon enough. For once, I bound out of bed before the others, too nervous to stay still any longer. I tossed and turned through the night, plagued with dreams of eyeless faces, drowned bodies, and ghosts. I never saw Finn, though; my horrible nightmares last night were all my own.

The day passes like molasses through a sieve, and by the time later afternoon rolls around and Maxine comes to fetch me from History class, my body is so full of nerves, I feel as if I might crawl right out of my skin.

I meet Lena up in our room, and we help each other dress. I came to school in my dingy work dress, and Lena came in her school uniform, so Maxine is kind enough to let us borrow her clothes. Maxine's dresses are beautiful, fine-seamed and dripping in family money.

We are all of similar enough sizes, and with some strategic pinning, the dresses won't look bad on us at all. If anything, it's fun to use my dressmaking skills once more. I'd nearly forgotten the particular satisfaction of creating a well-fitting garment.

Lena wears a gown of emerald green, dotted with small pink flowers, that ties in a chiffon scarf around her waist. I take my time winding her masses of shiny dark hair into a twist at the nape of her neck, but her hair is as stubborn as she is, and pieces keep springing free. I've never been talented at dressing hair, and Lena eyes me in the mirror as I curse and sigh and stick more pins in her hair.

Once I'm finished, she helps me into a cream-colored gown. The short gossamer sleeves are embroidered with delicate, near-invisible ivory blossoms in a motif that is echoed in the skirt. Vines of blooms climb up the edges of the floaty fabric, ending in the sash of light pink tied at my waist. Unlike Lena's dress, mine has a low neckline, and the bite of cool fall air drifting in from the window on my collarbones makes me feel dangerous.

Maxine marches into our room wearing a gown of light blue silk, with a dark cobalt coat thrown on over it. Her hair is pinned up and secured with a matching silk ribbon tied around her head like a halo. I'll never look so at ease in my skin as she does leaned up against the doorjamb.

"How did you get dressed so quickly?" Lena mumbles around the pin she has balanced between her teeth as she continues to put up my hair.

"I made some of the younger girls help me," Maxine says. "They were awfully jealous to have not been invited along."

"And your hair?" I ask.

"That little Cora is awfully talented. Her aunt was a lady's maid for a Rockefeller."

"Well, la di da," Lena murmurs, still pinning my hair up in something close enough to a bun.

We both look at my reflection in the mirror and shrug simultaneously. I look fine enough. I'll never have Maxine's icy beauty or Lena's lit-from-within glow, but I'm fine. I look fine.

As we walk out the door, Ruby turns up her nose and says it's un-American to think women should have the vote. Aurelia gives us a sad smile then nods in agreement.

Helen is waiting for us by the ambulance in a maroon traveling suit, her frizzy hair contained under a wide-brimmed felt hat.

"Thank you again for taking us along," I greet her.

Her face is annoyed at best. "Ah well, Maxine does love to get her way, does she not? Plus it's not like anyone will recognize you and Lena."

"But I'm from New York," I quickly remind her.

"Not this kind of New York."

Lena and I share an uncomfortable glance.

From the front seat Maxine rolls her eyes and mouths, *Ignore her.*

Helen loads us into the back of the rickety ambulance, and we take off through winding country roads into the city.

Only a few miles pass before the air grows heavy with the scent of rain, and the crackle of electricity speaks of lightning to come.

Helen hurtles our automobile across the Fifty-Ninth Street Bridge and into the streets of Manhattan around horses and pedestrians. My stomach is turning so badly, it's a relief when we park, even though the cobblestones are difficult to navigate in my borrowed shoes.

It's surreal to be back in the city after so long, and I can't help but wonder how everything about it has stayed the same. I have been profoundly changed by my time away, but the city has continued on without me.

Carriages rattle past us. Boys shout the day's news, evening papers clutched in their little hands. On the sidewalk we weave between people on their way home. I search for Oliver in their faces out of habit.

Next to me, Maxine and Lena are silent. Tethers of tense energy stretch between us. After a month in the open air of Queens, it's a relief to once again be surrounded by tall buildings. It feels like they're embracing me, welcoming me home.

Helen rattles on about how the city is bad for her nerves. The three of us manage to nod and smile on cue, but our minds are on the Resurrection. We make it to the meeting with only minutes to spare.

The New York Woman Suffrage Association holds their meeting in the dank basement of a Methodist church on West Thirteenth Street. The arched doorway is small and grim compared to the electric lights flashing on the rest of the street. We pad down a carpeted staircase and into a meeting room. On the walls, sweeping felt banners declare FORWARD! THROUGH THE DARKNESS. FORWARD! INTO THE LIGHT. And WOMEN NEED SUFFRAGE TO END SWEATSHOPS. Rows of simple wooden chairs sit facing an unoccupied podium. There is a hearty crowd of women, mostly in middle age, all white, milling about and mingling. Helen greets a few like old friends and introduces us with a warm smile.

"Anna"—she greets a young brunette woman with rosy cheeks— "this is my niece Maxine and a few of her school friends." She gestures to us, and we offer small waves.

A taller blonde with riotous curls springing from her low bun approaches us next. Her gray dress is adorned with VOTES FOR WOMEN pins.

"Ladies." Helen turns to us. "This is Ethel, Anna's sister, the election district captain."

Ethel can't be much older than Maxine; she must be particularly accomplished to be running a chapter like this so young.

Ethel laughs and replies, "Oh, I'm only the captain for now; once Alice gets out of prison, she'll be back at the helm. Let's just hope it's before my next arrest."

"Arrest?" I ask.

Understanding dawns on Ethel's face as she realizes I'm not joking. "Oh yes, we're thrown in prison quite frequently. Being a public nuisance, failure to pay fines, breaking and entering . . ." She lists the charges off on her fingers.

She finds my silent horror amusing. The sparkle in her foxlike hazel eyes is similar to Maxine's. "Sometimes prison's a nice reprieve from those pelting us with trash on the streets."

My mouth gapes as I imagine the strength it must take to bear something like that. I wonder if I'll ever be that brave.

She turns to Helen, and they continue chatting about the state of marches and strikes. Beside me, Lena shifts uncomfortably.

"What's the matter?" I whisper to her.

She shrugs her shoulders in response, and I jab her in the side with my elbow and give her a look. "Lena?"

"Look around," she whispers. "None of these women are looking at me."

I hadn't noticed. "I don't understand," I reply.

"These women don't care about me. They're fighting so that girls like you can vote alongside your rich, white husbands. Not girls like me." Any sadness in her eyes is quickly replaced with fury.

My face burns red with shame, because she's right. I didn't notice, nor would I have had she not pointed it out. The world is broken in so many ways. What good is it having magic if we can fix none of them? What good am I if I'm so self-absorbed I don't even notice?

But guilt without action doesn't do Lena any good.

"You want to know the stupidest thing?" she continues. "The Founding Fathers stole the model of democracy from the Iroquois Confederacy, bastardized it, and everyone called them geniuses. These women are doing more of the same. Only certain kinds of people get to be equal."

I reach down and take her hand in mine. "You deserve a better world than this one."

Her steely eyes set on mine. "So do we fight, or do we search for safety?" she asks.

"I think I want to fight," I say.

Lena casts a glance at the women around us. "Then we can't lose."

Before I can respond, Anna steps up to the podium at the front of the room and bangs a gavel. The noise echoes sharply through the meeting hall, and the women quiet and take their seats.

"Sisters, welcome," she greets them. "Today is a joyous occasion. Since our last meeting, California passed a suffrage amendment to their state constitution. How wonderful it is to have a victory to celebrate!"

Lena's hand falls from mine as I take a few steps backward. I linger near the stairs. Lena's eyes roam the room before meeting mine. She nods. I take advantage of the celebration to slip out, over dusty rugs, and up a narrow staircase, until I finally emerge into the dense humidity of New York before a storm. The smell of earth has settled thick in the air. Dark clouds roll in on the horizon, partially blocking out the last light of the dying day.

I walk the twelve blocks to the Commodore Club quickly, my deft, city-native feet carrying me through the seas of people, stepping around horse manure and garbage, avoiding carriages and cars. It is a ballet I know well. One I miss.

The club isn't far from the shop where I worked or the apartment I shared with my mother and William. I purposefully avoid those blocks, like a coward too afraid to look at the buildings through the eyes of the new person I've become.

I pass the exact corner where I ran into Oliver Callahan, what feels like a very long time ago. Somewhere across town he's probably warm and laughing in a dormitory, surrounded by classmates, and not thinking at all about magic daggers and speaking to ghosts.

I reach my destination a few blocks later; it's impossible to miss. The Commodore Club is everything the church where the suffragettes meet isn't. The building is not polite. It roars, taking up nearly a whole city block, punctuated by stark white pillars, like teeth in an open mouth. I pat the head of one of the stone lions on the stairs upon my approach. *Good evening, please don't devour me whole.*

I climb the granite steps to the carved oak double doors quickly, leaving no time to second-guess myself. I pick up the door knocker, a heavy brass stag, and I knock three times. After a heartbeat, an old man in a red velvet coat opens the door.

He's small, shorter than I am, and his scraggly white hair is combed over his egg-shaped head. His pencil-thin mustache is dark, like he might have drawn it on himself. In any other circumstance, it might have made me laugh.

"Evening, miss," he greets me, somehow looking down at me despite his inferior height. "What can I do for you?"

How stupid am I to just now realize my plan didn't go much beyond this moment? I thought Finn would be waiting outside for me, that perhaps he'd lead me through a back door like a detective in a novel. I've been so anxious about tonight, I've tried not to think about the details much at all. Perhaps I shouldn't have even knocked. Maybe I've ruined it already.

"Frances Hallowell, sir. Here to see Finn D'Arcy."

"The young Mr. D'Arcy did not inform us he'd be having a guest tonight," he drawls.

I shift my weight from foot to foot. What would Maxine do in this moment?

Before I can formulate a clever response, Finn appears at the top of the carpeted staircase. He's wearing a tuxedo and all the swagger that comes with it. He hasn't attempted to tame his curls, and the bruiselike shadows under his eyes are even more present in the electric light of the Commodore Club than they are in the dark of Forest Park. He looks handsome, dignified, dangerous.

At the sight of me, he cracks a grin, teeth straight and white, as well formed as the rest of him. "You came."

"I did."

He descends the stairs with slow deliberate steps. He confidently pushes past the small mustached man to take my arm in his. The contact of the bare crook of my elbow against the twill of his tuxedo sends a thrill up my spine. I stomp it down.

"A woman here, tonight of all nights, Mr. D'Arcy?" the doorman asks him, his tone thick with judgment.

"She's a guest of Boss's," he lies.

He takes me up the main staircase, through serpentine halls, past stag heads, stuffed boars, mounted swords, and something that I think might be a pickled human hand in a jar.

The walls are fitted with buzzing electric light sconces, but it hasn't stopped someone from lighting hundreds of white candles that drip wax on every flat surface.

Every muscle is tense with anxiety. My dress pinches me; pins dig into my skull; the heat of Finn so close to me is sending my stomach into somersaults. I concentrate on my breathing, inhaling and exhaling, trying to focus on the singular task at hand. I cannot afford to be distracted.

The emptiness is eerie. We don't pass another person, though occasionally I hear the door downstairs open and the raucous laughter of men floating in from the cold.

Finn and I reach a set of ornately carved mahogany doors, so tall they reach right up to the ceiling.

"You ready, Watson?" Finn asks with a smile. His eyes crinkle around the edges like something about to crack.

"If you are, Watson." I nod. My heart is hammering so hard, I wonder if he can hear it.

"Once you unlock the door, I'll search the office. You be the lookout. If you see someone coming, slam a door to warn me, and do your best to distract them. If they ask why you're here, tell them you're looking for Judge Callahan."

Oliver's father? "How do you know Judge Callahan?"

"We don't have time." He gestures at the brass doorknob. "I've never been able to pick this lock, nor can I manipulate objects like you can. You can open this door, Frances. I know it." The way he stares at me with such confidence, such belief, makes my chest swell with pride. It reminds me of the belief William always had in me.

I stare at the door, close my eyes.

"Say *dighlasáil*, please, Frances," I hear Finn whisper, as if from far away.

I obey. The word is less elegant out of my mouth, but at once I feel the ripple of magic, and the door unlocks with a satisfying click.

Finn nods. "Good girl." I swell with pride at his praises. I want so badly to be as good as he thinks I am.

He turns the knob, opens the door a crack, and slips inside. I'm left standing in the hallway, freezing cold and alone.

The first couple of minutes are the worst. I flinch every time the downstairs door opens. With no other outlet for my nervous energy, I pick my thumbnail until it bleeds.

"Everything all right?" I hiss through the closed door.

His voice is muffled. "Yes, just one more moment."

With no more thumb skin left to pick, I count to pass the time: twenty seconds, then sixty, then one hundred, then two hundred. There are footsteps in the hallway now. A ways down, but too near for comfort.

From behind the closed door, the office is silent.

"Please hurry," I whisper, perhaps too quiet for Finn to hear.

Voices join the footsteps. Male, of course. Low and rumbling, too far to make out individual words.

"Finn," I say under my breath, a prayer, a beg.

"Almost finished," he replies. From behind the door there is a tearing of paper, the slide of drawers closing, and the sound of smooth-soled tuxedo shoes on expensive carpet.

The steps from the hall get louder. Definitely too close.

Dread ripples through me.

With a flash of power, I hiss *dorrstanga* under my breath. It's a simple enough spell, one I learned in the context of housekeeping weeks ago.

Far down the hall, close to the stairs, my magic opens and slams a door so hard it would have shaken the floors of a less grand building.

Footsteps, faster this time, go off in the direction of the noise.

The relief I feel is only momentary.

Suddenly, from around the corner, comes a man who doesn't look nearly as startled to see me as I am to see him.

He's dressed like I imagine an Austro-Hungarian diplomat might dress. His outfit is a combination of rich blues and reds, punctuated by gold cuff links. The chain of a pocket watch is strung across the vest. The man is shaped like a barrel with an up-tipped chin. It is clear he's used to taking up space.

He smiles the terrifying smile of a man who knows he's completely in control.

"Kind of you to join us," he greets me.

I look around the hallway, attempt to break free the words lodged in my throat. "I'm not staying long," I blurt. "Just looking for Judge Callahan. It appears I've gotten lost."

He screws up his face into an expression of exaggerated sadness. "And not a one of our household staff was polite enough to accompany you? Trust me, my dear, heads will roll tomorrow, but for now let me show you the way myself."

He takes a step toward me, his hand outstretched.

I take a step back and glance at a massive ticking wall clock at the end of the hall. "You're too kind, sir, but I've only just seen the time, and my family will be wondering where I am. I hate to interrupt your evening. I'll contact the judge at his office tomorrow." It all comes out too fast, in a singular breath. I fake a smile and will myself to look sweet and small.

"Nonsense! You're here already! Let's make an evening of it!" He claps his hands together and takes a step toward me once more.

My back is against the wall now. The chair rail digs into my spine. It's too familiar, this feeling of a giant of a man leaning over me.

Damn it, Finn. Where are you?

As if summoned by my panic, Finn barrels out of the door.

"Finn," the large man greets him in a delighted voice. "What brings you up here? The festivities are about to begin."

"Ah, yes, sir. We were looking for the judge." Finn grabs me by the hand and tries to walk away, but the Austro-Hungarian diplomat stops him by placing a hand on his shoulder.

He sucks his teeth and smirks. "My office seems an unlikely place to start."

"You're right, sir. We had no success. I'll show Frances out now."

My hand inside Finn's is sweaty, and he grips it hard to keep it from shaking.

"The young, always in such a rush!" the diplomat booms. "In my day we knew how to show our guests hospitality. Please, dear, what is your name?"

I consider lying, but Finn doesn't give me the chance. "This is Frances Hallowell."

"A relation of our late William?" the diplomat asks.

I unclench my jaw to reply, "My brother." It's hard to believe my brother knew this man, that he lived in an entire world I knew nothing about.

"My condolences. He was a good boy. I am Boss Olan. Leader of our humble social club."

The lights in the hall flicker. I desperately need to be somewhere that isn't here. "I'd really best be going. Like I said, I have family waiting, and they'll be wondering where I am." I lie smoothly, but Boss Olan raises his eyebrows in amusement.

"Not a chance!" He grins, still looming over both Finn and me. "It's only polite we invite you to join our little party."

"Boss, Frances can't stay." Finn speaks up on my behalf.

"Oh don't be ridiculous." He smiles, but his eyes narrow on Finn. "Of course you can stay in my office if you'd prefer. I didn't know you could read well enough to learn a door-unlocking spell. I'm proud, really, my boy."

The tips of Finn's ears turn red. "I can read, sir."

Boss Olan laughs. "Oh, so you're just slow. Or you can't cast. Perhaps both?" He ruffles Finn's hair like he would a toddler's, but the force of the gesture bends Finn's neck sharply to the right. Finn takes it silently with a grimace.

Boss Olan turns his attention to me. "Come now, young Hallowell. I won't take no for an answer," he says with a flash of a smile that looks as if he means to eat me.

Panicked, I glance behind me at Finn, who nods reassuringly.

He pats his breast pocket. At least he's got the dagger.

Boss Olan in front of me and Finn behind me, we walk through a winding hallway past more mounted stag heads and gleaming trophy cases until we reach a back staircase. Noise and the heat of bodies radiate from down the stairs.

In a mansion like this, what sort of party is held in a basement?

I look back at Finn and mouth, *What do we do?*

His eyes are frightened as he leans forward and whispers in my ear, "You can handle anything you come across in that basement. You're brave, Frances. I know you are."

His response only sends my panic spiraling further. "What's in the basement, Finn?" I sound like a child, my voice full of fear I can't control.

But Finn doesn't answer. Boss Olan pushes open the doors, and my words are swallowed by the low roar of voices floating up the stairs.

Down, down we go on a staircase so narrow, I could stretch out both my arms and touch the walls on either side.

Before us stretches a cavernous basement. The dark wood-paneled walls are dotted with carved golden sconces that glow dimly and throw shadows. Hanging from the ceiling is a dusty crystal chandelier alight with melting candles. In the corner a man in a tuxedo plays a fiddle.

There are dozens of men in the room. Young, old, middle-aged, all rich. I can feel the money in the room, dripping off them like sweat.

More than one is puffing on a cigar, and the air burns with the smell of them. Glasses full of whiskey are clinked and swigged. Their eyes, set into all but identical doughy faces, are trained on me, simmering with raw unbridled want.

From the stairs, I can see over their heads to the middle of the room, where a circle of marble edged with gold is set into the floor, twelve or so feet across

"What is this place?" I whisper to myself as much as to Finn beside me.

But I already know the answer. I've just walked into a lion's den with no way out.

CHAPTER SEVENTEEN

As soon as I reach the bottom of the staircase, a crack echoes through the room.

In front of me, Boss Olan bangs his eagle-head walking stick on the flagstone floor three times. The crowd parts for him as silence falls over the room.

Sweat and tobacco smoke burn my eyes. I look up at the ceiling. *What have I done?*

"Gentleman!" he booms as he struts through the masses. "We are gathered here tonight for the most beloved of our many traditions: the *Cath Draíochta*."

The men cheer.

I turn to Finn, who stands next to me stock still and wide-eyed. "What on earth is the *Cath Draíochta*?"

My question snaps him back to reality. "A tradition to awaken the magic of the younger members. See if they're worth anything."

"Sounds like a perfect distraction. How do we get out of here?" I whip around, looking for the exit. We're not far from the stairs. We could still escape.

Finn shakes his head. "We can't."

Boss Olan reaches the front of the room and bangs his cane on the floor once more. It reverberates through the soles of my boots.

A hush falls, palpable and reverent.

Sickening panic rises in my chest. I tug on the hem of Finn's tuxedo jacket and look toward the exit. He shakes his head no again, a horrible look of resigned fear on his face, and that's what frightens me most of all.

"Your bets may be placed with Freddie," Boss Olan continues. "Cheating, as always, will be harshly prosecuted."

A ripple of laughter moves through the crowd. More tuxedo-clad men seem to be streaming in by the second. The room is thick with shoe polish, sour smoke, and cologne. I think I'm going to be sick.

Boss Olan smiles and cracks his cane against the floor yet again. "Let us begin."

The lights dim; then the chandelier above the marble circle sparks to life with a *snick*, illuminating the white ring in a spotlight.

The room takes a collective intake of breath. The fiddle stops. Everything stills. My stomach rolls.

Then the crowd parts, and a man struts into the ring. He's short and broad shouldered, wearing a brown suit and a scowl on his face. He paces the perimeter of the circle and throws his arms up. The crowd roars. I cannot leave, so I simply watch with mingled curiosity and fear.

On the other side of the ring there is a brief commotion before another man is shoved into the center. He's in a fine tuxedo, tripping over his shiny shoes. His head whips desperately back and forth, scanning the crowd.

Oliver goddamn Callahan.

Of course he's a part of this too. Underneath my initial flash of anger and frustration is pity. He looks as scared as I feel.

He attempts to walk away but is shoved back in by one of the crowd inching closer and closer to the golden circle on the floor. Although he's tall, he's too skinny, all elbows and spindly legs, useless in fighting off the men pushing him. His eyes dart like a rabbit's caught in a trap, as he's forced nearer to the center.

The crowd is getting restless. Someone shouts "Coward!" from the back of the room.

I can't hear him over the din, but he's saying something to the men holding him that might be *Please, no.*

And despite all my anger at Oliver, despite my suspicion seeing him here, despite our fraught history, my heart pangs for him, as William's voice rings in my ears. *Help him, Frances. He doesn't have any of our street smarts.*

Oliver's head makes a sickening cracking noise as it hits the marble. It happens so quickly, I don't even see him fall. I only see the dazed look in his eyes from where he lies on the floor. I really might be sick.

The other man in the ring looks down at him with disgust, and nudges him with the toe of his boot. "Get up!"

Oliver pushes himself up and spits blood onto the marble.

It's a ring. They're in a boxing ring.

The room erupts. Cheers, shouting, jeering. My ears are ringing, my mouth agape.

I turn to Finn in horror. "We have to help him!" I yell.

He leans down and whispers, "Just watch."

Oliver puts his fists up over his face, but he looks so young and so scared. And suddenly I am a child again, drinking vanilla floats with him, playing hide-and-seek. I see his boyish face as he sits on our stoop, laughing with William back when my world was just eight blocks wide and the most interesting thing I'd ever seen was the color of Oliver's eyes.

But before I can form another coherent thought, the pocket watch is ripped from the breast of the man next to me. It flies through the air and winds itself around one of Oliver's fists, jerking it down to his side.

Taking advantage of the distraction, Oliver's opponent stretches out his hand, and a glass of champagne flies out of the grip of a man next to the ring. It hovers in the air for a moment before shattering on the floor.

The largest shard goes flying at Oliver's cheek, but he dodges it with a duck to his left.

"Oliver!" I shout at him.

His eyes snap to mine. He does a double take.

"Frances?" he cries.

"What are you doing here?" I shout through the din.

I've done the worst possible thing by distracting him. His opponent uses his fists instead of magic this time and lands a blow square on Oliver's left cheek. By the way his eyes water, it's obvious he's never been punched before. William was his defender as much as he was mine.

The sight of an unwilling tear streaming down Oliver's rapidly swelling cheek makes me feel as if the wind has been knocked out of me, too.

I can't just stand and watch. Despite everything we've been through, or perhaps because of it, I push myself forward, shove through a wall of solid bodies and the riled-up disappointment of men who wanted to see more violence than this. All the while, I scream Oliver's name as Finn calls for me from behind, shouting at me to stop.

My brother wouldn't have stopped, and neither do I.

Despite every reasonable part of my body screaming for me to leave, I step into the ring.

Panic makes it easier to call the magic. Power swells as I send an entire bottle of whiskey flying off a shelf on the back wall and into the skull of Oliver's attacker. It only takes one blow. He crumples to the floor like a marionette cut from its strings.

The crowd goes wild. The floor vibrates with the stomping of feet. I've never used magic to intentionally hurt anyone before.

No, I correct myself. *You didn't hurt anyone—you* saved *someone.*

In front of me, Oliver is very still. His blood stains the bright white marble crimson.

I kneel and grab the lapels of his tuxedo. "Are you all right? Should I call a doctor?"

He turns his head and spits blood on the floor again. "At least ten men in this room are doctors."

Finn is suddenly behind me, stony faced. "You shouldn't'a done that."

Boss Olan's cane bangs twice against the floor, silencing the room.

"A loss for Mr. Callahan and Mr. Bertram it seems!" A roar rises from the crowd "Your bets are null and void, you dirty gamblers!" The roaring turns to laughter. Glasses are clinked. Oliver's blood runs close to my left shoe. His hands are shaking.

I seethe with anger at Finn and at myself. I risked so much coming here. I've been so stupid.

"No more of this. I am leaving," I say to Finn through gritted teeth. The stairs look blocked by men, but I'd guess it's our best bet.

"I'm sorry, Frances, I'm so sorry," Finn says. He looks pained like he did the other night when he declared I'd been haunting him his whole life.

Before I can ask him why, we're interrupted by the sharp rap of a cane against stone.

"Place your bets, gentlemen: next up is perhaps the most exciting match we've ever held." A murmur rolls through the crowd like thunder.

Oliver reaches for me as two men pick him up by the armpits and haul him out of the ring. He still looks dazed. I need to find a doctor to examine his head.

I take a step to follow as the largest man I've ever seen steps into the gleaming marble ring. He's not clad in a tuxedo like most of the other men; he's shirtless, the muscles of his expansive chest and arms on display. He's barefoot, too, pacing around the golden perimeter like a caged animal.

"Vlad the Impaler," the Hungarian Diplomat announces with unbridled glee. Whoops and hollers ripple through the crowd. "Versus . . ." He pauses for dramatic effect.

Finn is warm beside me, but I scan the room for the quickest path to the stairs. This whole thing is a dangerous waste of time.

"Frances Hallowell!" The room goes quiet. Every head turns toward me. I blink, certain I've misheard.

"Excuse me?" I turn to Finn.

Two men appear from the crowd behind me and grab me by my upper arms. They half shove, half carry me toward the center of the wretched ring.

Finn grabs on to my hand and holds it like a vise. I throw my shoulder into the man on my right, and Finn pulls and pulls on my other arm to no avail.

"Get your hands off her!" Oliver cries. He reaches for me but is thrown back by the crowd.

"Don't touch her!" Finn shouts. He's silenced by a punch to the face from the man on my left. His hand slips from mine.

"No, no, please—" I beg. "Finn! *Finn!*" In a moment of stillness in the rollicking chaos, our eyes lock.

The men shove, and I dig my heels in. My boots cut a line through the still-wet blood. I kick my legs, whipping my head wildly from side to side, searching desperately for a savior I know isn't coming.

I try to use the magic to call for something, anything to come flying off the back shelf again, but it doesn't obey.

I'm sorry, Finn mouths. Oliver is silent and horror-struck.

The men's faces blur into one. The marble ring in the center of the room is the eye in a hurricane of sharp-toothed laughs and wadded-up cash.

In it, Vlad paces. He smiles. The grin reminds me of the look on Mr. Hues's face minutes before I killed him.

I am a fool. And I am going to pay for it.

Vlad circles me.

I tremble like a prey animal. I am terrified. But more than that, I am so goddamn mad at myself.

A single bottle of whiskey will not take him down. It seems silly to have gotten this far only to be killed in a magical boxing match by a grown man who goes by the name Vlad the Impaler. It's unclear if the sound that escapes my lips is a hysterical peal of laughter or a sob.

There's a joke in here somewhere about wanting to see my brother again.

Vlad lunges.

I sidestep him. Shards of glass crunch under my boots.

Vlad lunges again.

A crystal from the chandelier above us flies at my eye. I dodge it at the last second with a duck to my right. I bite my tongue, and my mouth floods with blood. I'm sure the Sons are screaming, but I hear only the rush of blood in my ears.

I try to call the magic again, try to really focus, but it sends the whole shelf of alcohol on the back wall crashing down. The men in the audience shout as bottles rain down on them, but it does nothing to stop Vlad.

Every magic lesson I've ever had feels so far away. Everything I ever learned in a classroom or the woods is drowned out by the buzzing terror in my head.

Vlad steps toward me, I stumble back. I search for an exit, but the crowd is a writhing blur, so chaotic, I can no longer see Finn or Oliver.

There is no one coming to help me. I'm bobbing alone, lost at sea, and my lifeboat is the part of me that scares me most.

A shard of glass flies up from the floor and slashes at my exposed collarbone. I swat it away like a wasp. It leaves only a surface wound, but it stings like hell.

Vlad keeps coming at me, pushing me to the very edge of the circle. Someone presses their hands to my lower back and shoves me back in.

No.

No.

It's the sensation of a stranger's hands on me that does it. A switch flips, and all at once my fear is replaced with rage. It burns through my body like a spark on a fuse.

I will not suffer for their entertainment. They don't get to touch me.

Not now. Not anymore. *Not ever again.*

This time the magic doesn't spark to life under my skin. It explodes like a wildfire.

There is a deafening crack as every last glass in the room shatters.

The jeers stop for a fraction of a second.

But Vlad doesn't hesitate. He raises his hands and sends the shards flying at me in a torrent.

I call the power. I don't know what I say to it, only that we speak the same language.

A candle falls from the chandelier and sets a loose lock of my hair alight. I wink it out before it does any real damage and, in the same moment, magick a wooden chair from the corner hurtling at Vlad's head. He doesn't see it coming, and it splinters apart as it cracks over his skull.

The lessons in the woods with Finn return to me like day breaking.

Vlad is so huge, it doesn't stop him, but something shifts in his eyes. He's no longer doing this for the sake of the fight. He hates me. He wants to beat me.

I want to beat him more.

I don't hear the crowd anymore, but I feel their voices vibrating in my bones. My singular focus is on the man stalking me.

Vlad lunges his massive body toward me, and I send another shard of glass in his direction; it slices his forearm, but still he doesn't stop.

He's inches away now and burning with rage.

He lunges.

I dodge and spit out the blood filling my mouth.

He raises a fist, and I duck in the wrong direction. He blow lands squarely across my cheekbone.

A hiss goes through the crowd. Oliver screams my name, his voice breaking through the noise.

My eyes water fiercely. The punch burns more than I thought it would, though I'm probably in too much shock to feel the real pain of it yet. The blow only makes me angrier, only makes me want to fight harder.

He pulls his elbow back, preparing to land another blow.

I stare him down and command the tendrils of my soul to reach out and grab hold of his body.

He freezes, arm cocked back, eyes wide and terrified.

Again the crowd goes silent.

"Don't. Touch. Me," I whisper.

The same magic I felt two nights ago with Finn roars. It's alarming how similar fear and desire feel when it all comes down to it.

Vlad's ragged breathing hisses out of his nostrils, but the rest of his body is frozen. I can feel my hold on him. It is harder to channel this power, the power over his body, than it was to control the objects I sent flying at him. I'm beginning to learn how this different kind of magic feels in my body, how it burns in the back of my throat. Taking control of Vlad tastes like sucking on pennies, or maybe that's the blood in my mouth. I don't know how long I can hold him, but I don't let go.

My pulse radiates across my cheek. I can feel my eye swelling, but I refuse to cry in front of these men.

Boss Olan's hyena cackle breaks the silence of the room, and my hold on Vlad. I'm briefly afraid he'll take the opportunity to lunge at me again, but he stands still, just looking at me, his chest rising and falling.

"Wonderful!" Boss Olan cries. "Oh, how wonderful!"

I've ripped the delicate sleeve of Maxine's dress in the fight.

Boss Olan strides over to the ring and hoists my hand over my head in victory.

His hand is cold and clammy. I snatch mine away, and it sends a ripple of pain through my whole, aching body.

He leans over and whispers in my ear, "You and I are going to do great things together, Frances."

"Because you did such great things for my brother?" I hiss through clenched teeth.

I don't wait for his reply. I step out of the ring, arms in front of me, prepared to barrel through the wall of bodies enclosing me. But I don't have to fight my way out. The men part for me like the Red Sea.

How comfortable it is to be a thing that is feared.

I'm almost to the back staircase, far away from the crowd, when Finn catches up to me. "Frances, stop!"

I turn around, fury and sadness sluicing hot in my throat. "Looks like we can't protect each other, huh?"

"Frances, please." He takes two more steps toward me.

I back up until the cold of the basement wall bites into my exposed shoulder blades. He's so quick, I don't realize he's cornered me until it is too late.

Finn leans down, and the world goes a little quieter. He whispers, close, too close, "You were incredible."

I'm annoyed by his awe. "Did you find the dagger? I don't have much time."

From his pocket Finn pulls an ancient-looking blade, perhaps four inches long, with a pearl-encrusted handle.

I reach out to touch it. "Will it work?"

"There's only one way to find out." He brings his hand to his breast pocket. "But that's not all I found."

He pulls a folded-up bundle of yellowing pages from his coat pocket and unrolls it. It's a list of names.

"Membership rolls," Finn explains. "I wanted to see if the boys on Sheepshead Bay were related to the Sons. Perhaps another connection with your brother."

In the dark of the basement, it takes me a moment to scan down the list. *Frank Garza, Samuel Gantt, Theodore George, Vincenzo Gianetti, Lorenzo Gianetti, Matthew O'Farrell.*

My blood runs cold. "Two Gianettis, but not a Mario. There's an O'Farrell here too." The last names match those of the dead boys who washed up on the same beach where William was found. This is the definitive proof we need that the Sons, or those related to them, may be the target of a murderer.

Finn nods in agreement. "It's still something. They could be targeting relatives. Or maybe this list is out of date."

"So, what do we do next?" I whisper.

"We find out who killed William, who killed the others. Show them what a fearsome witch his sister is."

The room smells like a lightning storm, crackling hot with magic.

"I have to go." I want him to think I'm strong, but tears are pricking at my eyes. I'm shaky and angry, on the verge of crying. My eye hurts, and I need to be somewhere that isn't here.

"I'll come to you tonight. I want to make sure you're all right," Finn says.

I duck under the arm he has pressed to the wall and turn to leave. The basement feels like a hothouse filled with sweat, smoke, and men I don't want looking at me.

I have a foot on the stairs, ready to flee, when Oliver approaches from behind and tentatively lays a hand on my shoulder. I shake it off, and he snatches it away and curls it into a fist at his side.

"What on earth was that?" he asks me. He's breathing heavily, and his eyes dart around the basement. I remember how I felt as if my whole world shifted the moment I was told magic was real. I wish I had some way to explain it to him in a way that made any sense. I settle on "The world is strange."

"That was more than strange, Frances." At the sight of Finn, he blinks in surprise. "It's been a long time. Finn, right?"

"Nice to see you again," Finn replies through a strained smile.

I feel very small, standing between my brother's friends in this world he inhabited without me. Oliver breaks his stare from Finn and shifts his glance toward me. His eyes are still as kind as I've always remembered them to be. It's this familiarity that makes my shoulders release, my hands go limp. He nods up the stairs. "Let me walk with you?"

And I do. I follow him up the stairs but can still feel Finn's gaze boring through me as I climb the narrow passage. He doesn't follow.

My pounding heart slows with each step away from the basement. Oliver and I are almost to the front door when the sound of someone clearing their throat makes me turn.

Boss Olan rises from an armchair in front of a massive roaring fireplace.

I hadn't seen him leave the basement.

"Leaving so soon, Miss Hallowell?" He strokes the eagle head of his cane as he takes in Oliver at my side. "Oh, and you've found a friend."

"We're going," I say.

"A shame."

Magic hums under the surface of my skin. "You know you can't stop me."

"I don't wish to. You are here as our guest."

"And this is how you treat your guests?" I laugh bitterly. I can barely see through my swollen eye. A twin bruise blooms around Oliver's.

"You are an extraordinary creature, Frances. We want to help you. And, Oliver, dear boy, I am sorry if all that came as a shock. We were hoping you'd be . . . talented. It appears, like your father, you'll have to serve us in other ways."

Oliver clenches his jaw.

The windows are dark. The rain beats against the pavement in a torrent as the storm finally fractures from promise to reality. Still, I'd rather be outside standing in the river of sludge pouring down the street than here. From downstairs I can still hear sickening cracks, followed by elated cheers.

"What do you mean 'talented'?" Oliver sounds as angry as I've ever heard him. "Did my father know you were going to throw me into that ring? What sort of operation is this? What sort of tricks are you pulling?"

Boss Olan booms a laugh, leaning back with the force of it. The flickering fire has made this room too hot. "My dear boy, you'll understand in time. The *Cath Draíochta* isn't elegant, but it does have its purposes. I'm sorry you're sore you lost."

"I didn't *lose*. I'm not sore about anything. I simply wish to know what kind of organization it is you're running here. I was led to believe this was a social club." Oliver juts out his chin, defiant, like using a thousand words to ask a question when he could use only a few makes him sound grown-up.

"We are the ancient order of the Sons of Saint Druon, the kings of New York City, magicians of the highest order, general bon vivants, et cetera. We can be social. We can be many things."

"I doubt I'm the first person to tell you that's not a helpful description," I snipe.

Each of his fingers is encircled with a thick gold ring. The maroon of his silk jacket shines like the blood we left in puddles in the marble boxing ring. "Oh you are delightful, young Frances! Your brother was a delight too. I cannot wait for the things we'll do together."

I'm biting my lip so hard, it stings. I lick away the blood before asking, "What things?"

"You are stifled at your little school. They're teaching you small magic. You, my dear, were not meant to be a practitioner of small magic."

Are these my choices for magic, then? Housework or bare-knuckle boxing? It's too depressing a thought to accept.

I gesture to my swelling eye. "I'm not sure I find magical fights a more appealing venture than magical sewing."

Boss Olan laughs once more. "Real magic is power, and these parlor tricks help us hold on to that power. You leave those witches of yours, and we'll show you what we can really do."

It's absolutely terrifying, the part of me that wants what he's saying to be true. But my eye socket throbs, and I'm terrified Maxine and Lena have already left the city, and my mother taught me never to take the word of men in shiny shoes.

"I'm leaving now."

Boss Olan doesn't rise from his chair. He lazily lifts his pointer and middle fingers from the armrest, and instantly the fire in the hearth triples in size. Without pause, a cold wind whips through the room from nowhere, the grandfather clock in the hall gongs, a stack of mail rises from a side table in a perfect, swirling tornado, and then, most terrifyingly, my own feet begin to move, completely against my will. In jerking steps, Boss Olan brings me across the room to his side. It is not lost on me that he could force me to kneel at his feet if he wanted to. He doesn't. He looks up at me with the confidence of a man who believes he is untouchable.

Oliver shouts in protest, but I whip my head to him. "I can handle this, Oliver." I don't like Boss Olan, but I also don't fear him. At least not in this moment. He's just trying to make a point. I'm so desperate for any information, I'll let him make it. It's better to let men like Boss Olan think they've won.

Boss Olan stares up at me from where he sits; the flickering of the fireplace illuminates his face in ghoulish shadows. "The streets of this city run with blood from a war that's been going on since it was called New Amsterdam. Those witches will tell you pretty stories about duty, and sisterhood." He screws up his face like the word disgusts him. "But we alone can help you get everything you wish."

He releases his hold on me, and I lash out in return, manipulating his fingers back down onto the chair. He smiles at the force of it. I don't give him the satisfaction of a reaction.

I can't get out quickly enough. I don't look back as I tug Oliver with me.

Boss Olan calls after me from where he still sits in front of the roaring fire, "When you return to your little school and your little magic, remember what you did here, tonight. Remember, and come find us."

The blast of cold air as I throw open the front door is a relief. In the second before I slam it behind me, I hear one last chuckle from in front of the fireplace.

CHAPTER EIGHTEEN

Oliver and I step out on the rain-soaked street. The air is heavy with the smell of sewage and damp garbage.

Maxine's delicate dress sticks heavily to my skin as it becomes laden with rain.

My whole body still feels electric. For the first time in a very long time, I was brave. It's hard to be brave when you're sad, and I've been so sad for such a long time.

"Are you all right?" Oliver asks, but the thunderstorm carries his question down the gutter, where it washes away with all the other useless things.

I don't answer, so he tries another question.

"Why aren't you at the sanitarium?"

Ah yes, my cover story. How quickly I forgot that I'm supposed to be laid up with tuberculosis.

"How did you know about that?"

"Do you remember in the letter you wrote me, you said you went to the police station every Sunday at ten a.m. to ask about Will's case?" He looks down at his shoes. "I went a couple of weeks ago. I should have done it sooner, but I finally felt ready, and I wanted to see you after—" He sighs. "Well anyway, you never came, and when I asked an officer about you, he told me what happened. Some story about the owner of your shop being found dead and you getting diagnosed with tuberculosis all in the same day. Quite the story."

"Rotten luck," I mutter.

"You seem well enough now."

"I snuck out." It's a terrible lie. He doesn't believe me, and I don't blame him.

He takes a steadying breath. His hair is dark, wet and stuck to his forehead. I swear he's grown again. "It's the strangest thing—I tried to write to you, but no one could tell me the address. I wrote a dozen letters addressed to you, sent them around to every sanitarium in the state just to be thorough, but it doesn't seem you received any of them."

"You—you wrote me letters?" I ask. A small voice in the back of my head, the one I try to ignore, understands what he truly means: he tried to find me.

"Of course," he whispers.

And the way he says it makes me feel like I've been put into the ring again—emotions raging, raging like a church bell ringing in a storm. I don't have time for this, to sort through what it means. Instead, I shrug my shoulders. "You know how the mail can be," I offer as an excuse.

He narrows his eyes. It hurts to be looked at by him with so much skepticism, even though I deserve it. "Why are you here?" he asks.

"I was invited here by a friend. It was probably foolish to have come," I say.

He frowns. "Was it Finn?"

I let myself imagine for a moment that he's jealous of me spending time with a boy who isn't him. "I didn't realize you two were acquainted."

"I don't know him well enough to speak badly of him. I never understood why your brother seemed so taken with him and his friends. Perhaps they were more exciting than me."

It hadn't occurred to me until this moment that Oliver may have been hurt by William's obsession with the Sons of Saint Druon and his new job with them as much as I had been.

"So why'd you come here tonight?" I ask. Even in the dark of this rain-soaked street, the bruise blooming around his eye is visible. He always seemed so confident, so untouchable. Seeing him this lost makes me want to cry.

"The Commodore Club is where my father's gentleman's club meets. I was invited here tonight to meet with them. I thought perhaps he finally believed I was old enough to join them without embarrassing him. One moment I was drinking a scotch, the next I was being shoved into that basement, and—I feel like I'm losing my mind." He tips his head up to the sky, and lets the rain fall over his fine features, bruised now from the fight. "You did something in there. It was like . . . magic. That man inside called it magic." He can barely choke out the word.

"You didn't know?" Between his father and William, I'm shocked

Oliver has been left in the dark about all this. It must have been very lonely.

Oliver shakes the rainwater from his hair. "I'm beginning to think I don't know anything. The stupid thing is, I knew my father loved Will more than he loved me. But I was still so jealous he found him a position with the Sons, when he wouldn't even let me enter the building. Said I was too young to join, and didn't listen when I reminded him Will was only three months older than I was. But he was right. Will was better equipped to handle all this than me. He had a higher tolerance for the absurd, said it was annoying that I always needed things to make sense." Raindrops drip from his fingers, hanging heavily at his side. "I think I probably need to go home and vomit."

"I wish I had the right thing to say." I gesture to the air, as if my whirling hands could possibly communicate what I'm thinking. "You're not crazy; you're not seeing things."

"So it *was* magic?" Oliver sounds pained.

I shrug. "If that's the word you want to use."

His facial expression changes—like he's seeing me for the first time. It's enough to make me stumble backward.

"I'm sorry, Oliver. I wish I could stay, explain . . ." My voice trembles only slightly. I won't let my feelings get the best of me. Not when Maxine and Lena are waiting, if they haven't left yet, that is. God knows what trouble we'll be in. "I really do have somewhere to be." My boots squelch against the wet sidewalk as I turn and leave him alone for the second time in months

"I'm sorry, Frances," he calls after me. I'm so far down the block, his voice is barely audible over the rain.

"For what?" I shout. It's a moment that aches.

Oliver shrugs his shoulders. His tuxedo is soaked through. "Everything."

My heart beats wildly against my rib cage. I know what he means.

I run the twelve blocks to the Methodist church where the suffragette meeting is being held.

By the time I arrive, my hair is a soaked matted mess at the back of my head, and the hem of Maxine's beautiful dress is ruined with mud. I hope she will forgive me. I hope I can fix it.

The street is quiet, the rain dissipating by the second.

I step into the damp basement where women still mill about speaking to each other in small groups.

I catch bits and pieces of conversation as I pass them: "strikes," "sit-ins," "marches."

Maxine's eyes widen with horror as she sees me walk in.

"What on earth happened to you," she asks through her teeth.

"I was caught in the rain." I smile sweetly because Helen is glaring at us from across the room. But I don't think she means the rain; I think she means my mottled-purple eye socket.

Helen marches over at the sight of me. "Where have you been, Frances?"

I will myself to tear up, and it isn't difficult after the night I've had. I recite the story Maxine, Lena, and I came up with two days ago when we planned this deception.

I tell Helen I missed my friends at the shop so desperately, I couldn't help but leave the meeting to go see them.

"Your friends must not have been glad to see you." She eyes my swelling face.

"I tripped. The rain made the sidewalk slick."

"I can't say you didn't deserve it. No matter, we have larger matters to attend to."

She approaches the tall blonde I spoke with earlier. "Ethel, are you ready?" she asks in a low voice.

Ethel gulps. "I suppose as ready as I'll ever be."

With Ethel at her side, Helen leads us outside to where the ambulance is parked on the curb.

Even with Maxine up front, the back of the ambulance is awfully crowded with one more body.

"Sorry about your tuberculosis," Lena says to Ethel.

"Helen told me where we're off to. A professional courtesy."

"Well then I'm sorry about your magic."

Ethel sniffs. "Go on a hunger strike, come out with magical powers. I do feel bad about the guard, though."

"Don't."

The rest of the drive back to school is long and oppressively silent.

Helen seethes in the driver's seat, angry with me for disappearing during her carefully planned field trip.

Maxine seethes in the front seat, probably angry with me for ruining her dress.

Lena seethes in the back of the ambulance, rightfully angry with all those closed-minded suffragettes.

Ethel may be seething. I don't know her well enough to tell.

And I feel terrified, and *terrifying*.

My brain is at war with itself, unable to process all the things I learned about both magic and myself tonight. I can still feel the echo of it, how big it made me feel. I crave that feeling again already. It's intoxicating. But then I think of the crunch of the whisky bottle as it crashed into that man's skull, and the raw fear in my opponent's eyes as I seized his body, and I recoil. Tonight I was forced to confront magic's ability to do harm. And I was good at it. *What does that say about me?*

Boss Olan's offer to join them nags at the back of my mind. Would running away from Haxahaven to join a man who has made big promises make me exactly like my mother? Or would harnessing my power keep me from making her same mistakes?

Finally, we return to school. The gravel crunches as the ambulance slows to a stop. In the dark, the white columns of the school look blue.

Helen jumps out of the car.

"Frances, you're on kitchen duty for the next two weeks. Report to the dining hall at five in the morning tomorrow." As if I'm not worthy of another second of her attention, she stomps into Haxahaven without a look back, poor Ethel at her heels.

"See, I told you so," Maxine says. " Now you need to tell me everything that happened tonight." She drags Lena and me to her suite on the second floor.

I startle upon seeing a redheaded girl sitting on her canopy bed in a nightgown.

"I'm so sorry, darling, not tonight," Maxine says.

The girl's face crumples in disappointment, but she walks out the door without protest.

"Who was that?"

"May."

I drop it. We have more important things to discuss.

I pad across the lush navy carpet to Maxine's dressing table still covered in haphazardly placed necklaces and silver hairbrushes. There are magazines too, open to dog-eared pages of men in dandy's clothing, candy colored suits and striped neckties.

Like a magpie unable to resist shiny things, I run my fingertips across the cool rivets of a sapphire brooch.

"I've told you to take whatever you want."

Maxine's voice snaps me out of my trance.

"Any brooch you want, any dress, whatever strikes your fancy." Her voice is cold. "It's all useless. I'll be wearing this cape until the day I die." She sinks onto the bed, looking so exhausted, I don't remind her she's not actually wearing a cape at the moment.

I want to be out of this heavy, soaked mass of a ruined dress so badly I nearly take her up on her offer, but she begins speaking again before I can ask her to undo my buttons.

"So, Hallowell, what the hell happened tonight? I felt the magic do . . . something."

There is relief in telling Maxine and Lena. The story comes spilling out of me so quick, I'm tripping over my own words. I can't even look them in their shocked faces until I'm finished.

Lena stares at me, mouth agape. "Why didn't you just leave?"

I don't have an answer that makes sense. I don't think I could explain the responsibility I felt for Oliver, the weight of Finn's gaze, or worst of all, the exhilaration of using my magic.

"I don't know."

The look on Maxine's face is hard to decipher. She's pacing the room, pulling her hair out of its bun.

"What I felt . . . ," Maxine mutters. "I couldn't breathe, like someone had seized my chest."

"I don't know how I did it," I say. It wasn't much different from our practice in the woods, but it was *more*, like someone let a stopper out of a bottle that was only leaking before. For the first time I felt the true magnitude of this power. What I don't tell them is the terrible satisfaction it gave me. I still feel a little intoxicated. I can't tell them how hungry I am for more.

Finn was right. This magic is dangerous.

I'm afraid all of Maxine's pacing might wear a hole through the carpet.

"Frances, you can't let anyone find out about this. We take this to our graves. If Vykotsky were to learn about this . . ." Maxine trails off like the consequences are too terrible to speak aloud.

I shoot her a glare. "Oh yes, Maxine, Mrs. Vykotsky was the first person I thought I'd tell about our forbidden spells, and a magical bare-knuckle boxing match."

"Shut up."

My nerves are scraped bare after everything tonight; I'm not in the mood to tolerate Maxine's usual jabs. "I don't understand why you're being mean to me about this!" I shout too loud. The room goes silent as all three of us listen for someone stirring. The last thing we need is a knock on the door from whoever is patrolling the halls.

After a tense moment, Maxine sighs heavily and looks up at the ceiling. "I'm not trying to be mean," she whispers. "I just wish it were me."

It's as vulnerable as Maxine has ever been with us. I'm shocked to hear of all things, she's *jealous*.

"If I could give this power to you, I would," I reply, but I don't know if it's the truth. If it gets me one step closer to the resurrection spell, finding what happened to my brother, I would never give it up, not for a second.

Lena hardly speaks during the whole exchange. She just looks at me, her eyes narrowed, fiddling with a piece of dark hair that's come undone. Her unending stare is more unsettling than Maxine's frantic pacing.

When Maxine is convinced I can give her no more answers, Lena and I climb the stairs to our room together.

I'm frustrated and hurt. I needed to feel their support tonight; instead I feel chastised.

"Are you all right?" Lena asks me as I reach the door.

She looks like she needs a hug as badly as I do. "No. Are you?"

She frowns. "No."

I pull her into my arms, and it's awkward. I'm too angular and she's too tall, but it makes me feel a little better.

We exchange sad smiles and go quietly into the darkness, careful not to wake up Ruby and Aurelia.

I'm still uncomfortable from my conversation with Maxine. I'd pity her if I weren't so annoyed. It feels typical she'd find a way to make this about her.

I fall asleep quickly, the magic having burned through my energy like a flame on a wick.

I dream I'm standing in the lush field of the Blockula. Finn is waiting for me. The meadow is awash with tiny crimson blooms, as if the grass has been splattered with fresh blood. The light bends wrong here.

His white shirt is unbuttoned around the neck. A crescent of mottled purple is sketched beneath each of his eyes. I wonder when the last time he truly rested was.

"Hi, Finn." I wonder distantly if I could control his body in this dream landscape.

He fiddles with his fingers and casts a glance at the ground. "I never should have taken you. You could have died."

"But I didn't die."

Finn scrubs a hand across his jaw. There's something tortured in his eyes as they take me in. "Does your eye hurt?"

I bring the tips of my fingers to my eye socket. It's tender, here in the dream, but not unbearable. I'm not sure how real-life-pain translates into dream pain. His eye is swollen too, from where he got socked trying to stop them from dragging me into the ring.

"Does yours?"

He shrugs. "I've had worse." He takes a breath. "What you did tonight was . . . extraordinary." His voice is thick with awe. He's gazing at me like I'm magic itself. "Boss Olan invited you to join us, didn't he?"

"How did you know?"

"I just know him. He collects people with extraordinary power the way ordinary men collect stamps."

It's the exhausted way Finn says it that makes me wonder if that was what happened to him. A child with a broken leg taken by a man he didn't know across a great wide ocean to an unfamiliar city, he must have been terrified.

"Why would he need me? It seems the Sons have plenty of magic without me."

"All magic is complicated and individualistic. We have our own

Finders, and clairvoyants, and mind readers. But we don't have any-one who can manipulate like you other than Boss—he's been look-ing for a protégé, but none of us are powerful enough."

Powerful enough. The thought is thrilling and nauseating. I can't admit the truth to Finn, which is that I'm not convinced I have any particularly special power—I think Maxine or Lena or any of my classmates would have reacted the same as I did in that ring.

He chews on his lower lip. "So, are you going to accept his offer?"

"Has a witch been invited to join before?" The thought of leav-ing Haxahaven makes me uncomfortable. For all its flaws, it has become a sort of home, and after what I saw tonight, the Sons don't necessarily seem a better option than the one I currently have.

He furrows his brows. "Not that I know of."

"Do you want me to join?" This question makes me most ner-vous of all.

Finn thinks for a moment. "Of course I do."

"What if I don't feel like leaving quite yet. The food here is good."

Finn frowns. I thought he'd laugh. "What if leaving made it eas-ier to find out what happened to William, to the other boys?"

I should have known he'd use this. The one bartering chip he knows I can't turn down.

"I'm not convinced of it. Not yet." I don't know how to explain it to him without sounding weak. "Perhaps I'll feel different when I'm less bruised. Say what you will about the witches of Haxahaven, they've never punched me in the eye."

Finn exhales through his teeth. "I'll make them pay for what they did tonight."

I want to ask how he plans on exacting his revenge, but I doubt he'd take kindly to my condescension. It was made clear tonight just how little sway Finn holds within the Sons. "It's not worth it."

"Whatever it is you choose, we're in this together. I'll see you soon, Frances." Something violently real flickers in his hazel eyes.

My clever retort gets stuck in my throat.

I blink awake. My eye socket throbs.

Terrified and terrifying.

Before dawn, when the light is still purple, I wake for kitchen duty. I'm exhausted and frustrated with myself, but as punishments go, it's benign, so I button my cape, braid my hair, and sneak quietly out of the room so as not to wake my still-sleeping roommates.

Florence meets me at the door, much like the night when Maxine, Lena, and I first snuck out to meet Finn.

She raises an eyebrow. "Helen said a group of girls haven't given her this much trouble since Alice Roosevelt and her friends set a US senator on fire. What did you do?"

"I ran away to see my former school friends," I lie.

"And they punched you?" She chuckles, eyeing my bruised face. "I tripped."

"Come on then. I'll teach you how to make biscuits."

In addition to Florence, there's Ann, a plump woman as pale as the biscuit dough I'm kneading. Ann makes me scrub the ovens with a spell that levitates a scouring brush, but I don't mind it much. Cleaning has always given me a certain kind of satisfaction.

The kitchen is quiet, all bricked floors and glowing hearths. It's the heart of Haxahaven, if it has one at all.

The repetitive work gives me time to sort through the tangle of thoughts in my head.

Witches can manipulate other people.

I shouldn't be allowed to manipulate other people.

Do I even want to be able to manipulate other people?

I think I'm rather good at it.

A person who is better than me would feel terrible about what they did in the basement of the Commodore Club, instead of being desperate to try again. Good girls don't steal daggers and break whiskey bottles over people's heads. Good girls don't have a fire in their chest that begs for more things to burn.

Working in the kitchen is a little like early-morning tutoring, but without teachers who make me want to rip my own hair out with boredom. The way Florence can scramble a whole pan of eggs from across the kitchen with her mind, while stirring a pot of oats with her hands—it's the kind of practical magic work we're taught in Mrs. Roberts's class, efficient and quick, but Florence and Ann are more powerful than anyone I've ever seen.

"Can you move that broom over there, love?" Ann asks me on my second day.

I am not afraid of my power as it awakens in my chest. The broom falls from where it is propped on the wall. Moving a broom proves tricker than a person. Magic is an unpredictable, finicky thing.

"Good, but not quite what I was looking for," she says kindly. "Try this. *Soppa golvettia*," she murmurs under her breath.

The broom sweeps an elegant arc at her instruction.

With a clumsy tongue I repeat her words. *"Soppa golvettia."*

The broom floats off the floor, rotates in midair so that the bristles are facing downward, then makes a jerking sweeping motion across the floor.

Florence smiles and wipes her hands on her apron. "Good girl. Keep practicing."

And I do. Every morning I arrive in the kitchen, and every morning my control grows. I hop out of bed with excitement, motivated by my time with Ann and Florence each day. Every inch of progress made feels like getting to know myself better. By Wednesday I am able to sweep the whole floor without so much as elevating my heart rate.

Florence tells me I'm learning faster than any pupil she's ever seen. I swell with pride. "Is this what you girls are doing in the park? Practicing your sweeping?" she asks with a smile.

Florence is so kind, I almost want to tell her the truth. It might be a relief to tell an adult about everything. I can picture it now: she'd stroke my back and tell me everything is okay. She'd probably know what to do next. But she wouldn't help me with the Resurrection, so I smile back and say, "No, you're just a great teacher. Why don't you teach your own class?"

She purses her lips. At the stove, Ann goes still. "Mrs. Vykotsky believes Ann and I are of more use to the school here. We both disagree with Ana on a great deal. Call it different philosophies. But we share the same love for the girls here, don't we darling?"

Ann turns, a spatula gripped in her hand. "Yes, dear, we do."

During the day I sit quietly in my classes, and despite my efforts to pay attention, all I can focus on is the triviality of them.

I've started to openly lie in Mrs. Li's class. Talking about my absent father who I've never spared much thought for is easier than talking through the things that still ache inside me, so I spin tragic tales of missed birthdays and Christmases until Mrs. Li is satisfied with my pain.

The Sons of Saint Druon are correct about one thing. Haxahaven has no interest in teaching us to be powerful. Every lesson, every conversation, every skill taught is focused on keeping our powers under careful lock and key. Burn the magic off like leaking kerosene lest we all explode.

My morning lesson with Florence and Ann helps, but it doesn't scratch the same itch as the Commodore Club.

Maxine and Lena notice my mind wandering. We're all lying in Maxine's bed one night after dinner. My head on Maxine's stomach, her legs draped over Lena. Maxine is reading, Lena is stitching, and I'm just staring at the ceiling.

"A penny for your thoughts?" Maxine asks.

"They're not worth that much."

"Everything is always so dramatic with you." She sighs and returns to her book.

"What is it they say about the pot and the kettle?" I roll my eyes but hate that she's right. I hate the part of me that wants more than this. I am warm, with friends, in a school of goddamn magic. But it's not enough.

It's like my very soul is growing inside me. It yawns during lessons. By the time the world has gone dark, it's itching under my skin, begging for something to latch on to.

Horrible thoughts come like hail knocking on a window, slow at first, then constantly. *What if I made Maxine give me that last piece of pie? What if I made Lena stand up? What if I made Aurelia slap Ruby? What if, what if, what if . . .*

I try to brush them away, but the thoughts come back with more force the longer I ignore them, until they're screaming in my head, demanding to be heard. Most nights I retire to my room early, not staying up to talk and laugh in the sunroom like most of the girls my age. Kitchen duty makes a good excuse.

I stop sleeping.

I am terrified and terrifying.

CHAPTER NINETEEN

It shouldn't come as a surprise that Finn wants more too.

He comes to me in a dream, as handsome and exhausted as ever. We're in the Blockula again. It's dusk here, painted in brilliant orange and purples.

"It's been difficult to find you," he greets me. His hands are in his pockets, his curls wild.

I'm wearing my nightdress, hair undone around my shoulders. "Sleep hasn't come easy."

"I know the feeling. Your eye looks better." He gestures toward me. It's turned from a mottled purple to a sickly green. He has a matching shadow on his cheekbone.

I flip my hair as a joke. "Thank you, I think the green suits me." But he looks so serious tonight, the gesture doesn't get even the smallest smile out of him. His stony face makes me nervous.

"I don't have long, but I do have a question."

I try to keep my tone light, despite my anxiety. "Go on."

"Instead of our usual lesson this week, could you meet me just past the oak trees that line the path to Haxahaven. Six p.m.?" He pauses before tacking on the last part. "Alone."

The word sends a shower of nerves through me.

"That's right during dinner. I'm not sure. Why? Have you found something else? Is it the scrying mirror?"

"I have to go. I'll be waiting for you. I do hope you come."

And with that he's gone. I wake, angry with myself because I already know I'm going to do whatever it takes to meet him. Leaving in the daylight, during a meal is more dangerous than anything I've attempted at Haxahaven yet.

I tell Maxine that lessons with Finn are canceled this week, that he wants me to sneak out, believing that he's found something important for the spell.

Her face is disappointed, her answer noncommittal, but three days later she braids my hair while Lena shoves pillows under the covers of my bed.

"No amount of punching and fluffing is going to make that look like Frances," Maxine says in between tugging so hard my head is pulled backward.

"This was your plan!" Lena exclaims. She throws the quilt up over the pillows, and it kind of looks like a human body if I squint my eyes a little.

"I didn't say it was a good plan," Maxine retorts.

"Neither of you are filling me with much confidence." I sigh.

"As your friends, I feel it's our moral duty to tell you when you're being stupid about a boy," Maxine says.

"That's not fair. He—"

"And as your friends," she interrupts me, "it's our moral duty not to stop you."

She finishes my braid with a coil of black satin ribbon.

For a moment I wonder if this is what it feels like to have sisters, but Maxine interrupts the thought with a hard flick to the soft spot of my neck just below my ear. "What was that for?"

"For luck. You ready?" she presses her gate key into my palm.

"As I'll ever be." I toss my cape on, wishing I could wear something prettier than my uniform to meet Finn, but rule number one of sneaking out is don't draw attention to oneself, so this will have to do.

Maxine stops me with a hand on my shoulder as I reach the door to the kitchen, where I'll sneak out the side door. In the bustle of dinner hour, no one will stop me.

"You owe us a favor now—you do realize that?"

"You're keeping score?" I ask.

She tilts her head and raises her eyebrows.

"Ah, there's already something you want, isn't there?" I say.

It's fun, this push and pull. Maxine once told me not to be boring and I've tried not to be, but she must know in her heart I'll give her whatever it is she wants.

Finn is waiting for me down the road just as he promised he'd be. Leaning on the driver's-side door of a Model T in his black coat, he looks every inch the villain in a gothic novel, and although I am still upset about what happened in the Commodore Club, my heart hiccups at the sight of him.

"Right on time." His smile lights up his whole face like a sunbeam cutting through clouds.

"They don't call me Frances Hallowell: Haxahaven's Most Rebellious Pupil for nothing."

He laughs. "Who calls you that?"

"I thought you and I could start a trend." I bite the inside of my cheek to keep from returning his smile.

"All right, little rebel, hop in the machine—I want to get there before it gets dark."

"Did you steal this?"

"Borrowed." He says. I'm not sure if I believe him.

"Where are we going?"

"It's a surprise."

"Did you find something? Do the Sons have scrying mirrors? I looked in the library and didn't find much—"

Finn cuts me off with another laugh. "Not everything has to be about solving a murder, Frances."

I knit my brows together. "So you didn't find anything?"

"Just get in."

I do as I'm told, ignoring the ripple of frustration coursing through me. Finding out what happened to William is more than a murder mystery game to me.

We can't talk over the noise of the engine, so for twenty-five minutes I'm left with nothing but my anxiety for company.

The sky is a brilliant pink, a perfect fall sunset, when the automobile finally begins to slow.

Finn maneuvers the vehicle deftly down brownstone-lined streets, and then wider boulevards, until suddenly a beach comes into view. The water stretches out to the horizon, painted with the colors of the sunset. It's breathtaking.

He pulls the automobile over, hops out, and crosses to my side.

I've been to this area only once before, a special dress delivery for a client the winter I turned sixteen.

"What's at Coney Island?" I ask when he opens my door.

"Rides. Food. Merriment," he lists on his fingers.

I take the hand he offers and step out of the car. The air is thick with brine and fried food. "They didn't find another body?" I'm confused.

"No dead bodies. No mysterious documents. Just a little fun." He looks at me, his face open and hopeful.

I'm annoyed that I've been essentially tricked into sneaking out for nothing, but I'm also touched he put so much thought into doing something to make me happy. "I don't remember if I know how to have fun."

He smirks. "Well then let me remind you."

Luna Park on Coney Island is something out of a fairy tale. A quarter million electric lights have the dying day lit up like the middle of the afternoon. Around us floats a chorus of tinny carnival music punctuated by swooping roller-coaster screams.

We walk down the weathered gray pier, and the smell of seawater makes me feel lighter. I close my eyes and inhale deeply. *For one night, let this be enough.*

The ticket booth sits beneath a bright yellow crescent moon, bigger than the Haxahaven dining table, painted with the word LUNA. Behind the main marquee stretch the spires and turrets of the buildings of the park, laid out like a miniature European city.

Finn pulls a handful of coins out of his pocket and drops them on the ticket counter. "Two, please."

The man at the desk grins under his moustache, rips two red tickets off a roll as big as my head, and pushes them through the slot under the window. "Have fun, kids."

Finn's fingers brush my palm as he passes me mine. "Seventeen years in New York City and I've never been to the rides at Coney Island," I marvel.

"How lucky I am to be the one who takes you, then." The breeze off the ocean pushes Finn's curls into his face; he brushes them away with a smile that flashes white under the electric lights.

We pass through a metal turnstile and onto a boardwalk bustling with people wrapped in fall coats, scarves, and wool hats. I tug my cape around me, aware of how odd I must look among them.

Pinwheels taller than I am are illuminated with spinning red and green bulbs. A tower dotted with over a thousand white lights is posted in the middle as the centerpiece. The strange newness reminds me a little of my first magic class, the exhilarating knowledge that this world holds so many things I haven't yet seen.

Finn casts a glance at me, and the corners of his mouth hitch up. "You're pleased?" I hope I never get used to the charm of his accent; the way it makes everything he says sound like a song.

My nerves buzz like the electric lights. "I'm not sure." I'm foolish for letting myself have this moment.

It's like Finn can read my mind, because he reaches over and brushes my hand with his pinky. "You're allowed to be happy. It's what he'd want."

I sigh. "It just seems like such a waste that all this exists and he's not here to see it."

"I know what you mean, but nothing mattered to William more than your happiness."

"Did he say that?"

"No, I could just tell. It was the way he talked about you."

"Thank you." My words are clipped. It's hard to experience happiness without guilt, one of the more unexpected side effects of grief.

"I've upset you." He sounds distressed.

"No, no. I'm just . . . tired. Can we go ride something now?"

Finn looks down at me, an intense fondness in his eyes. "I think I know one you'll like."

Together we push through crowds and make our way across the park to a bright blue tent emblazoned with the words WITCHING WAVES.

A man perched on a barstool takes our tickets and waves us into a buggylike contraption, one of maybe a dozen haphazardly scattered around a ring about as big as an ice rink. The floor is made of sheets of corrugated steel, the walls around it of painted plywood.

The buggy is low to the ground; Finn grabs my hand to help me in as I navigate my skirts. It's a simple gesture, more politeness than anything, but it sends my heart kicking like a drum. He catches my eye, and for a fraction of a second I'm sure he feels it too, this electricity between us. He slides in next to me, pressed dangerously close. I'm wearing a wool skirt, and a chemise under that, but still I can feel the heat from his thigh against mine.

Maybe I can have this much. Maybe I can let myself appreciate the way the electric lights shine in Finn's hair like a halo. Maybe I can turn off the overthinking switch in my brain for one night and stop asking myself why I'm so afraid to feel something good.

More people file in behind us, a few other couples—some young, some old—two sisters with matching ribbons in their hair, a pair of rowdy boys close to my age.

The striped-shirt ticket taker looks bored as he shouts, "Keep your hands to yourself and inside the buggy at all times!" Then, without ceremony, he cranks a lever the length of my forearm.

There's a moment of anticipation as gears begin to click and whir underneath us; then the sheet of metal our buggy sits on top of pitches up, and our buggy is sent careening across the rink. Before we can hit the wall, another section of the floor lurches up, sending us flying in the other direction.

The whole floor comes alive like the ocean in a storm, there are buggies flying, and the rink fills with screams, whoops, and hollers. Organ music swells, a jerky rendition of "The Entertainer."

We crash into the buggy holding the sisters, and I don't know if I scream because I'm having fun or because I'm terrified. All I know is that my heart is in my throat, and Finn's hand is clutching my knee.

Finn is smiling, a grin of pure joy, laughing wildly every time our buggy crashes into another.

I love his smile. His bottom canines are just a little too sharp, like a vampire. Either I'd never noticed before this moment, or he's never smiled this wide for me to see in the oppressive gloom of the park.

I prefer this version of us. A Finn and Frances illuminated with a rainbow of electric lights, with freedom to laugh as loudly as they please. And for the first time since William died, my grief and mourning and all the fury that consumed me flies away and out of my reach. Like a hundred-pound weight has been lifted off my rib cage, and I'm finally able to take a full breath. I feel . . . *happy*.

But there's melancholy even in that. I'm terrified to face who I am without my sadness. What is left of me without it?

We ride the Witching Waves twice more, and after we get funnel cakes piled high with whipped cream and strawberries. Then Finn pushes me into something called Shoot the Chutes, which involves riding a small boat down a slide into a pool of water.

I laugh even when the wool of my skirt ends up soaked through. Finn's hand-knit sweater hangs damp and heavy off his shoulders.

"Any regrets, D'Arcy?" I laugh.

"Oh, a million. But regrets about tonight? None at all."

I blush, but I tell myself it's simply a survival mechanism, blood rushing in to fight the chill of my damp clothes.

Time moves faster outside of Haxahaven, and I'm surprised when the clock tower chimes nine.

"I need to be back by ten," I say to Finn.

"All right, Cinderella. A spun sugar for the road?"

"How could I refuse?"

Picking at an enormous cloud of the treat, we make our way to the Model T, parked a ways off the pier.

"Thank you for tonight," I say to break up the hollow sound of our feet against the boardwalk.

The lights of Luna Park glint off the navy blue ocean, which hits the shore with a soft hush, back and forth, like a lullaby. Above us, the starless sky is dark and quiet. If I listen carefully, I can still hear swooping screams, but in this moment, it is easy to imagine Finn and I are the only two people on earth.

"Well, I had some things to make up for, didn't I? Also I just wanted to spend some time with you. Not Haxahaven Frances, just regular Frances. I think sometimes you forget you're only seventeen."

"I feel a hundred and fifty. And also maybe five. An elderly toddler. The world's oldest idiot. I know too much and nothing at all."

He doesn't laugh at my joke but tilts his head to the side and looks at me. Quietly he whispers, "You're allowed to just be yourself sometimes."

His gaze is so intense. I break it like a coward and shake the thoughts girls aren't allowed to have out of my head. "It would be easier if I knew who 'myself' was supposed to be."

Finn stops on the moonlit boardwalk, we're far away from Luna Park now. Only the faintest jangle of music is still audible now.

Finn sits down, right there on the weatherworn dock, dangles his feet over the side, and pats the space next to him.

He places his hands in his lap and looks at me expectantly. "Well then let's get acquainted with her."

I sit down next to him, close enough we're nearly touching, unsure of what he means.

"What do you like to do for fun?" he asks.

I look at him, laughing. "What?"

He stares back. I want to touch him so badly, or maybe I just want him to want to touch me. We've never been alone together for so long in real life before. He's so much more vivid here than in the dream space. He's solid and alive.

His voice goes quieter. "It's a simple question."

I blink a few times, an attempt to come back to myself. I have a conversation to focus on; I can't lose myself in staring at the veins of his hands. "It's just, I don't have much time."

He raises a finger, correcting me. "Ah, but I didn't ask you how much time you have for fun. I asked what you like to do for fun."

I laugh. "Fair enough. Embroider and read . . . and sleep."

He's staring at me properly now. "What do you like to read?"

"In school I liked the Brontes. I admired their flair for the dramatic. Digging up your childhood sweetheart's bones because you miss them takes commitment."

At this he snickers. "Sounds like something I'll have to read."

"What about you? Do you have a favorite book?"

He shakes his curly head. "No, this is about you, not me. What's your favorite color?"

This answer comes more easily. "Lilac."

He drums his fingers against the dock. "Why?"

"It was the color of the only dress my mother ever sewed me. She made it for Easter when I was seven. I thought it was the prettiest thing I ever saw."

"Summer or winter?"

"Those two specific weeks each fall when the weather is cool enough you don't sweat, but not so cool you need a coat."

"Diamonds or rubies?"

I pause to think. "Garnet."

"That's against the rules." He grins.

"I wasn't aware there were rules to what I'm allowed to like." I nudge his shoulder with mine. I'd like to keep touching him, but I pull away.

He chews on his lip, pausing before his next question. "One place in New York you'd really like to see?"

"I've always wanted to buy a dress at a department store on Fifth Avenue." I can picture a store all lit up, with lush cream carpets. I'd walk in wearing a wide-brimmed hat festooned with feathers, and no one would think I didn't belong.

His hand inches closer to mine but doesn't close the gap. "One place in the world you'd really like to see?"

This one is harder. I rack my brain, and sigh. "I've never imagined a life in which I'd ever leave New York."

Finally, Finn leans over and rests his head on my shoulder. I go perfectly still, terrified to do something that might make him move. I like it so much, the warmth of his skull right next to mine.

"I'd like to show you Ireland."

"I'd like that too."

All the drive back to Haxahaven the game continues, with us shouting over the din of the engine.

"Favorite flower?"

"Hydrangeas."

"Best thing you've ever eaten?"

"The sticky buns at Haxahaven."

"The worst?"

"William once tricked me into eating a spoonful of congealed gravy. It was even worse than you're imagining."

Finn laughs and slaps a hand on the steering wheel. "Classic."

He pauses, opens his mouth, and closes it. "Worst fear?" he asks after a moment.

My stomach sinks. I wish I had an easy answer, like spiders or heights. Even being afraid of never finding William's killer would be an easier answer than the truth. I could lie, but I don't want to lie to Finn. He wouldn't lie to me.

"Never having a family again," I finally say.

The silence between us is stretched thin.

The car slows as we approach the oak-lined lane leading up to Haxahaven. "You'll have a family again, I promise."

"What about you? What's your worst fear?"

He thinks for a moment before saying, "Being nothing, being forgotten. Living in a basement working for men like Boss Olan forever."

"Never doing anything to make the world a better place," I say under my breath.

"Yes, exactly."

Finn parks outside the gate and walks with me across the expanse of the Haxahaven lawn. It's properly cold now, and my still-damp wool skirt isn't helping matters. I should be shivering, but Finn so close to me has set off what feels like a full-body blush.

"Can I ask you a question?" It's been weighing on me all night. "Why do you work for the Sons? After what happened in the basement of the Commodore Club, I don't understand why you or my brother would want to be members of something so . . . ugly."

"In the Sons' defense, you caught them on a particularly ugly night. The *Cath Draíochta* is an old tradition meant to awaken magic in some of the younger members. It rarely works, so in the modern age it's become more of an annual party. Nothing worse than anything you'd see in any other gentleman's club in the city. No one's died for at least twenty-five years."

"You're defending them?" I pick up my steps. Finn quickens his pace to match mine.

"No, no! The Sons can be brutish, but they also meet immigrant ships at the docks to pass out food and information about jobs. They welcome in men of all kinds, and work to give them access to a better life. They're too obsessed with tradition and politics, but their intentions are mostly good. I'd run things differently in a million ways, but they aren't evil."

His response paints a different picture of the Sons from the one I first imagined. It's easier to imagine William belonging to an organization like that. It's certainly more than the witches do. "How would you run things differently?" I raise my brows.

"Let in women, for one. Any who wish to join, not just you. Boss thinks he's doing you some kind of favor. He's too thickheaded to see you'd be doing him one. You're better than every last one of those lads. I hope one day you'll come prove it to them."

"Don't hold your breath."

Finn casts a sidelong glance at me and smiles. "I'm used to believing in impossible things, Frances. Remember, I once dreamed of you."

As we near the back door he stops. "What you said earlier about not knowing who you are . . . ," he murmurs. "You might not see it, but I do. You're fierce and kind. You're loyal and brave. You love deeply, and that terrifies you. And you have no idea how beautiful you look when you're casting."

My breath catches in my throat. I close my eyes for a fraction of a second, committing the words to memory. I never want to forget how this swell in my chest feels. When I flicker my eyes open, Finn is standing close to me, an intense look of longing on his beautiful face. His curls fall across his furrowed brow. His chest rises and falls too fast for how still we're standing. He leans forward a fraction of an inch.

"Frances." He says my name like a prayer, a sacred thing just for him.

I can't stop myself—I lean forward too. *I'm glad you found me,* I want to say, but I can't bear to shatter this moment with words.

He's so close, I can feel the heat of his breath.

Suddenly a flash of light makes me jump, awakens me from my trance. The kitchen door is open, spilling candlelight out onto the lawn.

"Frances honey, is that you?" Florence whispers from where she stands silhouetted against the doorframe.

I close my eyes, sigh. If only she'd opened the door two minutes later. "Yes, Florence, it's me."

Finn steps back and presses his lips together, then huffs out a laugh. "The coven calls." His voice is low. He walks me to the door and leaves me with a simple "Good night, Frances" and a brush of his fingers on my waist so light, it might be accidental.

"Ma'am." He nods to Florence. She stares him down as she shuts the door.

Alone in the kitchen now, she hands me a steaming cup of tea. "Be careful with that boy."

"There's nothing to worry about with him."

"There's always something to worry about with boys who look like that."

We're silent for a long moment. I sit down at the table. She stays standing, looking down at me with maternal concern.

"Why are you helping us?" I ask her.

"If I could stop you, I would, but I remember what it's like to be young. And if I can't help you make better decisions, I'll do my best to reduce the damage of the bad ones."

"How do you know this is a bad decision?" It comes out more defiant than I mean it to.

She shakes her head like there's so much I don't understand. "Just a feeling."

Lena is waiting up for me in our room. "You're later than you said you'd be," she whispers.

"I'm sorry."

"I was worried."

I sigh and sink down onto the bed. The drive and the Witching Waves and Finn's mouth so close to mine have left me rattled.

"Ruby threatened to tell. Maxine had to give her a necklace to buy her silence."

"Well I can't pay her back for that, if that's what she wants."

"You know that wasn't what I meant." Lena rolls over to face away from me.

"No, no. I'm sorry. I know it wasn't."

There's a long stretch of silence; then Lena whispers again. "Did you find anything else? Was it the mirror for the spell?"

A wave of embarrassment hits me square in the chest. I put my friends in danger tonight because I believed I was doing something worthwhile. Instead I ate spun sugar on a boardwalk and careened down a waterslide, but still I can't bring myself to regret it.

"No," I whisper. "It didn't pan out."

"You'll have better luck next time."

"I hope so."

The room is so still, I think Lena must have drifted off to sleep, but her voice cuts through the darkness once more.

"Frances?" she whispers.

"Yes, Lena?"

"Are you being careful?"

"Of course," I lie.

"All right."

"Why do you ask?" I whisper.

She sighs, then rolls over again. "I suppose . . . they teach the clairvoyants to suppress their visions, so it could just be that, but . . ." A soft tapping of rain starts at the window. "But I don't see your future anymore."

"My future?" The fizzy warmth I felt just minutes ago is replaced with dread.

"I don't usually see much. I used to see glimpses of us at dinner a few weeks from now, or us playing cards or talking in Maxine's room. Nothing remarkable. But lately, there's been nothing. Like . . . a blank space where you used to be."

I pull my quilt up to my chin to combat the chill that rolls through me. "Nothing at all?"

"Nothing at all," she confirms. "It probably doesn't mean anything. I just thought I'd mention it."

I pause, listening to the rain. "Are you telling me you've been cheating at cards this whole time?" I joke to break the tension, to help push down the fear climbing up my spine. For a second I secretly wish I was back at Luna Park, where flying felt like freedom.

Lena huffs a laugh. "I don't need magic to beat you. You're a rotten card player."

"Thank you for telling me," I whisper into my pillow.

Her voice is strained. "Please be careful."

I cling to her words like a life preserver. It's probably nothing.

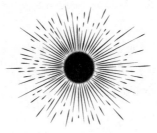

CHAPTER TWENTY

Mid-November marks the final death of orange fall leaves, and heralds the arrival of rain that freezes into ice on the lawn.

If I were a month, I think I'd be November, sad and cold and unremarkable, lacking the commitment required of being a fierce thing like January, like Maxine. Lena would be April, sunshine and rain, quiet and strong.

A few days after my jaunt to Coney Island, Maxine meets me after History class and asks me to follow her to the courtyard off the dining room.

The sky is gray and misty, but not cool enough to merit the wool Haxahaven cape, so I unbutton it and drape it over a stone bench.

"This weather is rather melancholy," I say.

"It seems fitting," she answers. "I hope you're ready to stop moping. I'm calling in my favor."

Maxine knows all about my night out with Finn. She wasn't as mad as I thought she'd be when I returned empty-handed, with nothing to report of new spells or bodies in the bay. I haven't yet had the heart to tell her about my future disappearing from Lena's visions. She'd either laugh it off or take it seriously, and I don't know which would be worse, so it remains Lena's and my secret.

"All right, spit it out."

"I want to practice what you did at the Commodore Club."

I'm taken aback. "I expected something like doing your laundry for a week."

"I'm offended you think I'm that boring."

"You want me to launch a bottle of whiskey at you?" I try to brush her off; it's easier than telling her I'm scared to try.

"No, stupid. I want you to try to manipulate my body."

My eyes snap to hers. "I'd rather do your laundry." To try to control Maxine is both intimate and invasive, in a way that makes me feel slimy, and like a bad friend. But more than that, I fear the way I still crave the exhilaration of the power. Using it feels like walking on the edge of a knife. One wrong move and I might slip and become someone I no longer recognize.

Before I can explain why it's a bad idea, Maxine mutters a word under her breath, and a tree branch comes flying at my head. I call the power and take control of the branch, but before it hits the ground, another is flying at me, then another, then another. She's stripping a young birch tree bare, hurling twigs and branches at me. I cannot stop them all—they scrape my exposed upper arms, and one even whips me across the face. I feel shock at first, then numb disbelief that she's doing this. Then comes the hot poker of anger.

"Stop!" I yell at her. I shield my face with my forearms, giving up on any attempt to use the magic to stop them.

"You can't stop the tree!" Maxine yells, full of glee. "You have to stop me!"

If she means this to be another sisterly bonding activity, she's failing. I'm not having any fun. "Christ, Maxine!" I wail. "This isn't funny!"

"I'm not trying to be funny," she taunts. She enchants the gravel next, and it comes at me, hitting my ankles one after another. Each pebble leaves a stinging welt in its wake.

"Stop!" I sweep my arm in an arc above my head. The sapling springs upright and stops moving all at once. I'm enraged at her outburst. She's like a child, throwing a fit because I won't play her stupid game. "Is this because you're jealous?"

She looks at me with disgust. "It's because I'm bored! If I had the power you have, I'd practice every single day. I wouldn't waste it moping."

Maxine doesn't know the hours I've spent in the library, or all the time I've spent alone in my room trying to manipulate hairpins. She also doesn't know about Boss Olan's offer. I'm so mad, I think about accepting it, leaving just to spite her.

"It's not my fault you're dissatisfied here," I snap.

Maxine scoffs. "We all bend over backward trying to help you, but the minute I ask you for a single thing, it's the end of the world. You act like you're the only person who has ever felt an emotion."

Her words sting. "You can't ask me to do this."

The fury in her eyes dims, her face falls, and all the power and determination leaches out of her. It's as if she's a star collapsing in on itself. She sinks down on the bench; her shoulders crumble inward. "It's not fair."

My anger retreats as quickly as it came. Her usually foxlike face is soft and flushed, like she might cry. I sit down on the bench next to her and put my arm around her bony shoulders. "I know."

"What makes you so special?" She looks at the ground as she says it. A single fat tear hits the stone bench.

"I don't know," I answer honestly. I wish I did.

If I could give the power inside me to Maxine, I don't know if I would. But I know how much it hurts to want more than what you have.

The interaction leaves a pit in my stomach that lasts until after dinner. If I am "gifted" with this power when others are not, what do I have to show for it? What have I really done? I'm wasting the gift I have when others like Maxine would do anything to possess it. And maybe Maxine would do more. Be better.

I peel off to my room as soon as the dishes are magically cleared from the table. I know who I need to see.

I fall into the dream space with all the grace of a Model T hurtling down a gravel road.

In this dream I'm in the basement of the Commodore Club. The torches on the wall flicker, and the puddle of crimson blood in the middle of the floor is still wet. Crystal glasses sit lined up on the bar, waiting to be smashed.

I walk to the bar and run my finger along the rim of one of the highball glasses. Suddenly it's filled with blood too. The room smells of it.

"Hiya, Frances." The sight of Finn's unruly hair and sharp cheekbones is a relief.

"Hi, Finn." My mouth forms a smile around his name. "How did you know I'd be here?"

"A hunch. I'm beginning to think all this time we're spending inside each other's heads is . . ." He doesn't finish the sentence. Is he thinking of the last moment we saw each other too? Has he too lost sleep, staring up at the ceiling in the dark thinking of the brush of his fingers at my waist?

I'm not sure what to say next. I wanted desperately to talk to him, but I don't know how to verbalize the slippery mass of bad feelings sitting heaving in my chest.

"Are you all right?" he asks.

"I'm fine."

"There's something you want. I can see it in your eyes," he teases.

It's been two weeks since the Commodore Club, a week since Coney Island, and I'm sick of waiting to make another move. "I want to find the scrying mirror for the Resurrection."

Finn raises his eyebrows. On my second day here, Maxine told me she'd once heard there was a magical black market in the city. If anyone knows more, it has to be Finn. I'm angry at myself for not thinking of this market and the possibility of the mirror being there sooner. "Do you know anything about a magical market in the city?"

Maybe I'm being delusional, maybe I'm being selfish, but I hope including Maxine in an adventure to the city will help her. I can't give her my powers, but we can continue to discover more of the magical world together. Two birds. One stone.

Finn chews on his lower lip for a moment. "It's on the Upper West Side. I've never been."

A thrill zips through me. "But it does exist?" I marvel at the idea that witches live dispersed through the city, enough of them to have a market, to have a whole world right under the noses of the non-magical.

"Yes, it's a place to trade in spells, magical objects, general mystical things. Boss and Vykotsky control most of the magical folk in the city, but there are enough hedge witches making a go of it on their own to merit a meeting place."

Excitement courses through me as I picture the market. "How soon can we go? Once we have the mirror, we only need the graveyard dust and something that belonged to William."

I still don't have a plan for that last one. My mother and I left our apartment quickly; William's belongings ended up on the curb or repossessed by the tenement board to settle our debts. I think one of our downstairs neighbors ended up with a few of his shirts; Finn and I could break in, try our luck. Or I could return to our old school and find a library book with his name in it, perhaps.

Finn interrupts my train of thought. "It's a market for witches—they don't allow Sons in. They'll spot me from a mile away. But I have a contact: ask for Miss Soraya when you get there."

"Get where?"

"It's in the basement of the natural history museum. The market is held on every full moon."

And with that, he is gone.

* * *

Despite our fight yesterday, Maxine doesn't flinch when I sit down next to her in the library.

"I have a present for you," I say.

She raises her eyebrows. "Oh?"

I'm eager to put everything from earlier behind us. "We're going on an adventure. The magical market you've heard about is real, and we're going to go."

She doesn't take much convincing. We take to the stacks. In the astrology section Maxine finds a hefty tome that tells us the next full moon is this Tuesday.

I trace my finger over the tiny ink illustration of the moon. "That's lucky."

"More than lucky," Maxine replies. "Helen will be gone this week for a family funeral upstate. I'll tell Vykotsky I've felt a new pupil and need the ambulance. You and Lena can come along."

"This feels too easy."

"Perhaps that means it's right," Maxine replies with a shrug.

"Surely they'll notice when we don't return with a new student," I say.

"I'll tell them I was wrong."

And so on Tuesday night, Lena and I meet Maxine in the back building where the ambulance is stored and crawl into the front bench seat, the three of us packed together like sardines.

"Tell me again where you learned to drive?" Lena asks, a nervous edge to her voice.

Maxine wiggles her eyebrows. "Helen taught me two years ago, and I've only crashed once."

Lena turns to Maxine, a horrified look on her face. "Once?"

"That man's leg healed fine, I assume."

With a turn of the key and a crank of the lever, the ambulance roars to life, drowning out our protests.

The dark drive from Queens to Manhattan doesn't take long, though crossing over the churning dark of the East River still makes my stomach turn.

These journeys into the city are beginning to feel routine. With Maxine and Lena beside me, I feel more at home than ever.

We pull up to the imposing American Museum of Natural History, and Maxine throws the ambulance into park on the curb.

The brownstone building stretches along most of West Seventy-Seventh Street. The sun has set, and electric streetlamps have the museum lit up like a Gothic castle. I half expect Lord Byron to greet us at the door.

"It's even creepier knowing it's full of dead things," Lena says.

If there is a market inside, there is no sign of it from here. The street is quiet. The windows of the museum are dark. We see no figures moving inside or out. The night is cold and clear. I shiver under my cape.

"How confident are we that Finn knew what he was talking about?" Maxine asks.

"He said the market isn't open to Sons," I say. "Maybe he was given bad information."

Maxine stomps her foot, either in frustration or to keep moving for warmth. "Well, we came all this way."

Together the three of us climb the marble steps to the main entrance. Lena tugs on the brass handle of the double doors. They rattle uselessly, locked.

"Perhaps there's another entrance," I offer.

"Or perhaps it's a test," Lena replies, peering down at the lock.

She extends her hands, whispers, *"Briseadh,"* and the door unlocks with a clink.

Maxine and I both raise our brows. "Well done," Maxine says.

Inside the museum is freezing and near pitch dark. The light from the street doesn't filter in well. It's all long shadows and black hallways. The checkered black-and-white floors look recently waxed. They stretch endlessly, branching off into exhibit halls. Above us, the ceiling is easily three times as high as the Haxahaven entryway. It is so quiet, even our breathing echoes. The girl I was just a month ago would have been terrified, but I set my shoulders square with the confidence there is nothing in this building more terrifying than the three of us.

"Well, Frances, what do we do now?" Maxine whispers.

It's a fair question. One I don't have the answer to. I look along the four dark halls extending from the atrium; none have any sign of life, as quiet as the dead animals they house.

The clicking sounds of feet on the marble floor make the three of us go still all at once. Lena has my hand in a vise. Maxine clutches my shoulder.

And then, from one of the many branching halls, appears a woman.

She's wearing a long black dress. Her dark hair is pinned back in a bun serious enough to match the look in her eyes. She's middle-aged, perhaps midforties.

"How'd you get out?" she asks us by way of greeting. The crystal necklaces she wears clack together with each step she takes.

"Does it matter?" Maxine stands up tall, no sign of the fear that had her clinging to me moments ago. "Regardless, we can't stay long."

"Finn said you were smart." The woman's face softens a bit. "I'm Miss Soraya. I suppose you'd better follow me."

Miss Soraya takes us down a nondescript staircase, then through a dim catalog room filled to the brim with shelves of dead birds. It stretches on for what must be the better part of a city block. Some of them are in jars that glow a little green in the low light. Others are laid out gently, their tiny dead feet wrapped in twine. This whole place gives me the creeps.

Miss Soraya stops at a dark wood shelf labeled RARE BIRDS OF NORTH AMERICA.

She smiles, but the corners of her mouth go out instead of up, so it isn't exactly reassuring. With a gloved hand, she feels along the shelf until she finds a seam. She pushes, and the wall swings back, revealing a secret door.

From somewhere beyond the door, comes the gentle rumble of voices, footsteps.

Anticipation tingles in my fingertips. I've gotten good at stepping into the unknown.

I follow her. Maxine and Lena, holding hands, are close behind.

The room we step into takes my breath away.

It is as big as a dance hall, but windowless. The floors and walls are gleaming tile, in a green so dark, it's almost black. Above us hang brass chandeliers, with cutouts in the shape of stars. In the center of the room is a white marble statue of Joan of Arc being burned at the stake.

Along the walls are stalls staffed by women, overflowing with objects that look more like a sparkly trash heap than goods for sale.

Piles of crystals, twisted-up pieces of metal, herbs, dripping candles, sculptures of hands, and stacks of dusty books.

About a dozen women of all kinds mill about, haggling, buying up magical supplies like they would meat at the market. Some remind me of my previous clients, dressed in well-tailored silks with pearls dripping off their necks, their sweeping hats adorned with flowers and feathers. Others are in factory clothes. One is in a black-and-white maid's uniform. They're tall and short, of all races and ages. Some keep to themselves. Some are gathered in small groups, chatting like old friends.

The smell of incense is so powerful, it makes my eyes water.

It's thrilling to see a place so alive with magic. Free of the sterility of Mrs. Vykotsky's school or the brutality of Boss Olan's club. Perhaps there is another option, a place I could belong.

Miss Soraya waves a wrinkled hand. "Welcome to the Bizarre Bazaar, ladies. On the right you'll find spell supplies. On the left you'll find magical objects. In the back you'll find whatever Yasmine Hawkins has scrounged up this week. Best of luck with whatever you Haxahaven girls get up to these days."

The sapphire necklace in the pocket of Maxine's overcoat jingles as we walk over to the first table. I'm not sure where to start, but I follow Maxine's confident steps. It's her job to cart girls off to a fake tuberculosis sanitarium—I suppose asking a stranger at a magical black market for a mirror can't be more difficult than that.

In awed silence Maxine, Lena, and I flit between tables. One is covered with tall tapers in all the shades of the rainbow. Another sells divination cards. At the table next to me, a middle-aged woman presses a hag stone into Lena's hands. She passes me one too. It's smooth like a river rock, but with an oblong hole through the center.

"I can't pay you," I reply, confused.

She shakes her head. "You need it more than I do."

I don't like the disquieting way she looks at us, like she knows something about us we don't.

Her expression is reflected on many women's faces in the market, some combination of pity and discomfort. I wonder how many of them once wore this same Haxahaven cape.

I push past my mild sense of unease. I could spend hours here, thumbing over copper coins, amulets, towers of crystal, tiny iron cauldrons—the objects seem endless.

Lena, Maxine, and I converge at a stall in the back corner of the market. The woman sitting behind the table has white hair down to her waist. She's selling candles etched with runes.

"Vykotsky know you're here?" She looks us up and down, her mouth turned in a frown.

"Of course." Maxine smiles sweetly.

"Oh the young, you all think you're such good liars. What are you looking for? Trouble? You look like you're looking for trouble."

"We're looking for a scrying mirror," I reply.

"Ah, so you are looking for trouble." She clucks. "Can't help you, I'm afraid."

Maxine pulls the necklace from her pocket. "Does this change your mind?"

The woman sighs heavily. "Not everything can be bought with money, dear."

"What can it be bought with?" I ask. There's nothing I wouldn't give.

"From the three of you? Nothing. It's for your own good."

"That seems to be an excuse only ever given to women," Maxine sneers.

The woman with the long white hair almost smiles. "Smart and looking for trouble. The three of you are dangerous indeed. I cannot help you. But perhaps Therese Theresi has less sense than I do."

"Where is she?" Lena asks.

"Three o'clock." She gestures with her head.

I open my mouth to say thank you, but before I can, Lena's hand pulls me away, and we slink off in the direction of someone who can, hopefully, help us.

Therese Theresi has a table covered in evil-eye charms; their blue irises gaze up at me. They match Therese's eyes, an unsettling shade of turquoise set against weathered skin. Next to her till there is a sign in black ink, but I don't read Greek, so I don't know what it says.

"We're looking for a mirror," Maxine says by way of greeting.

She continues her work thumbing through a deck of gold-edged cards, not looking up at us. "What kind of mirror, child?"

"A scrying mirror. Something old. Something that works."

"Working is subjective. It's all about intention. A bowl of grape juice works with the right intention."

Maxine puts her hands on her hips. "I don't want a bowl of grape juice—I want a scrying mirror."

Therese scrunches up her already extraordinarily wrinkled face, finally looking up at us. "Why?"

Maxine replies, "That's none of your business." At the same time Lena replies, "Normal things."

"What can you pay?" Therese asks in a thick, Greek accent.

"This." Maxine dangles the necklace from her elegant fingers.

Therese clicks her tongue, unimpressed. "I don't want your jewels." My heart sinks. If she won't take the necklace, we don't have anything else.

"Do you have the mirror or not?" Maxine asks. She taps the toe of her boot impatiently against the marble floors.

Therese looks at her through narrowed eyes, assessing and unnerving. "I have the mirror."

"What's the price?" I ask. I'm afraid to hear her answer.

She considers us, one by one. The way she studies me makes me want to crawl out of my own skin. What does she see underneath my trembling desperation?

"I need to know you're serious." She purses her lips. "I need to know you're committed to the kind of sisterhood this magic requires. Before you scry, you need an anchor. Can you be each other's anchors?"

I don't know what she means by anchor, but the seriousness of her tone frightens me. I felt so confident walking in, but seeing all of these objects, these women, makes me realize just how little I still understand about magic.

"Yes, yes, Lena and Frances are my anchors," Maxine sighs. She doesn't share my fear. "I adore them very much. We'll take the mirror now."

Therese shakes her head, her earrings jangle a tuneless song. "Not so fast, child," she scolds. "Tell me about your sisters."

"What about them?" Maxine replies, like she finds the question ridiculous.

"Tell me how they got their magic."

I don't know what I was expecting, but it wasn't this.

"The same way we all did." The tapping of her foot is getting louder, faster too. "Their souls are both a gift and a curse. We get it. Spare me the lecture, I beg you."

"No." Therese shakes her head. "Tell me about the day it happened."

"Frances killed a man. Lena might have too."

"I didn't." Lena speaks up from behind me.

"See?" Therese shakes her head again. "You don't know each other at all. How can there be trust without knowledge?"

"We know other things," Maxine says. "More important things."

"Nothing is more important than power," Therese retorts, and turns to me. "Tell your sisters how it happened."

I sigh. Maxine already knows about Mr. Hues, and Lena might as well. "My boss attacked me after hours in the shop where I worked. My scissors flew across the room and stabbed him. He died at my feet. Maxine picked me up the following morning." It's a little cathartic, telling the story like this to people who understand.

"And you?" Therese gestures to Lena, unfazed by the murder I described.

Lena takes a big, deep breath and closes her eyes. Her jaw clenches, and I can feel the hesitation brewing within her, the pain of recounting whatever happened. I almost think she's not going to say a word. Keep the truth buried within her forever until she says, cool and steady, "I suppose there's no point in keeping it a secret." Lena's eyes shift quickly to mine and Maxine's before meeting the witch's across from us. "I was once a student at a place called the Thomas School. We were beaten and screamed at. We were stripped of our names and our clothing. We weren't allowed to write our parents. In the winters, when students would die, but the ground was too frozen to dig graves, they'd stack the bodies in the attic. I had to share a cot with another girl, and at night she would cry so violently, she'd be sick. I was fifteen when they locked me in a shed for mouthing off to a teacher." Lena's voice hitches, but only slightly. "The nuns said to pray the devil out of me. But I didn't see the devil. I saw myself at Haxahaven. Maxine and Helen arrived three days later to test every pupil of the Thomas Indian School for tuberculosis. They only took me. Now"—she lifts her chin up toward Therese—"are you quite satisfied?"

Maxine's eyes are big and teary. She reaches out and grabs Lena's hand. They're sharing a memory I'll never understand.

A question escapes my lips: "Why? Why would they put you in a place like that?"

She shakes her head sadly. "How do you kill an entire people? You take away their children; you take away their language and their stories and their culture. But I am Onondaga. That's something they couldn't kill."

I take her other hand in mine. I thought coming here would help Maxine get out of her rut, but instead I've made Lena dig up painful things for my own purposes. She's reluctant to let us in emotionally, and now I understand why.

Therese smiles, but her eyes are glistening a little too. "See, you don't know each other much at all."

"I know I love them, doesn't that matter?" Maxine asks.

I didn't know she loved us.

"Can you love someone if you don't let them know you?" Therese replies. "Tell them your story."

"No."

Lena and I turn to Maxine at the same time.

"Why dwell on the past?" Maxine shakes her hand out of Lena's and purses her lips.

"You want a sorrowful tale from me? You won't get it," she snaps, and marches away from the table, cape fluttering behind her.

Lena and I run after her. The women at their booths around the market have quieted. Like a murder of crows, their eyes follow us.

Maxine darts across the market to a stand overflowing with crystals. She dumps her necklace on the table and begins to fill a velvet pouch with onyx, amber, and smoky quartz almost the exact shade of her eyes. She grabs a red candle next, then a black one. The woman at the stall watches her in bemused silence and tucks the sapphire necklace into the pocket of her overcoat.

"Do you have any spell books?" Maxine asks the woman. "I'm awfully bored. The more forbidden the better."

The woman laughs. "Does Ana Vykotsky know what a trouble-maker she has in you? No, dear, no books, but help yourself to what you can see."

Maxine rolls her eyes but grabs a bundle of dried lavender for good measure.

"Stop, Maxine. Good lord, what is wrong with you?" I run up behind her and place a hand on her shoulder. She shrugs me off immediately. I've never seen her so rattled.

Maxine turns to us. "We don't need her. The nosy old bat."

"We do," I say. "She has the mirror."

"You said we were coming here for a bit of fun. I'm having fun now." Her grin is exaggerated, awful and false.

Lena and I shared our stories; I'm at a loss for why Maxine won't do the same. It feels like a betrayal, sharp and baffling. But I know I can't force Maxine to do anything she doesn't want to do. I'll sneak out and come here again, or I'll use a bowl of grape juice and pray for the best. I want to see William and to stop the other murders more than anything, but I know when I've lost a battle.

When Maxine is thoroughly laden down with magical objects, we make our way to leave. The market isn't crowded, but the quiet voices of a few dozen women have the atrium buzzing like a beehive.

It's loud enough that I don't hear Therese until she's right behind us, tiny, hunched, and holding the mirror in her hands. She's breathing heavily, like she just ran the length of the room to reach us. She barely comes up to my chest, but her sudden appearance makes me jump.

"If you want it, it's yours. Go in peace." She doesn't acknowledge Maxine or me. It takes me a minute to realize what's happening. She presses the mirror into Lena's chest. Lena looks as baffled as I feel, holding it slightly away from her body like she's scared of it.

"I can't pay you," Lena replies.

"I don't ask for payment. Just come see me again, child."

Lena tilts her head. "Why?"

The old woman reaches up and pats her cheek. "I like the look of you. Perhaps we knew each other in another life."

"Thank you," I say.

The scowl that crosses her face makes me regret saying anything. "I'm not giving it to you. Better run along home before you're punished with something worse than detention."

Lena clutches the mirror against her chest all the way to the ambulance. It's awkward and silent between the three of us nearly the whole way home.

The drive feels long, but no one steps out of the ambulance upon arriving in the driveway. The three of us sit in the pitch dark, listening to the groaning of the engine as it winds down.

The evening is dark and cold. What few leaves remain are turned blue by the light of the moon. No noises come from the park over the wall. The edge of the mirror glints golden against the black of Lena's cape.

Finally Lena speaks. "I have one request." I raise my eyebrows, a useless expression in the dark. "Frances, the mirror is yours, but I'd like something in return."

"Anything."

"I want to start including the other girls in all this. It feels selfish to keep the lessons with Finn all to ourselves. It doesn't seem fair we're the only ones who should know more about"—she looks down at the mirror—"about this, about everything."

She's right, as Lena usually is. "You've got a deal."

Maxine marches past us straight through the double doors and right up the stairs, silent and steely. She never tells us her story.

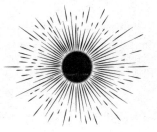

CHAPTER TWENTY-ONE

Gossip burns through the halls of Haxahaven like a spark on a fuse. It isn't difficult to find girls as hungry for more magic as we are.

Finn agrees to Lena's request as readily as I do. Sitting in the dream meadow, I ask him to teach more of us.

"I'm sorry I didn't think of it myself," he says. "Of course, I'll teach whoever wishes to learn."

I get the impression he wants to put the Commodore Club behind us, to return to the simplicity of our lessons in the woods. I'm excited to resume our lessons as well. I'm looking forward to seeing him because I love to learn, and not at all because of the way his hair curls under his ears or the way my name rolls off his lips.

It takes Maxine less than half a day to get over whatever it is she needs to get over. By lunch the next day she's chatting next to us, talking animatedly with the fork in her hand like nothing was ever wrong at all.

She's delighted by the new plan including the others in our lessons. "Maria is going to love this." She smiles between bites of galette.

Lena and I don't push her.

When night comes, we throw our black capes over our nightdresses and scurry through Haxahaven's eerie halls.

I swear sometimes I can hear something scratching at the walls when I can't sleep, and tonight, as I climb down the stairs with Lena by my side, my unease is the same. I tamp it down, tell myself I'm not a coward.

Everyone in our cohort except Ruby and Rebecca are waiting for us at the kitchen doors, as silent as ghosts.

The kitchen is empty, no Florence or Ann. I wonder if Maxine has their permission or if she just believes she can count on them not to tell on us if we get caught.

"Where's Rebecca?" I whisper to no one in particular.

"It's after sundown on Friday. She doesn't practice magic on the Sabbath," Cora whispers back.

It's a better reason than Ruby gave, which was that she wasn't interested in belonging to a club she wasn't the president of.

In single file, just like we were going to class after breakfast, we walk out of Haxahaven, through the gate, and into Forest Park.

In silence, we crunch down the dirt path to the forest. No whooping hollers like the Blockula, not even a nervous laugh or two. Whatever unease ripples through the air tonight, the other girls feel too.

The night sighs as we step off the path and into the dark cover of trees. We shuffle through the underbrush a few dozen feet before the clearing appears.

"Why aren't we at the Blockula?" Mabel asks. A bitterly cold wind rips through the trees. We shuffle closer together for warmth.

"This is creepy," Sara agrees.

"Why did you bring us here, Maxine?" Maria piles on.

Maxine stops and sets her lantern on the wet leaves of the ground. "My sisters"—she greets us, committed as always to the bit—"tonight we're gathered to exercise our magic without apology. We give thanks to the woods for the gift it has given us."

"Allow me to translate Maxine's dramatics," I say. "A friend of my late brother's has been helping us in the woods after hours. The magic he knows is different from the magic at school. He's offered to help teach all of you, as well."

"Help us how?" Cora asks.

"Does it have to be here? I'm freezing," Alicia whines.

"You've already been training with him, and you waited until now to include us? " Cora snipes.

This isn't going at all how I planned; it's nothing like The Blockula.

Maxine sidles up to me and hisses through gritted teeth "Where is Finn?"

I tense my jaw to keep my teeth from chattering. "He said he'd be here—maybe we're just early."

"You know we can't be out for long." Her delicate hands curl into fists at her side.

"I know, Maxine," I whisper. The longer it takes for him to appear, the more anxious I get.

"It's *cold*. If we were a real coven, we'd have a bonfire," Sara whines. She tugs her cape around her. Cora clings to her from behind, huddling together to keep from shivering.

"Well, when you find a real coven that stupid, I'm sure they'd love to have you join them. You'll fit right in." Maxine smiles, viciously.

"Can we please do something, anything at all, I beg you." Maria speaks up, she's putting on a brave face, most of them are, but I can see my own anxiety reflected in their eyes.

"We can't wait for him forever," Maxine adds so quietly, only I can hear. I nod in worried agreement.

With a frustrated huff, she pulls *The Elemental* from her satchel and opens it to a page I recognize.

"Gather round, gather round," she calls to our classmates. They seem grateful for something to do other than shuffling around the underbrush freezing to death.

Illuminated in the lantern light is the spell we did during our first lesson with Finn, the one with the leaves and the flame that's supposed to show you the first initial of your true love.

There's a twinge of bitter frustration at the memory of the spell failing for me, but the shouts of exuberance from my classmates nearly make me forget.

Maxine demonstrates first, to a chorus of awed exclamations. She gathers the leaves from the ground, says the spell, and sets them alight. Just like last time, an *M* curls from the smoke, visible in the flickering firelight against the dark sky.

If I'm not mistaken, both May and Maria smile to themselves.

There are squeals of delight, and off my classmates set, bending down to gather handfuls of dried leaves for themselves.

It's extraordinary how quickly their moods change. It warms my

heart to see my friends happy, but it doesn't stop anxiety from gnaw-
ing at me. I can't help but worry about Finn. What if the person
who killed my brother and the other boys got to him? The thought
of Finn's lifeless body washed up on the beach pops into my head. I
blink, clearing the horrible image, and swallow down the bile in my
throat. *He's fine,* I tell myself. *He has to be fine.*

Maxine shepherds the girls into a single-file line, each clutching
their leaves, anticipation in their eyes. Cora goes first, an *A* spiraling
into the sky. Then Aurelia: her hands tremble as she lowers them to
the flame. She lets out a relieved sigh as an *L* appears. A smile bright
as day spreads across her face. I smile too at the sight of her joy. In
line the girls chat about their predictions. Alicia is sure hers will be
a *B* for Bernard, her childhood sweetheart. Sara hopes it's an *E* for
Edwin, a boy she knew when she worked at the factory.

I stand back and watch them, a feeling of contentment washing
over me, until Lena's hand is on mine. It's ice cold, and she's gripping
on to me like her life depends on it.

"We shouldn't be here. They know. They're coming." She's shaking.

My mouth goes dry. "Who is coming, Lena?"

The lantern in my hand shatters with a pop. Glass shards fly at
my legs, stinging as they pierce the fabric of my skirt to meet skin.
There is a moment of shock, then the pain sets in.

The flame jumps to the ground, where it sets a pile of dry leaves
alight in an instant. Maria jumps into action and stomps them out.
I'm too shocked, my ears too full of screaming to do much of anything.

The forest smells of smoke and mistakes.

"I'm sorry, I'm sorry, I'm sorry," Lena whimpers. She doesn't sound anything like herself. "I should have seen—I didn't see until now."

I push her long hair back and cup her face in my hands. "Didn't see what, Lena?" I try to remain calm for her, but I'm panicking too.

"How will we get back?" Cora whines.

"Shh," I hiss. I think I hear the sound of leaves rustling. Something in these woods is deeply wrong.

There is a flickering of light between the aspens. Relief washes through me.

"Finn!" I call. I say a silent prayer that this is all a misunderstanding, that Finn will burst through the trees, a grin on his face, and make this all right.

"Frances, wait—" Maxine hisses. But it's too late.

The footsteps grow closer; the lantern bobs toward us.

"Who's there?" Maxine calls.

Lantern in hand, Helen crosses into the clearing. "I'm disappointed in you, Maxine.

The ten of us stare at Helen with identical wide-eyed faces and the knowledge that we are ruined.

I really might vomit.

Maxine mutters a curse word under her breath. Whatever Maria says is in Spanish, but by her tone I assume it's a curse as well. Cora and Sara immediately burst into tears. Mabel wraps her arms around them and allows them to sob into her tiny shoulders. Lena and I react the same, standing as still as statues, as if we can rewind time by refusing to acknowledge the present.

Helen looks over all of us like a disappointed mother. It is with relief that I see she hasn't spotted *The Elemental*. Maxine's eyes too flit to her bag, where the book lies open, but partially hidden.

Helen walks to the perimeter of the clearing, but the ten of us stay put until she clicks her tongue and chirps, "Come along then, girls. Mrs. Vykotsky is waiting for you."

The mention of Mrs. Vykotsky sends true fear through me. I have a sinking feeling this punishment will be worse than kitchen duty.

The wounds on my legs are superficial, but they sting terribly against the cold night air.

We follow Helen's bobbing yellow lantern through the trees and back to school. The only sounds are the snapping of twigs and hitched breathing.

A sliver of light escapes from underneath Mrs. Vykotsky's office door. It cuts across the marble entryway like a knife.

Helen knocks twice, and Mrs. Vykotsky's icy voice replies, "Come in. All of you."

CHAPTER TWENTY-TWO

We shuffle in, eyes on the floor. Cora and Sara are still snif-fling a little. Maxine takes the sunken chair closest to Mrs. Vykotsky, and Maria sits next to her. Lena, Sara, Cora, Mabel, and the others I don't know well stand behind them.

Helen takes up her post by the door, as if any of us are foolish enough to try to run.

Lena reaches over to stop Sara's hand from shaking.

Blood trickles down my shins.

The headmistress is dressed exactly how she dresses in daylight, right down to her flawless pompadour and unwrinkled black dress. I wonder if she ever sleeps or if she's like a vampire, sitting forever in this chair waiting for pupils to scold.

She clicks her tongue as she casts a leveling gaze over us. "I am disappointed, but I cannot say I am surprised." She looks at Maxine, who recoils like she's waiting for a blow to land. "You, of all people, Miss DuPre, should know better."

Mrs. Vykotsky looks up at Lena next. "And you, Miss Jamison, this seems uncharacteristically foolish. You have so much to lose."

"How did you find us?" Maxine asks.

"There is nothing that goes on under this roof I don't know about. And you are hardly the first group of girls at Haxahaven to be curious about the . . . *darker* aspects of magic. But we couldn't let this go on any longer. The lanterns in the woods were becoming a fire hazard, and poor Helen was so sick of trekking through that awful park—and the gasoline you were using in the ambulance was simply wasteful. And of course, Frances complicates things."

The blood in my veins goes as cold as the blood running down my shins.

Mrs. Vykotsky turns her icy gaze on me. "You really must exercise better control of yourself, Frances."

I stare at her in stunned silence. I didn't anticipate being called upon like this. My classmates turn to look at me too, and I wish I was anywhere but here.

She continues, a smug look on her face. "There was once a witch who became rather notable for her ability to control the bodies of others. Her name was Gudrun the Sorceress, and her own coven burned her alive in 1066 when she was nineteen. Would you like that? Would you like to be burned alive?"

I assume her question is hypothetical, but the silence stretches on and on. My classmates' faces have turned to expressions of confusion and disgust. Finally I give her an answer. "No, ma'am."

"That's what I thought."

Beside me, Sara sucks in a noisy breath to keep her nose from running.

"Oh, will you stop your sniveling, Miss Kowalski?" Mrs. Vykotsky snaps. She fans her bony hands out across the papers scattered on her desk. "It is late and I am very tired, so let's take care of this quickly. Miss Rosales, the allowance the school pays your family both in the city and in Puerto Rico will be cut off permanently. Yours on the reservation, too, Miss Jamison."

"No, please!" Maria shouts. "They won't be able to eat; my sister will have to leave school!"

My heart cracks at the panic in her voice.

"Well perhaps you should have thought of Josephina before you broke the rules. Maybe she will join us here sooner than you think."

Maria's lip trembles, but she does not argue further.

Lena stands stock still, but the vials on the back shelf rattle. She scrunches her eyes closed, and they quiet.

I can do nothing but watch in horror as the truth dawns on me. When I first arrived, I thought the stipends for the families of working-class girls were the most generous thing I'd ever heard of. Now I recognize them for the tool of obedience they truly are. I've never before been grateful that I have nothing left to lose, no job, no family, nothing I care any particular amount about, other than William and my mother. It's perfectly, horrifyingly evil to control the students this way. I don't know if I've ever been more frightened of anything than I am of the unfeeling expression on Mrs. Vykotsky's face. What kind of person could destroy someone's life without blinking?

She glances up at Sara and Cora, who stand trembling like leaves beside me. Mabel holds her head high; she clenches her jaw hard.

"You too, girls," Mrs. Vykotsky says. "Your family's allowance is also being suspended. I have no interest in your tragic stories or your tears. Because this is your first offence, the allowance will be reinstated after three months, pending a flawless record."

Sara and Cora nod vigorously, tears still streaming down their rosy cheeks.

On and on she goes through all eight girls, ruining their families' lives with a self-satisfied smirk.

I keep my teeth clenched. The blood on my legs has dried, and it itches. I want nothing more than to scrub this horrible night off me.

After what feels like a long while, Mrs. Vykotsky leans back in her chair and presses her hands together as if in prayer as she examines Maxine. "Oh, Miss DuPre, you always are an interesting case."

Maxine's glare back is a direct challenge. "My family is based in Paris now, and you've never paid them a stipend," she snarls.

"Your driving privileges are revoked. As is the leniency I've afforded you until now. It's time to grow up. Another infraction and we'll take your solo room away as well. You can sleep on May's floor. Or is it Maria you've been spending so much time with? I never can keep up."

Both May's and Maria's eyes go wide at this. Maxine stares down at the floor. A single sniff escapes her. I've never before seen her look small.

"You need to learn you're not in charge here. It's time to be humbled," Mrs. Vykotsky chirps with a smirk.

I am next. A part of me is morbidly curious to find out what she thinks is important enough to me to punish me with.

"Ah, Miss Hallowell, you have been a fascinating pupil, so quiet in your classes, but not untalented. You don't yet understand that we are trying to help you."

She waits for me to respond, but I don't give her the satisfaction.

Mrs. Vykotsky glances at Helen, then back to me.

"Is the magic you're learning not enough for you? Are you not satisfied with having power most would sell their souls for? Are you truly that selfish, Miss Hallowell?"

"Not selfish, ma'am. Curious." Maybe I am selfish, but it isn't for wanting to learn magic.

"You want to see what this power of yours can do?" Mrs. Vykotsky sneers. "If you insist on learning a difficult lesson for your-self, I'm sure a teaching moment can be arranged."

I don't know what to make of her threat, but it sends ice sluicing in my veins.

"You sweet girls," she continues in a voice that's anything but sweet. "I remember what it was like to be young. But something you have to learn is that you don't always know best. Magic, like all urges, is to be controlled."

With sharp teeth digging into bottom lips and tear-streaked faces we nod.

"Very good." She claps her hands against the mahogany of her desk. "You girls should be off to bed. Miss Hallowell, we will have a chat tomorrow."

It makes me feel itchy all over to think of how closely we've been watched without our knowledge.

Maxine once warned me that at Haxahaven someone was always

listening. I was naive not to have taken her warning to heart. She was reckless to not have heeded her own advice.

Mrs. Vykotsky dismisses us, and no one says anything to the others as we climb the stairs to our rooms. It's quiet for a minute—the only sounds are our feet against the carpet and Sara's and Cora's incessant sniffling.

Things turn sour at the second-floor landing. Cora turns to me, Maxine, and Lena—her sadness becoming anger. "I hope you know that this is all your fault."

I open my mouth to respond but close it when I realize I have no response. She's right.

"I'm sorry." Lena's voice is strained, her eyes big and sad.

Maxine stomps into her room and slams the door. Maria follows her inside, and the sound of muffled shouting comes soon after.

Alicia shakes her head at me in disgust before marching off to her own room. May follows her, her narrow shoulders slumped.

I wish I could tell them I would do anything to take tonight back, but my regret fixes nothing. No amount of guilt in the world can turn back time.

In our room, Lena holds a candle while I pick the remaining slivers of glass from where they've embedded themselves in my legs. The only sound is the clinking of the shards against the porcelain bowl and Ruby's snoring.

My emotions are boiling over—rage, mixed with sadness, mixed with embarrassment. There's a deep sense of frustration, too, at getting so close to having everything I wanted—magical education, friends, justice for my brother—only to have it all ripped away. *Stupid. I've been so stupid.*

Lena plinks another shard of glass from my calf into the bowl. "Thank you," I whisper to her.

She doesn't look up, just continues her work. "I feel like it's my fault," she says.

I shake my head. "It's Mrs. Vykotsky's fault."

"I should have seen it coming."

I extend a hand and place it on her forearm. "You know as well as I do that's ridiculous."

The crease between her eyebrows disappears, but the sadness in her eyes remains, just another thing I can't fix.

I wash the dried blood away and slide into bed feeling raw all over.

I toss and turn for hours, and by the sound of Lena's ruffling sheets, she does too.

When sleep comes, it comes violently, like being thrown into an icy river with chains bound around my ankles.

Finn is waiting for me, standing in the woods around a raging bonfire. I'm so relieved to see him alive and in one piece, I burst into tears.

Confusion, then worry crosses his face. "Are you all right? Wait, of course you're not. That's a silly question."

I hiccup in a breath, "No—no, I'm fine, it's just—" I sob again despite my best attempt to swallow it down. "Where were you?"

He closes the distance between us and wraps me in a tight hug. A vague sense of surprise that he can touch me in this dream space is overtaken by the relief that floods through my body at his embrace.

"What happened?" he asks into my unbound hair.

"We went to meet you in the woods tonight. Me and all the others, but you weren't there," I sob.

He rubs my back in slow circles.

"I came as soon as I could, but by the time I arrived, all I found was broken glass and a burned-out patch of ground. What did they do?"

He just listens and nods until the story is done and the tears are finished.

"I'm so sorry, Fran." He sighs as if my story is weighing on him like a physical thing.

I laugh through the hiccuping sobs. "I hate when people call me Fran."

"Franny?"

"I hate that one too," I say into his chest.

He unwraps his arms, and I immediately miss the warmth of them. "Why were you late tonight?" I ask him. I pray there wasn't another body found.

He takes a seat on a log; a breeze that smells of dying roses rushes through the trees. "Someone threw a brick through the window of the drawing room with a severed finger attached." His tone is grave.

I blink in surprise and revulsion. "I'm sorry? A severed finger tied to a brick?"

He nods, looking a little pale. "One of the more disturbing things I've witnessed at the Commodore Club."

"Do you think it's related to the boys on Sheepshead Bay?" With Mrs. Vykotsky's eyes always on me, how will I ever be able to do the resurrection spell now? The thought of coming this far only to fail makes me nauseous.

Finn's soft voice breaks into my thoughts before more tears pool in my eyes. "I think it would be foolish to dismiss it."

I shudder. "What did the others say?"

"Boss had Higgins take it to our contact in the police commissioner's office. They said they'd look into it."

"Will they genuinely look into it?" I know better than to believe the police.

He pulls a hand through his hair, making his curls look even more disheveled than usual. "Who's to say?"

The breeze stops, giving way to grim stillness.

"I should have never told you about the finger through the window. Now you'll never come to train with us at the Commodore Club." The sentence has the cadence of a joke, but the edge in his voice tips his hand.

"You know I can't leave Haxahaven. But you should also know it takes more than a finger to scare me off."

"You still want to stay, even after tonight?" I hate the way he's looking at me, like I'm a fool.

"It isn't that I want to stay. It's that I have to. I don't know what Mrs. Vykotsky will do to my mother or my friends if I run off."

"Boss is desperate to have someone with your abilities join, and I think having you would be the grandest thing in the world, so what if I encouraged him to sweeten the deal? If you come join us, there's a good chance we'll be able to release your mother from the hospital. We have the political connections to make it happen."

It's the most tempting offer I've been given so far. I briefly savor the thought of me and my mother both back in Manhattan, her free of her real sanitarium, me free of my fake one. But I long ago learned that when things sound too good to be true, they usually are. Finn's intentions may be pure, but without a plan, his offer is empty.

"Perhaps," I say, noncommittal.

"All I ask is for the opportunity to try."

The way he looks at me makes me want to hide under my hair. I feel particularly raw tonight after the dressing-down by Mrs. Vykotsky and the crying jag in front of Finn.

I want him to take me into his arms again and tell me I'm special and good and tonight wasn't my fault.

I realize I haven't responded to him. We're staring at each other; his face is so earnest, I'm tempted to do anything he wants me to.

I wake up with a jolt, gasping for breath, the ghost of Finn's arms still around me.

Mrs. Vykotksy lets me stew for a few days, she's awful enough to release the anticipation of waiting for a punishment is torture in itself. Then, finally, one morning Helen comes to fetch me from the dining room, a false smile on her face. "Now, please, Frances," is all she says.

In her herb-choked office, Mrs. Vykotsky sits as stony as ever, but her eyes shine with the fury of a lightning storm.

I'm struck with a wave of fierce hatred, seeing her sitting there at her desk, smug and self-righteous.

"Sit," she commands as soon as I enter.

I do as I'm told.

"Good morning, Miss Hallowell. I do believe I've come up with a solution to the unfortunate tiff we seem to have found ourselves in," she chirps. "You want to do magic in the real world? You want to see what happens to girls who think they're invincible?"

"I don't think I'm invincible, ma'am." My voice is flat. I refuse to give her the satisfaction of getting a rise out of me.

She huffs out what might be a laugh. "You're seventeen. Of course you think you're invincible. I was young once, as difficult as that may be to believe."

I don't reply, and she takes it as an invitation to continue. "Next Saturday Governor Dix will be holding a fundraiser for Senate candidate James O'Gorman. You'll attend this fundraiser with Helen and have the city commissioner sign paperwork renewing Haxahaven as a licensed, state-sponsored hospital, another measure we use to keep us safe. The commissioner has other loyalties and has been resistant to our attempts to negotiate the renewal of our charter."

I was expecting worse than this. I should feel relief, but it only makes me more anxious. "I thought you were going to throw me to the wolves."

She purses her lips. "Perhaps I am.

"It's a lesson, Frances. This is how it began with your mother. The trips into the woods, the recklessness. I'm trying to teach you limits, give you as much freedom as I'm able, and save you from losing control like she did. This is for your own good; you'll see that in time. Every witch who ever burned was once a girl just like you, one who thought she could change the world."

I hate her for using my mother against me like this, for speaking about her like she knew her at all. I chew on the inside of my cheek until it bleeds.

She continues her lecture. "You might even enjoy the fundraiser. I've heard such great things about your power." It doesn't sound like a compliment from her. I think back to her warning about Gudrun the Sorceress.

"I'll do my best." She's setting me up for failure, almost certainly, but perhaps I'll surprise her, like I've continually surprised myself.

"Sometimes we get what we wish for, Miss Hallowell." She smiles like curdled milk. "Please shut the door on your way out."

In Practical Applications class, I'm so unnerved by my meeting with Mrs. Vykotsky, I pierce the pad of my thumb with a sewing needle. As I watch the blood seep into the fabric, I think that in this moment, it hurts to be alive.

Later I find Lena in the dining room, feet propped up, reading a book at the head of the table.

"How are you?" My voice echoes off the walls of the empty room. It feels too still without the rush of mealtime. Guilt eats away at me at the sight of her face. What's happened to her family, I can't help feel that I am mostly to blame. I won't be surprised if she never talks to me again. But she does.

"Rotten, you?"

"Mrs. Vykotsky is going to send me to a political fundraiser to manipulate a signature out of a commissioner. My punishment for the woods."

"Hmm" is Lena's only reply. I don't blame her—it's such a minor, stupid consequence compared to what happened to her and the others.

I carefully sit down next to her. "What's on your mind?"

She reaches into the pocket of her uniform pinafore and pulls out two diamond-stud earrings. "Maxine gave me these to send to my parents now that the stipend from the school is cut off."

"That was kind of her." I wish I had something, anything, to offer Lena. But as usual, I come up empty.

Lena frowns. "I suppose. But I'm terrified to send them. I'm afraid if my family tries to sell them, they'll be accused of theft."

"Oh. I hadn't thought of that."

"Maxine didn't either. It's something the two of you will never understand. You can traipse around New York, you can break school rules, sneak out, lie, and steal. But the stakes are different for me. The consequences are bigger."

My stomach sinks. "I'm so sorry, Lena, for getting you into all this. If I could take it all back, I would."

She shrugs. "I don't need to explain to you that I can no longer be involved in any of this."

I reach out and squeeze her hand like she's squeezed mine so many times. And I realize there is something that I can offer Lena. I can let her free of the mess I've made, absolve her of any misplaced guilt, any lingering kindness I don't deserve. "You don't owe me anything."

Lena's voice is heavy. "Sneaking out was fun at first. It felt almost like a way to get back at this place for all the pain and frustration, but I can't do it anymore."

Something in my throat quivers. "I'm so sorry I put you in this position. I was selfish."

"It's not your fault." She sighs. "I was not about to back out on an opportunity to learn what it means to feel powerful. And I won't have you owning the choices I made." She takes a deep breath and rubs the jewels between her thumb and forefinger. I can barely hear her when she whispers, "I just want to go home before the world ends."

"Then we run away?" I quickly offer, my back straightening. "I'll help."

She shakes her head. "Vykotsky would find us."

"So we ask her. We explain."

"I've tried. She's told me I'm mad and not yet prepared to return to the stresses of everyday life."

"Does Maxine know?"

"Yes. She has her own reasons she can't leave."

The dining room feels very small. The walls are closing in on me. The walls outside have never looked higher. The place I once thought was my salvation is turning into a prison.

"You deserve a better world than this one, Lena. But I'd walk to the ends of it with you, barbed wire and all."

Mrs. Vykotsky is nothing if not a master of punishment. The morning of the fundraiser she informs me at breakfast I am to borrow a dress from Ruby's closet, and I need to ask Ruby for it myself.

There's little I dislike more than needing to ask for things from others, but asking for something from ice queen Ruby herself is a special kind of torture.

I find her after lunch sitting in the sunroom, holding court with a gaggle of fawning girls.

When I ask to borrow a dress, she snickers audibly and says, "You know I'd really rather not."

I snort. This is what I get for asking instead of just stealing it.

"I need it for an event I'm attending tonight . . . at Mrs. Vykotsky's request."

Ruby looks at me out of the corner of her eye and says, "Fine, just not the pink one."

"Understood."

Lena and Maxine meet me in my room a few hours later to help me dress. Maxine selects a dress of Ruby's for me, insisting she has better taste than I do. It's midnight blue with a golden sash around the waist and delicately embroidered constellations along the fluttering sleeves. It takes me an hour to tack up the hem and take in the shoulders in a way that will be easy to unpin later. The wide boat neck reveals a swath of my chest that feels scandalous. The satin is cool against my legs.

Lena pins my hair into a twist, and Maxine produces a golden diadem to place on my head.

I look like a lost princess. It is preferable to looking like a very scared witch. I wonder what William would think of his sister if he saw me now.

I glance at Maxine in the mirror. "My mother sent it on my fourteenth birthday," she tells me. "It looks better with your dark hair."

I wish more than ever that I could have my friends by my side tonight. When I walked into the basement of the Commodore Club alone, I was uncertain of my power but sure of my own judgment. Now I have a more secure grasp on what it is I'm capable of, but I'm nothing but a child in this war with players and conflicts much more complicated than I understand.

I borrow a small evening bag from Maxine and place the blue mittens Finn knit me inside, which is silly, but they make me feel safe.

Lena and Maxine walk me to the foyer, where Helen is waiting for me. She's wearing a simple high-necked black gown and a single ostrich feather tucked into her slightly-poufier-than-average bun.

With a sharp nod, she greets Lena and Maxine. "Girls."

Maxine squeezes my hand just once before I walk through the door and out into the bitter evening.

CHAPTER TWENTY-THREE

I've lived in New York City my entire life, but I've never been inside the Hotel Astor. I never thought I'd climb the white marble steps in a ball gown, gold woven in my hair. Then, I never thought I'd be a witch, either, so I am learning to temper my expectations of what this life is turning out to be.

It's frustrating to be this close to my brother's grave. Mere blocks away lies the graveyard dust I so desperately need, but Helen's leash is tight tonight and sneaking away will not be possible.

Silent men open the glass double doors as we approach, but before we enter, Helen stops me with a cold hand on my bare arms. "Tonight, your name is Juliet, and I am your aunt Gertrude. We are guests of Assemblyman Bush of Elmira. Understood?"

"Understood." I say through gritted teeth. I'm so nervous, I'm about to crawl out of my skin, but Helen doesn't need to know that.

The music of a string quartet envelops us as we walk inside, and a white-gloved hand appears from nowhere to hand me a flute of champagne. I down it almost immediately. It burns, but less than whatever was in the kitchen jar Maxine once stole. That night in the field feels like it happened to a different person.

Sparkling chandeliers clink above our heads. The lobby is abuzz with women in silk gowns and their tuxedo-clad escorts, and I have to weave between them and porcelain vases the size of children to traverse the room. The whole place smells like old flowers and new money.

Helen and I are ushered through the halls of the first floor until we reach the Grand Ballroom.

The cavernous space is packed to the brim with the highest echelons of New York society. Stepping into the ballroom is like stepping into a bottle of lukewarm champagne, all fizzy and golden, but off somehow.

I stand in the doorway for a moment, struck with the stark contrast of this electric-lit room and the apartment building I lived in for so long, not far from here, where my former neighbors are sitting this moment, fighting off cockroaches in the candle-flickered dark before their evening meal.

The ballroom could hold one hundred of my old apartments. The soaring ceiling is set with a honeycomb of glass and modern steel beams, and the room is decorated in dark wood, date palms, and heavy gold mirrors. I could probably steal a pewter salt and pepper shaker and feed my old neighborhood for a week.

Helen gives our false names to a large man standing guard at the door to prevent any riffraff from coming in. Then she tugs at my dress, a strained smile on her face. "Come now, Juliet."

The cool silk of the dress and the tightly laced corset make me stand up straighter than I ever have in my life. This is women's armor. Metal boning, slick ribbons, and an unwavering smile.

Shiny guests mill around a maze of round tables draped in white tablecloths. Helen and I find the place cards marked GERTRUDE GELDING and JULIET GELDING. We smile politely at those who pass by us and make quiet conversation with each other. Helen leans over to me and whispers as old men and their young wives float past.

"That's Mr. and Mrs. Goodhue Livingston, they must be back from their home in New Orleans. Miss Anna Douglas Graham, about to be married off to some English duke with a crumbling castle desperately in need of her father's money. Over there in pink is Mrs. Chisholm, wife of Hugh Chisholm. . . ." I tune out her drawling; I've never understood why the society section of the papers exists. Why should I care if a family I've never met has let a house in the Hamptons for the summer? This room is like the society pages come to life, but I can't politely tell Helen I simply don't care, so I nod along silently.

The diamonds around the necks of the women look like trapped rainbows, they blur as I pull my eyes in and out of focus. I stop as a tall figure draws my attention.

The sight of Oliver Callahan from across the room sends a shower of nerves careening through my body. Of course he'd be here. It's just my luck.

He's in the corner standing by his mother, a haunted look in his eye and a champagne flute in his hand. It takes him a moment to notice me staring, but when he does, I resist the urge to look away. I meet his eye boldly. He takes a step toward me, but I shake my head almost imperceptibly with a nod toward Helen. He seems to understand, because he steps back and returns to speaking with his mother, but anyone watching closely would see the way he keeps glancing at me. He doesn't drink the champagne.

Oliver is tall and broad shouldered in his tuxedo. His spine is so much straighter than it was the last time I saw him, terrified in the basement of the Commodore Club. He looks at home here among these powerful people with their money. If the world were different and he were just a judge's son and I were just a madwoman's daughter, he would never walk into a place like this with me on his arm. It's not his fault, but it's easier to be angry with him than feel anything else. Anger, at least, I understand.

Dinner is served by white-gloved men who move in perfect synchronization, but the food goes to sawdust in my mouth. Men with identical faces get up at a podium and give speeches about the need for a thriving and safe city. These men look nothing like the city I know, which is confusing because they repeatedly claim to represent us all. When they speak of thriving industry, they speak of the money to be made in factory advancements, not of those losing their limbs working the lines. When they speak of growth, they speak of their own bank accounts, not of the opportunities for those whose hands built this from stolen marshland into the shining something it is today. The crowd applauds and toasts them. The longer it goes on the sicker I feel.

We're less than two miles away from the apartment I spent nearly all my life in, but I've never recognized New York less.

At one point a man with a white mustache large enough to make up for the lack of hair on his head, drags his date up to the podium. "Gentlemen, would you look at her!" he exclaims. The gentlemen laugh and jeer like it's the funniest joke they've ever heard. The poor woman has the kind of smile every other woman in the room recognizes. One that says, *I want you to leave me alone, but think it was your idea. I am a pleasant thing, unworthy of this kind of focused attention.* It's a magic trick that seldom works.

The women in this room exist only in their relationship to men: mothers, daughters, wives. But the men are simply men, and their power is never stronger than when they give themselves a fancy room, a podium, and a seemingly endless supply of cash.

Finally, the speeches are done, and Helen leans over and whispers to me, "It's time."

I give her a nod, and she smiles more for the sake of those at our table than for me. "I'm going to point out Commissioner Murphy. You're going to be very charming, and you are going to get him to go to room two ten with us, where we will make him sign the necessary paperwork. Do you understand?"

Be very charming? I'd laugh if I weren't so revolted. No one has ever once looked at me and thought, *What a very charming girl.* "What do you propose I say?"

"Just tell him you'd like a word with him in private," she says with a tight smile. Disgust rolls through me at her implication.

We don't make it more than four steps across the ballroom before an old woman in a pale blue gown grabs Helen by the elbow.

"Gertrude Gelding? Is that you?"

Helen smiles warmly and attempts to ignore the woman. The

woman refuses to be ignored. "Gertrude, it's me, Dottie Maynard!"

Helen turns. "Oh yes, hello, Dottie, it is good to see you. If you'll excuse me . . ."

Dottie Maynard has a bouffant that looks more like a bird's nest than human hair, and it serves as an appropriate home to her tiara set with sapphires the size of robins' eggs.

"Gertrude, I haven't seen you since Mr. Gelding and Albert passed. How long ago was that?"

The tight smile on Helen's face disappears. "Thirteen years."

"Good lord, has it really been that long?" Dottie exclaims. She reaches out and grabs both of Helen's hands in her old wizened ones. "And now you've reappeared! There hasn't been this much to talk about since Mrs. Howland Randall threw that fancy-dress party at her house on Madison Avenue during Lent. Of course that was idle gossip, and your situation is a family tragedy, but . . ."

A tap on my shoulder makes me jump.

Oliver stands behind me.

"Another field trip?" He raises his brows. Helen is still trying to get rid of the insatiably chatty Dottie, who is now asking if Helen has been at the family estate on the Cape and that's why they haven't seen her around town in so long.

"I'm here on sanitarium business." I know it's a stupid response, and by the look on Oliver's face he does too.

"I wasn't aware sanitariums had much business at political fund-raisers."

"Well . . . they do."

His confident mask falls. "Frances, please, just tell me what is going on," he implores. "I can handle it. Whatever it is."

I shake my head; Maxine's borrowed tiara is giving me a headache. "Don't say things that aren't true."

"I'm not—" He turns his head up at the sparkling ceiling and shoves his hands in the silk-lined pockets of his tuxedo pants. "I don't know how else to say it. I failed William. I won't fail you, too. I couldn't live with myself."

I find the strength to look up at him, and the emotion in his green eyes makes something in my chest spark awake. For a moment I think it's the magic—the fizzy warmth is similar—but this is something different. So I do something stupid. I decide to warn him.

I take two steps closer to him and lower my voice so that only he can hear. "Oliver, I need you to listen to me carefully. There may be someone who is targeting young men connected to the Sons of Saint Druon . . . your father's social club, I mean."

He looks down at me; there is more curiosity than fear in his eyes. "How do you know this?"

"I don't for certain. It's just a hunch."

"Seems like you've had a lot of time at the sanitarium to . . . think." I swear I can hear his heart thudding through the jacket of his tux. It's been years since I've been this close to him.

He's daring me to tell him the truth, but I don't take the bait. "Not much to do but keep up with current events."

"So if someone is targeting the Sons, what should I do?"

"I'm not sure yet. Be safe. Don't go anywhere with anyone you don't know. Don't walk alone. Carry a blade."

At the last suggestion Oliver laughs a little. "You really think I have it in me to stab someone, Frances?"

I resist a smile. "Perhaps not."

He shakes his head. "Absolutely not. I once fainted at the sight of a classmate's bloody nose."

"I remember." I know exactly the seventh-grade fight he's talking about. Oliver and I share a past tightly braided together, so many memories intertwined. "But you seemed at least a little tough in that basement." It's foolish of me to bring it up, but I relish the way he narrows his eyes at me like I know a secret he desperately wants to know too.

"Me? A man punched me in the eye, and it took all I had not to cry. But you . . ."

I bite my lower lip so hard it stings.

Oliver leans down even closer. I smell mint and laundry soap. The glint in his eyes is a question I can't answer. "Please, Frances," he whispers.

"I can't." My neck hurts from gazing up at him. The panicked noises in my head drown out whatever I'm feeling. "I couldn't explain it even if I wanted to. You can't protect me from this, Oliver. Please don't try."

"Frances—" he begins, but we both simultaneously jump apart as a new figure approaches us.

Suddenly Finn in all his finery and unruly hair is standing beside us, and the nerves come careening once more. I feel a sickening wave of guilt at Finn witnessing me so close to Oliver. It feels like something I should apologize for. I want to explain to him that it wasn't what it looked like. *But what did it look like?*

If Finn is upset by what he saw, he doesn't let on. His face is as open and friendly as it always is. "Hiya, Frances. Fancy meeting you here. And Oliver Callahan, once again."

Oliver is the kind of boy who looks as if he was born in a white button-down shirt. Finn, on the other hand, looks more like a snake donning camouflage.

I probably deserve this, the nausea and vague, pointless guilt at the sight of the two of them together.

Oliver extends a hand. "An unexpected pleasure."

They hold each other's hands too tight and too long. Finn's knuckles are bruised.

"What's wrong with your hand?" I ask under my breath.

"An accident." He smiles, looking at Oliver, not at me.

My head throbs where the combs of the tiara dig into my temples, or perhaps it's the champagne or the dread that has wormed its way into every part of my body.

As if to have an excuse to break eye contact with Finn, Oliver takes a glance at the watch in the breast pocket of his jacket.

My heart stutters a beat as recognition hits me like a punch to the chest. I would recognize that tarnished gold chain anywhere.

"Was that William's?" I ask. I make an effort to keep my voice steady. I'm suddenly angry again, at all the things Oliver has made me feel.

I raged when my mother wouldn't tell me where the watch had gone after William died. "What use do girls have for watches?" she asked me. "To tell the time," I replied. It was one of the last times we spoke.

I thought perhaps she'd sold it. To see that she gifted it to Oliver behind my back hurts more.

"Ah, yes. My most prized possession." He beams.

As if possessed, I reach for it. For as long as I've known about the Resurrection, one thing has nagged at me. I didn't know where to find an object of my brother's. I wasn't completely without ideas, but none of them were good. My newest was to break into our old apartment and cut out a square of wallpaper.

But this watch, gleaming inches from me, is perfect. The graveyard dust is blocks from here. Then we'd have everything we need. Suddenly it's within my grasp. I'm near giddy with the knowledge.

I just need Oliver to—

I jump, snapped out of my trance. Helen, having extracted herself from Dottie, appears at my side and grips me tightly by the elbow.

Oliver flips the front of the watch closed and places it back in his breast pocket.

"Frances, tell your friends goodbye. We really ought to be going," Helen clucks.

"Goodbye," I call over my shoulder as she drags me across the ballroom like an unruly child. I leave Finn and Oliver staring wordlessly at each other, their perfect mouths in straight lines.

"I didn't realize you'd have friends here," Helen quips.

"In my defense, neither did I. Is your real name Gertrude?" I snipe in return.

"It was a long time ago."

I smile serenely so that anyone who sees us in the ballroom would think us an aunt and niece having a lovely evening, but my response comes through gritted teeth. "And you didn't think it was important to tell me?"

Helen, calm as ever, replies, "No. Now please focus on the task at hand."

Commissioner Murphy is a slip of a man with a pointy face and fluffy white hair that sticks out from his head as if he's been struck by lightning. He's standing by the podium next to Boss Olan, Governor Dix, and James O'Gorman, the candidate for Senate.

From the perimeter of the room, Helen and I watch them like snakes in the grass. It's a small relief to be a predator instead of the prey. "Just wait one moment," Helen tells me. She's right. One moment is all it takes before Commissioner Murphy steps away from his companions and toward the buffet on the back wall.

"Smile pretty, Frances," Helen whispers.

With Helen at my heels, I wander as casually as I can muster over to the buffet. I don't want to extend my hand to the man, but I do. Brushing my fingers against the twill of his coat feels like plunging my hand into a nest of spiders.

The magic in my chest scratches like a caged animal. It has been reined in so long, and here, with so many people to take hold of, it begs to be let loose. I tighten my grip on it.

Not yet.

If I fail at this, I will be punished by Mrs. Vykotsky, but what's worse is I will be found out by every single fish-eyed man in this room. It's been a while since men like this have had a witch to burn. I wonder how desperately they hunger for a new one.

"Hello, Commissioner Murphy." I do my best impression of Ruby.

"Well, hello miss, I do not believe we are acquainted."

"Frances Hallowell, sir. You're needed." I'm afraid my smile looks more like a grimace.

"Needed on what business?"

I have only one card to play. "A request of the Sons."

He doesn't bite. "Now's not the best time, sweetheart."

"It will only be a minute, Commissioner."

He looks to his companions, then back to me. "I'll tell you what. You meet me in the lobby tonight around ten, and we'll discuss whatever it is you need then, darling."

Darling, sweetheart. I truly hate this man. "Ten won't work, I'm afraid. It has to be now."

He narrows his eyes in suspicion. "Then I'm afraid I can't help you."

I use the trick Finn used on me in the basement of the Commodore Club, and with a few well-planned steps Commissioner Murphy doesn't realize I've blocked his tiny figure from the view of his companions. He's backed up against the wall.

I've learned spellwork at Haxahaven; I've learned advanced magic with Finn. But I learned in the basement of the Commodore Club that the magic to manipulate others doesn't respond to simple words. It responds to feelings deep in my soul. I channel the deepest river of emotion, the part of my soul that feels most and least like me. I close my eyes for a fraction of a moment and picture what it is I need Commissioner Murphy to do. With new clarity, I open them and take hold of his body. I don't have time to feel guilty for the flash of fear in his eyes.

Fighting the men in the *Cath Draíochta* was messy. This use of the magic, making Commissioner Murphy take measured steps and weave through a crowd, is like attempting to do surgery with a dull ax.

The commissioner is graceless as I force him to walk in front of me. The ladies he bumps into gasp a little but brush off his rudeness and blank face as drunkenness.

Helen follows as I walk the commissioner out of the ballroom, up the stairs, and onto the near-abandoned second floor.

Helen waves her hand in front of room 210, and the lock unlatches with a click. She magicks the door open, and the three of us step inside the hotel room. The room looks like it was built for a French king, decorated with heavy carved furniture, an imposing canopy bed, and plush deep red carpet. In the corner of the room there is even a knee-high marble statue of a cherub.

"That could have been more subtle, Frances," Helen scolds me.

I unleash Commissioner Murphy and heave in a breath. My chest is sticky with sweat; the world around me sways. I sink down onto the bed and put my head in between my knees.

"What is the meaning of this?" Commissioner Murphy exclaims the moment I let him go. He slams down a Bible resting on the black marble sideboard for good measure. The noise makes me flinch.

Helen riffles through her handbag, drawing out a contract and a fountain pen "You know what this is about, Paul."

"What are you witches doing in Queens?" the Commissioner replies.

"We've been in Queens for over two hundred years."

"And what have you accomplished? Tax fraud? Etiquette lessons? Pseudoscience?"

"Safety."

The tiny man laughs cruelly. "You know what true safety is? It's power. It's money."

"We didn't come here to ask for your advice," Helen snaps. "You're going to sign the contract. You aren't leaving this room until the ink is dry."

"And your tiny puppet master is going to make me?" He gestures to where I sit collapsed on myself.

I try to shoot him a menacing glare, but with my face as green as it is, I'm not sure I cut a threatening figure.

Helen jerks her chin at me, telling me that, yes, using her "tiny puppet master" is exactly what she intends to do.

"It doesn't look like she's up to manipulating much of anything right now. Even if she could manage it, I'll claim it's a forgery."

"And we'll claim that you're a liar. Or that you were too drunk to remember signing. We could put every last one of your verifiable signatures into question, all while systematically destroying your reputation. Unless you'd like to tell the public we forced you to sign with magic?"

"Why won't you sign it?" I ask, still hunched over and breathing heavily. Mrs. Vykotsky made it sound like it had never been an issue before. I didn't expect the magical underworld of New York City to rely so deeply on paperwork.

"Boss's orders." He huffs. "Under strict instruction not to cooperate with the witches. They have something he wants, something Ana Vykotsky won't give him."

Am I the thing she won't give him? I didn't even know they spoke.

The thought makes me feel sick. I sit up a little straighter and turn the focus of my power to Commissioner Murphy. The magic, usually hot like a spotlight, flickers with no more power than a candle contained within my rib cage. I've never pushed it this far before.

With the set of his jaw and his scowl at Helen, I know we're not going to make any progress talking. It's time to get the signature and leave. With all the noise he's making, I can't imagine we have long before others come looking.

I raise my own right hand, and his rises along with it. It's a little like looking in a mirror.

I hold his arm, but I don't have the strength to control his whole body, so, with his arm still raised, he stumbles to the door.

Helen steps in front of him "Frances!" she screams.

Speaking a single word is a herculean effort. "Can't—" I choke.

"Frances!" Helen shouts once more as the city commissioner reaches for the doorknob. His hand never reaches it, but the door flies open anyway, revealing a stunned Finn.

To his credit, he shoves the skeletal commissioner back through the doorway and slams the door behind him.

"What's going on?" he exclaims at the same moment Helen screams, "Get out!"

Finn looks from me to Helen to the commissioner, then back to me. "What is this, Frances?"

The commissioner takes advantage of the chaos to lunge for the door.

"No!" Helen shouts.

Finn blocks the doorway with the expanse of his shoulders. I rise from the bed, and with all my concentration, I hold the commissioner's body still.

"Helen, now," I say through my teeth. Finn just watches the scene wide-eyed and still.

Every muscle in my body screams as I force the commissioner to walk over to the sideboard to sign the hospital charter.

Controlling his legs feels like one of those dreams where I'm trying to run away, but my body won't obey me.

He fights against the pen Helen shoves into his unwilling hand, but still I hold him. Helen and Mrs. Vykotsky's plan was poorly thought out, or they overestimated my ability, because I cannot make him sign the document. I don't know how. I could manipulate his hand, but all I would manage to get is a scrawl of ink across the paper. Not the commissioner's verifiable signature. Perhaps this was simply an exercise to scare me, or to scare him.

Carefully, like I'm slowing down the cranking of my sewing machine, I loosen my hold on him. I do my very best to free just his right hand from my control, but I don't quite know how.

It all happens in a flash. Helen's scream pierces the room before I see the fountain pen sticking out of her arm. The commissioner stumbles backward toward the door, but the wisp of the commissioner is no match for the bulk of Finn's chest.

I stand from the bed and seize the commissioner's body with my power, but I can't hold him for long.

My hold on him snaps like a fraying thread.

The commissioner wheels around to face Helen, who is still staring, a little dumbstruck, at the fountain pen sticking out of her bicep.

The dagger the commissioner produces from his breast pocket glints like the crystals on the chandeliers in the ballroom below.

Finn and I gasp.

The commissioner lunges at Helen, but his empty fist falls harmlessly with a dull thud against her breastbone. The dagger he held just moments before floats above his hand, pointed at Helen's heart. Before the commissioner has time to take another breath, Helen uses her magic to spin the dagger in midair and sink it into the hollow of his sternum.

Dark blood blooms on his crisp white shirt. He looks down at it, a curious expression on his face. He collapses on the floor and coughs hollowly again and again. The three of us watch in silent horror as he gasps in one final gurgling breath and then, like a sigh, life exits his body.

It's physically painful to watch. I stumble to the bed, sitting on the edge and dropping my forehead to my knees. The bed sinks as Finn sits down next to me. The hissing of Helen's curse words make me think she's just yanked the pen out of her arm.

I can't bear to look at her or the body in the middle of the floor, so I keep my head down as I choke, "You killed him . . . you killed him . . . you didn't say we'd kill him."

Finn rubs my back in soft circles and mutters, "There, there, you're all right now," under his breath over and over. Which doesn't help, because it only reminds me that I've made myself look weak and incapable in front of him.

Helen kneels before me and places her non-bloody hand on my knee. "Frances, compose yourself. Listen to me very carefully. We need to leave this room. Now."

Next she turns to Finn, whose hand has gone still against my back.

"And if you think I don't know who you are, Mr. D'Arcy, you are mistaken. You seem fond of Miss Hallowell. I'm sure you'd hate to see her in trouble. You aren't going to tell anyone about this, are you?"

"No, ma'am."

Helen smiles sweetly. The blood from her stab wound runs down her arm, dribbling through the gaps in her fingers. "Of course you aren't. Be a good lad; grab that carpet there," she commands him, pointing to where the commissioner lies very still, his blood leaking out of his chest into a puddle around him.

Finn gets to work rolling the commissioner's body up, while I put my head back down and try unsuccessfully to steady my breathing.

"Why didn't he stop you?" I ask Helen after a moment.

"He doesn't have magic," Finn huffs from where he's crouched on the floor. "The Sons value power. There are so many different kinds. Some wield . . . political influence."

From the bathroom, where Helen holds a towel over her bleeding arm, she snorts.

"What do we do now?" I ask.

Helen peers at Finn. "He looks strong. How far are the docks?"

Getting Commissioner Murphy's body out of the hotel is a challenge. We don't want the elevator operator to see the carpet in Finn's arms. At best, he'll think us carpet thieves. At worst, he'll notice the obvious shape of a body.

Helen creeps down the hall, leaving Finn and me sitting in silence with the body.

After a moment, she rounds the corner, declaring she's found the service stairs. It doesn't take us long to haul the body down one flight and out into the alley.

The hotel room was never rented under our names, and the bloody carpet, the only evidence of the killing, we take with us.

On our way to the river, we give Commissioner Murphy a funeral march through the streets of the city he once ruled.

On a Saturday night in New York City there are stranger sights than two women in ball gowns and a young man in a tuxedo carrying a rolled-up carpet over his shoulder. We don't draw much attention. We only need to make it six blocks; the docks are a straight shot down West Forty-Fifth. Finn knows the way.

We pass young men in dingy coats, coins jangling in their pockets, en route to the nickelodeons in Times Square. Past them rush more young men in top hats on their way to see Gibson girls or picture shows. Jolly piano music pours from the open doors of theaters, harmonizing with the wailing of feral cats.

Helen, Finn, the body of Commissioner Murphy, and I turn the corner toward the docks. The smell of rotting fish guides us like a compass. None of us speak.

My face is still swollen and pulsating after my crying jag, and judging by Finn's concerned glances in my direction, I look as upset as I feel.

Helen doesn't look at either of us. She just keeps marching on, her eyes on a singular target, the dark water ready to swallow our victim.

The docks aren't empty, but the women leaning against the brick walls and their companions don't pay us much attention as we duck behind a dry dock, blocking ourselves from view.

Finn dumps the carpet with a huff, and Helen unrolls it with a kick, revealing the commissioner's lifeless body. His mouth lolls open, but his eyes are closed, thank God.

Helen pulls the commissioner's bloodstained dagger out of her beaded handbag and crouches down.

It takes me a moment to realize what she's doing, taking the dagger and sawing, sawing, sawing at his wrists.

It's ugly work, cutting through sinew, veins, and milky-white joints.

She's cutting off his hands.

I turn around and vomit champagne into an overturned crate.

"Don't be dramatic, Frances," Helen says, not letting her eyes leave her work. "The last thing we need is the police identifying his body quickly. Removing his hands will stop them from using his fingerprints."

Finn places his hand firmly on my shoulder, and we share a knowing glance.

So this is it, the confirmation I need. All the news articles of the boys on Sheepshead Bay come rushing back to me in a torrent.

The blood on her hands is slick and dark. I've never heard anything worse than the snapping of skin and bone.

She makes quick work of it.

Like a skilled surgeon.

Like someone who has done this before.

Helen nods to Finn, and he helps her roll the commissioner's body from the dock into the water, while I stare at the dark horizon and ask the stars to give me a different life.

The body that was once Commissioner Murphy plops as it hits the water. I dart my eyes down just quick enough to see a pale handless arm sinking into the dark water.

I swallow down the sob and the bile in my throat, but the image is one I'll never be able to scrub from my brain.

They dump the carpet, too, then the hands, individually. They hit the river with two small splashes.

When Helen is finished, she wipes her hands with a handkerchief and tosses that into the river as well. It floats away, a specter on the water.

We walk away much quicker than we came, now that we're unencumbered with the body, but my guilt feels just as heavy.

At a street corner two blocks from the river, Helen turns to Finn and says, "You understand if you say anything about what happened tonight, you will do irreparable harm to the tenuous peace that exists between our two organizations. There are players much older than you who have been doing this for a lot longer. Don't try anything tricky. You'll fail."

"Yes, ma'am," Finn answers.

"Good." Helen nods.

The farther we walk from the docks, the more people crowd the streets. It's brighter here too, illuminated with flickering gas lamps. I feel like an imposter, walking among normal people going about their evenings like I didn't just dispose of a body.

"Finny!" a male voice shouts from across the street. I'm so on edge, I just about jump out of my skin.

From the corner of my eye I see a short blond boy, perhaps nineteen, bounding across traffic, dodging a horse and carriage, a wide smile on his face.

Finn slows his pace. He's just ahead of us, so we slow to match it.

"Finny boy, there you are! We've been looking for you! We were just headed back to the club. Patterson swiped a bottle of whiskey off the bar, and we still have so much planning to do for the—"

"Ah, of course!" Finn stops the boy. He doesn't acknowledge Helen or me. It's probably not wise for him to be seen by other members of the Sons cavorting with witches.

I step to weave around him, but his shoulder slams into mine, causing me to stumble. I drop my beaded bag.

"Oh, miss, I'm sorry. I didn't see you there!" Finn exclaims. We both bend down to pick up the bag. Crouched on the ground, he leans in so close, only I can hear him. "I'll be waiting outside the gates tonight. Please be careful."

His statement fills me with both terror and relief, because Finn saw what I saw tonight, and he knows what I now know with bone-aching certainty.

I can no longer stay at Haxahaven.

Finn takes one look back at me as he walks down the street; his eyes grave. I nod, just once to communicate my understanding.

Helen and I march on back to where the ambulance is parked outside the hotel. She takes my arm in hers and tugs me in close. What must look like a show of maternal affection to passersby is closer to a death grip. The hold of her arm in mine feels like a threat, like a reminder she controls me.

"You're hurting me," I whisper through clenched teeth.

"You failed tonight, Frances," she whispers in return, her tone poisonous.

Her response fills me with rage. "I suspect that was the point. Perhaps I would have succeeded if you'd bothered to teach us anything."

"We teach you how to stay safe."

"Yes, thank you. I feel so safe, Helen," I say disdainfully. "Or should I say Gertrude?"

"Gertrude is dead," she replies flatly.

For blocks we walk down the street arm in arm, weaving through other pedestrians out for a night in the theater district. Above us, electric lights advertising the Ziegfeld Follies twinkle.

"Did you kill Gertrude, too?" I snap.

"Typhoid did when it took her husband and son from her." Helen looks up at the billboards, glassy-eyed and far away.

My words stick in my throat for a moment, but the anger doesn't wane no matter how tragic her past.

"You put me in danger to prove a point," I say. She and Mrs. Vykotsky have been so self-righteous about keeping us safe, but the minute they had a chance to use me for their own gain, they took it.

"I apologize for the way things got out of hand this evening." Her arm on mine is still too tight. I don't believe her apology.

"If you hurt any of my friends because of what happened tonight, I swear to God, I'll burn that wretched place to the ground." I don't know if I mean it, but by the fear that flashes across Helen's face at my threat, she does.

"You can't burn down the world for taking the things you love from you. I tried."

We're back to the ambulance now, where it sits parked on a curb outside the hotel. People are pouring out of the main entrance, their drunken conversations filling the night with noise. The fundraiser must be over. They're so happy, unaware that one of them is now dead.

Helen opens the driver's-side door and slides in.

My hands hesitate on the handle of the door. I know what I have to do. I've known it since I saw my brother's pocket watch in Oliver's hands.

I take a deep breath. I look up at the stars.

And then I step into the crowd—and run.

The city does what it has always done; it makes me invisible.

CHAPTER TWENTY-FOUR

Like a river, I let the current of the crowd carry me away from the ambulance, my heart beating faster with each step.

From behind me, I hear Helen shouting, enraged. *"Frances!"* she screams over and over again. *"Frances!"* My name is carried away by the sound of the crowd, floated off on the breeze by the jangling music spilling from theaters until it becomes just another noise.

I pick up my footsteps until I'm running at a full sprint, and I don't look back. I duck through alleys and dart around corners, dodging passersby who clutch their pearls and look at me with horror.

It's only when I'm doubled over—gasping for breath, sure Helen isn't chasing me—that I allow myself to take stock of my surroundings. I need a plan, even if it's a half-baked one.

I'm in midtown, a good hour's walk from Columbia. If I know

anything about Oliver, he's home safe in his bed at this hour. He was never the type to close down a party, raging past midnight.

The subway is closed this time of night, but I can hail a petty cab. This close to the theater district it isn't difficult. One stops in less than two minutes.

I rip one of Maxine's delicate bracelets off my wrist. "Columbia University, please. You'll take this for payment?"

The driver eyes go wide at the sight of it. "Yes, ma'am." He nods. "No escort this evening?"

"He went home ill," I lie.

He huffs in acknowledgement and drives on. He's not chatty. I'm grateful for it.

All the ride, my brain buzzes with possibilities. If it is the witches of Haxahaven killing the boys on Sheepshead Bay, I need to know who was involved. Is it just Helen? Certainly Mrs. Vykotsky is part of it too. But who else? Surely Ann or Florence. *But what about Maxine?* She spends so much time alone with Helen, out doing god knows what.

It's too horrible a thought to dwell on.

I need more than ever to speak to my brother, to learn the truth. Only then can I make things right.

By the time we arrive uptown, every one of my cuticles is bloody. My jaw aches from being clenched. *One step at a time.* I hear William's voice in my head.

The jingling reins slow the horse to a stop. The driver sees me off with a polite nod and a "be careful, dear."

I feel a little sorry I have zero intention of heeding his fatherly advice.

It's a navy-blue dark outside, the moon covered by gray clouds. This part of the city feels dead compared to the theater district. The quiet is heavy. I found comfort in the crowds of midtown. The empty, wide boulevards uptown make me feel exposed, like I have nowhere to hide.

The imposing, ivy-covered buildings of Columbia University might as well whisper, *Frances Hallowell, this is not a place for girls like you.*

I've been here once before, back when William was alive, to deliver a Christmas present to Oliver. William had saved for weeks to buy his best friend a book of sports statistics. It seemed like a boring gift to me, but Oliver clutched it to his chest with delight upon opening it.

I loved that day. It was the first time I'd seen Oliver in months, and I'd been thrilled my brother had asked me to come along. I remember my boots crunching down this same brick path. It was covered in snow then, and the sky was a clear, bright blue. Five months later my brother would be dead. And now, eleven months later, his sister is back to rob the place.

Oliver's dormitory is an intimidating fifteen-story brick building near Morningside Park. This late, the paths winding through the campus are empty, but inside the building, windows glow with students studying after dinner and faculty advisors waiting to catch the honorable young men of Columbia University breaking the rules.

I circle the building once to find the diamond-paned first-floor window I'm nearly positive belongs to Oliver. I remember the slightly cracked glass in the left corner from when my brother and I visited. I found it odd that such a nice university would let cracks go unfixed.

I press my face to the cold glass and cup my hands around my eyes to see better. The glass is foggy with time and frost, so the image is warped, like trying to look through the bottom of a pop bottle.

The room is dark, just a single low lantern flickering. I hear no noise, see no movement. I pray he is asleep.

I steel myself. *"Briseadh,"* I whisper to the window. The lock obeys my order and unlatches with a thunk.

As slow as I'm able, I pry the window open. It squeaks terribly. Curse this old school and its rusty window hinges.

Nothing stirs from inside, so I press on. What will I do if he isn't home? Hide and wait?

And what will I do if he is home? Greet him like there's nothing unusual about climbing in his window late at night?

I have no time left to contemplate. The window is open. I hike my heavy, beaded skirts around my knees, and climb inside.

The room is small, dancing in shadows cast by the single lantern. And sitting up in bed, wearing a nightshirt, holding a book, is a very startled-looking Oliver Callahan.

"Hello," he greets me, wide-eyed, like he doesn't know what else to say. But a sliver of amusement cracks his face—watching me in all my fancy-dressed glory sneak into a boy's dormitory at such a late hour. "Aren't you full of surprises this evening?"

"Hello," I reply, like any part of this is normal.

We stare at each other for a moment. I'm calmer than I thought I'd be.

Oliver opens his mouth, then closes it. He opens it again. "To what do I owe the pleasure?"

I picture another life in which I'm an ordinary girl sneaking into his dormitory simply because I want to spend more time with him. We'd arrange this secret meeting with passed notes and stolen moments. Perhaps if my brother had lived, Oliver and I could have grown together naturally, like I'd always wanted. I can almost picture it, like the echo of a memory, a different version of Frances and a different version of Oliver. Both a little less broken, embracing in this same room.

I snap back to reality. "I wanted to see you." It's mostly the truth. His face softens, but I can tell he's unsettled by my sudden appearance.

"I don't often have pretty girls crawling through my window." *Pretty.*

"Not often?" I reply. "But it has happened a nonzero amount of times?"

Oliver furrows his brow and laughs a little, like he's baffled by this entire conversation. I don't blame him. "Is that what you came here to talk about, Frances?"

I sink down into the wooden chair at his desk. Like everything in this room, it's tidy. The pencils are lined up in an even row, his papers in a stack. His blazer hangs unwrinkled on the back of the chair. But for all the room's cleanliness, it isn't cold. There's a threadbare red quilt on the bed, and a painting of a sunlit landscape hung above the door. The whole place is paneled in oak. His room is small and soft. It smells too much like him, feels too much like him.

"No, that's not why I came."

"Are you in trouble?" The concern on his face is genuine. It hurts with an acuity so fierce it nearly knocks the wind out of me—the realization that he's trying to take care of me.

336

"No."

He knits his brows together and snaps his book shut. "You look like you're in trouble."

"I'm not." It comes out sounding petulant.

He pulls himself out from under the blankets and sits on the edge of his bed, so close our knees nearly touch.

Oliver sighs. "I cannot let you go like I let William go. Let me help you, Frances."

It's uncomfortable, this fizzy, soft nervousness that comes with looking at his face, so I choose to feel anger instead. I poke at the familiar rage, and it rises as I think of all my unanswered letters in the months after William's death, all the days I spent alone at the police station. They would have taken Oliver more seriously. Perhaps they would have solved the murder months ago, saved the other boys from the same fate. The world listens to boys like Oliver Callahan. "You abandoned me," I reply.

His fine features crumble like he might cry. "I'm sorry." He breathes as if the words have been trapped in his throat for the six months William has been gone. "It hurt, Frances. It hurt to look at you. It hurt to think about. I cared so much, and I couldn't take it. I'm sorry. I'm so *so* sorry." His dark admission hangs in the room for a moment.

But now is not the time to make amends. "I don't need your apologies."

I hate the way he's looking at me like a thing that needs saving. And I hate that some small childish part of me craves his protection.

"I understand nothing I say will ever be enough to express my deep regret." He pauses and sighs, like the weight of the world rests on his shoulders. "Will was always the one who was good with words. I never seem to be able to find quite the right ones."

I didn't think Oliver Callahan had the ability to break my heart anymore, but here it is, breaking.

It was one thing to have Maxine and Lena and Finn help me with the quest for the Resurrection, but it's another to be here with someone who misses William as much as I do.

Grief is lonely.

I lean forward; our knees brush, just barely. "I miss him too."

"Sometimes I wonder if I'll ever feel better." Oliver's green eyes well with tears, and it cracks through the facade of my anger. It's easy to forget why I came here tonight at all. My only thought is that I'd do anything to keep him from crying.

"I think we'll feel differently one day. Perhaps not better, but different."

"I thought we'd grow old together." He sighs. "Be old men sitting on a balcony, feeding pigeons."

I smile at the image. "I think none of us get the future we imagine for ourselves. How strange it is that life always turns out to be a different thing entirely from the one you pictured."

What would it be like to embrace him? Would it make him look a little less shattered? Could I press the pieces of his broken heart back together?

"Are you ever going to tell me what's going on?" he asks.

I know he's not asking about me breaking in; he's not even asking about the tuberculosis. He's asking about what happened in that basement. He's not going to let this go. Which is fair. I probably wouldn't either.

"Frances, please." It's more an exhale than my name, like it's a word that always exists in his lungs.

I want to tell him so badly, but that's not why I'm here. "I need something."

His answer is immediate. "Anything."

"I need my brother's watch."

He looks confused. "Will's watch?"

I hope he gives it willingly. The thought of using magic on Oliver makes me sick, but I'll do it if I have to. "Yes. I can't explain, but it's urgent."

Oliver worries his lower lip. The gears in his brain whir behind his eyes. He's thinking hard. After a long moment he rises. "All right."

He pulls open the top drawer of the table next to his bed. There sits my brother's watch, carefully placed.

Oliver presses it in my hand. "I'll ask only once more: please let me help you with whatever is going on." His eyes are dark and syrupy, Coca-Cola on a hot summer day a lifetime ago.

"I wish it were that simple." I wrap my fingers around the smooth, cool watch. It's heavy in my hand. I'm reminded of the night William went missing, when I woke up the next morning to his unslept-in bed and his pocket watch on the kitchen table. It wasn't like him to go somewhere without it. I left for work, annoyed at him for being so careless with his things. When I came home and the watch still hadn't been moved, my annoyance turned into full-blown panic.

It took them three days to find his body.

I rise and walk to the window, still cracked open, leaking cool air into the cozy room.

Oliver looks startled. "You're not staying?"

I'm confused. "Why would I stay?"

"I just thought after seeing you tonight, perhaps you'd come for more than the watch, that you'd wanted to see me, too. . . ."

The feeling I've tried so hard to tamp down swells in my chest. "Thank you for the watch."

He gathers the courage to look me in the eye. "Remember when I said I used to picture Will and me growing old together, feeding pigeons on a balcony?"

"Yes?"

His gaze bores into mine, resurrecting dead butterflies. "I'd picture you, too. In my future, I mean."

My cheeks burn red. How different would my life be now if he'd looked at me like this a year ago? How would sixteen-year-old Frances have reacted to getting the thing she wanted most, the thing she only let herself imagine late at night?

But tonight is not a night to dwell on feelings; I still have so much to do. "Thank you for the watch."

I place a leg on the windowsill and turn to say goodbye. I find Oliver, hand outstretched, staring at me like he has so much left to say. I accept his hand, warm and soft, and climb through the window. His fingers linger on mine just a moment too long.

"Good night, Frances."

I hail a petty cab two blocks away. "Forest Park, Queens," I greet the driver.

"That's a long way," he replies. I rip the borrowed sapphire necklace from my neck and pass it through the barrier. I hesitate, giving away Maxine's jewels like this, her gifts. But, remembering the way she clasped the necklace onto my neck—*They are yours,* she whispered. *Do with them what you wish*—allows me to extend my hand out farther. "Will this do?"

"Lady, I'd take you to California for this," he replies and flicks the reins. I jerk back against the seat as the horses begin to trot.

The watch in my hand gives me a renewed sense of determination.

The ride back to school is longer in a carriage than an ambulance. I'd fall asleep if my nerves weren't so rattled. Instead, I count down the objects the entirety of the ride. *The watch, the dagger, the mirror, the graveyard dust, the book.*

I have the watch. The book is next. It will be easier to sneak into Haxahaven while it is still dark than wait until morning.

Soon this will all be finished.

After nearly an hour, the driver drops me on the far edge of the school wall. The street is abandoned. I hear nothing except the rustle of trees and the swishing of beads on my dress.

I round the corner, preparing to unlock the gate when a figure moving in the corner of my eye makes me jump.

"Calm down, it's just me." Finn's Irish brogue cuts through the darkness. His bow tie is slung untied around his neck, his tuxedo shirt unbuttoned two buttons, exposing his collarbones. He looks as exhausted as I feel. "I thought you'd be inside. Where are you coming from?"

I hold up the pocket watch. "Getting this. One of the last items we need for the spell."

If he recognizes the watch as the same one Oliver had at the fundraiser, he doesn't let on. I don't know why I don't want to tell him I was in Oliver's dormitory. It feels like a betrayal, somehow.

"Well done." Finn gives me a nod. "Helen left you in the city?"

"I ran away." The look of pride that crosses his face makes me smile. I want Finn to think I'm as bold and brave as he is.

"And now you're back to break in?" He looks impressed.

"I don't need much time. Just wait here, please."

Finn shoves his hands into his pockets, he looks worried. "You're sure you won't get caught?"

I hope the smile I flash looks confident. "I'm rather an expert at sneaking in and out of Haxahaven, I'll have you know." He doesn't need to know it isn't entirely the truth. I'd rather he think me as assured as I pretend to be.

I leave him at the gate, and alone I march forward into the darkness.

The school looks so much bigger at night.

I picture myself as I was the first day I arrived here. I was trembling then, too.

But I know more now than I did then.

With a flash of magic, I unlock the gate and march back into Haxahaven for what I pray is the final time.

CHAPTER TWENTY-FIVE

The foyer is quiet and cavernous. Everyone retired to bed long ago. I take in the sweeping staircases, the dark chandeliers. I want to commit this to memory, this place that was once my home.

I don't know who is on patrol tonight, but they are nowhere to be found. I wonder if Helen has returned yet to tell them I fled. Perhaps they're out looking for me now.

I creep upstairs to my room, where Lena is sitting up in her bed, her dark hair loose around her shoulders.

"How was it?" she whispers as I walk through the door.

I'm shocked she waited up for me. I remember how it felt the night I killed Mr. Hues, how lonely it was walking into an apartment of sleeping girls with no one to help me. Lena's voice in the dark offers me more relief than I can say.

"I'm leaving," I whisper as quietly as I am able.

I crouch under my bed and pull the scrying mirror from its hiding place. The little black cat who once scared the living daylights out of me is under there too, eyeing me judgmentally. I give it a pat on the head. It nuzzles against my hand like it knows I'm saying goodbye.

"What?" Lena hisses. She leans forward on her knees. "You can't just *leave*."

I'm surprised by her shock; I hoped she'd be excited. "Finn is waiting outside the gates. I only came back for the mirror, the book, and you and Maxine." *I wouldn't leave you behind.*

Lena bounds out of bed and shoves me by my shoulders into the quiet hall. She shuts the door to our room slowly, silently. The portraits on the dark walls seem to watch us. I can't be out of here soon enough.

"Why are you leaving? What's the rush? Sleep on it, please, I beg you."

I tell her about the commissioner and Helen sawing his hands from his body. The blood runs from her face as understanding dawns on her.

She looks sick as she says, "You think she's responsible for the bodies washing up on the bay?"

"I know Mrs. Vykotsky and Boss Olan are in conflict. Helen sure looked like this is something she'd done before. What if she's the one who killed my brother, Lena? We can't stay here."

"Where will you go?"

"The Sons of Saint Druon," I say. Her face scrunches up in disgust at the name. "But we don't have to stay forever. We'll go wherever we want, Paris, California, Japan!"

I'm hopeful, underneath the sickening anxiety, that I could have a future. I will solve my brother's murder. Stay with the Sons long enough for them to help my mother, as Finn once promised. I could move on. I could have a life. I could finally do right by the ones I love.

The sorrowful look on Lena's face snaps me back to reality. "I don't want to go to the Sons of Saint Druon, or Paris, or California or Japan. I've told you: the only place I want to go from here is home. I can't go with you."

I didn't expect this. My eyes well with tears. "Please, Lena—" I'd do anything to convince her. I search my brain for the right words, but nothing comes.

She shakes her head sadly. "I've had visions of myself leaving, but it's not tonight. It's not like this. I'm sorry, Frances."

"But it could be tonight. Let's go—let's go together." I'm holding both her hands in mine, staring into her eyes. My words fall short, but maybe she can see it in my face, how desperately I want her to come with me. "You have to come. What if they hurt you? You don't know what they're capable of; you weren't there tonight. *Please, Lena.*"

Her bottom lip quivers. "This isn't how I leave."

I suck a deep breath in through my nose. My whole chest aches from the effort it takes to keep from sobbing. "I don't know how to do this without you." My voice breaks, and the tears come steadily, rushing down my cheeks. I was so sure of myself just moments ago, but I don't know if the right decisions are supposed to hurt this much.

Tears from Lena's eyes spill over too. "This isn't the end for us."

"How do you know that?" I hiccup. "You can't see my future."

Lena gives me a watery smile. "It's just a feeling. A plain old, regular feeling."

I pull her into a tight hug; it feels so inadequate. We hold each other until her nightgown is damp with my tears. I don't want to let her go; I don't know if I'm strong enough.

Lena pulls away first.

"Until we meet again." I have to believe in a future where we are together once more.

"Until we meet again," she echoes.

She sneaks back into the room that was once ours, but that I have no intention of ever entering again. The click of the door behind her shatters my heart.

I run down the stairs, clutching the mirror to my chest, and creep into Maxine's room.

She's asleep, wearing a striped pajama shirt, her silvery hair sprawled out against the pillow, illuminated in starlight.

Silently I crouch at the edge of her bed. First, I pull *The Elemental* from where it rests under her bed, beneath a pile of strategically discarded clothing. I prop it up with the mirror by the door. Perhaps it's a rotten thing to do, taking it while she sleeps, but I refuse to take the risk that she won't let me have it.

Next I whisper, "Psst, Maxine. Wake up." The skin of her hand is cold where I grab to shake her awake.

She comes to with a gasp. "Frances, Jesus Christ?" Her eyes widen in horror at my tear-stained face.

"I'm leaving." I mean it to come out dignified, strong, but it comes out as a pathetic sniffle.

She blinks a few times, her eyes heavy with sleep. "What?"

I shake her shoulder. "Maxine, get up, let's go."

She finally sits up, voice thick with sleep. "Where are you going? What is happening?"

Like I told Lena, I tell Maxine what happened to the commissioner, about Helen and the hands, about the way I ran like hell. Like Lena, her eyes go wide with horror.

"Dopey old Helen sawed a man's hands off?" she asks.

I'm getting annoyed at how slow she's being on the uptake. "Yes, please, Maxine, Finn is waiting. Let's go."

Then she asks the question I'm dreading most. "What about Lena?"

The pieces of my broken heart ache. "She's not coming."

Maxine takes a deep breath, the way an adult does when they're preparing to give a child bad news. "You know I can't go with you."

I don't want to do this by myself. I'm so sick of being by myself.

"Please, Maxine, I can't lose you, too."

"You aren't losing me. You could stay. You need to stay." She scrubs a hand across her face in frustration.

"You can't honestly be suggesting that after everything that's happened."

She throws up her hands in exasperation. "This place is my home!"

"They're murderers!" I spit back.

"That's not entirely fair. It sounds like Helen was provoked."

"Was she provoked every time she dumped another handless boy in the river? She might have killed my *brother*, Maxine."

She is fully awake now, sitting upright, her eyes wide and full of anger. "That is a completely unreasonable accusation and you know it. You truly believe Helen, *Helen*, whose interests include knitting periodicals and being the world's worst watercolorist, is a killer?"

It feels like I'm in one of those nightmares where you're trying to speak, but no one can hear you. I don't know how to make her understand.

"I know what I saw tonight." The color in my cheeks rises. "You truly don't believe me?"

"I believe you . . ." She trails off like she doesn't believe me much at all.

"You believe me, but you won't leave with me."

Her face crumples. "I wish I could."

"Then do it, Maxine. Leave this place behind. Be more than this, like you're always talking about! You want more power; you've told me as much. We could become as powerful as we want. We could stop wasting our time on floral arrangements and needle threading and make a difference." I'm so filled with anger that my body shakes.

She leans forward on her knees and grabs my wrists. Her eyes search mine. "Don't leave, Frances. Please. Not with him."

"With him?" I'm stunned by the turn in the conversation.

"I don't trust him." She pauses and swallows hard. "There's something I've never told you. I didn't just find *The Elemental*. I *dreamed* it."

"So?" I don't understand what she's implying about Finn, but I don't like it.

"Surely you don't think it's a coincidence?"

"It sounds like a lot more of a coincidence than witnessing Helen murder a man. God, you're always going to defend them, aren't you?"

348

"Don't say 'them' like you're not one of us," Maxine quickly shoots back.

The most awful thought I've ever had bubbles back up to the surface. There is no more suppressing it. I think of all the time Maxine spends alone with Helen in the city, all the ways she defends them at any cost. It's a spiral I can't stop. My head aches. It's all so clear now. I take a careful step back.

"Are you part of this? Are you helping Helen? Do you all really hate the Sons that much? You hate them so much you'd kill them?" The accusation comes out as a whisper.

Maxine's face turns to horror. The air between us goes still and cold. "How dare you."

I don't want to believe it. I love Maxine too much. But her silence feels like a confession.

I have nothing left to say to her. I back farther away, toward the door, gathering the mirror and book in my arms. If Maxine notices the book I've stolen, she doesn't say. Rage too large to hold inside my body any longer, I rip the diadem from my head and hurl it at her. It lands at the base of her bed.

With my back turned, she whispers once more. "I loved you. I thought of you as a sister." She takes a shaky breath, then snaps, "Get out."

"I loved you, too," I say under my breath, so low I'm not sure she hears me.

I close the door right as she begins to cry.

CHAPTER TWENTY-SIX

F inn is waiting at the gates where I left him.

He's leaning against the Model T, smoking a cigarette. I've never seen him smoke before; the smoke curls between his long fingers.

"You were gone a long time. Was everything all right?"

He must see the devastation on my face, because he pulls me into his chest and lets me fall apart.

Against the warmth of his beating heart, I sob into his shirt, dampening it with my tears. After a moment, he nudges me. "You have everything you need?"

I give a pathetic nod.

Finn brushes my hair back from where it's plastered to my face with tears. "Then we need to go, love."

I imagined I'd feel relief pulling away from Haxahaven, but

there's nothing but a deep ache, like someone has scooped out my chest cavity and left it in a bloody mess all over the school's fine marble floors.

I can't stop picturing Lena's and Maxine's faces. I even think of Sara, Cora, Maria, May, Aurelia, and Ruby. All the girls I kept at arm's length, I didn't imagine I'd miss them at all.

But then I remember the sound of Helen sawing through muscle, how casually she pulled the dagger out of her handbag, and I know that I am making the right choice.

Tomorrow I do the resurrection spell. I will get answers from my brother himself, and then I will stop the killings; I will find peace. I will make a better world than this one.

Finn spends the entire drive into the city with his hand gripping my knee like he's reassuring himself I'm truly here. The heavy beading of my dress makes me feel like I'm suffocating.

"Can we make a detour?" I ask Finn as we enter Lower Manhattan.

"Sure thing, where to?"

I give him the directions to the final place on my list tonight.

After my brother's body was found, the Callahans paid to have him laid to rest. There isn't much space for bodies on the island of Manhattan. My mother and I planned to have him cremated, but the Callahans insisted. At the time I remember thinking it was odd, but now I'm grateful.

The cemetery isn't far from the Commodore Club. Finn follows my instructions diligently, without question.

He slows the car in front of a wrought-iron gate set between two redbrick buildings. It's strange, which is saying a lot for a city filled with strange things. There are dozens of graveyards on the island, but this one is newer. It would be easy to walk right by, if not for the skull welded right into the bars.

Finn cuts the engine and turns to look at me. His hands grip the steering wheel so hard, his knuckles are white.

"Well . . ." He takes a minute to gather his thoughts. "We have your brother's watch, the mirror, the book—and the dagger is shoved under my mattress back at the club. If I were a betting man, I'd bet you've taken me to where William rests."

My chest is tight with emotion. "It's the last thing we need."

Finn gives a solemn nod. "Would you like me to go with you?"

I shake my head, but his kindness softens some of the hurt. "I think I'd like to do this on my own."

"I'll keep watch." He reaches over and gives my hand a squeeze of encouragement right before I hop out.

I'm surprised the gate isn't locked. It greets me with a low whine as I push it open.

The soft night has washed the cemetery in silver light as if from another world. There's something about the quiet of this place that makes me want to sink to my knees and ask for forgiveness. It is still here, so far removed from the street just feet behind me. And in the stillness, I am utterly alone.

I remember now why I don't come visit; I don't feel my brother here.

William couldn't stand still for longer than thirty seconds. He would have hated the idea of eternal rest.

The tombstones sit in rows. Many have gone crooked with time, but my brother's is new. It sits on the edge of the small plot, dignified and cold, nothing like William was in life.

WILLIAM JOHN HALLOWELL

BELOVED SON, BROTHER, FRIEND

I trace my fingers over the words. They're too sterile, so unlike my bright light of a brother.

"I saw Oliver tonight," I whisper out loud. I don't know why I do it.

The cold grave gives me no answer.

I sigh, press my forehead to the stone. I'm so tired, I ache down to my bones. "He misses you too."

A single, pointless tear escapes. I wipe it away with the heel of my hand.

I scoop a fistful of dirt and drop it into my fine beaded bag.

I rise from the ground, brush the dirt from my dress, and steady myself with a breath.

It's done, William, I think. I've done it. I've gotten every object needed for the Resurrection. Now all that's left is to gather every last ounce of my courage.

"I'll see you soon," I half sigh, half wish. Lifting my fingers to my lips, I kiss them and place them on the cold tombstone.

"I promise."

I stride out of the cemetery and back into Finn's waiting automobile.

We drive the final few minutes to the Commodore Club in silence, both lost in our own thoughts.

Finn gently parks the machine against the curb, and we make our way up the marble steps. He pauses right before we enter through the double doors.

"I'm so proud of you," he whispers.

I'm surprised to find the same tiny bald doorman in the foyer this late at night. Finn passes him the mirror and the book and kindly asks him to place them in his room. It makes me uncomfortable to hand them off to a stranger, but I follow Finn's lead. My brother's watch I keep clutched in my sweaty palm. I have no intention of ever letting it go.

Finn's hand rests in my other, warm and steady against mine. It makes me feel less like I'm being swallowed whole by this building.

Together we go up the grand staircase to a study paneled in dark wood. In the corner is a taxidermy leopard, posing in an eternal snarl. I'm too tired to be frightened of this place. I suspect that will come in the morning.

We pause at the same door I remember well from the first night I came here. I shoot Finn a questioning look.

He squeezes my hand in reassurance. "We'll need to see Boss. He'll be thrilled to have you." *Have me.*

I open my mouth to protest. A conversation with Boss Olan is the last possible thing I want to do tonight, but Finn knocks on the door before I get a single word out.

"Come in," a booming voice instructs.

Boss Olan looks as grand as ever sitting behind his desk. Illuminated by stained glass Tiffany lamps, papers spread in front of him, in a well-tailored suit as if it's the middle of the workday, not the middle of the night.

He smiles as we enter. "Why, Mr. D'Arcy, it looks as if you've brought me a present."

Finn nods. "Aye, Boss. Thought you'd be pleased. Frances here has finally decided to join us."

"Well, Miss Hallowell," Boss Olan booms, clapping his hands together. "I cannot tell you how delighted I am that you're here. We have extraordinary plans for you. Together, we'll remake the world." He laughs, openmouthed like a jackal.

I steel myself. One final performance for the night. It's best if Boss Olan thinks I'm a sweet girl, one without plans of my own, so I smile and bow my head in gratitude. "I only wish to be of service. We can work out particulars in the morning."

"Of course, of course!" He slaps his hands down on his desk like he can think of nothing more wonderful.

I have no intention of helping him remake the kind of world he desires. Away from Haxahaven at last, I will learn what I can. I will get justice. And then I will leave. I ignore the nagging fearful thing in the back of my brain that says it might not be that easy.

"Mr. D'Arcy, the poor lady looks exhausted. Won't you get her to a guest suite so she can get some rest. We have so much work to do, we need you in tip-top shape."

"Oh, I'd hate to be a nuisance," I say as sweetly as I can muster.

"Nonsense! Be a good girl!" Boss Olan exclaims.

The wink he exchanges with Finn as we exit the study is so like Mr. Hues's that for a moment I'm filled with rage.

We're at the door when he stops Finn. "Mr. D'Arcy, you didn't happen to see the commissioner downstairs did you? He hasn't made his report to me, that old drunk."

"No, sir, haven't seen him." There is no hesitation in Finn's voice.

Boss nods and returns to his papers. We shut the heavy door behind us with a thud.

Finn takes me to a guest room one floor up. Covered in burgundy velvets and rich mahogany, it looks like someone took Boss Olan's wardrobe and turned it into a bedroom.

It's past two a.m. now. My eyes are heavy with sleep. I run my thumb over the smooth brass of the watch. "Tomorrow?" I ask Finn. "We'll do the spell tomorrow?"

"If that's what you want, love."

We hover awkwardly in the doorway. "I'll bring you some clothes in the morning. We'll make a plan then."

I curse under my breath.

A look of concern crosses his face. "What is it?"

"I don't think I can get out of this dress by myself. Lena helped me get into it." God, I miss her so much already. I tug the clasps at the neck. "I could rip it, probably."

"Stop, stop." Finn steps inside and closes the door behind him. "I'll help, of course I'll help."

"You don't have to—" I protest, but he's already behind me.

"I know my way around a row of buttons and a corset. I'll make quick work of it."

The thought of him being with another girl, unbuttoning someone else's dress makes me sick to my stomach. I don't like the idea of him touching anyone who isn't me.

He starts between my shoulder blades. His cool fingers are agonizingly slow as he undoes the buttons one by one. I'm covered in goose bumps at a single brush of his fingertip. I pray he doesn't notice.

When he's done, I slip the heavy dress off my shoulders. It falls to the floor with a slump much too loud for this quiet room.

"Well done." My voice is too high. "Corset next. Start with the laces at the base of my spine."

He laughs. "Like I said, I've done this before."

"I'm trying to forget." It's meant to be a joke, but it comes out strained.

I can't see him, but I know he's smirking. "Are you jealous?"

He tugs on the strings with a deep exhale. That makes one of us. I can't breathe at all.

Slowly, so slowly he undoes the laces. Each brush of his knuckles against my vertebrae feels like something I need to ask forgiveness for.

"All done." His voice is rough.

I tug at the corset, and it drops to the floor with the dress, leaving me in nothing but my chemise.

I turn to face him. He's so close, I can see the flecks of gold in his eyes.

He does not step away; we do not break eye contact as I run my fingers through my already undone hair, searching for any loose pins.

Silence. More terrible, sinful silence. It echoes in my ears, and for a moment the only thing I feel is a painful stab of loneliness.

His gaze flickers from my eyes to my lips and back again. He leans in a fraction of an inch.

He lifts a hand and thumbs at the thin fabric at my hip. *"Frances,"* he sighs.

I want to say his name back. I want to lean in, close the distance between us; I want to want this.

But I can't do it. Not tonight, when my nerves feel scrubbed raw and my face is swollen from crying. It's all too much.

I gasp sharply and turn my head from him.

Finn steps back—the spell between us is broken.

Wordlessly he makes his way for the door, but I don't want him to go.

"Will you stay with me tonight?" I don't recognize my own voice.

He turns to me, closes his eyes for a moment, exhales. "My bedroom is in the basement."

My face flushes red. "I shouldn't have asked."

"No, no—" He stumbles. "If you want me to stay, I will stay."

"It's just, I've had quite a night. This place is new. I'm—" I struggle for the right words. *I'm heartbroken* is the closest I come to an accurate description. *Please don't let me be alone.*

He nods. "I understand."

He walks over to the bed and throws a pillow on the floor. "I'll sleep right here. I'm not going anywhere." He's a gentleman about it—of course he is.

I slide into the cool covers as he rises and presses the button for the lights. There is rustling as he undresses in the dark.

As my eyes adjust to the low light, I see him lying next to the bed on the floor in nothing but his slacks and undershirt.

He looks up at me, eyes large and searching. "Go to sleep, love. You deserve some rest."

I almost invite him into bed with me. Having his warm, solid form next to mine would be such a comfort.

But my bravery for tonight is spent. "Good night," I whisper.

"Good night, Frances."

I lie awake for a while, listening to his steady breathing. Then I doze off into oblivion. I have no dreams.

I sleep for what feels like a very long time. I wake up heavy limbed and confused in an unfamiliar room.

I am greeted by a freshly bathed Finn at the end of my bed, grinning and holding a white tea gown.

It all rushes back to me: the commissioner, Oliver, Lena, Maxine. It doesn't feel real yet, like when you bang your elbow and it takes a minute for the pain to set in. I'm still numb and waiting.

But Finn looks so delighted to see me, I put on a brave face. "Good morning," I greet him.

"It's nearly lunchtime." He laughs.

"You let me sleep that long?" I'm embarrassed.

"I wanted you to get your rest, but it's best you eat. You'll need your strength for tonight."

At the mention of tonight I'm fully awake. "We'll do the spell?"

Finn gives me a confident nod. "After most of the lads are asleep, there's a room in the basement where no one will bother us."

I've worked so hard for this, I didn't think I'd be this terrified when the moment finally came.

He tosses the dress on the bed. "Up with you."

The lace is much finer than anything I've ever owned. "Did you commit robbery for me?"

"I'll never confess. Go on, get up and I'll take you down to meet the lads."

He waits outside the door while I dress. The tea gown is a little too small, pinching me at the waist, but I don't tell him so.

The dining room at the Commodore Club is similar to the one at Haxahaven, but this one is filled with taxidermy predators and young men with pale, beady-eyed faces. They all greet Finn with whoops and hollers of "Aye! Finny boy!"

Finn stays protectively close to me, his fingertips always a breath away from the edge of my skirt.

They introduce themselves to me with throaty voices, without ever looking me in the eye. They all seem to be named James.

I'm grateful I don't recognize Vlad or Bertram in their midst—the men Oliver and I were forced to fight the night of the *Cath Draíochta*—but my comfort is short lived.

There's something near feral about the boys' interactions with each other. The way they jab their elbows into the ribs of the boys next to them, their bared teeth as they laugh at jokes made at another's expense. It's all so *loud*.

For minutes no one pays attention to me. I sit, hands folded in my lap, feeling small and uncomfortable. Finn laughs with his friends and drops a plate of food in front of me. "Eat," he commands with a smile.

It's after I've taken my first bite of potatoes that one of the boys finally speaks to me. "You've finally joined us, eh, Frances?" one of the Jameses asks with a laugh. "You're all Finn talks about. Maybe now that you're here, we'll hear the end of it!"

By the time I've chewed and swallowed, ready to answer his question, he's turned away, already in another conversation with the boy next to him about something someone I don't know did last week. By the way they slap their knees, it must have been hilarious.

A blond levitates a piece of chicken off his plate and directly into the face of the boy next to him. Everyone at the table laughs like it's the funniest thing they've ever seen.

"You see?" Finn leans over to me. "They're so excited you're here. They've been waiting for you."

It's meant to be comforting, but it only makes me nauseous. I don't see what Finn is seeing, and I don't like the idea of these men thinking about me at all. I don't want to exist in their heads in any capacity.

I'm so anxious about finally performing the Resurrection, I barely touch my food. Finn nudges me with his elbow. "It's going to be all right, you know."

"I know," I lie.

I think of Lena and Maxine, sitting down to lunch in the Haxahaven dining room at this very moment. Is my chair next to them empty, or have I already been replaced? Did Maxine tell Lena about my accusations? If I suspect Maxine is capable of such terrible things, why do I still miss her so much?

After lunch I retire to my upstairs bedroom to wait and wait some more. Finn is gone for hours, while I pace laps around the plush carpet.

I watch the sunset over the city from the window. The November sky is painted in a brilliant orange, giving way to soft pinks, fading to purple, and then finally dark blue. All the while I think of my brother. My anxiety increases with each new star that pops into the sky. We're so close now.

It's only when Orion crests the horizon and I can no longer stand the sound of my own thoughts in my head that I hear a gentle knock on the door.

"You ready?" Finn's voice is soft.

I reach down for his hand, and find it already at my side. I lace my fingers through his and picture my brother in a light-filled dream meadow, whole and waiting for us. "As I'll ever be."

CHAPTER TWENTY-SEVEN

In silence we cross the headquarters of the Sons of Saint Druon together. We walk through the basement where the *Cath Draíochta* was held, then down another flight of rough wood stairs. The stairway is ancient-looking, dug through the bedrock. It smells of iron and rain. The temperature drops by a degree each step we take into the dark.

I clutch the mirror and the spell book to my chest; the beaded bag containing the watch and dirt from my brother's grave dangles from my wrist. I've wrapped a wool blanket around my shoulders, but it doesn't do much to stop me from shaking.

The cellar the stairs lead to looks to be as old as the city itself.

It's perhaps fifteen by fifteen. Big enough that I can't touch the opposite walls with my arms outstretched, but small enough that I feel as if I've been swallowed by a beast made of mud and shelves of dusty wine bottles.

It's dark, too; the only light is Finn's kerosene lamp. With shaking hands, I prop the scrying mirror in the corner. It reflects the light of Finn's lantern, twin flames dancing in the dark.

Maybe it's the unbearably low ceiling or the silence pressing on my ears, but I've never before heard my heartbeat this loudly.

Finn lowers himself to the dirt floor and pats the space next to him. I tug the blanket tighter to stop my hands from shaking.

"Let's begin." His voice is low and so much steadier than I feel.

"All right." It comes out as a whisper.

"We don't have to do this if you're not ready."

I don't think I'll ever be ready for what we're about to do, but that's not the point. "We need to know for certain who killed him. We need to stop them from killing again." We don't have the luxury of waiting around, not when wasted time could mean another boy's life lost. I don't tell him a simpler truth—that I miss my brother and am both terrified and elated at the idea of seeing him again.

I sit down next to Finn and watch him open to the page that has consumed all my thoughts.

The book's ancient spine cracks, like it, too, has been waiting for this.

The ground is hard and cold. The damp of the cellar takes root in my lungs. My heart is in my throat.

I have the feeling I am standing on the edge of a cliff, sick with anticipation of the unknown.

Finn places a warm hand on top of mine. I grip it like a life preserver on a vast dark ocean. What was it the old woman at the market said about anchors?

There's a diagram of objects drawn on the onionskin paper,

sketched so lightly that I can barely make it out.

In a five-pointed star, I lay out the items. I dump the pile of graveyard dust to the right of the mirror, the pocket watch to the left. To my direct left I place the dagger. Then, completing the pentagram, I lay the book open to my right.

Finn's eyes lock onto mine. "No matter what happens, Frances, I am here for you," he says.

I picture my brother's face, alive and smiling. He had wrinkles in the corners of his eyes from how often they were scrunched up in laughter. He had dimples and crooked bottom teeth and my exact same nose.

What if he doesn't look the same? What if he looks waterlogged and dead?

I nod. The words won't come. I feel as if I'm about to vomit. Everything I've worked for is fanned out in front of me, but what is the punishment for breaking the very laws of existence? What does the world do to girls who speak to the dead? How will I move on when all this is over?

Deep in my soul I know it doesn't matter what the consequences are. I'd do anything for my brother, and this is the very last thing I can do for him. The final act of the love that's eating my heart alive.

"Let's begin," I say; it echoes off the walls.

I pull the book from Finn's lap onto my own, and I begin to read.

I've read over the spell at least a dozen times, but the words are still clumsy on my tongue.

"Tras thar an veil agus tabhair dom an méid a cailleadh ionas go faimais níos mó ama a labhairt."

The familiar stirring in my gut I expect when I say a magic spell doesn't come. Instead there is only the blank, yawning emptiness of nothing.

In the center of the room the lamp flickers, illuminating the fact that nothing has changed.

I pause, staring at Finn and myself illuminated in the mirror, praying for something to happen. But nothing sparks, nothing changes—I'm just stuck staring at my own disappointed face.

Panic rises in my chest. I've never fully stopped to consider what I'd do if the spell didn't work. I haven't allowed myself to consider the possibility.

"It didn't work." I say it out loud more for myself than for Finn.

"Try it again," he urges. "Close your eyes, really focus."

I do as he says. With practice, the words come more easily.

I shut my eyes so tight, I see stars. *Please please please,* I pray. *Please let it work. Please please.*

I open my eyes. The basement is still and cold. There is only me and Finn reflected in the mirror. He's concerned too. I can see it in his face.

"Why isn't it working?" My voice breaks on the last word, and tears begin to fall hot and fast down my face. *No no no.* This can't be right.

"I don't know." Finn puts his arm around my shoulder, but it doesn't give me any comfort. "Try again," he encourages gently.

I pull the lantern closer to the book. I study the diagram. Read every frantic note in English scrawled in the margin.

Only effective if done soon after departure from this plane
Best under waning moon
Graveyard dust no more than five days old
RISKY.

Best in the company of others

We've done everything right. Everything except for one thing.

Only effective if done soon after departure from this plane.

It's the note in the margin that stands out the boldest, as if mocking me. William has been gone for months. Maybe it's too late; maybe I've lost my chance.

I say the spell faster, with more desperation than ever, but still there is nothing. Everything is hollow and quiet. It's heartbreakingly ordinary. The mirror reflects my devastated face. I thought I was powerful; I thought I was different. But I'm just as useless as I've always been.

"I don't understand." I'm sobbing in earnest now. I don't know what to do. I never truly imagined we'd fail.

The basement is silent except for my hiccuping, childish crying. I suppose it was all too good to be true, the idea that I could speak to my brother once more, that I could find meaning in his senseless death. That I could solve it and be a hero. It was a fairy tale I told myself to survive, and I'm a fool for having believed it.

I curl into a fetal position on the hard dirt floor and let the sadness rack my body. It's a relief, in some ways, to let the tidal wave of pain I've kept at bay for the last six months wash over me. *He's gone, he's gone. He's gone forever, to some place I'll never reach.* This was the whole point of everything. Of sneaking out of Haxahaven, of practicing in secret, of putting everyone at risk. And now I have nothing to show for it. *Nothing.*

Finn's soft voice is an anchor. Without it I'd be lost completely; I'd let this feeling carry me away.

"Frances." He strokes my shoulder. "Don't give up on me yet, Frances."

"The spell doesn't work. It's broken. It's all so goddamn broken," I sob.

He takes a breath. "We might have another option."

Another option. I cling to the words and push myself up off the ground. Finn points to a note written in Gaelic, the one I can't read. "This one references another spell. There's something else we could try."

Hope bubbles up from despair. *Anything. I'll try anything.*

He flips the pages of *The Elemental* to one of the very last pages and lets out a sigh. "We could bind our magic. Together, we might be strong enough."

I blink through my tears. "Bind our magic?"

Finn studies the page. "It's forbidden. It's dangerous. It's like a . . . marriage." He struggles to get the word out. "It ties us together, our souls, I mean."

I'm still confused—I don't understand what I'd be doing to him. "I couldn't ask you to do that for me."

Finn looks at me, his eyes wide. "Frances, I'd do anything for you."

I close my eyes for a moment. I think of the first time I met Finn in the park. A light in the darkness. I could certainly do worse.

From between my tears I let out a laugh. "I never thought I'd be wed at seventeen."

Finn smiles up at me through thick lashes, but I can tell he's as scared as I am. "I've always enjoyed surprising you."

He lays the spell book at the base of the lantern and takes a steadying breath.

I look over the spell. It looks like any other in the book, with delicate drawings of hands and rope and a spell in a strange language.

I've long been a creature of desperation. Agreeing to this doesn't seem any worse than agreeing to do the Resurrection in the first place.

"Can we undo it once it's done?" I ask.

"I don't know," he answers honestly.

"Go on then," I urge him. I don't know how to return to the world if I can't complete this spell. I will finish this tonight, or I will burn my soul to ashes trying.

He swallows. His confident veneer is stripped, revealing the nervous eighteen-year-old underneath. But he is brave for me. We'll be brave for each other. "No matter what happens, I'm here."

Without further discussion he rips through the hem of his white shirt, producing a thick ribbon of fabric.

"Give me your hand." His eyes are wild with the flickering lantern flame.

He adjusts himself so he's sitting cross-legged directly across from me, and he takes my right hand in his.

He drapes the ripped shirt hem over our clasped hands, where it dangles on each side.

"The original spell is in Gaelic," he explains. "But I think it will be more powerful if we recite it in English, so we both understand the meaning."

I nod in agreement.

With his left hand, Finn gathers the two ends of the shirt hem and, in an elegant figure eight, winds them around our joined hands, tying them in a knot at the base of my wrist.

He leans forward and places his forehead against mine. The heat from his skull unravels the tension between my eyebrows. And then he begins.

"I, Finn James D'Arcy, give myself to you, Frances Victoria Hallowell. All that I am and will be is yours, from this life onto the next. My soul, and all that is within it, belongs to you."

I let the words work their way inside me. They find their home somewhere in the left chamber of my heart, where I know I'll carry them forever.

"Your turn," he whispers.

I close my eyes and speak the words deliberately. "I, Frances Victoria Hallowell, give myself to you, Finn James D'Arcy. All that I am and will be is yours, from this life onto the next. My soul, and all that is within it, belongs to you."

Saying the words breaks my heart for reasons I cannot name, but Finn gives my tied-up hand a reassuring squeeze. With his left hand, he points to the spell book and a line of Gaelic words at the bottom of the page.

"Now say this."

I obey. *"Déantar é. Is leatsa tú."*

With those words, something happens. The temperature of the basement drops even further, and a shudder like a November wind courses through my body. My heart feels suddenly hollowed out. I dry heave, but nothing comes up. My hand, still tied to Finn's, is shaking.

"Did we do it wrong?" I choke out to Finn, who looks somehow more golden in the light of the lantern.

"There's only one way to find out."

He turns back to the Resurrection.

"Together this time?" he asks, looking into my tear-streaked face.

"Together."

His deep Irish brogue joins my quiet American accent. The spell feels different now; I can feel the magic within me reaching out, a spark begging for something to light on fire.

Upon the last three words, *"ama a labhairt,"* something strange happens to the scrying mirror. The glass ripples like waves of dark water, no longer reflecting the room, but something silvery and strange and not of this world.

Then, like fog parting, the cloudiness dissipates, and in the mirror is *him*. Reflected, just as if he were standing on the other side, is my brother. It knocks the wind out of me to see his face in such perfect detail. Closely cropped brown hair, eyes that always looked ready for a laugh, the same straight nose as the one on my face.

I let out an exclamation somewhere between a wail and a shout of joy. I scramble closer to the mirror on my hands and knees.

"William." His name comes out as a sob, and the tears begin falling once more.

"Hello, Frances." It's the voice I never thought I'd hear again.

I was afraid the Resurrection all might be an illusion, an untruth spun with magic, but there's something about the particular line of his grin that is so unmistakably William. Real, this is real.

I have one million things to say, but the only thing I can manage is "I'm sorry, I'm *so, so* sorry."

"Sorry for what, sis?" He's looking at me in that fond, sort of patronizing way he did in life. He's slouching, too, in the way our mother used to nag him about. There's a freckle next to his nose that I'd forgotten. "People die. It appears I was one of them." It's just like him, to treat his death as casually as he treated everything else.

"But I didn't save you."

He laughs—his chest rises and falls with it. "I didn't save me either. No one could have." He shrugs, and the gesture is so *William*, it devastates me.

There are so many questions on the tip of my tongue, but all I can think about is time. "How long do we have?"

He presses his lips together and exhales. It's a smile of pity. "Not long, I think, sis."

I wish we had more time. There's so much I want to tell him about magic and Haxahaven and Oliver and our mother, and the millions of other things he's missed.

"I miss you. You don't know how much I miss you. I can't lose you again. One day you were just gone, and I can't have you be *gone* again."

"Will it make you feel better if I say I'm at peace?"

I swallow the lump in my throat. I don't want to waste the time I have with tears. I want to crawl inside the glass, throw my arms around him, and let every broken piece of my heart finally rest.

"You need to move on. God, that's a cliché. Being dead has made me a cliché." He laughs. "But it hasn't made me any less right."

"Where are you?" I press my hands to the mirror; it's so cold, it feels like being burned. I jerk away.

William knits his eyebrows together in concern but keeps his tone as jokey as ever. "You know I can't say. I've always thought you worried too much about me. Stop worrying so much."

From behind the glass he closes his eyes. He's becoming more translucent by the moment.

I don't know how if my heart will stand losing him again.

"You can't leave yet. We need more time. What happened the night you died?"

"It's the stupidest thing. I hardly know. I'd worked a late shift and was walking home like I always did. Something hit me hard from behind. There was a gloved hand over my mouth. It was scratchy. The river was cold, but only for a minute. I barely felt a thing. Next thing I knew I was dead. Didn't even have time to turn around."

Disappointment surges through me. When I imagined this moment, I always pictured him giving me a name, a full description, something I could take action on. "You don't know who did it?"

He shakes his head. "I'm afraid I can't help you." It's just like William, to be so nonchalant about his own murder.

"Did you see a woman, maybe? About forty? Or a taller, younger one?"

He sighs. "I didn't see a thing. I was gazing at the river. I heard someone whistling a tune. It was a beautiful night, and then, *boom*, lights out."

Some part of me wonders if he's lying to spare my feelings.

"So what do I do?" I ask my brother in the very last moments I'll ever have with him. "What do I do in a world without you?"

He smiles, and the moment is perfect, except it's not, because he's dead and I'm still here.

"You *live*, silly."

"I don't know how." I can barely speak for holding back tears.

"You were always the smart Hallowell. I don't want you to feel any guilt about my death. Go live your life enough for the both of us. Don't for one single second feel guilty that you can't change the past."

There's nothing I wouldn't give to step into that mirror and switch places with him. "You were always the brave one."

He's fading quickly—parts of him are curling and evaporating like smoke on the wind. "Now it has to be you."

"I don't know how," I repeat, tears spilling hot down my cheeks.

"So you'll do what you've always done. You'll *learn*."

My chest is caving in on itself. "Please don't leave me," I sob.

"You know I'd never do that." He smiles one last time, and then he is gone.

"No," I cry. Finn is behind me, holding my shoulders as I collapse over my knees, sobs racking my body. "No!" I shake him off and crawl to where the spell book lies on the dirt behind us.

"*Tras thar an veil agus tabhair dom an méid a cailleadh ionas go faimais níos mó ama a labhairt.*" I recite the spell between gasping sobs. It sounds like I'm begging. I suppose I am.

"Stop, love, you'll hyperventilate." Finn tries to take the book from me.

"No!" I scream at him. "I need more time!"

I snatch the book back from him and crawl to the mirror. Again I recite the spell, but nothing comes. Nothing stirs within me.

I try a third time.

A fourth time.

In the reflection of the mirror, Finn looks on with pity.

Again and again I recite the spell and beg the universe to break the rules for me just one more time.

Finn places a gentle hand on my shoulder. "C'mon, Frances."

I press my forehead to the cold mirror and let the horrible truth take root inside me.

I've lost William again, and this time it's forever.

CHAPTER TWENTY-EIGHT

I collapse and cry so hard, it seems unbelievable it doesn't shatter every bone in my body.

Finn holds me until my eyes are all but swelled shut. "You did it, Frances."

I should find peace in knowing he felt no pain. Maybe that will come when I don't feel quite so ruined for having lost him a second time.

Finn lets me cry for what feels like a long time. When the tears slow and I'm strong enough to look up at him, he picks me up off the floor and supports me back up the basement stairs. His chest is solid. It's nice to have something steady to cling to.

He takes me to his room, small and windowless, not much bigger than a closet. The narrow space contains a cot and a desk, which is covered in books, skeins of yarn, and scrawled notes in familiar handwriting.

Leaned up against the wall is a scuffed-up fiddle and a fraying bow.

"I didn't know you played," I say in a weak voice. I don't want to cry anymore. I feel hollowed out and desperate to think of anything other than how bad I feel.

"I don't much anymore."

He guides me to his bed, the only place to sit down with much comfort. I lie back and roll to my side. My body feels so heavy, but my mind is alert with the kind of clarity that comes after crying. "What do we do now?" I ask him.

He lies down on the bed next to me, so we're facing each other. Our noses are almost but not quite touching. "We have a lifetime to figure that out."

I gaze at Finn's fine profile. I could spend hours examining the slope of his nose.

He cards my hair with his hands. Soft and steady, without urgency or pressure, simply touching me like I'm a thing worth touching.

It's strange to know I've existed for him for so long, when he is so new to me.

We sit quietly until my hands stop shaking and my breathing slows. It's only then I ask him the question I've wanted to ask him for a very long time.

"Am I what you imagined I'd be when you saw me in your dreams all those years ago?"

Finn bites his lower lip. Finally he answers, "You're better."

"In what way?"

"You're real."

And then, before I have a chance to overthink it, he turns his head and presses his lips to mine.

His kiss is urgent and reckless. I rise to meet it with a recklessness of my own. His hands wind through my hair, finding their way to the nape of my neck. He tugs a little, pulling my head back, and trails his mouth down my neck, liquid and hot down my jackrabbit pulse. I grasp at the expanse of his shoulders. It would be so easy to lose myself to this feeling. I want to drown in it and never come up.

When he finishes his work on my neck, his mouth slots against mine once more. His tongue darts in between my lips.

I allow every one of his touches to push the sorrowful thoughts from my mind. I could become nothing, no one. I crave more, this heat of oblivion.

The hand that isn't in my hair presses hard against the small of my back, pulling me closer to him.

He rolls, and suddenly I'm under him, the weight and warmth of him is overwhelming. He is everywhere.

I think I want this.

I want to want this. It's safety and comfort and peace. The grief in my head is quieted in the moment, replaced with Finn—his touch, his urgency . . . his need.

Finn's kiss sends fire through my veins, but my heart echoes like the halls of an empty cathedral.

He rolls so we are lying side to side once more.

I pull back, panting and flushed.

Pupils blown out and awestruck, his eyes are sparkly even in the low light of his basement room.

This moment feels inevitable, and in that there is comfort.

"Thank you," I whisper. I close my eyes and curl against his chest. His heart is beating fast. It makes me blush.

"For what?" he whispers against my hair.

"Not giving up on me."

He places a kiss on top of my head. "We're together now, you and I. It's going to stay that way."

The room is dark when I wake with a start, but I feel it must be close to dawn.

Next to me, Finn's breathing is steady. He looks so much younger in sleep. There's a constellation of freckles across the bridge of his nose so faint, they're only visible this close. I feel a deep sense of possessiveness when I look at him, like I want to spend the rest of my life making sure nothing else ever hurts him.

Suddenly there is an unmistakable tug in my rib cage, demanding I go up to the foyer. I don't know how I know—I just do.

I feel it again. Like there's a string attached to my sternum. The sensation is nauseating. *Come on,* it says. *Come with me.*

I grab a knotty knit sweater of Finn's off his desk chair and pull it over my dress.

Finn doesn't stir as I leave the room and creep quietly up the stairs.

Through the hall windows, the first pale pink light of dawn leaks. The Commodore Club is quiet.

I wrap my arms tight around my middle and follow more serpentine halls until I reach a swinging door that will lead me to the main foyer.

I take a breath and push through.

Pacing the gleaming wood floors is a very concerned-looking Mrs. Vykotsky. She's in the same buttoned-up, stiff, high-necked black dress and velvet cape she always wears, except she's added a wide-brimmed hat to the ensemble. Haloed in streaming light, the moonstone brooch at her throat throws rainbows along the stern line of her jaw. She cuts a frightening figure with her hands on her hips and the look of maternal disapproval etched on her face.

I should be less shocked she's found me here, but her presence still shakes me to my core.

"I am disappointed but not surprised," she says by way of greeting.

There is fear, and then comes anger, a fire sparking from long-burning embers of rage. How dare she follow me here like she has any claim to me at all. "I'm not going back with you."

"Don't be stubborn, dear. I thought perhaps with a little time you'd come to your senses on your own. It is unfortunate to find I was mistaken." She clicks her tongue.

"How did you know where I was?"

She turns her nose up at me. "I don't know what it is that makes young girls think you're so unknowable. You're incredibly predictable."

She can condescend to me all she wants, but I am no longer her pupil, and this is not her school. "You can insult me if you'd like, but I'm not coming back with you."

She arches a brow. "Now, I wouldn't be so sure about that. You do seem to care genuinely about Miss Jamison and Miss DuPre."

Fear rolls through me. "Are you threatening them?"

Just then the sound of a walking stick thumping down the stairs makes us both pause.

In a dressing gown and gold-threaded slippers is Boss Olan, who doesn't look at all baffled by the scene before him.

"Hello, Ana," he greets her.

"I'm fetching my pupil. We'll be gone soon," she replies.

Though Boss Olan towers over her in stature, Mrs. Vykotsky's presence still looms large over all of us. I suspect the whole city block just shivered at the ice in her voice.

"The young Miss Hallowell has made her choice. And you know the rules, Ana," Boss Olan says.

"As do you, George." They're on a first-name basis with each other—it surprises me. I feel like an interloper witnessing their conversation. I wonder if I could sneak away, back to the basement.

"Then you know you can't step foot in this building, not after Billy."

"And, as per our mutual agreement after the McKinney boy incident, you know you can't harm any of my pupils."

Billy? Her pupils?

Boss Olan stays on the stairs, looming over Mrs. Vykotsky. "Miss Hallowell came to us on her own volition. Seems she's not impressed with the operation you have going on in the outer boroughs."

Mrs. Vykotsky proves impossible to talk down to. She somehow manages to speak to Boss Olan as if he were an ordinary man with no magic, no threats ready to be carried out. "Miss Hallowell is confused. She doesn't understand what it is you do."

I can't stand them speaking in code about things I don't understand. I gather my courage and interrupt them. "What is it that you do?"

Mrs. Vykotsky answers before Boss Olan can. "They'll destroy the world if you let them, Frances. Did you know they own twentyseven factories in the city? Did you know they staff them with children? They control most of the judges in the city and half of the city council. The Sons of Saint Druon would do anything to remain in control. They worship nothing except money and their own reflections."

"What is it they say about glass houses, Ana?" Boss Olan replies. "Does the young Miss Hallowell know what you've done?"

I'm standing between Mrs. Vykotsky in the foyer and Boss Olan on the landing. I wish I could ask them to sit down and discuss magic and my future and our differences over a cup of tea, but something about their posture tells me that isn't going to happen.

I hesitate to ask the question, afraid of the answer. But I have to know. "What have you done?"

Her voice goes a little quieter, her posture slumped, just barely, like the memory is heavy to carry. "Nothing that wasn't merited, and it was a very long time ago."

Boss Olan stomps—it makes me jump. "She killed poor Billy McKinney and dumped his body in the East River."

Dumped his body in the East River.

Everything is happening so fast, I file the information away for later. I can't keep up with the conversation happening in front of me.

"After you and Billy burned my sister's coven to the ground with her inside!" Mrs. Vykotsky shouts with a pain that reaches to the very depths of her being.

I'm reminded of my second day at Haxahaven; it feels so long ago. I sat in the low chair across from Mrs. Vykotsky's desk, and she told me of a coven burned to the ground with salt and gunpowder, all thirteen witches still inside. She said the fire was why she kept us out of Manhattan; it was why we couldn't develop our magic into anything of significance.

Boss Olan slams his walking stick down on the stairs in anger.

"And did torturing Billy and ruining my knee make you feel any better about your big sister being dead?" Boss Olan shouts at her with a cruel laugh.

Of all the questions I have about the conversation, I am only able to vocalize the most trivial; 1845 was so long ago. "How old were you when you killed him?" I ask Mrs. Vykotsky.

She regains her composure and clasps her hands together. It's all so polite. "They killed my elder sister when she was seventeen and I was five. I waited until I was seventeen to get my revenge. I made sure Billy knew I was coming."

Her reply sends a chill down my spine. "Why'd they kill her?" I ask. I'm not sure I want to know the answer.

This time it's Boss Olan who answers. "Because they were harming our business ventures and putting all of us at risk."

Here it is, six decades of bitterness and rivalry leaking like a chemical spill all over the fine carpets of the Commodore Club.

"You've always been a liar," Mrs. Vykotsky sneers. "You killed them to make a statement. You killed them to send us the message that you ruled this city and there was nothing we could do."

Killed them. I try to keep track of the body count in my head. Mrs. Vykotsky killed Billy. The Sons killed her sister and her sister's coven.

Then my brother. Then the handless boys on Sheepshead Bay. Then the commissioner.

On and on for sixty-six years.

Who else is dead because of this? How much blood has been spilled?

"No, that was just a bonus," Boss Olan says with a wicked grin. The look Mrs. Vykotsky gives him speaks of death itself.

She marches over to me and tugs me by the arm, hard. "That's enough ugliness. Frances, we're going."

"No—" I rip my arm from her grip.

"Don't make this harder than it needs to be, dear."

I take a step back. "No, I won't go with you." My voice is steady despite the fear coursing through me like an ice-cold river.

"Would you rather I turn you in to the authorities?" she threatens.

I call her bluff. "Yes."

"And why is that?" she asks me with the indulgent patience of a school teacher.

"Because if I'm going to be in prison, I'd rather my jailer be someone who isn't you. That school you're running is as good as a cell, the way you—"

She sighs in frustration. Then from out of her pocket floats a delicate silver chain. More quickly than I can process, she uses magic to wind it around my wrists. It's so tight, my hands go almost immediately numb.

I struggle against it, first physically, then with the magic boiling in my chest. I lash out with power, but nothing happens—the chain does not budge.

Boss Olan watches through narrowed eyes as I struggle.

I try to take hold of Mrs. Vykotsky's body with my magic, but she rips out of my control almost immediately. She makes it look so easy, like she's just swatting a fly away.

"Please—" I turn to Boss Olan, pleading with him. I hate asking for his help, but I'm not going back to Haxahaven with her. *I won't.*

He shrugs, like he means to see how the fight between us plays out.

383

"The automobile is waiting, dear." She gives the chain around my wrists a hard tug. I stumble forward.

"Finn!" I scream, but I doubt he can hear me in the basement. *"Finn!"*

Panic rises in my chest. I dig my heels into the wood floors.

Like he's bored of all this, Boss Olan says, "The girl is allowed to stay."

Mrs. Vykotsky barks out a laugh. "Come, Frances." She tugs me to the door.

"Finn!" I scream once more, head whipping around like an animal caught in a trap.

Boss Olan waves his hands, and the lock on the front door turns with a click. "I said she's allowed to stay."

It all happens so quickly. Mrs. Vykotsky flings the door open with her magic; then Boss Olan sweeps the rug out from under her feet, leaving her sputtering on the floor. He must release the chain around my wrist, because it unfurls in a blink. I shake my hands as the blood rushes back, a blessed relief.

The coatrack flies at Boss Olan as he flings Mrs. Vykotsky against the wall; she stumbles, but does not fall. The hall table collapses at some point, though I'm not sure which one of them is responsible.

Quicker than I can process, the room is thrown into chaos. The front window shatters; furniture is levitated, then crashes with a bang. I duck out of the way of a ring of keys spiraling through the air. I turn to make a break for it, hoping I can use this momentary distraction to get away, but I run directly into Finn's chest. He's come sprinting into the room, hair flying, panting and wide-eyed.

I shout, "You can't let her take me, please. They're killing Sons!"

At this Mrs. Vykotsky and Boss Olan stop. The storm quiets, leaving rubble strewn across the formerly elegant entryway.

"Is this true, Ana?" Boss pants.

She sighs like I've inconvenienced her. "The commissioner? Helen made it clear we were defending ourselves."

Finn places a hand on my shoulder, but I'm so singularly focused on Mrs. Vykotsky, I barely feel it.

The foyer chandelier shakes, the crystals clinking against each other like a swarm of cicadas as my rage becomes too big for my body to hold. And because I have nothing else to lose, I ask the question I've been dying to ask her. "And what about my brother? Were you all defending yourselves then, too? He had *no* magic! He was an ordinary person. He was a *person*. And you threw him in the river like trash. *Why.*" I beg, "Tell me why you did it."

Mrs. Vykotsky and I stare each other down. The snickering look on her face is an admission of guilt in itself. The chandelier shakes and shakes, the sun peeks above the buildings, throwing a single golden sunbeam into the entryway, and I wish more than I've ever wished anything in my entire life that Mrs. Vykotsky were dead. Not only for what I believe she did to my brother, but for all the girls at Haxahaven. Punishing them—hurting the ones they love to make a point.

For Lena, her family. Maxine and those she cares for. Aurelia, Maria.

My mother.

Mrs. Vykotsky starts to say something. "Your brother was . . ." But her lips are barely able to form the next words.

I wish I'd never met her. I wish Haxahaven had another headmistress. I wish my brother was still alive. I wish—

I wish she was dead instead of him.

I wish she was dead.

The magic part of me snarls awake, lashing out like the crack of a whip.

Noooo! But I can't harness this, the wild, awful power.

Suddenly her neck snaps sharply to the left, and she crumples like a rag doll onto the fine entryway floor.

My chest heaves. My heart thump-thumps against my rib cage. The air becomes hard to breath.

No! No! No!

Finn reaches out to catch me, but I slip through his arms, collapsing to my knees.

My ears ring; everything goes fuzzy.

How did I let everything go so wrong again?

Boss Olan does nothing but raise his eyebrows. The weight of his stare pushes down on me as he hovers over Finn and me. "Looks as if Haxahaven has broken our treaty yet again. Killing helpless members of the Sons." His voice swirls in my mind. "I am sorry, Frances. Your brother was a good lad."

Ripples of shock and sadness burst like a rusted-out pipe. Finn cradles my head against his chest. I don't recognize my voice as I repeat over and over again, "Did I kill her? I didn't mean to kill her. I didn't mean to. Didn't mean to . . ."

Soon other men pour into the room, drawn by the noise of the fight that ended less than two minutes ago. How quickly I always seem to ruin things.

Without much discussion they carry Mrs. Vykotsky's body away. Boss Olan takes her shoulders, and one of the larger Jameses takes her feet. Almost as if this is nothing new—a dead body in the Commodore Club.

The hem of her black dress rises as they lift her, revealing pale blue stockings.

I can picture her putting them on this morning, not knowing it was her last. I'm struck with a wave of guilt and regret so fierce, I don't know if I'll ever be able to stand to look at myself again. She was right in the end, I realize. I refused to heed any of her lectures regarding how dangerous my uncontrolled power was, and now I've killed her with it.

Every emotion I'm feeling must be splashed across my face, because Finn whispers, "You did the right thing."

I push him away, afraid of what I might do. I don't trust the magic swirling inside me. "But I didn't mean to do it," I rasp.

Finn isn't afraid, though. He inches closer, cups my chin in his rough hands. "The right thing is you and me, ridding the world of anyone who has ever harmed us." His eyes are gold and silver, the brightest green that flashes with hope. He stares at me, hard. I'm shaking so badly that Finn scoops one of my arms over his shoulders and helps me back down to his room in the basement.

I flop onto his bed and stare at the ceiling. The place my brother spoke to me from last night looked peaceful. After all the things I've done, I doubt I'll be joining him there. *What would he think of me now?*

I killed her. The thought pounds in my head over and over again, like a nail hammered into my skull. There is no escaping what I've done. Killing Mr. Hues was different. This was, was . . . *I don't know.*

Finn breaks the long silence. "She won't be coming after you now—trying to take you back to that prison of a school. Think of the grand life we'll have now. We can do whatever we want. Go wherever we choose. No more rules to follow, or walls to keep us in."

I peer up at him. "You don't think I'm irredeemable?"

I want so badly to be saved by him, to be forgiven by anyone for what I've done. *Tell me I'm special. Tell me I'm good.*

He huffs out a sad laugh. "I killed my step-da. One bullet in the skull on my way out of town. Boss helped me dump his body in a bog the same day he came for me in Ireland. I hopped on the ship for New York the next day. I've never once regretted it." He reaches for my hands, clutches them so tightly, my fingers go numb. "Do you think *I'm* irredeemable? It's all right when the reasons are good."

Of course I don't think that. His stepfather was cruel in ways that I can't imagine. "But that's different, Finn."

Finn sighs. "I don't think it was."

I shake my head, rub my temples to stop the ache pulsing behind my eyelids. What will happen to Haxahaven now that she is gone?

I thought there would be more peace in knowing the truth of what happened to my brother. I never imagined it would involve this much blood on my hands.

Finn's windowless room blocks out the light, and by the time I wake, I have no idea whether it's night or day. All I know is that I'm alone.

My bare feet touch the cold cement floor and I tug the too-long sleeves of Finn's sweater over my shaking hands. My head still aches and my stomach is still in knots, but I don't want to sleep anymore, afraid of what nightmares I might find waiting for me.

I pick through the pile of clothing strewn across his floor until I find a pair of socks, obviously knit by Finn, and pull them on to stop my shivering.

I trail a finger along the water-ringed wood of his desk, savoring the peek inside his life when I'm not around.

Littered with books and papers and yarn, something on the far-left lower corner catches my eye, something I didn't spot last night.

Etched deep into the wood with a penknife is a word. The edges of the letters are sharp and angry, like they've been carved out repeatedly for a very long time. A knife digging into wood, tracing the same letters over and over again.

A name.

My name.

FRANCES.

I peer out the door. The basement is eerily still. "Finn?" I hiss down the lamp-lit hall.

Nothing.

I creep up the staircase. "Finn?" I call once more. The knob on the door at the top of the stairs turns easily, but the door itself won't open. With my shoulder I shove and muscle the door until whatever is blocking it slides enough for me to shimmy out. I trip on a human leg and crash onto the floor, landing halfway on top of a very cold, very dead Boss Olan.

CHAPTER TWENTY-NINE

I don't scream out, but I do say, "What?" very matter-of-factly, like Boss himself could answer me.

His eagle-headed walking stick is still grasped in his right hand, and there's a gunshot wound in the center of his forehead. He was so alive when I saw him just hours ago.

I push up off the floor, shaking, terrified. A frightening thought creeps into my head. *I did this.* The witches have found out what happened to Mrs. Vykotsky, and this is their revenge. Killing the leader of the Sons. It takes everything I have to focus on finding an exit. The witches could still be in the Commodore Club, and I don't want them to find me here. I trust Finn will come to me, as he always does. That is, if he isn't dead too. But that possibility is too horrible to entertain.

On quiet feet, I travel as fast as I'm able down the hallway, past silent lounges and billiards rooms.

From upstairs, I hear muffled shouting that shifts to the dull thud of bodies slamming into one another.

I have no time to dwell on my horror. With pure animal instinct, the only thing in my head is *run, run, run.*

I make a break for the front door, but the brass handle won't turn, like it's locked from the outside. Knowing there is no time for creative magic, no room for error, I extend my hand and whisper, *"Briseadh,"* but the spell doesn't work. The window above the door is shattered from Mrs. Vykotsky and Boss Olan's previous fight, but it's too high to reach.

I curse under my breath and shatter the narrow window next to the door with the handle of the first umbrella I find. Glass rains down at my feet.

"Frances!" Finn's brogue calls me from the top of the stairs.

My head snaps to him, and relief floods through me at the sight of him alive. "Finn!"

"Frances, go back to the basement." He's breathless, sweaty, and covered in blood I hope isn't his own.

"We need to leave!" I shout.

"I said go back to the basement!" The sound of shattering glass and more shouting draws his attention.

"Are the witches here?" I step forward. "Maybe I can talk to them. Explain what happened to—"

"Frances, I beg you," Finn interrupts "Go back to the basement. I'll come to you soon." And with that he runs back down the hall and out of sight.

I will not go back to the basement. But with one foot out the window and one still in the foyer of the Commodore Club I am faced with a choice: fight or run.

His words echo in my head. *We're together now, you and I. It's going to stay that way.*

My choice was made the night I went to meet Finn in Forest Park.

I run up the stairs.

The sound of the scuffle isn't difficult to follow. I race down the hall, passing room after silent room of bodies draped over couches or sprawled in front of stately portraits. Whatever has happened in the Commodore Club is nothing short of a massacre. What have they done?

What have I done?

The pop of a gunshot rattles my bones, and I run even faster. Down the hall, in an elegant bedroom, I find Finn and three of the Jameses. One of them is holding a smoking pistol, and at his feet is a body with a large red stain spreading across its back.

"Very good," Finn states casually to the gun-holding James. He freezes when he sees me in the doorway.

I freeze too, taking in the scene before me. I shut my eyes, as if I can wish this all away, but I know what gunpowder smells like, and I've heard a man die before.

There in the middle of it all is my gorgeous, lovely, sweet Finn. A boy with freckles on his nose. A boy who knit my friends and me mittens, who bought me spun sugar just to see me smile. Who is here now, with blood on his shoes and a look on his face so hardened, I barely recognize him.

"I told you to go to the basement, Frances." His sparkly eyes have gone dark; worry creases his brow.

A sick feeling sluices in my chest as I realize I don't know Finn as well as I thought I did. The boy I thought I knew would never speak to me like this. "Don't tell me what to do."

He throws his hands up in the air. "I'm trying to keep you safe."

"From what?" I demand. A childish part of me hopes he has a perfectly reasonable explanation for all this. That he'll kiss me on the forehead and make everything better.

"You didn't tell her?" One of the Jameses nudges him in the rib cage with an elbow.

"Frances knows what she needs to," Finn replies in a low voice.

I scan the room: the bodies are all men. "I don't know anything," I whisper, but that's not true. Looking at Finn, the tension in his face, the body at his feet, I'm putting the pieces together.

"Finn," I beg him, "please."

The Jameses exchange the grins of foxes who have broken into a chicken coop. "It's Boss D'Arcy now that the old bastard's dead. Show some respect."

"Boss D'Arcy?"

No. No, no.

"Finn will do fine, boys," Finn answers, looking straight at me.

I step toward him. "What are they talking about?"

Finn sighs like I'm an inconvenience. It shatters something inside of me.

"I don't have time to explain it all right now. I just really, really need you to trust me."

In this moment there is nothing more I want than to trust him, but I can't ignore the slippery feeling in my gut.

"Tell me what's going on," I beg him, desperate and pathetic.

One of the Jameses visibly rolls his eyes. Finn sighs and sinks down into an armchair in the corner of the room.

"You ever heard of a coup?" the shortest James says.

"A coup?" I ask Finn. I won't believe anything until I hear it from him.

Finn's eyebrow lifts as his hand rakes through his messy hair. "The Sons of Saint Druon were due for a change. You saw the way they ran things. It was unfair."

I shake my head, trying to understand. "You mean the *Cath Draíochta*?"

Finn snickers and looks at me as if I'm a naive little girl. "Those with magic . . . *us*, Frances, we're special. *We* should be the ones in charge. I'm doing this for us, love. Truly. Please, just trust me."

There's that word again, "trust." I don't trust anything in this moment. I'm not even sure I trust myself.

"So you killed them? You killed the Sons who don't have magic?" The words taste traitorous on my tongue. I can't believe I'm saying them. Asking Finn—my Finn—these questions.

The short James speaks again. "They killed us first. Once Finn discovered what they were doing to the factory workers, we couldn't sit by and do nothing. They were offering our kin jobs, only to make them work with shoddy equipment that took their limbs. Then they dumped their bodies to avoid a labor investigation. They didn't even let Walt bury his little brother Johnny. They deserve this and more."

Johnny O'Farrell, found handless on Sheepshead Bay.

The Jameses mutter and nod their heads in agreement.

Finn whips his head around to glare at the boy who spoke.

394

I stare up at Finn in horror. My ears ring for a moment as I attempt to process what I've heard. Surely I can't be understanding right. "The boys on Sheepshead Bay were victims of *factory accidents*? How do you know?"

He's breathing so heavily. "We don't have confirmation on all of them. I found the documents the night you and I broke into Boss's office. We confirmed the cause of death with the city coroner. I guess after the Triangle Shirtwaist disaster there's been a great deal more manufacturing oversight. Boss Olan and the factory managers wanted to avoid an investigation. It made more sense to dump them. But that doesn't mean the witches didn't kill your brother. He never worked at a factory, Frances. Vykotksy deserved what she got."

For a moment it's like I'm watching this all happen to someone else, like I'm out of my body floating on the ceiling. *Finn knew*, I realize. Finn knew why those boys were washing up on the beach, and he never once told me. Instead he let me traipse around the city, put myself and my friends in danger. Sure, I'd still have wanted to use the resurrection spell to speak to my brother, but I would have made different choices if I hadn't believed that speaking to him and solving his murder could save more lives.

Oh God, Maxine. I picture her devastated face as I accused her of being responsible for killing the Sons.

I come back to my body. "Of course that's what it means!" I shout. Rage and horror burn through me like a wildfire. "You lied to me?"

Finn crosses the room and takes my hands in his. They're cold and clammy. I want to pull away, but he grips hard. "The entire system is rotten. Everyone at the top was corrupt. We can build a better world now. One where magicians can live without secrets, one where we can rule justly, like we were meant to."

"A mansion full of bodies is not my idea of a better world," I reply.

He closes his eyes in an expression of frustration. "This was a necessary sacrifice. You and I, we're going to rule the city . . . the world . . . side by side, just like we spoke about." His wide-eyed optimism might be infectious were it not for the blood staining his clothes and the body at his feet.

"I didn't ask for this." I didn't know he wanted this. I didn't know this power-hungry, brutal side of Finn at all.

"You didn't have to." He reaches up to brush a lock of hair from my face. It is in this moment that I realize I'm still wearing his sweater and socks. "I'm sorry I kept this from you, but I didn't want to scare you—your heart is so soft."

It doesn't feel soft now. It feels shattered.

He continues, excited. "Once we've cleared the high council, we'll rule everything, love. The judges, the mayor, the factories. And that's just the beginning."

"We're going to be kings," a blond James adds, gazing at Finn with the reverence of a choirboy.

Finn nods. "Soon the world will be as it should, with the magical ruling over the non-magical."

My heart sinks. The whole world is crumbling, and I can't stop it—I'm as powerless as the body lying on the floor in front of me.

"I've never wanted to rule over anyone," I answer. "I don't want to be a part of this."

"That's because you're so sweet." Finn looks at me with pity, like an aversion to killing is a weakness.

"Listen, love," he continues. "We have the power to remake the world. Make it different, better. This is what William wanted. You, changing things."

I scan the room, the weapons in the boys' hands, the blood, the body, see how proud Finn stands as the coordinator of it all, and at once I understand. Finn would burn the world to the ground to get what he wants, but I have no interest in helping him turn the world into ashes.

"My brother wouldn't want this," I whisper. Finally, he allows me to take my hands from his. "I don't know who you are," I say more to myself than to him. Speaking the words aloud makes it real.

Finn purses his lips, clenches his jaw. A look of hatred crosses his face, so intense, it feels as if I'm looking at a stranger. "Would you prefer I be more like Oliver Callahan?" His anger mixes with a genuine look of hurt, which only confuses me more. "I see the way you look at him," Finn scoffs. "I could be your future. Let me be your future."

Finn runs a hand through his sweaty curls. "Join us. There's so much left to do."

I could say no. I could walk away, run from Finn, from magic, from myself. But would he really let me just march out the door?

"Remember," he says, holding his hand out to mine. "You and I are tethered together. What we did in the basement. There is no escaping that." He smiles at me, and I know he's right. There is a small, foolish part of my heart that wonders if Finn is not yet irredeemable. An even worse part of me thinks maybe it's where I'm meant to be—by his side. I've killed twice now. I can't temper my anger, take hold of the power I have swirling inside me; I can control others against their will. Maybe I am just like him.

The tether of energy between us tugs me closer to him. Is this where I belong? There is nowhere else for me to go. Would Maxine and Lena ever forgive me for what I did to Mrs. Vykotsky? The other witches? And Oliver. *No.* He'd never understand me now. And I have no intention of dragging the one good thing about me into the middle of a magical war. Do I really have another choice?

"All right," I reply.

Finn's face crumbles in relief, and he throws a heavy arm around my shoulder. "I know this is hard for you, but you'll understand in time."

I smile sweetly, like he wants me to, slip on my shoes and a coat and follow him out the door. I smile the smile of a girl who is nothing like me.

You foolish girl. Mrs. Vykotsky's voice rings in my head.

The street is dark and cold, but I am relieved to be out of the death-filled Commodore Club.

"What's your plan?" I say to Finn with an intentional touch of his shoulder. Let him think I'm a sweet girl. He doesn't yet need to know my heart is nothing but a burned-out shell, filled with the smoke of things I used to love.

"We've taken care of all the council members we could. Their meeting this afternoon was like shooting fish in a barrel. But there were a few that couldn't come, so the boys will go to them. You and I are going to take care of some paperwork."

"Paperwork?"

"Mayor Gaynor is in Boss Olan's pocket. He'll never agree to work with me now that Boss Olan is out."

I don't correct him that by "out" he means "dead."

"So he's going to sign his resignation," Finn continues.

I think of the last time I was tasked with making a man sign his name against his will. "Have you had this idea since the night with the commissioner?"

"You were so powerful, Frances. I can do great things, now that we're one."

He turns to the four Jameses milling about the sidewalk, cracking their knuckles. One is twirling a butterfly knife. "You know where you're going, lads?"

"We're off to the Callahan place." The blond James gestures to the tall James.

"And we're off to the Tilfords'."

"Most of the lads are already headed up to that school," a short redhead adds.

Finn gives them a sharp nod, and the four of them take off like a shot down the street.

"The Callahans'? *That school?*" My false sweetness evaporates, replaced again with terror. Just when I think I have a handle on what Finn's planning, he plays another card. He's been playing all along.

He loops his arm through mine and tugs me forcefully in the opposite direction from where the Jameses ran. I try to shake him off, but I stumble over my shoes. He's so much bigger than me.

"It's fine," he says darkly. "You and I have our own tasks to worry about. And besides, we're finally alone again, eh?"

He leans in to kiss me, but I recoil from his touch. "What are they doing at the Callahans'? What are they doing at Haxahaven?" Finn's mouth is so dangerously close to mine, I almost bite him.

"I always said if I was in charge, I'd recruit the witches to join us. We'll give them the opportunity to learn real magic, just like you and I always wanted. Think of what we could accomplish together, the witches and the Sons. We could do anything."

"But you'll kill anyone who gets in your way?" I think of encouraging Mrs. Roberts, kind Florence, and gentle Ann. They'd never join him.

"Every war has casualties." He shrugs. "If they choose to die rather than join us, that's their business."

The gesture fills me with white-hot rage. I need to get out of here, to warn them.

"I won't let you touch them." I scarcely recognize my own voice. I try to unleash my power, to take hold of Finn's body, but it feels less like a flame and more like smoke from a snuffed candle.

An electric shock zips from the tips of my fingers, through the joint at my elbow and into my shoulder. My arm jerks away from Finn's, entirely out of my control.

I try again to take hold of him, but the magic doesn't come when I call.

Next I try to levitate a rock to hurl at him. It's a simple spell, one I've done a hundred times, but nothing happens.

Finn watches quietly as I struggle. There's a stab of panic. "What have you done?" I ask in horror.

"I did what you asked of me, love. You used our magic to speak to your brother. Now I use our magic to do this."

Sickness rolls through me as I fight understanding what I already know deep down. *"This?"*

Finn's smile is awful and hungry. There's nothing sweet about his grin now. "Your magic within me has made me the most powerful magician in New York. No one can stop me. No one can stop *us*."

"What did you do, Finn?" It comes out as a whisper.

He sighs, annoyed I'm not getting it. He takes a step forward in an attempt to grasp my hands in his. I rip away from him. "When we bound ourselves—which, I'll remind you, is what you asked for— you bound your magic to me. Your power lives in me now. Isn't that something? Isn't it incredible, what we've done?"

Panic rises in me as the horrible truth settles. "How?"

"The binding spell gave me control over your power as if it were my own. It transferred it from your body to mine. I own all of it. It is mine to do with as I please."

"But you said the words too." I'm confused.

Finn smiles, as pleased with himself as ever. "Your vows were different than mine, love. You pledged all of yourself to me. I made no such promises."

"I'm powerless? It's all gone?"

"Oh, darling, I'd never do that to you. I'll give it back eventually. Once you see that I'm right."

And here is the full force of the truth I've been fighting. *He's stolen it. He's stolen my power. And it's my own fault.*

"You can give it back, though, can't you?" My lips tremble as I try to push out the words.

He shrugs. "In theory."

"You tricked me?" I nearly double over in pain, but I refuse to be weak in front of him.

"I did what you asked of me. It's what partners do."

I want to slap the smug look off his face. I'm on the verge of vomiting. The violation of it all makes me want to crawl out of my own skin. "Give it back, Finn. Give it back now. It belongs to me."

He shakes his head slowly. It's like looking at a stranger. "No. Not yet. Not until I'm sure you understand what this means for us. I must be sure that you will stay. You'll see in time, Frances. I'm positive of it. Just be patient, love."

"Was this your plan all along? Did you care for me at all?"

A look of genuine hurt crosses Finn's face. Whatever it is we've felt for each other, the betrayal we're both experiencing is violently real. I'm not the person he wanted either.

"Can't the answer to both questions be yes?" he replies.

I want to cry.

I want to kill him.

I want to kiss him and beg him to make it all better, and that's what hurts the most.

He throws his hands up in exasperation. "You know what's so stupid about all of this?" His voice is rough and annoyed. "I could just make the mayor sign the paperwork in his dreams, like I had you write those damned notes left on your pillow. But I wanted you to be a part of this. I wanted to do this together!"

I can't process all this information in such a short time. "You . . . you made me write the notes to myself?"

"A fancy trick. One of the reasons I was so valuable to Boss Olan."

I don't understand. "It wasn't my handwriting."

With wicked, flashing eyes he responds, "Of course not, it was mine. Your pen, your paper, your hand, *my* words.

The sick bile of betrayal stings my throat. My own body was something I thought I had complete control over. He's taken even that from me.

I turn away from him, terrified to spill the ugly tears welling in my eyes.

"Frances, please," he begs me. His tone is softer, like it used to be. "Help me. We're so close. Then the world will be as it should be, and you and I will be together."

"How do you know how the world should be?" My voice cracks.

"I've been seeing you in my dreams since before I knew you were real. This is fate."

How I wish I had that much confidence in anything. I certainly don't have it in Finn.

"Will you answer me one question?" I ask.

"Anything."

"Why you?"

He steps back as if I've slapped him. "Why did they pick you to lead? Ruler of the city seems like an awfully big role for an eighteen-year-old."

His eyebrows furrow together. "They didn't pick me. *I* picked them to help me." He accentuates every word, makes sure they're implanted in my skull. "Truth is, I've been planning this for a long while. With you by my side."

Maybe it's the way he looks at me—so filled with purpose and rage and misplaced reverence. How right he believes he is. This isn't the boy who brought my brother home drunk last year—the boy I've always wanted him to be. William's voice breaks through the roiling panic of my thoughts.

Run.

"I'll never rule by your side." I turn on the heel of my borrowed shoes and sprint as quickly as my aching legs will carry me in the direction of the Callahans'.

"Frances!" Finn runs after me and grabs me roughly by the elbow.

"Don't touch me!" I swing my arm to throw him off.

"Frances, Frances, stop," Finn huffs. "Just . . . enter through the back door. They'll have someone posted at the front. And take out Jack first. He's the most powerful, but he does his best magic with metal, so get the knives out of reach as quickly as you can. He always keeps a dagger in his breast pocket."

I struggle against his grip, try to wiggle through. I don't understand what he's doing. What he's saying.

"Jack is the blond one. Frances, focus. The blond one—"

"Why are you telling me this?" I snap at him.

He opens his mouth, then closes it. For a breath he looks like the boy who knit me mittens. With a sad sigh he shakes his head slightly and takes off running in the other direction.

I'm confused as I watch him leave, but I have no time to dwell. I just run and run and run all the way to the Callahans' brownstone. I pay no attention to the people of New York, who look at me, scandalized, as I sprint down the street. It's nearly fifteen blocks, and with each step I imagine the consequences of not making it in time, of Judge Callahan with a bullet in his skull, or generous Mrs. Callahan, dead in her fine drawing room. I have no money for a petty cab or the subway; my only choice is to push past the burning in my legs and pray I'm not too late.

I approach the brownstone from the back alley. Finn could have been lying to me; he's good at it. But the particular sadness in his eyes makes me believe he was telling the truth.

I climb their back garden wall. A single flickering gas lamp set into the back of the brownstone illuminates only the porch, so I jump to the ground blind. Gravel crunches as I land roughly. My right ankle collapses under me with a sharp twinge. I swear under my breath but hop up as quickly as I'm able. I have no time.

I run through the garden, thinking of Oliver and vanilla ice cream and baseball and secret smiles and embarrassed glances.

Please, please. Please.

Without Mrs. Callahan I would never have learned to sew. My brother cared for Judge Callahan, and that is enough for me. I won't let them be murdered in their home.

When I get to the French doors, I find them locked. I whisper *"briseadh"* out of habit, but nothing happens. My magic is all but gone now—I can feel the hollow it's left in my chest.

I try the kitchen window next. I grasp the cool metal of the sill and give it a shove; the window rises without resistance. I sigh in relief and wriggle through the gap. It scrapes my shoulder and snags Finn's borrowed sweater.

Finn was correct: there was no one guarding the back of the house.

The relief is short-lived. There are muffled voices arguing from down the hall.

I haven't been inside this house since my brother was alive.

Limping a little, I race into the parlor and find the blond named Jack and the tall James standing over Judge Callahan, Mrs. Callahan, and Oliver. Their hands are tied behind their backs, and they're all on their knees. Mrs. Callahan is weeping. The judge looks furious. Oliver is trying to calm his mother down, which is hard to do with a rag shoved in his mouth. His panicked eyes go wide at the sight of me barreling into the room.

Oliver has lived at Columbia since starting school—I hadn't expected to find him here. The sight of him tied up devastates me.

"What's Finn's girl doing here?" Jack sneers.

"Let them go. I demand it." My voice sounds stronger than I feel.

"And why would we do that?"

"Finn's orders."

The boys share a look. They mutter something. The smaller one shakes his head. "You're a liar."

There's no point in arguing with them. "Fine, then because I'll kill you if you don't." I don't want to mean it, but if it came down to it to save Oliver, I think I could.

The boys exchange another glance, and Jack takes a step toward me.

"I wouldn't do that if I were you," I bluster. "You're going to remove the dagger from your breast pocket, or I'll snap his neck." I gesture to his companion with a jerk of my chin. "You know what I can do." I hope they don't call my bluff.

He reaches into his jacket slowly. Every one of my senses is on high alert. He drops the dagger to the floor, and as quick as I am able, I bend down and pick it up. I clutch the knife tightly and point the blade toward Jack, who looks at me with disdain. His companion looks a little more out of his depth. If I had to guess, I'd say this was his first home invasion.

"Untie them," I demand.

Jack takes a few steps toward the Callahans while I keep the

406

silver dagger trained on him. I'm so focused on Jack that I don't see James lunge at me until his knife is at my throat. It's a kitchen knife, less elegant than the pretty dagger I have in my hand, but the sharp edge still bites into the skin at my throat.

Damn it.

"Drop the dagger," Jack demands as he rises from untying Mrs. Callahan's wrists.

I don't have time to think. I plunge the dagger into James's thigh. He screams and drops the knife at my throat. With the very last drops of my power, fueled by pure desperation, I magick the knife up off the floor and into my left hand. The whole thing happens in the space of seconds. James howls in the corner, trying to stanch the bleeding in his leg, and Jack stands frozen in the center of the parlor.

I take two steps over to him. I grip the handle of the kitchen knife, my fingers wrapped tight around it. Then I draw my arm back, and with as much momentum as I can muster, I punch him as hard as I can in the temple, the blunt end of the knife's handle hitting the soft spot. The blow lands. He crumples to the floor. James goes down just as easily.

It was a trick William taught me a long time ago. He told me if anyone ever gave me trouble, one sharp blow right to the side of their head would knock them out. I've never tried it before this moment. I can't believe it worked so well.

I run to the Callahans and saw through their ropes with sloppy panic. I don't know how long Finn's cronies will stay unconscious, and I'd really like to avoid killing them.

"Thank you, thank you!" Mrs. Callahan cries when I remove the rag from her mouth.

"No time!" I exclaim. I free the judge and Oliver next.

"Frances, what are you doing here?" Oliver asks me with equal parts awe and fear.

"Finn—" I begin like there's any possible way I could make him understand. Something akin to hurt crosses Oliver's face. "I'll explain later—tie them up."

Oliver and the judge make quick work of Jack's and James's wrists and ankles, but Oliver barely takes his eyes off me, stealing worried glances between knots. He and his father haul them over their shoulders and lock them in the hall closet, leaving me and a weeping Mrs. Callahan in the parlor alone.

"Why aren't you calling the police?" she sobs. I rub her back in half-hearted circles, but I don't answer her. I wouldn't know how to begin telling her that the magical secret society her husband belongs to has been taken over by a group of young magicians, and we can't call the police because we don't know whose side they're on.

Oliver and his father return to the parlor a moment later. "My dear girl," Judge Callahan booms. "You have saved us."

I'm still out of breath from the fight and the run over. "There's been a coup. Most of the Sons' council has been killed. Don't trust anyone. Don't open the door. Leave in the morning if you can. I have to go."

"Wait!" Oliver calls after me. "If you're leaving, I'm going with you." The cuffs on his fine white shirt are a tiny bit too short, exposing rope burns around his wrists.

"No you're not." I push past him. I have to get back to Haxahaven, and I don't have time to explain.

"No." He steps in front of me. "I'm no longer accepting that as an answer. I'm not going to let you disappear on me again promising to explain something later. I've done what you've asked of me, because I will do *anything* you ask of me, but . . . Jesus. Frances, please let me help you." He sucks in a deep breath through his nose and closes the space between us in two lengthy strides. "You don't have to do this on your own."

There was a time when I would have collapsed into his arms, but Finn has taught me what trusting people can cost. "You don't owe this to William. Let me go."

"William?" Oliver asks in genuine surprise. "This isn't about William, Frances. And it's not about owing anyone anything. I mean . . ." He shakes his head in disbelief as his eyes pierce through me. This is a different Oliver than I'm used to. This is assertiveness and truth and determination wrapped up in years of history and tenderness. He steps even closer, his hand lifting my jaw so my eyes meet his own. "This is about me and *you*."

My face glows hot. I file his words away for later. But he doesn't know who I am now. What I've done. My heart aches the more his eyes bore into me. I can't stand what he might see if he stares a second longer. I turn away from him.

"How far is the train from here?"

A brilliant smile spreads across his face. He snatches an overcoat from the coatrack in the living room. "I have a Cadillac—it will be faster. You can show me the way." He shrugs the coat over his broad shoulders.

Oliver ignores his mother's cries, begging him to "Stop. Wait! Think about what you are doing," as we race out of the house and into the dark night.

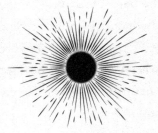

CHAPTER THIRTY

The drive to Haxahaven seems to take three times as long as it usually does. For the better part of an hour, I'm bombarded with horrible visions of my friends being tortured and killed.

Over the din of the engine Oliver speaks just once, breaking the silence between us. "Is it true what those boys said?" he shouts.

"What who said?" I've heard so many boys say so many things.

"That you're Finn's girl?" He keeps his eyes focused on the road.

I'd laugh if I weren't so laden down with dread. "No, it's not true."

It's so brief, I could be imagining it, but I'm fairly sure he smiles.

I make Oliver park the Cadillac a ways down from the circular drive, so they don't hear us approach.

"Stay in the car," I hiss at him.

"Fat chance," he replies.

I hand him the elegant dagger I stole from Jack because I know there's no talking him out of it, and he needs the weapon more than I do.

He smiles sadly. "You really think I have it in me to stab someone, Frances?"

The first sign that something is terribly amiss at Haxahaven is the front iron gate, swinging wide open. They're here, then—that's for certain.

Together, Oliver and I creep across the gravel drive. In the dark Haxahaven looms like a specter.

We sneak in the side door to the kitchen, like I've snuck in so many times before. We find it empty, benches scraped clean, like no one has been here in a while.

There is no one on the stairs, no one in the sunroom. It fills me with a deep sense of wrongness.

Then, suddenly, the sound of muffled shouting echoes through the hall. Oliver and I don't speak, we just exchange a glance and take off running in the direction of the dining room.

There is no one guarding the doorway. Finn's men seem to be semiskilled killers but dreadful strategists. Oliver and I linger in the darkness outside the door to the dining room, where my classmates, all one hundred of them, are huddled together, surrounded by twenty or so members of the Sons of Saint Druon.

One hundred poorly trained witches are no match for twenty well-trained Sons. Our instructors are nowhere to be found.

Out in front of the girls, just as I expected she'd be, is Maxine. The shouting I heard was her.

"We won't go with you." She's screaming, and her arms are splayed out, defending the younger girls behind her. Lena is right next to her. The sight of them nearly makes me cry, I've missed them so much. I want to crawl to them and beg for forgiveness, but that will come later.

"Frances!" Mabel shouts. She's the first person to spot me as I enter the dining room. The Sons of Saint Druon turn to me, the same disdainful sneering look on their faces. I recognize some of them, but not all.

"If it isn't Finn's little princess," one of the Sons greets me.

"You know these men?" Maria asks from where she sits, huddled with the other Haxahaven girls.

"Shut up!" a tall boy I haven't seen before shouts. "Didn't I tell you little witches not to speak unless spoken to?"

I have one advantage; I've beaten Finn here. These boys don't yet know I am not one of them.

"Hello, boys," I say demurely. "Now is this really necessary? You don't need the guns, surely."

The men look to one another, unsure what to do.

"I thought we were friends," I continue. My classmates look at me with horror.

"We report to Finn, not to you," one of the men says.

"But she is Finn's girl," another counters.

"I don't care whose girl she is," the tall boy screams. "The witches are under orders to come with us. We can't keep the teachers locked up for much longer, we need to leave, let's just take them and go."

My classmates cry out in a chorus of terrified objections.

I steady my breathing. They want to take my classmates away. This is all my doing, and now it's my responsibility to fix it. "There's no need to be rash." I take careful steps toward them, my arms up in front of me, a sweet smile plastered to my face.

I flick a glance to Lena and Maxine. They look back at me, Maxine with rage, Lena with pity.

If I survive tonight, I will spend the rest of my life trying to make things right between us. I pray I have the chance.

Maxine uses the distraction to spring from where she's crouched on the floor and magicks the closest guard's knife into her hand.

Someone else, I can't tell who, sends an antique pistol one of the boys is holding and slams it against the wall. It crumples to the floor in a twist of metal.

Then, everywhere, there is chaos. Screams and sobs. Fists connecting with eye sockets. Magic sparks and bangs. Lena and Cora spring into action, shepherding some of the younger girls to safety through the kitchen.

Oliver and Aurelia haul Ruby up by the armpits and drag her across the floor. Oliver's hand is pressed to her bleeding shoulder; the blood spurts between his fingertips. She must have been hit in the chaos. He catches my eye in the side doorway. *Go*, I mouth to him. He nods in understanding and disappears into the hall.

It's as if the *Cath Draíochta* has sprung to life in the Haxahaven dining room. Objects fly about. Sconces crash to the floor; books weave through the air. It's a hurricane of magic and fear and power. There is blood on the walls. All around is the guttural sound of people being hit.

Suddenly a gunshot rings out.

Standing in the doorway, his smoking pistol aimed at the ceiling, is Finn. He's wearing an overcoat, a hat, and gloves. At the sight of me, the tight line of his brows smooth in relief.

"Frances, thank God you're safe." I don't share the same relief in seeing him, only slippery, bitter fear. His tone sharpens as he turns to his cronies. "Boys, is this what we discussed?"

Some of them mutter, "No, sir."

The room smells of blood and gunpowder. Sons of Saint Druon watch Finn, and the witches of Haxahaven watch me. Oliver has returned from the kitchen. He clutches the pearl-handled dagger in his fist. He's desperately out of his depth in a room where he is the only one who possesses no magic, though you'd never know it by the determined look in his eye.

"Boys!" Finn calls to his cronies scattered across the room. "Please remember we came here for collaboration. Magical lives are valuable. I'll be back in one moment. No one do anything while I'm gone, or you'll have me to answer to!"

Finn shoves his pistol in the waistband of his pants and crosses the room. He takes both my hands in his and says, "We need to talk." He drags me out into the dark foyer, pulling harder than he needs to, and though I don't want to leave my friends alone, they're probably safer with Finn out of the room.

His gloved hand against mine is itchy and wrong.

Scratchy.

Cold wraps its claws around me. I feel like I'm being dunked in icy waters as my brother's words about his death come flooding back to me. *Something hit me hard from behind. There was a gloved hand over my mouth. It was scratchy.*

Scratchy.

I didn't see a thing. I was gazing at the river. I heard someone whistling a tune. It was a beautiful night, and then, boom, lights out.

The first night I met Finn in the park comes to me, crystal clear and ice cold. I remember it so well now, the way his whistling ghosted through the trees.

Darkness circles my thoughts. My legs are barely able to keep me upright as the realization smacks me with a terrible wave of sadness and horror. I've never felt this lost, this empty before.

The cavernous marble foyer of Haxahaven is deadly silent. The only light is a beam of moonlight streaming in through the window above the door. It cuts a silvery line across Finn's sharp face, turning one of his hazel eyes golden.

I look at him, horrified, like I'm seeing him clearly for the first time. *"No."* It's guttural, primal, and afraid.

His eyes go wide. And he knows. I don't know if it's the connection of the spell or the ordinary magic of how well we understand each other, but all at once he knows I know the truth.

It was Finn who killed my brother.

Blood drains from his face. "I need you to understand . . . what I did, I did for us," he says quickly, as if he could possibly justify this.

"What did you do, Finn?" I ask in a voice very small, considering the storm raging within me. I want him to say it. I need to hear his admission.

"He didn't love you." He puts his hand over his heart. "Not like I do."

"You killed him." As soon as the words leave my mouth, I know they're true.

"I saw how he treated you."

Every part of me grows colder, numb. "Saw how he treated me?"

Finn nods—he's eager to tell his twisted side of the story. "He came home drunk and left running the entire household to you. He didn't appreciate you."

"We were bickering like brother and sister . . . so you killed him."

"I've always known we were fated to be together. Your mother was a witch. You appeared in my dreams. All I needed was to awaken your magic, make you see. William dying was supposed to help you. He wasn't even magical, Frances. Your life, our life together is worth one thousand of him."

For someone who has spent half my life imagining the worst-case scenario, I didn't see this coming. "You were his friend. He helped you. *Jesus Finn*, he trusted you. We both did."

Two Hallowells made the same mistake twice in trusting Finn. We let the same vampire in from the cold. And we both paid for it.

Something shifts in his face. What is meant to be beseeching only looks unhinged. "Yes, but you mattered more."

I can almost see it through his eyes. I am the girl he saw for so long in his dreams. He thought he knew me before we'd even spoken. In his entitlement to me, to my life, he took everything from me.

He continues, "I'm sorry I did it, if it helps at all. But don't you see, Frances"—his voice rises—"the things I would do for you? I'd do *anything*."

"I need to hear you say it." I cut him off. "Tell me what you did to my brother." The words taste like poison.

Finn sighs. "No you don't, love."

"If you are truly sorry, you will tell me."

He steps toward me; I step back. "If that's what you'd like." He shuffles feet and swallows, hard. "A brick to the head. It knocked him out cold. He sank quickly. He didn't suffer. I'm not a monster."

A brick to the head.

There it is, then. The confession.

Our definitions of *monster* are different.

And Finn might not understand why William's death didn't awaken my magic, but I do. Magic is the expansion of one's soul, and mine died the night he killed my brother. For four months I stumbled through a fog, going through the motions of my life. Killing Mr. Hues demanded I be present for the first time since my brother's death. There is no beauty in trauma, but there is urgency in it.

"You planted the book in Maxine's dreams, didn't you?" I interrupt him. You wanted us to find you, to need you. You weren't afraid of the Resurrection because you knew he didn't see you. Was it all a plan to bind my magic to you?"

Finn shrugs. "I needed it more than you did."

The boy I thought I loved is a monster.

I ruin everything I ever touch.

A crash rings out from the dining room, then screaming. I run in the direction of the chaos, leaving Finn and my shattered heart behind me.

Maxine stands on the dining table.

Maria sniffling, but standing tall, holds her fists raised.

Lena shields a group of girls, her arms stretched wide, sending objects flying in front of them in figure eights like a shield.

The fighting is bloody and loud. I can't tell who is winning and who is losing. I can think only in short clips.

Stop.

Breathe.

Run.

Fix this.

Save them.

The sound of a wall sconce shattering draws my attention. Maxine stands with a fistful of dinner forks, ready to send another careening at the tall man stalking toward Maria.

Finn runs into the room after me and with a booming voice shouts, "Stop!"

His men obey him and turn expectantly to their leader.

Finn trains his gaze on me. "I made a mistake with William, Frances. But you will have a whole lifetime to find forgiveness. Just leave here with me and your friends will be safe. I promise."

"And if I don't?"

"Then my men will kill them all, and you will still leave with me. The choice is yours."

I have no magic left. The witches of Haxahaven would fight, but we are poorly trained and we would lose. He leaves me with no choice.

My classmates and friends all look to me. From the corner, someone moans as they float in and out of consciousness. I do not know if it is a witch or a Son, but I know that it is my fault. The moment I stepped into the halls of this school, I damned them all. If I have to leave with the person who killed my brother to save them, then that's what I'll do. It's my punishment, and it's one I deserve. If the prison I was always going to end up in is a life tethered to Finn, then so be it.

I look up at him with empty eyes. "Give me a moment to say goodbye?"

Finn closes his eyes in relief and smiles, dimples cracking his perfect face. He nods. "I'm not heartless. But no more than fifteen minutes. Go to the kitchen and help those that are wounded. Hurry."

Aurelia and May carry a girl into the kitchen. I catch Lena's eye and gesture for her and the other girls to follow them.

Like a miserable, silent parade, the Haxahaven witches shuffle into the vast room. How I wish I could go back to the days of Florence teaching me to sweep the floors.

With heavy footfalls, Finn's men come to stand guard outside the door.

"I'm not going with them," Mabel says the minute we're out of earshot.

"Me either," Maria echoes. Sara and Cora nod in agreement.

"I'd never ask you to do that," I whisper. "Just . . . give me a moment."

I dart to Maxine and Lena huddled in the corner.

My apology comes out in a single exhale. I'm tripping over my words, desperate to make them understand. "I'm sorry. He tricked me, I'm stupid, I'm *so* stupid, you were right, I'm sorry, I'm sorry."

They throw their arms around me. Maxine's hair smells of gunpowder and Lena is shaking and it's all my fault.

"He killed my brother. He stole my magic. I'm such a fool." My voice trembles.

Lena pulls back, horror-struck.

Maxine sighs heavily. "I didn't want to be right."

There isn't time to say all the things I want to say, so I settle on, "Thank you for being my friends. I believe you two are the best thing that's ever happened to me. I never deserved you."

Maxine pushes me away. "Enough of this. We don't have time to waste." Maxine—always the fighter. "How did he steal your magic?"

"He bound us together"—the words come quickly—"using a spell from *The Elemental.*" I glance at the clock. I don't have long before Finn comes looking for me, and I have so much I need to tell them. "I'll do whatever I can to stop him, but I couldn't leave without letting you know how sorry I am, and how dearly I love you."

Maxine puts a hand to her temple. "Jesus, Frances, stop trying to say goodbye. I'm thinking."

"If the spell worked once . . ." Lena trails off.

"Then it will work again." Maxine finishes her thought.

It takes me a moment to catch up. "You can't possibly be thinking of giving me your power," I say. I'm shocked they'd consider it. "I'd refuse it. I don't deserve it."

"You're the only one close enough to him to stop him," Lena explains. "You can't disagree that it's a practical decision."

I shake my head. "I won't take it from you. I refuse."

Maxine looks around the kitchen. She's counting each girl, mouthing the numbers. Then she quirks a smile. "But what about a drop from all of us?"

"They wouldn't." After everything I put them through, how could they?

Lena rests her soft hand on mine, looks me straight in the eye. "They would."

And she's right.

I explain the spell to Maxine and Lena. They explain the spell to the girls huddled in the kitchen, and each and every single one of them agrees to help me. Their yeses echo through the room. Some are friends, like Mabel and Maria. Some I barely know, like Rachel, and a tiny redhead I've never said a word to. Even Sara and Cora agree to help.

"But will it work?" I ask.

Maxine shrugs. "There's only one way to find out."

Faster than I can believe, the group of us spread out in a circle on the brick floor of the kitchen. I lean against the oven. It's still warm.

"We need fabric to bind our hands," I explain. I'm racking my panicked brain to remember as much of the spell as possible.

Maxine flings open a drawer and produces a paring knife. One by one, it's passed around the circle. Each girl rips the hem of her Haxahaven cape, producing a ribbon of black fabric.

Maxine and Lena sit on either side of me. They tie our hands first, but the gesture ripples through the circle like a wave. Soon we are all bound.

"You don't have to do this," I tell them. "I don't know what will happen." Guilt mingles with panic. Am I just as bad as Finn for agreeing to this? Or is this friendship, accepting love even when you don't feel you deserve it?

"Come on, Frances. We don't have time," Maxine prods.

"We're not afraid. Get on with it," Sara insists.

I take a deep breath. I can already feel the power of my friends. It buzzes like an electric light. It's rare and it's holy and it belongs to them.

For as long as I live, which might not be much longer, I'll work to deserve them giving even the tiniest drop of themselves to me.

"Together, we'll say the vow, and then the spell," I explain. My voice is shaking. Thirteen pairs of eyes stare at me. My hands are hot, as if the current is already connecting us.

They nod in understanding. I go first, even though I know I have nothing to give them.

If magic has taught me one thing, it's that words are powerful, so I make one change. I no longer use the words "yours" and "you" but "ours" and "us."

"I, Frances Victoria Hallowell, give myself to you. All that I am and will be is ours, from this life onto the next. My soul, and all that is within it, belongs to us. *Déantar éh.*"

The kitchen is dark but crackles with static.

A chorus of voices echo in response to mine.

"All that I am and will be is ours, from this life onto the next. My soul, and all that is within it, belongs to us. *Déantar é,*" they recite. My loyal sisters. My brilliant, brave friends.

Heat starts in my hands, blooming up my arms. With each of their words, a light unfurls in my chest growing, *growing*, and then, like a snap, the spell is done, and I can breathe again.

"Did it work?" Sara asks.

They watch in silence as I reach out with my magic and levitate the paring knife discarded in the middle of the circle.

Relief floods through me. I feel at home in my body once more. "Thank you. *Thank you.*" It comes out in tears. Lena squeezes my hand. Maxine lays her head on my shoulder.

I think perhaps this is how we survive in the world. Passing little bits of our magic back and forth to each other when the world takes it from us. It's survival. It's love. It's family.

"I'll never be able to thank you enough," I tell them.

The spell between us is broken as the kitchen doors swing open and Finn appears once more.

He leans against the doorframe and sucks on his teeth. "It's time to go, love."

Maxine, Lena, and I share a glance that speaks of death.

I follow Finn and leave my heart behind me.

The November air has turned the dew to frost so cold it rivals the splintering ice in my veins. Indifferent stars hang above our heads, and I pray to the deep nothingness for strength. The deep nothingness answers with the voice of my brother.

Be brave.

If I cannot be brave for myself, I will be brave for my classmates who were so brave for me.

Finn takes me by the hand, and I need every last bit of strength I have not to recoil at his touch.

"Let's go home, love. Lots to do in the morning."

"You swear you'll leave Haxahaven be?"

"As long as you cooperate," he says with a sickening smile. "I think they'll be more use to us like this, eh? And it will be a comfort to you to know they're up here, tucked away from the big bad world."

But he's right. I will cooperate. I will leave this place hand in hand with my brother's murderer if it means the girls at Haxahaven will survive. Let Finn think I'm a girl who needs protecting from the evils of the world and her own tender heart.

Just then Oliver's voice cuts through the darkness like a knife. "Stop!" he shouts from the porch. "I won't let you take her with you!"

Poor, sweet, brave Oliver. How is it possible that he still thinks I'm someone worth running after?

Lena and Maxine sprint out behind him. "Stop!" Maxine says.

Oliver ignores her and climbs down the porch steps onto the gravel drive. "Frances, please."

"Take care of this, will you, boys?" Finn says with a jerk of his chin.

A roil of pure terror goes through me. "Stop, *stop!*"

My cries are swallowed by the sound of a gun firing into the body of Oliver Callahan.

He doesn't scream when the bullet hits him. Rather, he looks at his bleeding stomach with a furrowed brow.

My body knows what it's doing before my mind does. I run for him, screaming so loud it echoes off the nothingness of the night.

Oliver falls to the ground.

There are so many of Finn's men and so few of us.

Maxine is fierce and beautiful. She manipulates gun after gun, magicking them right out of the Sons' hands, but she cannot manipulate bodies, and she is no match for the fist that connects with her cheekbone and knocks her to the ground.

Lena makes it the farthest. She sprints at Finn with a knife in her hand.

I take hold of the first man who lunges at her and bring him down, but I don't see the second until he crashes into her.

By the sound of his screams, she's able to land one solid blow with the knife, but the man is enormous on top of her, and she has no more knives.

"Please!" I scream at Finn again and again, but still he does nothing. Maxine screams; men close in on Lena. Oliver's body is a dark splotch on the lawn, sickeningly still. Memories of our childhood together flash before my mind. Of William, of the three of us. He was all I had to hold on to from the past, and now . . . Suddenly the rest of the witches spill out the front doors. I see Finn's men ready to fight. Panic and anger and fear burst through me, and just then, like a dam breaking on a raging river, my very soul pours out of my body, and I am everywhere. I am everyone. It is so strange, this new magic that is both mine and not mine.

I feel Maxine's vibrant love and exquisite pain. I see flashes of the faces of the girls she loves. Their kisses in dark corners and the way they tangle together in empty bedrooms just as dawn is breaking. I feel her sense of duty and her desire for adventure locked in battle with each other.

I see Lena's grandmother's lined face and the way her parents looked the last time she saw them so many years ago. I know her heart-wrenching homesickness and feeling of isolation. I feel her fierce pride and unrelenting ambition, the deep well of kindness that is her heart.

I know Oliver's overwhelming goodness, his self-doubt. I see myself through his eyes. The way he looks at me like I'm the most magical thing he's ever seen, even though he's seen real magic. I feel now how desperately he misses William. How he talks to him when no one else is around.

But it's Finn I feel the most. The bottomless pit of his want. His willingness to do anything to create the world he thinks is just. The strange warm spot he has in his cunning heart just for me.

All this information floods into my mind in the space of half a heartbeat.

Pain rips through my head. My vision tunnels.

My soul cannot contain this much; my body cannot take it. My grip on the magic is slipping. My soul has stretched so far from my body, it could slide right out and never return. I could join William, wherever he is. The torment of this life would be over. It would be so easy to give in. The relief of death begs me to accept it; like waves of the ocean, it laps at my feet. Death is warm and soft, and living is so, so hard.

The air here is particularly heavy. On it floats William's voice, as clear as I've ever heard it. *Hold on,* he says.

I will not leave this world a half-done, unrealized thing.

For the first time in a very long time, I want desperately to live.

Hold on. And then a burst of energy, of stars and light and emotions hazy with power.

With a gasp, I come to, lying on my back on Haxahaven's lawn, gazing up at the cold stars, everything just as it was, except the lawn is silent and almost empty and the air here is warm. I stand and find only Finn across from me.

He looks terribly broken.

"This is a dream, then?" I ask him.

He pushes himself up off the ground and brushes the dirt from his trousers. "I suppose so. You screamed like a bloody banshee, then collapsed. The next thing I knew, we were both here."

"You killed my brother." The words taste like poison in my mouth.

He puts his hands up as if in surrender and takes a step toward me. "Aye, but I'm sorry I did it."

"Not that sorry. You're about to kill my friends," I reply.

"Only because you forced my hand. I love you, Frances. No one will ever love you as much as I do."

Only the tiniest, most broken parts of me believe him. "If this is being loved by you, I don't want it. I don't want any of it."

Finn throws his hands up. "And you think I do? Love is a weakness!"

I shake my head. "No, Finn. Wanting to control the people you love is a weakness."

His face crumples, and he looks so much like the same boy who was sleeping next to me just last night. "Do you think you could ever forgive me?"

Saintlike, I step toward Finn and draw him into an embrace. But he has forgotten the first magic lesson he ever gave me: in my dreams I am the creator and the destroyer of worlds.

I picture the pearl-handled dagger, and there it appears in my hand.

Finn's chest is solid and warm against mine. His heart kicks under his shirt. I let myself have this moment—for a breath I hold him. I close my eyes and rest my head on his shoulder.

And then I count down the beats of his heart.

Three.

Two.

One.

I plunge the knife into his back.

CHAPTER THIRTY-ONE

I blink back into consciousness, back to the world that is solid and real. I gasp for air; it's like I'm drowning, and my head has finally cracked the surface of a cold pond.

First there is screaming, horrible and frantic. I blink my eyes open, but the starlight is dim, and the lawn is washed in darkness as black as ink.

The screaming isn't coming from me but from Finn, who is collapsed on the ground next to me. Very alive, no visible stab wounds, but howling in pain like an injured animal. The sound is so heart piercing, I have to remind myself to feel no sympathy for him.

With aching arms, I push myself up off the ground.

Before I collapsed into the dream, my power was a candle trying to stay alight in the wind. Now it is a bonfire. Like tongues of flame, my magic reaches out and takes hold of all twenty of Finn's

men. The control comes as easy as breathing. Something in me has
been unlocked.

I slam them to the ground with a rib-shattering crack. I am in
control of their souls. I am in control of my own.

"You will leave Haxahaven and never return. Do you understand?"

Their moans of pain turn into words of affirmation, and without further hesitation they take off, some hobbling, some running,
in the direction of the dirt road that will take them back into the city.

I hope I don't come to regret letting them live.

I stand over Finn and despise the sight of him. I hate each angle
of his perfect face.

Once Finn's men are out of sight, I crouch over his ashen form.
He's gone still and sweaty, but his eyes are open.

"What have you done to me?" he pants. "The magic . . . I can't
feel it."

"Maybe it's because you're a soulless monster."

"Kill me," he gasps. "I can't live like this."

"I should kill you," I say so quietly, only he can hear. "I should
want to." I lean down and press my lips to his forehead. "But not yet."

I rise from the ground and don't look back. I walk across the
lawn, letting Finn's crumpled form fade from view into the darkness,
among other shadowy broken things where he belongs.

My steps pick up quicker and quicker until I'm running full
tilt to Lena, Maxine, and Oliver across the lawn, lying agonizingly still.

They're laid out in a constellation. Lena is bleeding from the
head. Oliver's shirt is more blood than fabric. Maxine's left eye is

swelled shut. I reach them, and my soul, having expanded to the corners of possibility, sighs in relief. "I'm sorry," I sob.

And then the darkness swallows me, full and complete.

Everything hurts.

I wake in my usual bed, covered in cold sweat and the creak that comes with being asleep for a long time.

I can't move my limbs. My throat burns.

The images come flooding back to me all at once: Oliver being shot, the dagger going into Finn's back, how it felt to know someone's soul.

Lena calls from her bed. "Are you finally awake?"

"How long have I been out?" My voice cracks with disuse.

"Three days," I hear Maxine say from across the room. She's sitting on Ruby's bed, sporting a violently purple shiner and flipping through *Vanity Fair*. "You look terrible."

"I'm sorry, Maxine. I can't believe I ever thought you could have had something to do with William's death," I croak.

She silences me with a small shake of her head. "It's all forgiven. Obviously a terrible thing to be accused of, but I do quite like that you thought I might have been interesting enough to be leading a second life as a late-night murderess."

A pang of hurt peals through my chest like a church bell at the sight of Ruby's unslept-in bed.

"Ruby?" I ask.

"Alive, she went home yesterday," Lena replies.

"And Oliver?"

A knock on the door startles us, and Florence strides in. No

longer in her gray muslin kitchen dress, but a silk crepe gown of turquoise blue, the Haxahaven cape buttoned across her chest.

She smiles when she sees me awake. "I'm glad to see you up."

"Florence is taking over as interim headmistress," Maxine explains.

"A fine choice." My throat burns with every word. "Where
is Oliver?"

"Can you walk?" Maxine asks me.

I'm unsure if my shaky joints will hold me, but it doesn't stop me
from rising from my bed. "Take me to him."

They've laid out Oliver in Maxine's room. He looks like a ghost,
pale as death under her canopy.

I stumble to him and collapse on my knees at his bedside.

His green eyes flutter open.

"Oh, thank God," I sigh. I've never seen anything better than the
rise and fall of his chest, *alive*.

He moves his hand weakly to touch mine.

"Are you crying?" He manages a weak laugh.

"No," I sniff.

"Good. I still have a million questions about magic you once
promised to answer."

He smiles, and his face is brighter than the afternoon sun.

Whatever exists between us feels deeply inevitable. An incor-
ruptible truth. As unstoppable as tree roots pushing up through city
concrete. And now we have all the time in the world.

There are thousands of things I want to say to him, but I put my
faith in the stars that we will have time to say them. For now, holding
his hand and listening to our synchronous breathing is enough.

But there is something I still have to do.

431

I ask to meet with Florence, Maxine, and Lena later that night. I need to tell them what I've done.

I pass Mrs. Vykotsky's office door on the way down the stairs, and I feel a stab of guilt so sharp I nearly collapse.

Lena, Maxine, and Florence meet me at the small circular breakfast table in the kitchen. I make a pot of tea, clutching the mug as if the warmth could leach back into the parts I feel most broken, and I begin.

The three of them listen with patient kindness as I tell them what I did to Mrs. Vykotsky. How I killed her. How she didn't deserve it. How I understand if they choose to never speak to me again.

They keep their faces neutral, nodding at all the right moments.

It's Florence who pats my hand once I've finished. "It sounds like it was an accident."

"Yes, but—" I begin.

She doesn't offer me false smiles or coddling. She simply says, "We learn from our mistakes, Frances. They don't make us irredeemable."

Tears stream down my face. I didn't realize I was crying. I am so sick of crying; I hope not to do it again for a very long time.

I look between Maxine and Lena. "You don't think I'm a monster?"

Lena shakes her head. "Of course not."

Maxine agrees. "I think you're plenty of things, but monster doesn't make the list."

I clutch my teacup. Mrs. Vykotsky's death is something heavy I will carry with me all the days of my life. But for now, this is enough.

"You girls did a very brave thing," Florence says. "I regret I wasn't there to fight alongside you, but I had to get the little ones out of the school after Helen fled."

"She fled?" I ask.

"We think she felt something coming. It was an act of cowardice," Florence explains.

Maxine sighs. "Good riddance."

"Who healed Oliver?" I ask. "Can I thank them?"

"Magic isn't much good at fixing broken bodies, so Maxine called up an old Haxahaven pupil who is now a medical student in the city. She said the bullet missed anything important. As long as he avoids infection, he'll be fine. It was nothing short of a miracle that boy lived."

"Thank you." I steal a glance at Maxine to my right. "I don't know what else to say."

"What do we do now?" Maxine asks.

"I wish to build a new Haxahaven," Florence says. "One where magic isn't treated as a disease, and where girls can grow up nurtured. Ann and I intend to train the girls of Haxahaven, truly train them for whatever it is that's coming. And I would be honored to have the three of you by our side."

Lena doesn't need a beat to consider Florence's offer. "Thank you, ma'am, but I'm going home to my family. Haxahaven was never a place I intended to stay."

"I understand, Lena," Florence answers. "You have my full support. We'll do whatever we can to help you reunite with them."

"Thank you," Lena says.

Maxine shrugs. "Haxahaven is my home. I'll stay."

To be a witch is to have power in a world where women have

none. I've witnessed the Sons of Saint Druon use their magic to entertain, to grab power, to subjugate and do terrible things.

But the witches of Haxahaven did nothing with theirs. The nothingness feels just as ugly. "Yes," I finally say. "Yes, I will join you."

Lena leaves for home on a cold Tuesday. I cry. She doesn't, though she does hug me and promise to write.

Aurelia returns home to her family just days later, and, unable to take the sight of my roommates' empty beds, I move into Mabel's room. She talks in her sleep, but her gentle voice reminds me I'm not alone in the darkness, so I don't mind much.

Oliver's gunshot wound heals slowly, as gunshot wounds do. The judge and Mrs. Callahan, having left for an extended stay at their Paris home, deem Haxahaven an appropriate place for him to convalesce. It is, after all, a sanitarium. With a diet of biscuits and the fussing of all the younger girls playing nurse, he's up and walking in less than a week.

We take to strolling the path that borders the woods after breakfast, just the two of us. We walk in companionable silence. I think he craves the reprieve of giggling sighs. The novelty of a boy at Haxahaven hasn't quite worn off yet.

My magic feels both bigger and smaller now. Less like a chained animal, more like a muscle. It has taken hold at the base of my power, growing and twisting like the roots of a tree with the witch I was then and what I am now. Knowing parts of it belong to the people I love, I no longer fear it.

I learn to believe in miracles. The forgiveness of my friends is holy, and when we laugh together, it is a promise to build a better world. Haxahaven becomes a place of joy. Filled to the brim with laughing girls and sloppy magic, I allow it to heal me.

We make plans to get my mother proper care and an apartment in the city.

Helen once told me I couldn't burn down the world for taking the things I loved from me. Helen was wrong in many regards, but in that she was right. I take the endless well of love I have for my brother, and I whisper to it, a prayer to stop eating me alive. I learn to give it away. To the homesick Haxahaven girls. To my friends. To myself. I think the only choice any of us has is to take our pain and make a world that hurts its inhabitants a little less.

I don't dream of Finn. I don't dream at all; it's like I've lost the ability entirely.

When the fighting was over, and my unconscious body was dragged inside by Florence and Ann, they found only a pearl-handled dagger in the place where Finn had once lain. I can't think about him for long without being overcome by a sadness that reaches straight to my bones. I hope anger comes in time. It would be easier to understand.

I think about William every second of every day, but the thoughts feel lighter with Oliver here to share them with me. I do not profess to know much about the afterlife, but here in the mess he left behind, I promise the stars that I will live enough life for the both of us. Death is senseless, but perhaps life doesn't have to be.

Oliver and I are on our morning walk one day when he turns to me, his hands shoved in his pockets, a scarf wrapped around his neck. The air is cool; his breath comes in puffs of vapor. The sky is a brilliant December gray, so bright, I have to squint up at him. It's a single perfect moment, the two of us here, our boots crunching in the snow.

"Will always said you were going to change the world, you know that?"

I smile. "It sounds like something he'd say."

Haloed by winter tree branches, Oliver gazes down at me like I'm magic. "I think he was right."

I look past Oliver to the road that leads back into the city. "I hope so. There's so much left to do."

June 1912

Dearest Frances,

It feels rather quaint to be writing you a letter with ink and paper after all the time we spent inside each other's heads.

I think of you every second. So much of me feels empty now that you're so far away. How ridiculous I am to love someone who has taken so much from me.

But time will march on, and we will be reunited, as the universe always fated it to be. There is so much happening here in Europe. What I'm building, I'm building for us.

The clairvoyants say you'll be here soon.

I pray they are right, because we have so much to discuss. So much left to do together.

Every night I dream of your lips on mine, my love.

My soul feels empty, but we will remedy that upon

our reunion. I look forward to reclaiming all that you've taken from me.

So many cogs are turning, but still my heart beats only for you.

We belong to each other—never forget that. In your heart, you know it as well as I do.

Soon, Frances, we will be together again. Together, as we were always meant to be.

Love,
Finn James D'Arcy

ACKNOWLEDGMENTS

Writing the acknowledgments to my first book feels overwhelming, like attempting to thank the universe for conspiring to allow the exact conditions needed to make all of my dreams come true. Thank you feels too small, but it's what I'll start with. Thank you, thank you, thank you.

To Hillary Jacobson, your belief in me is the greatest gift I've ever been given. Thank you for always being in my corner and for guiding me into the world of publishing with grace and unfailing kindness. The term "dream agent" seems too small for all you do, so I guess we just have to work on one hundred more books together until I find the right words for all you mean to me.

To my editor, Nicole Ellul, for somehow always knowing exactly what it was I was trying to say. Your ability to cut to the heart of stories is so magical, I'm not entirely unconvinced you're a witch yourself.

To the entire team at Simon & Schuster Books for Young Readers, Amanda Ramirez, Katrina Groover, Cassie Malmo, Justin Chanda, Kendra Levin, Lauren Hoffman, Chrissy Noh, Victor Iannone, Anna Jarzab, Emily Ritter, Lauren Castner, thank you for believing in this book and me from the jump, and for welcoming me so warmly into the S&S family.

ACKNOWLEDGMENTS

To Heather Palisi, Faceout Studio, and Tom Daly for making both the inside and outside of this book so, so pretty (like . . . the prettiest thing I've ever seen.)

To Brian D. Luster and Kathleen Smith for fixing all my commas (and so much more.)

To Roxanne Edouard, Savanna Wicks, Liz Dennis and Josie Freedman for working so hard on behalf of this story, it means more than I can say.

To Stacey Parshall Jensen for her time, care, and incredible notes.

Although this is fundamentally a fantasy novel, I'd like to thank those who assisted in the historical research, and acknowledge that any errors are my own. Thank you to the research librarians and newspaper archival teams at the Library of Congress, the Google Research Ngram Viewer team and the NYC Tenement Museum.

To the booksellers, librarians, bloggers, and reviewers who had a hand in getting this book out into the world. There is nothing that means more to a debut author than your kindness, support, and enthusiasm. To Adalyn Grace, Alexis Henderson, Adrienne Young, Jessica Spotswood and Ashley Poston for reading early copies of this book and leaving such kind words. I look up to each of you so much.

To the Pitch Wars organizers and the class of 2017. Thank you to McKelle George and Heather Cashman, my mentors who taught me from the ground up what it meant to edit a book, and my writing big sister Kristin Lambert for being with me through it all, there's no one else I'd want to go on this journey with.

To every teacher who told me I was a writer before I knew it myself; Mrs. Larson, Mrs. Mattson, Ms. Ide, Mrs. Bona and Mrs. Sidesinger.

ACKNOWLEDGMENTS

To my friends who were endlessly patient and unfailingly supportive, how lucky I am to have a coven of my own.

To Allison Rich for living me while I wrote the majority of this book, and somehow still loving me, even though I turned our home into a coffee cup graveyard and left gummy worm dust on the couch.

To Sabrina McClain for believing in me the most and for her uncanny ability to spot plot holes. To Kosoko Jackson for making me laugh when I felt like crying. To Lindsay Landgraf Hess for reading a draft of this story years ago and giving me the encouragement I needed to keep going. To Kristin Dwyer, whose friendship feels like a gift and for responding to every unhinged 2 am text.

To Emilie Sowers, this book feels as much yours as it is mine. It would not exist without you or your endless faith in me. I don't know much about the universe, but I'll always be grateful to it for giving me you. I could write one million words about friendship and never capture exactly what it is yours means to me.

To Casey McQuiston, whose brilliant mind is only eclipsed by their giant heart. I'm so glad I found you in this lifetime, I'm sure we've known each other in so many. I have you, I'm good forever.

To Charles Wilson, who makes sure our home is filled with snacks and fall-scented candles. You're more than I ever let myself hope for. Thank you for loving me in the endless, unconditional ways I thought I'd only ever get to read about.

To my family, whose love is the closest thing to magic I'll ever experience.

To my parents who spent countless hours reading to me, who filled our home with stories and art

Mom, your love makes me brave. Thank you for always cheering me on the loudest. Dad, you're the most creative person I've ever known. It is from you that I learned to love creating something from nothing.

To my brother Thomas and his wife, Sayaka, thank you for always being the first to celebrate with me.

To my sister Hannah, who taught me what hard work looks like.

To my grandmothers; Jo, brilliant and kind, forced to leave school at fourteen, who taught me never to take my access to education for granted, and Polly, born before women had the right to vote, locked up in a tuberculosis sanitarium for years of her twenties, whose life inspired much of this book. I wish I'd gotten to hear your stories.

And finally, to Leah. My twin. My first and forever best friend. I wrote you a book. I really hope you like it.

I began this book with a Mary Oliver quote, and it feels right to end it with one, too.

"Instructions for living a life:
Pay attention.
Be astonished.
Tell about it."

If this book has found its way into your hands, I am astonished. Thank you for going on this journey with me.